Wan

MW01255921

Vanda is giving away *Juliana (Book 1: 1941-1944)* & a fascinating true story about a six year old boy.

The story is *exclusive* to her VIP readers group.

Details can be found at the end of OLYMPUS NIGHTS ON THE SQUARE.

Praise for the first Volume of *Juliana*
(*Book 1*)

"What a pleasure it was to read Volume One! I love the author's vision. Her research brought the settings alive. Once upon a time, I would have pursued Juliana myself. She's a fully developed character. I look forward to seeing her in future volumes"—Lee Lynch, author of *Rainbow Gap* & *The Swashbuckler*.

"*Juliana* is the opening act in a series of stories that will cover, discover and recover LGBT history ... Vanda's clean-shaven style in *Juliana* amplifies the creative ways in which lesbians and gays in the 1940s compartmentalized their identities like meals in an automat ... I can't wait for the next edition of yestergays' news to come out"—Allison Fradkin—*Curve Magazine*

"In Vanda's engaging novel, in the summer of 1941, Alice Huffman arrives in New York City with dreams of making it as an actress. Though stardom proves elusive, Al connects with a new circle of friends in the entertainment business, and she's immediately enchanted by Juliana, an enigmatic lounge singer.

"As World War II begins, Al and Juliana cross paths repeatedly and a complicated relationship develops. This romance provides a fascinating entry into New York's gay community during a rarely explored era"—*Publishers Weekly*

"Vanda creates a historical novel about a time period in which we know very little about queerness—WWII ... Vanda's narrative, prowess of timely language, and setting and character development lend a poignant message: to be queer was to be anti-American."—July Westhale, *Lambda Literary Review*.

"Vanda's research includes not only attitudes, specific places and the music of the times (that in itself is fun), but the lingo, the slang, the clothes will put you right in the groove"—Sandra deHelen, *LgbtSr*, author of LGBTQ thriller *Till Darkness Comes* and the Shirley Combs/Dr. Mary Watson mystery series.

"Juliana is a captivating piece of history and romance, a time capsule that captures all the tumult and thrill of wartime America in the early 1940s"—*Indie Reader*

"Imagine the first songbird crush you had—for me it was K.D Lang—and then, imagine that person seducing you. Put on some Irving Berlin songs of the 1940s and let the magic begin"—Roberta Arnold, *Sinister Wisdom*

"Juliana is a masterful work of historical fiction that leads you through the early 1940s with substance and style. It is an LGBT coming of age story, a tale of sexual awakening (and as such, should be reserved for more mature audiences) that really opened my eyes to some of the truths of gay history.

"The author makes very effective use of period language to set the tone and the scene, and even though some of the language may be offensive or hard to read, it is valuable to understand this time in history"—Braver, *On-line Book Club*.

2017, <u>Saints and Sinners</u>, Finalist, Emerging Writer Award.

2017, *Juliana* was shortlisted for the <u>Chanticleer International Book Award: Goethe Novel Award</u>

2016, *Juliana* received an <u>Indie Reader Approval Sticker</u>.

What I'm Doing and Why

I'M WRITING THE story of gays, lesbians, transgenders, bisexuals, questioners, and those who claim no gender at all because I must. These are my people. I'm writing it because this history, and hence, LGBT culture, is in danger of being lost.

Many younger people, gay and straight, are not aware of the battles that were fought to get to the level of acceptance that gays enjoy now. LGBT history did not begin with Stonewall. Too many people only know of that one event, and nothing of what led to that explosion. They don't know there are people walking around today, damaged, still carrying the scars of what went on before. They don't know of the pain that some carried to their grave.

A study completed 60 years after World War II found that almost 15% of closeted LGBT veterans had attempted suicide. (Paolino, 2017) [1]

My series of novels will show what occurred in the decades before *and* after Stonewall. The Stonewall riots were not the end of the story, either. Gays were not suddenly embraced after the riots happened. There were decades of struggle still ahead.

Despite this being a long struggle for rights and dignity, it's not a sad story. Just like every other minority group, LGBTs have always had their own culture, their own language, their own traditions, and their own inside jokes. They've also had their own unsung heroes. Imagine if we didn't know who Martin Luther King Jr. was. This would be a travesty. But how many of you know who Frank Kameny was? The answer to that will be in Book VI.

I began this series in the 1940s with *Juliana, Books 1 & 2, 1941-1944*. This current volume begins with the early Post-War years (1945-1955.) Future books will cover the later decades. The same characters will move and grow through each new time period. Gradually, new characters from different generations will add their own perspectives to those who began the series.

And, as always, history is never simply history: Past truly is Prologue.

* * *

---

[1] Before Stonewall, there was Juliana: Historical Novel Explores LGBT Life During WW2, The Verge of Jordan, May 29, 2017

A few weeks ago, I was presented with the opportunity to promote my book on a particular site. I began filling out the form by answering the usual questions: my name, the title of my book, etc. I then came to some questions that were not so usual. "Are there gay or lesbian characters in your book?" "Are these characters minor characters?" "Are these characters major?"

I thought such questions were odd, but I answered them. At the end of the form they said they couldn't guarantee that my book would be featured on their site. This is the case with many free sites, so I didn't think much of it. They also included a statement saying that if my book wasn't chosen, they couldn't tell me why." This *was* unusual. Then, I noticed that one of the genre choices listed for their site was "Christian."

It now came as no surprise that my book was not chosen to be featured, and I told them this. It's funny, though. I've been around long enough to remember a time when the word "Christian" meant "loving." That was a long time ago.

The second reason I must continue to write this series becomes clear with the next scenario. Two weeks ago, a friend walked out of a Greenwich Village gay bar in the late evening. He was accosted by three guys, who called him "faggot." One guy beat him up badly, while the other two stood nearby, laughing and repeating "faggot."

Knowing this history is important for both gay and straight. It's already starting to repeat itself.

How We Got Here

A SMALL NUMBER of you, in your reviews, were concerned that *Juliana (Volume 1: 1941-1944)* might be considered "racist," "homophobic," and "ableist." It's good that you were concerned. It shows how far we've come, even though we haven't come far enough. Yes, there is homophobia, racism, and ableism in the first volume of *Juliana*, but that doesn't mean the *book* is homophobic, racist, or ableist. When Al refers to her fiancé, Henry, as "crippled" in Book 2, she is not insulting him; rather, she is using the terminology of the nineteen-forties. Hence, her language reflects the time in which she lives, not the time in which the book was written. This is history; I can't change the facts.

If you thought *Juliana (Book 1)* had homophobia and racism in it, then be prepared for Book 2. Let me paraphrase Margo Channing (Bette Davis) in the 1950 film, *All About Eve*, "Fasten your seat belts; it's going to a bumpy book." In *Olympus Nights on the Square,* you are likely to run into every horrifying "ism" you can imagine. There will certainly be racism and homophobia, but there will also be anti-semitism, transphobia and sexism. This is the reality of our world's history. As the Ghost of Christmas Past in Dickens' *A Christmas Carol* told Ebenezer Scrooge: "These are the shadows of things that have been. That they are what they are, do not blame me."

Still, I think it would be a grievous error to sit back congratulating ourselves on our enlightened views while denigrating those who went before. The people from the past struggled with issues that needed to be struggled with. There would be no PC language or PC thinking today if it hadn't been for them. Have we resolved all the issues of our past? Of course not. History isn't a series of dates; it's a process that we're all a part of. We're creating history right now. Which way it goes depends on us.

In Memory

of

My Spiritual Mom

Karen L. Sands

OLYMPUS NIGHTS ON THE SQUARE

JULIANA SERIES - BOOK 2: LGBT LIFE IN THE EARLY POST-WAR YEARS (1945-1955)

VANDA WRITER

SANS MERCI PRESS

Chapter 1

May 1945

WHEN THE GERMANS surrendered in May of '45, we knew the war was almost over. Juliana and I went to Times Square to watch the lights return. I wore a simple day dress. I couldn't wear trousers outside my apartment anymore. Everything was going back to the way it used to be, but wearing dresses ... I just felt funny in them, like they weren't quite me. I didn't remember feeling that way before the war, but now ... Juliana looked gorgeously feminine as usual, in her white cotton dress with the blue flowers splashed across it. She always knew exactly the right thing to wear for looking like herself. We still couldn't get nylons, but the air felt cool against our bare legs, so it was okay.

The square was choking with people. It was an ordinary, dark night with all the lights dimmed or off. Hundreds of us waited for them to come back on after they'd been off for more than three years. Juliana and I stood sandwiched between a huge marine with tattoos on his hands and a broad GI with a smile filled with too many teeth. We couldn't move, but it didn't matter.

An electric charge ran through the crowd, uniting us. It seemed as though we waited forever that night. Then, one by one, the lights popped on. There was the Four Roses ad, and the Pepsi-Cola ad in red, white and blue, and the lights on storefronts, hotels, movie theaters, and Broadway theaters. The whole world was suddenly ablaze, making the night into day. It was the light Manhattan was famous for, but had been snuffed out for too long a time.

A group of foreign soldiers broke into "God Bless America." Army hats and cheers flew into the air. Sailors and GIs pulled women into their arms and kissed them. Hitler was dead and his Nazis defeated. The United States of America was the greatest country in the whole world!

The big marine with tattooed hands grabbed me and kissed me on the lips. I spun out of his arms toward Juliana who'd just been released by her own GI. We ran toward each other filled with love and freedom and ... stopped. *We* couldn't do that.

Chapter 2

THE SOLDIERS WERE coming home. They hurried to cast aside uniforms and don civvies: jackets with wide lapels, pants with wide legs, everything as wide as the air. They married the girls who'd been waiting for them and moved into prefab houses, while Bill Levitt tore up the potato fields in Long Island to build his first Levittown for the rest of them.

All along MacDougal Street, signs decorated the buildings—*Welcome Home, Leon*; *Welcome Home, James*; and *Welcome Home, Smitty*, but there was no, *Welcome Home, Max*. No one but me knew he was even home. He'd practically snuck back in, not wanting anyone to see him, and had been hiding in my place for the last couple months like a criminal. His crime: enlisting in the army when his country needed him.

We stood at the bottom of the stairwell of what had originally been Max's basement apartment; Virginia had lived there now for the past two years while Max was away fighting in the war.

"Max, I don't belong here." I backed out of the stairwell. "You can do this by yourself."

"Stay right here." Max pulled me back. "You're the one who told her I was home."

"I had to. She thought you were dead. How long did you think you could avoid her by hiding in my apartment?"

"I would've told her I was home. In a year or two. She thinks of me as someone important. The way I used to be. The army ... Did you know before they shipped me off to that hospital, they put me in a cage in the middle of the camp with others—like me, in their own cages. Oh, God." He turned his eyes away from me.

I squeezed his arm. "It's over, Max."

"Is it?"

"She's gonna understand."

"Should I knock?"

"I think so."

He knocked. "I always imagined I'd be in uniform when I saw her again. She liked me in uniform. *I* liked me in uniform."

When the army gave him that blue discharge, they took away his uniform and gave him a cheap shirt and a pair of pants that were too short for his legs. Nothing about Max was cheap. Always the best of everything, even when he couldn't afford it. As we stood waiting, I noticed how good he looked in his custom-made, black suit from the thirties and his pre-war silk tie. Had to be pre-war. Who could get silk these days? He'd trimmed his mustache so that he was back to looking a little like Clark Gable. I wore a simple yellow cotton dress. Max insisted I let him do something with my flyaway hair; he put a couple of Victory curls on top of my head. I looked ridiculous.

The door creaked open.

"Virginia," Max said in a gasp of terror.

"Max." Any anger she might have held toward him wasn't there. She wore a satin shirtwaist dress with a blue paisley pattern, and by the length—to her calves—I knew she bought it before the war. She hated the knee-length skirts the war board mandated for saving material. Her brown curls were swept onto her head in the popular updo.

"Are you truly here?" She touched the side of his face lightly as if afraid he was an apparition that would soon fade.

Max smiled. "I'm here, Virginia."

"Come in. You too, Al. I've made some iced tea."

"I'll help you," I said.

"You sit. It's already prepared." She scurried from the room.

Max and I sat on his familiar overstuffed chairs. The place smelled of flowers instead of his stale cigarette smoke. While Virginia went for the tea, I watched Max's eyes scan the room. "Different, isn't it?"

"I'd say so. Where's my David? She's got her African violets where he should be. And the other statue, the one I had on the piano."

"Shh," I whispered. "They're perfectly safe. I put them in your bedroom."

He sighed. "How could I have been so stupid?" he whispered.

"You weren't stupid, Max. You told me the guys in your group were always camping it up, and nobody seemed to care so—"

"Not the love letter. The love. How could Maxwell P. Harlington III let himself fall for some cute, scared, nineteen-year-old kid who thought he was grown up enough to fight in a war?"

"You're gonna find him again."

"Am I? Should I?"

I looked toward the kitchen to be sure Virginia wasn't coming. "I'm gonna drink my tea fast and go. You should tell her by yourself."

"Don't drink too fast." His hands were shaking as he pushed a Gitanes Brunes into the cigarette holder he always used.

Virginia returned and placed a silver tray with our tea on the coffee table. "I have honey there," she said, pointing. "We still can't get sugar, but maybe the honey—"

"That's fine," I dribbled some honey into my glass.

"I don't have lemons, either."

"No one has lemons these days, Virginia," I reminded her. "It's okay."

"I just want Max to be happy."

"I am, Virginia. I'm here, not there."

"Yes, I suppose … that must have been awful for you."

"Yes."

We fell into an uncomfortable silence. Max chewed on his cigarette holder without lighting the cigarette. Virginia smiled too pleasantly, and the clock on the mantle ticked too rhythmically, and too loud.

"So, Max …" Virginia finally broke through the afternoon quiet. "You're home."

Max flicked a silver lighter at his Gitanes, "Yes." He coughed out a puff of smoke. "These things are so strong they're gonna kill me."

"I thought you would wear your uniform. You look so lovely in it."

"Yes, well, that's what I wanted to, uh …" Was he going to do it now? I didn't want to be here for this.

"I missed your letters," Virginia continued. "They just stopped coming."

Every week Virginia received a letter from Max. She'd keep the latest one tucked away in her brassiere, near her heart. When she and I were alone in the kitchen at the Stage Door Canteen, she'd slip it out and read it like she was reciting Lady Macbeth from a stage. For close to six months, no letters came from Max. I knew now that it was because Max was in an army hospital-prison, labeled a sexual psychopath, and couldn't write to her.

"Oh, Max, let me show you." She jumped up.

Max followed her to the window where his David once was. She moved her African violets off the windowsill. "Look," she pointed to the service banner with the blue star hanging in the window. "I hung it for you. I know I'm not your wife, or your sister, or … I'm only your …" she whispered, "beard,[2] but …"

Max turned her to face him. "Don't call yourself that. After all these years, you must know you're more to me than that. Thank you for hanging that for me. I'm sure it's what got me home."

"I thought I lost you." Tears slid down her face.

He lightly brushed her lips with his own. She knew it would never be more, but that afternoon, she glowed like any woman whose soldier had come home from the war.

I tiptoed out.

---

[2] A woman who poses as a wife or girlfriend for a gay man so that his homosexuality isn't discovered. More on this in Juliana (Book 1, 1941-1944) p. 365.

Chapter 3

I LOVED WATCHING Juliana put oil, or lotion, or whatever on her legs. I lay on her bed—in the bedroom that was only hers, not the one she shared with *him*—watching her through the open bathroom door, her foot propped up on the closed toilet seat. I wore my new vest, a pair of gray trousers with the zipper in *front*—Juliana's tailor made them—and a tie with my fedora pushed way back on my head like a gumshoe in a crime picture.

Juliana's hands slowly glided up from her delicate ankles, the lotion sliding over her perfectly shaped calves, her long fingers moving on to her slightly-muscled thighs. She pushed the lace of her underpants leg up a bit so she could massage the oil into that delicious place I loved to kiss, the place where her thigh met her rear. Then she started on the other leg.

"What *is* that stuff you're putting on your legs?" I asked.

"Dorothy Gray's Satura Lotion," Juliana answered. "It captures the dew from the air to prevent aging. It's been scientifically shown to …"

"Okay, that's more than I wanted to know."

She straightened up, drawing her white satin robe around her almost-nude body.

"Do you put that stuff on your legs so they'll be soft for me?"

"No. I put this *lotion* on my legs, so they'll be soft for *me*."

"Not for *him*?"

She gave me one of her "don't start" looks and took out another jar of stuff. She dipped her fingers in and rubbed it on her neck. "Orange flower tonic," she said to the question marks in my eyes. "To prevent double chin." She sighed, "I'm almost thirty. I can hardly say the words."

"You're only twenty-eight."

She studied herself in the mirror as if expecting her face to suddenly collapse. "I just hope Richard comes home with a list of fresh songs for me to sing. There isn't a moment to waste."

"When does he get in?"

"He wasn't sure which ship they'd be putting him on. A few days."

She finished with the orange flower tonic and moved to the end table next to her bed. She took her hairbrush from the top drawer and stood near the bed brushing, in long strokes, the coal-black waves that bounced around her shoulders.

As she brushed, the robe fell open, and I could see her breasts. I kneeled on the bed, and put my arms around her waist, pulling her close to me. I kissed her stomach and started pulling her underpants down with my teeth, but she stepped back. "You better not. I went to confession yesterday. I need to take Holy Communion today."

"Are we sinners?"

"You know my thoughts on that."

"If we're such sinners, why don't we—you—just stop. Not that I want you to, 'cause I don't, but—"

"I can't help what I am." She leaned over the dresser, looking into the mirror and putting on eyeliner.

"Well, if you can't help who you are, then how can God expect you to be somebody else?"

She made a loud sigh. "You've got to go to college."

"College? What does college have to do with it?"

"You keep asking me questions I can't answer." She wiggled into her girdle and hooked up her stockings. She hiked up her robe to her waist and twisted in front of the mirror. "Seams straight?" she asked.

"As always."

Leaning over the dresser, she closed one eyelid and pulled a dark pencil across it.

I lay back on the bed, my hands under my head. "I don't think college would give me answers to these kinds of questions."

"You still should go." She dabbed on brown eye shadow. "You're the college type, and I think you'd like it. You need to start thinking about your future. You're not getting any younger, you know. At twenty-two, you're almost too old to go."

She ran deep-red, almost-maroon lipstick over her lips and blotted them with a tissue.

"Once Richard comes home for good, I guess I won't see you often."

"You can come to the rehearsal studio and watch me rehearse. Richard likes you. Right after the New Year's Eve party, he said he thought you were good for me."

"So, he gave you permission to have sex with me?"

"Ha, ha, funny, funny. He goes on lots of business trips during the year. *And* there's his mother and sister in Omaha. I never go with him on those visits."

"I don't like you having a secret life that doesn't include me."

"It's not secret, Al. It's business. He manages my career." She threw her robe onto the chair near the dresser and put on her blue bra with the lacy top. She pulled her light-blue dress over her head and cinched the matching belt. "Actually, *you're* my secret life."

"Are you going to let him make love to you?"

She picked up her lipstick and put it in the drawer. She picked up the mascara and put that in the drawer. When she went for the eye shadow I said, "Well?"

She put the eye shadow away and looked at me through the mirror. "That isn't a very nice question to ask a person."

"You are."

"He's my husband. A wife has certain duties …"

"Yeah, yeah, my mother tried to tell me all about those *unpleasant duties* when I almost got married. You remember my almost-wedding, don't you? You were there. You kissed me when Henry walked—"

"No. *You* kissed me. I merely responded."

"Do you like it with him?"

She pulled on her left glove, then her right.

"You do!" I said, slamming my fists against the bed.

"I didn't say that. I don't know how to answer your questions." She looked in the mirror to fix the hatpin to the top of her wide-brimmed blue hat.

"It seems like a simple enough question. Not a question I have to go to *college* to get answered. Either you do, or you don't."

"I can't talk about this right before communion. I haven't been to church in weeks, and with Richard coming home …"

She slipped her feet into the heels with the straps that went across her foot. Such a delicate movement, a slender foot slipping into a high-heeled shoe. "How do I look?" she asked, standing at the end of the bed.

"Beautiful. You always look beautiful."

"Not—old?"

"Oh, Juliana." I threw a pillow at her.

She stepped out of the way of the pillow and picked up her handbag from the bed, letting it dangle from her wrist.

"Juliana, I …"

"Yes?" She was giving herself one last look in the mirror, adjusting things.

"You know—the way I feel, uh … for you and …"

"Alice," she sighed.

"Uh, oh. You never call me Alice. Here it comes."

"You know I don't want to hear about those feelings. They'll pass. A woman cannot feel that way for another woman. Those feelings are for husbands so that the couple can have babies. Let's not bring it up again."

"Yeah, sure." She'd just sliced open my stomach with her nail file. Again.

"Don't look like that." She sat on the bed and ran her fingernails up my inner thigh. "I hate it when you look at me with those puppy-dog eyes. We can still have fun, can't we?"

"Uh, Juliana," I was looking at her hand still moving around my inner thigh, getting dangerously—or deliciously, depending on your perspective—close to … "Unless you plan on dumping church and finishing things, you'd better not …"

"Oh." She pulled her hand away, "Sorry. Reflex." She jumped up. "We have all of today to be together. Tell you what. When I get home, I'll fix us a lunch and we'll eat in the park. And tonight, let's go to Tony's for drinks. We'll ask Riley and Warren to join us. They're always up for a club."

"I guess we do have to ask *them*, don't we?"

"We can't go unescorted, but once we're seated, Riley will be with Warren and you'll be with me."

"Sure. It'll be fun."

"Exactly," she spun around. "Tonight, we shall be terribly gay. And when we get home … who knows what loveliness we shall make." She winked at me and headed for the door.

I crawled to the edge of the bed. "A kiss?"

"No. I'm going to church."

* * *

Richard came home unexpectedly that afternoon, so we didn't go on a picnic or to Tony's, and we didn't make any loveliness that night; I didn't see Juliana alone again for four years.

Chapter 4

July 1945

MAX MOVED BACK to MacDougal Street and Virginia moved back to the uptown mansion with her mother. Max gave up on the dream he'd written to Virginia about during the war—the dream to own a world-class nightclub that would rival the Copa. Disqualified for government loans, he had no money to begin again. Most nights, he played the piano in a quiet little bar on Third Street, next to a dimly-lit establishment with no sign; we all knew it was gay. He may have given up on his dream, but my mind wouldn't let go of it.

I sat on my couch in my Milligan Place apartment night after night, thinking. There had to be a way. The fern on the shelf next to *War and Peace* was wilting from my lack of attention. "Dreamer," I heard my mother say one night. That's what she called me when she wasn't calling me demon. "You never pay attention to what's real. You make up stuff in your head." She was crazy and always seeing demons chasing her, so I figured I didn't have to pay a lot of attention to her opinion.

The Japanese would surrender any day now. The war would be over. For so many years, it'd been the center of our lives. I could barely remember a time when it didn't determine everything—what we wore, what we ate, what we talked about. I wasn't sure I'd know how to live without it. Or that I wanted to. Oh, that's ridiculous. Of course I wanted it to end. That's all I thought about the whole time we'd been going through it, and yet, now ... there was talk of the Stage Door Canteen closing soon. What would I do? The war and the Canteen gave me purpose. Without them ...? A cold chill came through the July heat and pierced my chest. I reached out and grabbed Max's dream. It was the only thing that could warm me, but he didn't believe in it anymore. What if *I* did? What if *I* opened a nightclub? Oh sure, Max couldn't get the money, but I thought I could. Big sigh.

I got up from the couch and walked over to the open window. The air was so still, it couldn't budge the filmy curtain I had hanging there. I looked down on the little tree in the courtyard. I always got a sense of strength from that tree growing right through the cement. If that tree could do that, then why couldn't I …? Maybe Max just wasn't thinking right about this. Maybe there was another way we could … If I had my own nightclub, I could hire Juliana. Yes, that's it! I jumped around my living room. No, wait! I skidded to a stop in front of the coffee table. There's more. Of course. I knew what I had to do. In one flash it was all there, right in front of me. *I* would make Juliana a star! No, not just some star. A huge one. Bigger than even *she* could imagine! Yes! That's it. Then she'd choose *me*. She'd have to. I'd be giving her the one thing she really wanted. There would be no reason to stay with Richard. She'd leave him, and she and I would be together FOREVER! I jumped around the room again, then skidded to a stop.

How? How would I make her into a star? I didn't know. Those dark feelings crawled up my legs. The ones that made me think of knives and Mom and … No! I didn't want to think about that. I'd figure it out somehow. I could do this. From some deep down place within me came a whisper, "Queer."

"No!" I shouted. "This doesn't make me that."

* * *

One night, at Max's place, he was looking sad and running his fingers over the keys of his piano, I said, "When I was a little kid, about eight … On one of the nights when my mother threw me out of the house and locked the door, I had to spend the night under our porch—"

"She really did that to you?" Max asked.

"Yeah. Anyway, one of those times, I …"

"How many times did she do that?"

"I don't know. Lots. Listen. It was cold and wet under the porch, so maybe it was to keep myself warm, I started thinking things. Things to do with my future. And under that porch, I decided I had to do something absolutely, completely wonderful with my life."

"Like what?" He played a chord.

"That was the problem. I didn't know. I used to think maybe it was acting the classics on a Broadway stage, so I came to New York City. Then I found out that didn't feel right for me. But working at the Stage Door Canteen with the stars, and the bands, and listening to your stories …"

"You think running a night club might be it?"

"Could be."

"It's not. Running a nightclub is dirty. Hidden under all that glamour is a pile of filth I wouldn't want you knowing about. I was selfish to even bring you into my so-called dream." He gulped down the scotch sitting in a shot glass on top of the piano.

"Virginia!" I squawked.

"What?"

"That's where you can get the money for your club. Virginia."

"No. She needs her father's inheritance so her witch of a mother doesn't keep her prisoner in that mansion for the rest of her life." His fingers played a running scale up the keyboard.

"But you'll make her more money."

"You have no idea how risky owning a club is. I could fail." His fingers ran down the scale.

"Max Harlington the Third never talks of failure. Max Harlington is the boy wonder of Broadway! Where is your arrogance? You were always the most arrogant, conceited—"

"Before the war! Before the damn army …!"

"But you won't fail."

"I could! Dammit, Al." He slammed his fingers down on the keys in a loud chord.

"Don't!" I yelled back, slamming *my* hand on the keys even louder, making an awful sound. "And dammit, yourself."

"Don't curse; it's not lady-like."

Chapter 5

August 1945

"COME IN, AL." Shirl stood at her desk to welcome me, a cigar dangling from her mouth. She wore her usual dark suit and tie. "Why did you want to meet in my office? You should be at the pictures with the air conditioning. We could've met at my home in the evening when it's cooler. Mercy would love to see you."

"I just came from Gimbels, where it's plenty cool, and I'd do just about anything to escape that crummy job. This is business, Shirl, so I thought your office was the best place."

"Hmm, business. Have a seat." Shirl and I sat with her large wooden desk between us. I took off my gloves and placed them in my purse.

Shirl was the most obvious person to approach for start-up capital. She'd been a major investor in Max's first club, but she lost her whole investment in '37, when the club slowly died. Max had crossed Shirl off his list of potential investors, but I didn't.

"So, it's over," Shirl sighed. "After all these years, it's over, but … Have you read people's reactions in the *Times* editorials?" Shirl reached into her desk drawer and pulled out a rumpled *New York Times*.

"Yeah. It's hard to believe they ended it—that way."

"One man says in here." She opened the newspaper to a dog-eared page. "'We have, meanwhile, sunk to the spiritual level of the Nazis.' Do you think that's true?"

"Well, we did kill 200,000 men, women, and children, but … you know? I can't feel it. I can think it, but I can't feel it. I know I should feel some big thing inside me, but I don't. I don't know what to feel. It's amazing to me that those men in the paper could express what they did. And now we're hearing what the Germans did to the Jews. What am I supposed to feel about all this?"

"One of these guys says …" Shirl read, "'It may strike us back …'" She looked up from her reading. "And yet, … my nephew—the only relative I have who'll speak to me—a good kid—was on a troopship heading for the invasion of Japan. I know it's selfish, but I keep wondering if he's alive today, because now there'll be no invasion of Japan." She closed her eyes.

"I know."

The silence between us sunk deep into the humidity that hovered in the room. It seemed as if we should pray, but we didn't.

"Well …" Shirl sighed, throwing the newspaper into the trash can beside her desk. "Are you still volunteering at the Canteen?"

"Yeah, but it's going to close soon. The Theater Wing is opening an acting school for veterans, and the teachers are all going to be celebrities, so there's no place for me. It's not what I want anyway. I gained a lot of experience working there. I worked with budgets, personnel, Broadway stars, orchestras, bands …"

"Are you applying for a job? Because I don't have—"

"I want to open a night club."

Shirl sat way back in her seat, a smile forming around her cigar. "How old are you?"

"My age has nothing to do with it. I want you to look at these plans." I held out the plans Max had drawn up on my living room floor.

"Are you even old enough to drink?" she asked without taking the plans.

"You're laughing at me and I don't like that."

Shirl sat up straight in her chair. "I'm sorry." She stamped out her cigar in the ashtray. "Let me see what you've got there."

I handed her the papers. She shook out a pair of glasses from her breast pocket and secured them onto her ears.

I couldn't believe I'd spoken back to Shirl. No one ever spoke back to Shirl. I got up to walk around, but there wasn't far to go.

I'd never been in Shirl's office before. I usually went to her home on Bleecker Street. That way, I could visit with her and her "special friend" Mercy, too. Shirl's office was on the tenth floor of a building on Madison Avenue and Fortieth. It was a small room, only big enough for a desk, three straight-back chairs, and a file cabinet. Shirl had no tolerance for ostentation.

She was taking a long time studying the papers, and I thought I was going to faint from anxiety and humidity. I leaned against the sill of the window that looked out onto Madison Avenue, counting the steady stream of cars. In my imagination, I saw Juliana singing in Max's nightclub, a halo of stage light surrounding her.

My mind floated back to a time when I was first getting to know Juliana. We sat on her couch, drinking Turkish tea in little glasses. She said the sultan's son had given the special tea glasses to her mother, because he'd fallen in love with her. It was a hopeless love, though, because her mother was already married to Juliana's father.

Juliana had taken my hand in hers that night and led me to the music room. She pulled out a record from a brown sleeve and placed it on her Victrola. "I made this record—'My Romance'—a while ago," she told me. "Mind if I play it while I sing?"

"I'd love to hear it."

She played the piano with the record and sang. Then she let the record play without her. "Let's dance."

"No. I … don't dance very well." I was scared to touch her; she was so beautiful.

"Put your arms around my neck." I did, but I shook inside. She pulled me close and our bodies touched. My heart pounded, and I could hardly breathe. She sang right to me, her perfume floating around me. This glamorous, movie star-type woman was singing to *me*. "See? You're doing it," she said as she guided me over the rug.

Inside me, I felt breathless and giddy … and then … she kissed me. Right on the lips. My tongue met hers, and a vibration shot down to that place, and—

"Al? Hello, Al, are you still with me?"

"Huh? Oh. Shirl. Sorry. I was thinking."

"Must've been some pretty fascinating thoughts." Shirl held up the papers. "These are good."

"I know." I sat down, ready to talk business. Of course, talking business meant I had to tell her the truth. "Those plans were mostly done by Max, but I—"

"No." She stood to hand back the plans to me.

I stood too, trying to be as tall as her, not taking the plans. "Hear me out. Max has changed. He's more serious now. You can ask Virginia."

"*She* would never say anything against Max."

"True, but I think this time he can do it. I think he can make you a wealthy woman."

"I'm already a wealthy woman."

"A fabulously wealthy woman."

"It's sweet you want to help a friend, but you weren't there when he let his club die. Lots of the clubs were struggling. It was the depression, after all. Many went under, but there were some that thrived. The Onyx, for one, and Café

Society, Downtown. Café Society first opened its doors in the middle of the depression, and they're still going great guns today. These clubs helped people to endure those bad times. Everything was dirt-cheap, but the owners managed to keep going. After the repeal of prohibition, that was no easy job with all the new state liquor laws. Max was a handsome, talented boy, a powerhouse, but he squandered his gifts on too much liquor and marijuana."

"Max smoked reefer?"

"You didn't know that, did you? There's a lot you don't know. The boys were his downfall. He was always giving them money or jobs they weren't qualified for, or taking some score on an exotic trip where he spent thousands of dollars impressing the ne'er-do-well. He'd be gone for weeks, while his club foundered."

"But—" I tried to interject.

"It's not only the money I lost," Shirl went on, "my faith in Max was shattered."

"But the war changed things inside him. He's even nice to Virginia."

"I doubt—"

"He wouldn't take money from her to make his dream come true. No money for his dream, Shirl! He was afraid he'd lose it, and she'd be stuck with that mother of hers. Would he have cared about that before the war?"

"I suppose not, but—"

"He can do it. He's learned his lesson. Everyone deserves a second chance. Don't they?"

"Well—"

"You're a fair woman. Everyone knows that about you. How can you condemn him forever? Forever, Shirl."

"I lost a lot of money, and a lot of faith."

"It's not like you to be so unforgiving. That's not the Shirl I know. That's not the Shirl who's always been my heroine."

"Now, really, Al—"

"It's true. Who do I always come to when Juliana makes me certifiable? Who is the wisest woman I know? Please don't crush my faith in you. Who else will I look up to? You know how awful my real mother is."

She sighed, "*You're* not playing fair." She sat down.

I smiled my cutest, sincerest smile. "Couldn't you *think* about it? That's all I'm asking. For you to think about it. You could do that much, couldn't you? For me?"

Another sigh. "Well, if you put it like that, I suppose I …"

"And then you'll talk to him, right? One meeting. That's all. He didn't ask me to come. He doesn't even know I'm meeting with you. *One* meeting. What could you lose?"

"Time. Time is a very valuable commodity. Don't you forget that." She lit her cigar again and blew out a cloud of smoke. "I'll tell you what. I'll see Max here in my office next Wednesday noon, but I want you to come with him."

"That's fine with me. I don't know much about business, but …"

"Don't sell yourself short."

* * *

"Max," Shirl said, leaning across the desk, chewing on her cigar. "I'll give you forty percent of what you need *if,* and this is non-negotiable, Al is given twenty-five percent ownership in the club and kept on as an assistant manager, so she can keep an eye on you. I'll loan her the money for her share at a respectable rate."

"Fine," Max said.

"Are you certifiable?" This was happening too fast. "Me? A part owner of a club?"

"Anyone who can talk Shirl into investing her money with *me* is ready to be a part owner in a club."

"Agreed." Shirl nodded.

"But what if it doesn't work? How will I ever pay you back?"

"So, now that *your* tail is on the line right next to mine, you're not so confident, heh?" Max smiled, flicking an ash off his cigarette into Shirl's ashtray.

"Welcome to the risky world of business," Shirl said.

"Have your lawyers draw up the papers, and messenger them over to my apartment," Max said to Shirl.

"And Al," Shirl looked at me sternly, "I expect you to keep a sharp eye on this man. If he strays, and, you know what I mean, it's your head. You understand?"

"Uh … well …"

* * *

As we stepped from Shirl's building into the bright afternoon sun, Max stopped to light an Old Gold and put on his hat. He'd gotten a new suit—wide legs with cuffs and a broad-shouldered suit jacket with big lapels—especially for this meeting. He had no intention of appearing in Shirl's office in anything less than the latest. "Well, we did it!" I said. "We're gonna open a club."

"Maybe," Max said. He had a far off look.

"Maybe? We got the money. Okay, we still need thirty-five percent, but I can ask Virginia for ten. I know she wants to help, and ten percent isn't so much. She won't get stuck with that mother if things don't go how I know they're gonna. And sure, we still need twenty-five percent more, but ..." Max stood there smoking, looking up at the cloudless sky. "Max? We did it. Why aren't we cheering?"

"We didn't do it, Al. The blue discharge?"

"We got around that by getting the money without asking the government, so—"

"We need a liquor license. *And* cabaret licenses. It's illegal for homosexuals to own establishments that serve liquor."

"Then lie."

He laughed. "My goodness, you're certainly learning this business fast. Yes, we'll be doing a lot of that, but my blue discharge announces to the world exactly what I am, and the big guys are gonna check."

"But you said our problem was money; you didn't say—"

"I never thought you'd get the money."

"Then we can't ...?" My dream of Juliana perched on a star began to drip wax.

"There's one thing I can try. If that doesn't work—"

"It will! It will! What is it?"

* * *

"Calm down, Robert," Max said into the phone. We were both huddled in a phone booth at the Walgreen's Drug Store in Times Square. "I'm not asking you to get involved again. I only want you to sign a couple little papers. I know it's risky, but it'll be plenty risky if you don't. I don't want to threaten you, but ...you don't even have to see me. I'll get the paperwork ready, and you can meet with my assistant. You'll be the owner in name only. I promise. After it's done, you'll go back to Teaneck, and continue living happily ever after with your wife, two boys, and delightfully dull job at the bank. How do you stand it after all you and I had? Don't you miss the nude sunbathing at The Grove?—Okay, okay. Tomorrow noon. Meet Al at Child's—Yes, *he'll* have the papers. Sign them, and your 'normal' life will remain intact."

He hung up the phone.

"Yes?" Holding my breath.

"Yes."

Chapter 6

September 1945

WHEN I GOT off the elevator at the Carnegie Studios, I heard Juliana singing. It was like she'd magically hooked a string to the center of my heart and was reeling me in. She was singing "Till the End of Time." I stood in the hallway, pretending she was singing to me. I dreaded pushing through that closed door, because once I did, I'd feel all the reasons why she *shouldn't* be singing that song.

Inside, it was even warmer than in the hallway. The August heat was hanging on to September. The tall windows were open, but only a dry, dusty breeze occasionally blew in. Juliana stood on a low stage near the piano, singing and smiling at Johnny, her accompanist. She wore a simple light green shirtwaist, a few of the top buttons undone. She'd bobby-pinned her hair off her neck, but a few strands hung loose around her face. There was a lot of bare skin showing. I loved it.

Still singing, she smiled at me. I gripped the back of a chair in the last row and sat down. Richard, in shirtsleeves, his jacket hanging over the back of his chair, sat in the front row, nodding to the music.

What a fool. He obviously didn't know Juliana couldn't handle the ballads. I bet he's given her a whole line-up of ballads. If I was preparing her for an engagement, I'd have her rehearsing funny songs, and sexy songs, and songs where she could show off her dancing, but not ballads. It was like she had some kind of psychological block against them. Her voice always sounded terrific, but still the ballads came out stiff, with little expression, or she made them sound comical when they weren't supposed to be. The only love song she sang well was "My Romance," and it had some silly lines she could play with. I wondered what Sigmund Freud would've said about this. Of course, no one was going to get Juliana on an analyst's couch, so whoever directed her had to work around her "problem." I wondered why Richard insisted on directing her himself. He could easily afford a topnotch professional. That's what I'll get her. The best.

She finished the song. "Al," she called. "Richard, do you mind?"

Richard turned in his seat. "Hey, Alice, I didn't know you'd come in. Sure. Let's take a break." Johnny took a sip from the glass on top of the piano.

Richard put on his jacket with the wide lapels and tightened his tie. He was a few inches shorter than Juliana and had a receding hairline. He wasn't fat, but he was round. He wore the expected baggy pants that all the men wore. "Alice, how nice to see you. Don't you look nice. Blue is your color."

"That's what I've been told." I put on my plastic smile. I hated when people commented on my clothing. It made me feel like they thought there was nothing more to me.

"Gosh, I haven't seen you in such a long time." Richard said, as if we were old friends. I'd only met him once, two and a half years ago. "Since the New Year's Eve Party," he said. "Isn't this heat something? It doesn't quit. I thought by September it would cool off."

"I heard it's going up to ninety-five tomorrow," I added. Why was I participating in this stupid conversation? Juliana stood behind him smiling at me.

"You know, it's not so much the heat," Richard went on. "It's this New York humidity."

"Uh, Richard …" Juliana tapped him on the shoulder.

"Am I monopolizing your friend? I'm sorry. I'm so glad you stopped by, Alice. You're the kind of friend I want for my Julie. Sensible, hard working. Julie, why haven't you asked Alice over to the house?"

"I have," Juliana said. "She's always busy."

The thought of visiting her when *he* was there was too much. I couldn't pretend she was my "girlfriend." So I always said no.

"Well, I'm glad to see you now," Richard said. "What did you think of the song Juliana just sang?"

"Perry Como."

"Very good! You keep up with *Billboard*. He's on the charts with it right now. Doesn't Juliana do a beautiful job with that song?"

"Oh, uh … very nice."

"Wait till you see the whole act. Lots of romantic ballads."

"What a good idea."

"Richard, dear," Juliana interrupted. "I haven't seen Al in four months. Do you mind?"

"Oh, no, you two girls go ahead. But we have to get back to work in a few minutes. Not a moment to waste. Alice, do come to the house for lunch some Sunday. Convince her, Julie."

He left us standing there opposite each other. With her hair pinned up off her neck, and the open buttons, she looked like one of those gorgeous farm girls you see in the pictures. The kind that completely knocks the socks off the traveling salesman. I supposed the traveling salesman was me. For a few seconds, I was silent, watching her breathe. A light speckling of sweat dotted her chest as her breasts went up and down. It was hard to collect my thoughts. I tried not to stare at her wedding ring.

"How can you look like that in this heat?" I asked.

"Like what? A mess?"

"You're not capable of looking like a mess even when you are a mess, and you know it."

"You hated it. The way I sang that song."

"Well, uh … hate's a strong word. It's too bad you can't sing opera, though. That's your best."

"Opera in a nightclub? I'd get laughed out of the business."

"Maybe. I've missed you."

"Really? And yet you never come to see me."

"You said he had lots of business trips to go on, but …"

"Since he's been home he's been focusing on my career, less on his own; he hasn't gone on many business trips."

"How thoughtful. And you think he can get your career going?"

"It's obvious *you* don't."

"Remember how we used to be? During the war? I know it's a terrible thing to say. It was such a serious, deadly … but … I miss it. The war. How we were."

"I know," she said softly, looking over at Richard, who stood near the piano, talking to Johnny. "Every moment mattered. Life was … much more alive." She sighed, "Now, everything is a steady stream of ordinary."

"And we were together. At least some of the time."

"Yes."

"Remember that day at Reggios?" I asked.

"We can't talk about that here," she whispered with a big grin, having the same memory as me.

"You weren't wearing underwear."

"Al." She nodded in the direction of Richard.

"I was so shocked when you told me, but excited too. And then when we were seated, and I put my hand on your knee under the table I—"

"Al—"

"I ran my hand inch by inch up your leg—"

"Al, it's warm enough in here without you—"

"And then I touched your—"

She took in a deep breath. "I better get back before I … Maybe we could meet somewhere." I watched her scurry away, wishing I could grab her back.

Chapter 7

MAX FOUND A cheap, worn-out building in Times Square, on 42nd Street—the crummiest street in the city. One cold September morning, the wind whipping our coats, we stood comparing Max's dream building with the one we saw in front of us. That pile of rubble didn't look like it could ever end up as a fancy nightclub.

"You sure this is a good idea?" I asked before we bought it. "We're in the middle of Hell's Kitchen."

"The Latin Quarter and The Diamond Horseshow aren't far," he said.

"Far enough. And *they're* beautiful. This building is … Everyone, especially tourists, thinks of Fifty-Second Street as the place for nightclubs."

"We can't afford that."

"But what if no one comes to our place?"

Max stared straight ahead, as if he could see our nightclub already standing there. "We'd lose all our money," he said, matter-of-factly. "We'd owe a lot of dough, without having any way to pay it back. No one would ever trust us again. We'd pretty much be ruined."

"Oh, gosh." I looked up to see if there was a grin on his face. There wasn't.

"But remember, Al, *you're* the one who said we could do this."

"And we can! We can." *Can't we?*

Our building was sandwiched between two run-down grinder movie houses with marquees whose picture titles weren't always polite. The whole street smelled of popcorn and hot dogs because it was lined with cheap eating places like Nedick's, Hector's Cafeteria, and the automat. In the street, clouds of white smoke poured from manhole covers. The subway station had a ferocious ventilating machine that tore the hats off people's heads as soon as they entered. The city had huge signs at the entrance saying, "HOLD ONTO YOUR HATS." Soldiers and sailors, in spite of the war being over, still mobbed the area, trying to see all of New York City in twenty-four hours. Tourists poured in to see hit plays like *The Glass Menagerie*, which was changing the whole way we thought about theater even if the *New York Times* did think the language was too flowery.

It wasn't terribly unusual to see a veteran who'd lost a leg or arm in the war leaning against a building with a cup. Carlitos' newsstand, along with all the others in the Square, was lined with muscle magazines, tell-all rags, and the daily newspapers. You had to be a veteran or blind to own a newsstand. Carlitos was definitely not blind; he was always catching sneaking peeks at his magazines.

Back in the days when I was really poor, Carlitos was always yelling at me for standing at his newsstand, reading his latest *Cue*. It was the only way I could keep up with Juliana's career. I mean, I was only looking at one column in the whole dang mag, so why should I buy it? I was buying unhomogenized milk to save the two cents, so I wasn't gonna spend money to read one lousy column in a magazine. Carlitos didn't see things same as me. "Hey girlie, no reading the merchandise. I'm tryin' to make a livin' here," he'd say and then tighten his tie. The tie thing meant he might call the cops, so I high-tailed it outta there.

Down the block from where Max was building his club was Hubert's Dime Museum. Its front had creepy pictures of people screaming and twisting themselves into knots. A guy near the door yelled, "Laaadies and Gentlemen, be mystified, be horrified, for only fifteen cents. See the amazing Alberta, half-man, half-woman; faint at the sight of Ethel, the Bearded Lady."

Hubert's Dime Museum, which mysteriously cost fifteen cents to enter, was famous for its flea circus; but I never saw that 'cause as soon as I saw Ethel, the Bearded Lady, I ran out, terrified. She reminded me of that dream I'd have sometimes where I'd wake up and see I'd grown a beard during the night.

The out-of-town boys, in tight blue jeans and open shirts, would strut down the street and end up in front of our place. "Come on, Max," I said one afternoon, grabbing his arm when I saw him eyeing one of the boys. "We have work to do *inside*, and you promised Shirl."

"No, I didn't. *You* did. But you're right. Bad for business." He reluctantly headed back inside to talk over plans with the contractor.

Soldiers and civilians overflowed the bars, and if they didn't have the price, would leer at prostitutes parading their wares up and down the street. Businessmen on holiday from the Midwest in their trilby hats escorted the girls to the many hotels for transients. The war was over, so you never saw a woman on the street in slacks anymore. The nancy boys—Max hated *them*—dressed up for the evening in make-up and flashy outfits to strut the square. They always managed to score as long as there were no cops around.

Despite this odd collection of humanity choking the streets of Times Square, there never was one speck of trash anywhere. We were the post-war generation, and during that first year, we were filled with nothing but hope.

Chapter 8

February 1946

OVER THE NEXT few months, the club was transformed from an ugly building into a glamorous work of art with fountains on both sides of the stage spraying upward toward the high-beamed ceiling. A huge dance floor, made of the best wood, surrounded the stage on three sides. There were reproductions of famous Greek statues sprinkled among the tables, chairs and banquettes. When customers entered his club, Max wanted them to feel like they were leaving the earth and being elevated to Mt. Olympus, which was the name he ultimately chose—Max's Mt. Olympus.

With the club almost physically ready, Max began thinking about the entertainment. He started grooming me to work with talent, so I could be in charge of hiring some of the back-up people and could one day be a talent manager like he'd been in the thirties. Once he trained me, I'd know enough to make Juliana into a star. Of course, I couldn't tell Max that was my dream. Juliana and Max hadn't spoken since before the war, when she married Richard. Max taught me how to choose the Maxine Goddesses, or The Maxines for short; they were the chorus babes he expected to outdo the Copa Girls.

"You've never been to the *Folies Bergere*, have you?" he asked. We sat at a table with notepaper and a pile of the girls' pictures in front of us. The girls we were auditioning lined the walls and snaked around the room in tights and leotards.

"What's the folly berger?"

"*Folies Bergere*," he pronounced, in what I suspected was perfect French. "It's a nightclub in Paris. They have the most beautiful girls in the world. We must have girls just as beautiful. First, we're going to send home any girl who is less than 5'8". We want tall, leggy girls. Watch. Learn."

Max pulled on his gray suit jacket that he'd folded over the back of his chair and walked to the line of girls; he tapped the shoulders of the ones he deemed too short and pointed them toward the door.

"The next thing I want you to learn is how to choose the right breasts."

"What?" A warm pink ran up my face. I'd never heard a man say that word right out in public, and right to a girl's face.

"Girls at the *Folies Bergere* all have about the same breast size. Wait! I'll show you." Max sprinted toward his office and came back with a thin book. "This is a souvenir program from the *Folies Bergere* in '35." He thumbed through the pages. "Here. Look at this." He pointed.

"Max! Those girls have no tops on!"

"I know. Do you see the size of their breasts?"

"No." I had my hands over my eyes.

He pulled my hands from my face. "Look! This is important."

"You're not going to make the Maxine Goddesses do that, are you? We'll get closed down."

"That's the way they do it in Paris. We can't do that here. Our girls will wear gowns that show off their figures. Sometimes, custom-made togas to match the theme. The pictures in this program will give you an idea of the breast size we're going for. Not too big, not too small. I'll choose today, but I want you to study this program and choose next time. It'll be part of your job."

I flopped into my seat. He couldn't be serious. He wanted me to look at girls' breasts as part of my job? Besides my own, Juliana's were the only ones I'd ever seen, and I liked looking at them, but ... I stared down at the pictures. I'd never seen pictures like these before. Page after page of girls wearing nothing on top but necklaces! *How was I gonna do this job?*

Next, we went on to the roundness of rear ends. When we got down to about sixty girls, we *finally* did the singing and dancing, the best part.

Max and I agreed a lot on which girls were the good singers and dancers, and by the end of the day, we had thirty girls who would be the first Maxine Goddesses. Max said I had a good ear. I knew that must be true 'cause I loved sounds and could always hear the quietest sounds before everybody else. Like seagulls way out over the ocean. Before I could see them, I could feel their vibrations through my skin. That's how I knew Juliana shouldn't be singing ballads.

While Max was hiring chorus girls and the finest musicians for the orchestra, he also looked for a head chef who would oversee the kitchen and create delicacies that could only be eaten at Max's Mt. Olympus. Before we even opened, our club was filled with the most delightful scents because prospective chefs were in our kitchen trying out their masterpieces on Max and me. Besides the head chef, Max hired two assistant cooks and a renowned Chinese chef he'd lured away from the Stork Club to cook the Chinese food nightclubs were expected to offer.

He hired a maitre'd, a hatcheck girl, and cigarette and camera girls. He even hired a fortuneteller, though he didn't believe in them. Every nightclub had one, so his would too. He hired waiters, cleaners, and bathroom attendants. He expected me to sit in on every one of those interviews to learn, and I did. Except—when he was expecting a guy who was gonna sell him some cigarette coin-ops. For that, Max told me to go out and get lunch. Without him. I headed for the front door, but, at the last minute, I ducked behind a wall. A round guy in a gray suit, his trench coat open, and his porkpie hat pushed way back on his head, shoved himself through the glass door, not even taking his hat off. A cigar dangled from his mouth. He held out a stubby hand. "Hey, there, you must be Mr. Harlin'ton."

"Yes," Max said, barely touching the man's fingers.

"Moose Mantelli from Paramount Automat. Sorry de boss, Mr. Miniaci could not be wit' us today, very occupado, but he'll be here for openin' night wit' some of his friends."

Max was staring at the guy behind Moose Mantelli. "Oh," Mr. Mantelli said, "Dis here's my cousin, Jimmy. I'm teachin' him de business." Jimmy was a big guy whose left eye, cheek, and lips were kind of flattened and melted together, so he hardly had a face on that side; it looked like he'd been burned in a terrible fire. He wasn't so easy to look at. He wore a wide-brimmed fedora that covered his eyes. When he took it off, you could see thick brown hair covering his forehead; his left eye was stuck half-closed with no lashes and his hands were shoved deep into his overcoat pockets. Max put out a hand to shake and Jimmy slid out his. There was no thumb. Only a nub of flesh that wiggled. I swallowed down my gasp. Max took the thumbless hand in his, and I thought I was gonna be sick.

Jimmy stayed put, while Moose walked past Max into the main room, looking around. He whistled his approval. "Well, you done pretty damn good for yerself, Mr. Harlin'ton. So, where ya want my guys to put 'em. In here?"

"No!" Max said, panicked. He closed his eyes, calming himself. "Uh, well, Mr. Mantelli, I'm sure you know that would spoil the décor." He plastered a big smile on his face.

"Oh, yeah. Deckor. I know 'bout dat."

"I thought, perhaps, in this hallway down here." Max led the way. Jimmy followed, and I crept behind them, wondering what was happening and why I couldn't know about it.

"It's kinda outta de way," Mr. Mantelli said. "You t'ink folks'll find 'em?"

"The men's room's down there." Max pointed.

"Good t'inkin', Mr. Harlin'ton. You gotch yerself a good head for dis sorta t'ing, doncha? Should we sez ya gonna take four?"

"Well, uh, with four … will the bonus from four cover my short fall?"

"Let's t'row in a juke box too."

"But this is a club. With live music."

"Dem 'musical' guys gotta take a break sometime. Don't dey?"

"But we have a relief—"

"How many can I put ya down for?" He flicked a long ash from his cigar onto the rug.

"One?" Max said, hesitantly.

"How 'bout we sez two? You got dem udder rooms upstairs."

"Why didn't *I* think of that?" Max sighed.

"I'll get dis order in right away and have you up and runnin' in no time." He patted Max on the back, and they headed toward the post I hid behind. I scrambled to slide into the kitchen. Jimmy's one good eye watched me. He moved toward me, and that face … my heart thumped. *Was he gonna kill me?* I opened my mouth to yell for Max, but nothing came out. Jimmy nodded at me and left to stand by Moose.

I heard Mr. Mantelli saying to Max. "Glad to have ya in the neighborhood, Mr. Harlin'ton. Guys da likes of you gives a place class."

Max walked Mr. Mantelli, with Jimmy behind him, to the glass door, and then turned back down the hall. He leaned against the doorsill of the kitchen. "Al, what are you doing?"

"Who are those guys?"

Max sighed. "This isn't something you should think about."

"I'm part owner. I gotta know."

"They're … friends. In the club business, you need 'friends' like that to stay in business. We won't talk about this anymore." He walked away.

* * *

On February 14, 1946, Valentine's Day, in Times Square, surrounded by ugly buildings, Max opened the Mt. Olympus. It was the fanciest, swankiest place in the area.

For the opening, Max had everything decorated in red, white, and blue, with the theme of soldiers coming home to their sweethearts.

Max hired "The Incomparable Hildegarde," the highest paid supper club singer in the business, to be the headliner. We were terrified her salary would break us, and I tried to talk him out of it. I was having those visions of me moving into my own cardboard box down on the Bowery. But Max knew he had to take the risk if he was gonna compete with the top clubs. We held our breaths.

Limousines crowded the block to drop off grand dames, dripping in furs and diamonds, on the arms of some of the richest, most powerful men in the country. Moose Mantelli introduced me to Mr. Miniaci and Mr. Frank Costello. Moose was always a disheveled mess with crumbs sticking to his lapels, but Mr. Costello and Mr. Miniaci, the owner of Paramount Automat, were clean, and they wore expensive tuxedos that fit real good, and they smelled good too. Mr. Miniaci came with his wife, who was dressed in a silk Balenciaga— Max told me that's what it was—and a silver fox stole. Moose's cousin Jimmy wore a tux, and had his hands stuck deep in his pockets. That face. No date. *He* was scary.

Hildegarde's name was emblazoned across the marquee in red and white neon. Still, I don't think Hildegarde's enormous popularity was the only reason Max insisted on hiring her. I think it was his own private joke. Although we would never be a club that openly catered to homosexuals, having Hildegarde as our first singer was like a coded invitation to gays who knew how to be discreet and blend in. Hildegarde was one of their secret icons. They were there that night, invisible to the straights, but there, despite the State Liquor Authority's law against serving alcohol to immoral persons like homosexuals.

We needn't have worried about Hildegarde's salary. She knocked the audience on its rear, and the next morning, all the papers had stories on it. *The Herald Tribune* asked, "Can Broadway Golden Boy Do It Again?" *The New York Post* said, "You can't keep a good man down, and that good man is Max Harlington." Even Walter Winchell stepped away from the Stork Club to gush over Max's return. Max was on his way. Now, if only I could convince him to hire Juliana.

Chapter 9

June 1946

THE MT. OLYMPUS grew to be a popular nightspot, but not as big as Max dreamt it. It wasn't rivaling clubs like "21" and El Morocco, and The Copa wasn't intimidated. Yet.

I rode around in taxis, and sometimes limousines, as part of my job. With Max's help, I learned to wear gowns, and furs, and pearls. I had to wear the Dior New Look with its flared skirts that were kept bouncy by the frilly petticoats underneath. I'd resisted as long I could. I even joined The Little Below the Knee Club, which protested the mid-calf length of the New Look skirts coming out of Paris and influencing Ready-to-Wear. Christian Dior, in Paris, thought it was a great idea to put women back into long, puffy skirts with petticoats after years of wearing the mannish wartime styles. A lot of us didn't want to go back to clothes that restricted our freedom of movement, so we kept wearing our skirts a little below the knee. When Dior visited New York, our club organized a march down Fifth Avenue against him. I felt like a traitor wearing those New Look dresses Max told me to wear.

During the day, to look serious to the men at business meetings, I wore suit jackets and school marm blouses like Dorothy Arzner, the picture director. Only I didn't wear a tie like she did. Max would've bounced me out of our place for sure if I ever wore a tie.

As part of my job, I met with agents and personal managers of nightclub talent that included singers, dancers, comics, and jugglers. Max regularly introduced me to Senators, Congressmen, Broadway and Hollywood stars—Lucille Ball came in with a male friend one night. I loved her in that radio program, "My Favorite Husband," so I got her autograph even though Max told me never to do that. I met jazz celebrities and gangsters. Moose Mantelli was there most nights with his crowd and a different lavishly-dressed lady. Next to him was always his cousin, Jimmy. The legless Vet told me that in certain circles, Jimmy was known as Jimmy "the Crusher" Mantelli.

One night, during the dinner hour, our doorman came looking for Max. He always stayed outside under the awning in his black jacket with the gold epaulets, greeting our guests, so it was strange seeing him inside. "What is it, Georgio? Max is having drinks with Mayor O'Dwyer."

"Coppers. Outta side. They wanna him." Georgio had an Italian accent, and a headful of gray ringlets. "Missa Al, I needa this job. The coppers say he needa bringa his papers."

"He'll be right there." My heart beat in my throat as I practically ran to the bar. "Max!" I pushed myself between him and Mayor O'Dwyer.

"Al, what are you doing?" Max admonished. "I'm having a conversation. With the mayor."

"I'm sorry." I bowed to the mayor. "Max, it's important."

"You go ahead, Max," the mayor said. "You don't want to upset this sweet young thing." He patted my rear. "I've gotta go after this shot anyway."

Max slid from his stool. "Al, what's so important you'd interrupt me with Mayor O'Dwyer? We need him."

"The police!" I whispered. "They wanna see your papers. Outside in the squad car."

"It's nothing. You gotta be calm about these things. They only want to see our cabaret and liquor licenses."

"But your name isn't on those. They're gonna close us down."

I hurried beside Max as he sprinted to his office. "Where are you going? The cops are in the other direction."

Max lifted a wood panel from the wall near the molding and reached into a safe in there. He counted out a fistful of large bills. "No. They're not," he said, placing the bills in an envelope.

"What?"

"You asked if they're going to close us down. They're not." He locked the safe and stood. "I suppose it's time for you to know about this, but I don't ever want you to have anything to do with it. You have clean hands. Keep them that way. We need to make regular payments to the cops so that no one asks to look at those licenses up close."

He hurried from the office and pushed through our heavy double doors. *Calm. He told me to be calm. Oh gosh, I'm gonna die.*

A few minutes later, Max came back with …

Walter Winchell! Was I *really* seeing him? I'd only seen him in magazine pictures. His mostly-bald head had strings of hair crisscrossing his scalp. I didn't know he was bald. In the magazine pictures, he always had his hat on. There he is! The real Walter Winchell! Walking toward me!

"Walter, I'd like you to meet my assistant, Alice Huffman," Max said as the two men approached. "Alice, this is Walter Winchell."

"Uh, uh, yes, I—I …"

"Nice meeting you," he said. "Assistant? But she's a girl."

"Yes, yes, I—I …" I blathered.

"She's not usually so tongue tied," Max said. "You've got her starstruck, Walter. Let me show you to our table. Will June be joining us?"

"No, the old ball and chain set me loose tonight."

I stared as the two men ambled down to the front tables. I couldn't believe I was in the same room with … and I sounded like a jerk. Dang! What was the matter with me?

He was a hero in my neighborhood. My father adored him. When Winchell came on the radio, you didn't talk on the phone, or eat dinner, or go to a movie. You listened. He was a champion of the poor.

I sauntered down to the front to watch Max having a drink with him. I wished I was a waiter, so I could wait on him. I stood near the mobsters' table at ringside, trying to catch Mr. Winchell's words. I knew they'd be brilliant. I couldn't hear a thing. Moose's voice bellowed through the dining room. "I heard he's musical."

Frank Costello laughed, "No kiddin'? Dat guy's a for-real faggot? I can't stand dem guys. Shoulda shot their gawddamn balls off."

"I'd do dat for ya myself, Mr. Costello," Moose said, "Wit' pleasure. If one dem comes anywheres near youse guys—Pow!"

Frank said, "I hate dem dames day go wit, too. Ya know da ones dat wear dem 'comfor'able shoes.'"

They laughed. The woman choking Moose's arm giggled. "I t'ought you liked dem bull dykes, sweetie."

"Only if dere da softer variety," Moose said, "and dere's two of dem, and they invite me to jern in."

They laughed again, but Mr. Miniaci stopped them. "Gentlemen! Dere's ladies present. I am glad my Rose ain't here tonight listenin' to dis fowlness."

"Sorry, Mr. Miniaci, I swear to Gawd on my mudder's grave," Moose said, bowing. "I woulda never bring no fowlness to your dearest Rose, the soil of dis eart'. Forgiveness ladies."

"Ah, fuhget it," his date said. "Day got any beer here?"

I stopped trying to listen to Walter Winchell. Now, I was worried they were talking about Max.

Even though I traveled in these circles, I knew I wasn't a part of it all. I ached for Juliana, and tried to follow her career. She appeared in small clubs around the country and did gigs in Indiana, North Dakota, and once in Okefenokie, Georgia. Max got a big laugh out of Okefenokie. He couldn't believe her dope of a husband would book her there. He grumbled as he read one of her New York reviews in the *Daily Compass*. "Juliana is a delight with the funny, cute songs, but she never seems able to shake up a ballad ..."

"What does this guy know?" Max said, slapping the newspaper. "He used to bus tables for me in the thirties. Now, he thinks he's a critic?"

"He's right," I mumbled to myself.

For a while I continued to go to Juliana's rehearsals, but it got too painful watching her husband direct her wrong. It was like watching a car crash over and over into a brick wall with my beautiful Juliana inside being mangled in the wreckage. Finally, I stopped going. I didn't go to her local engagements, either. I wondered if she noticed I wasn't there anymore. Maybe she replaced me with some cuter eighteen-year-old from the country like I'd once been. It wouldn't be long before I surprised her with my plan to make her a star. I was learning as fast as I could. I hoped by the time I was ready she'd still want me.

I got invited to exclusive parties, but, to Max's dismay, I rarely went. No matter how much I charmed these people, I knew I would never truly be one of them. My favorite thing about being the assistant manager at the Mt. Olympus was leaving work at two in the morning, four on Fridays and Saturdays when the city still burst with life and color. I liked returning home to my Greenwich Village apartment when the light was just starting to break through the night sky, and no one walked on the streets but me.

Chapter 10

March 1948

AS PART OF my training, Max took me around to meet the top club owners on Swing Street, or as they called it, "The Street." The Street was where Max wanted to be. Fifty-Second between 5th and 6th Avenues, or thereabouts. Most, but not all, were jazz clubs. There was Jules Podell at the Copa Cabana, Sherman Billingsly at the Stork Club, Jimmy Ryan at Jimmy Ryans', and Joe Helbock at The Onyx. They all had been palsy-walsy with Max back in the "old days" and were glad he was coming back. They didn't have much to say to me. A girl club owner? Really? Max kept telling me someday I'd show them. *Yeah, I would! When I made Juliana a star.*

There was a light snow falling the night Max and I dressed up and took a cab to Café Society, Uptown. When Max couldn't convince the Rogers-Hammerstein Office to take a look at Tommie, my friend from the Stage Door Canteen, for the chorus of *Annie Get Your Gun*, he knew he had to do something. Max's reputation from the late thirties was getting in his way.

Tommie was hurting for dough, so Max got him a job waiting tables with his friend, Barney Josephson, owner of Café Society, Uptown and Downtown. Tommie wasn't too happy about that, but he needed the cash, so he took the job. But Max put Tommie there for a reason. He knew Barney gave newcomers a chance. He'd given Billie Holiday her start at the downtown club, on Sheridan Square in the late thirties. Juliana had appeared downtown before the war. Max told me Barney was a good person for me to know. That snowy night, when Max and I stood under The Café Society, Uptown awning waiting in line to enter, we knew this was it—Tommie's big chance. He wasn't going to be waiting tables that night.

Inside, white and Negro couples bebopped around the tables. It was a little before the ten o'clock show, and the place was packed. We had to wait in line to get to the hatcheck girl. Standing there, watching the dancing couples, I thought how strange it was to see colored customers sitting and dancing right alongside white customers. Café Society, Up and Downtown, were about the only nightclubs to let colored *customers* in; but Negroes were allowed to entertain in all the clubs.

The ceiling was cathedral-high with balconies and elaborately painted murals around the perimeter. The colors were a swirling thrill of aliveness.

"Beautiful, isn't it? Not like Barney's downtown place. That place is much more casual."

"Juliana appeared there."

"I know. When Barney bought this place, he hadn't dug the other place out of hock yet, but he was a big risk-taker. The risk paid off. Both places are going great guns."

"Like us. In a few years. Maybe we should let Negro customers into our club too."

"You don't think we're taking on enough risk with my little 'army discharge' secret? We need another thing for them to get us on?"

"Oh."

As we neared the hatcheck girl's booth, Max helped me out of my stole and took off his own hat and overcoat, handing them to the girl. As soon as we moved away from hatcheck, Barney Josephson came dashing up to us. "Max!" He shook Max's hand vigorously. "It's good to have you back with us."

Barney Josephson was a slender man with gray hair receding from his forehead. He wore, what was obviously an expensive three-piece suit—not a tuxedo like Max—and brown and white, two-toned shoes.

"You're here for your boy," Barney continued. "The rehearsal with the band this afternoon was flawless, *and* he told me he's been cast in Garson Kanin's new one, *Born Yesterday*."

"That's right," Max said. "Gar and I go way back. He's opening the day after tomorrow. I want you to meet my assistant manager, Miss Alice Huffman."

"Assistant? That's a fancy title for a secretary."

"She's not a secretary; she's a manager. She's also part owner of the Mt. Olympus."

"The war sure brought on lots of changes." He stuck out his hand to me. "You think you're up for the job, Miss Huffman?"

"I have to be. I have a lot to lose."

"Good. Having something to lose will keep you sharp. I didn't have two dimes to rub together when I started this place, and now look."

"I hope I'm as lucky, Mr. Josephson."

"Luck had *nothing* to do with it. Oh, what am I saying? Of course it did. Without luck, Miss Huffman, you'll never get here, to The Street. And without luck, you'll never stay here."

"Barney knows what he's talking about," Max said. "We better go to our table, Barn. Nice seeing—"

"Mr. Josephson," I said, resisting Max's attempt to pull me away. "Do you remember Juliana? She sang in Café Society, Downtown before the war."

"Yes, I do."

"Well …?" I waited, expecting him to say more; he didn't.

"Let's go, Al." Max pulled on my sleeve. As we weaved in and out of the dancers circulating around the tables, he asked. "You're still thinking about Juliana? Forget her."

He might as well have asked me to forget breathing.

"That's so strange," I said to Max, as we sat at a table. Edmund Hall and his sextet were playing the pre-show music.

"What's strange?" Max asked, fitting a cigarette into his holder. "Oh, look, Tommie's first on the bill." He pushed the program toward me and lit his cigarette. "He's going by his real name—Tom Clanton. My boy is growing up."

"Juliana sang in Barney Josephson's downtown cafe back in '41, but he didn't have much to say about her."

"What's strange about that? That was six years ago. Barney sees hundreds of singers. He probably barely remembers her."

"No. I've talked to people. If he hired her he had to like her, and talent he likes, he keeps on, sometimes months, even years, like Edmund Hammond on stage now. He's not like the other owners who keep a singer for a few days and then throw them out like yesterday's fish. *Plus,* Juliana's gorgeous, and Barney is known for … you know."

A spotlight rose to follow Tommie onto the stage. *Please God, don't let Tommie forget the words.* He wore black tails and a stiff-collared tuxedo shirt with a black tie. He sang into the microphone, "Fly Me to the Moon." I knew Max had been working with him, but I couldn't believe how polished he looked on stage. I always saw him as the kid who helped me at the Stage Door Canteen, the kid who flapped his hands around, never trying to hide his limp wrists. Now he was masculine, no limp wrists. The piano player and drummer picked up the pace, and Tommie moved to the faster rhythm. He stepped off the stage, and the girls at the front tables sitting with their dates sighed. He winked at them as he exited.

The audience went nuts with clapping, including me. Max looked so proud. Bobbysoxers sitting in the balcony flopped over the bannister, screaming; their dates didn't look pleased. If only they knew.

Tommie came back for an encore, singing and snapping his fingers to "I Can't Give You Anything but Love, Baby." Practically the whole audience was on its feet dancing.

"Well, Miss Huffman," Max said, "will you do me the honor?"

"You mean you and me?"

"Unless you have someone else you want me to dance with." He took my hand and led me to an open space. Dancing with Max made me feel like I was a good dancer too.

After Tommie left the stage, Café Society regular, Sister Rosetta Tharpe, a colored gospel singer, came out singing her special combination of gospel and blues while she played the guitar.

As the house lights came up, Tommie gracefully snaked around the tables, flapping his hands in his usual way. "Well?" he asked, as he slid into a chair at our table, gracefully placing one leg over the other. He'd changed into a tan jacket and tie.

"You were terrific," I said.

He grinned, looking like the sweet Tommie I'd always known. "So, Max?" This was the person whose opinion counted most.

"You were good, kid."

"Yeah?" he squealed. "Tell me again."

Max ruffled his hair. "You were good, Tom Clanton. Darn good."

Tommie grabbed Max's hand and kissed his thumb.

"Need a lift home?"

"I made a friend here. He's walking me home in the moonlight." He nodded toward the corner of the room. A thin young man in glasses and a blue suit with wide lapels leaned against the wall.

While we waited in line at hatcheck, I saw Barney near the exit surrounded by patrons telling him they'd loved the show; one of them was the brilliant actress Eve Le Galliene, who I saw in *Hedda Gabler* on Broadway in February. Max had told me once she was "that way."

"Al," Max said, "go and say hello to Miss LeGalliene."

"I don't know her."

"Introduce yourself. Invite her to the club. That's how you get successful in this business. Hobnobbing with celebrities."

I took a few tentative steps toward her. She was such a famous actress. What would I say to her? "Miss, Miss …" I whispered to the floor and ran back to Max. "That's not something I do."

"You're going to have to—"

"Al! Al!" Angela Lansbury came running toward me. "Al, how simply brilliant to see you after all these years," she said in her English accent. I ran to her and we embraced. Flash from cameras danced around us.

"How have you been?" I asked. "What am I saying? You've been terrific. Two Oscar nominations and a Golden Globe. I loved you in *The Picture of Dorian Gray.*"

"Yes, but I simply must thank you for the kindness you showed me when I was new to the States and first came to the Stage Door Canteen. I didn't know a soul. A babe in a foreign land, and you welcomed me."

"I didn't do much."

"Oh, but you did. I must be on my way, but let's meet for lunch."

Max cleared his throat from behind me.

"Oh! Angela, this is Max Harlington, owner of the Mt. Olympus."

"Hello, Mr. Harlington. I've heard many nice things about your club." She shook his hand. "Al, didn't I hear something about you being the manager over there?"

"Assistant."

"Well, I'm sure you'll be chief in no time. Won't she, Mr. Harlington?"

"Yes, of course. And I hope while you're in town you'll be my guest at the Mt. Olympus."

"That sounds lovely. I'll see what I can do, but now I must hurry off. Lunch, Al? How about next week before I go back to L.A.? Here's my card. Give me a call. Cheery-bye." She dashed from the room with a group of people buzzing around her.

"Not something you do, huh?" Max said.

"Well …"

The crowd around Barney began to thin. "I'll be right back," I said to Max, as he took our coats and his hat from the hatcheck girl.

"Al, what are you …?"

I ran to where Barney stood, surrounded. I waited for Miss Le Galliene to leave and then barged through the crowd of important people who now stared at me.

"Sorry," I said to their disapproving eyes. "I uh—"

"Don't apologize," Barney said. "Be as tough as your inclination. Don't sit on your instincts. If you do, you'll never make it in this business. So, what'd you want?"

I felt eyes boring into the back of my head as I stepped away from the crowd. "I wanted to ask you something. Over here?" I walked away from the group, and he followed me. "I wanted to know—"

"You're Alice, right?"

"Most folks call me Al."

"Okay, Al. So?"

"Before, when I mentioned Juliana, you acted as if you barely remembered her, and I couldn't see how—"

"I remember Juliana well. She's a beautiful woman. That's not easy to forget, but besides beauty she has talent. The problem is she doesn't seem sure how to use it. Sometimes she was inconsistent in her delivery."

"The ballads."

"Yes! I'm impressed. I would've kept her on, given her time to work on her act, but she left after a week. I don't have contracts with my performers so—"

"You mean *she* was the one who decided to leave? Why?"

"I have a theory, if you'd like to hear."

"Yeah!"

"Excuse me, Barney," a young man said. "The phone for you. Leon."

"Tell him I'll be right there." He turned to me. "I have to take this. It's my brother. But wait. I'll only be a sec, and then we'll have a drink and talk."

Max, holding my fur, pushed through the exiting crowd. "Al, what are you doing?"

"Oh." I laughed. "I forgot you were waiting. Barney's gonna tell me something about Juliana. You can go if you want."

"I'm not leaving you by yourself, but why are you pursuing—"

Barney hurried back to us, pulling on his overcoat, his gray fedora plopped haphazardly on his head. "I can't talk now. My brother. Subpoenaed to appear before the House Un-American Activities Committee. They want to send him to prison."

Chapter 11

December 1948

IT WAS NOT a good day, and it wasn't because of the snow. I moved *Billboard Magazine* off my desk onto the chair and thumbed through the mountain of papers I had to get through. Jergen's Lotion had dropped Walter Winchell's radio show. Jergens had been sponsoring his show for twenty-six years. What was he gonna do?

Thick snow flew past my window. It was my job to keep up with the dailies, weeklies, monthlies, anything that was going on in the entertainment industry, so we could stay ahead of things. Today my job was too hard. Under the load of papers, I found a letter from Tommie. That made me smile. Maybe it would help to read it now.

Earlier in the year, Tommie had opened in *Born Yesterday*. He only had a small part, but got terrific reviews for being the prissiest assistant hotel manager you'd ever expect to see on a Broadway stage. It'd been Max's idea. Max knew audiences loved to laugh at swishy men, so that's what Tommie became. *Their* idea of the sissy. No one ever suspected anything. After all, he was only acting. When the play transferred to The Henry Miller Theater, Tommie wasn't with them. He'd signed a contract with RKO, Hollywood. I opened the letter.

"Al, I met George Cukor last week, and yesterday I went to his Sunday soirée! We swam naked in his pool. You would've perished if you saw all the naked lady movie stars there. Telling you that is my little present for you. There were a couple of beautiful boys in the pool that I had my eyes on. That was a present for me."

I folded the letter back into the envelope. I'd read the rest when I was home and could concentrate. I leaned back in my chair. Then, restless, I got up to look out the window. The snow had made uneven piles along the sidewalk. Cars inched down the street.

I missed Barney. Over the past few months, I'd been spending more time with Barney Josephson. I guess you could say we'd become, I don't know, friends? I'd go to Café Society, Uptown and we'd talk. There was always some blues musician rehearsing in the background. Barney told me about his mother and father, his brother, Leon, and his older siblings who were born in Russia. Barney was born in what he called "The Valley of the Israelites," Trenton, New Jersey. I loved his stories. When he told them, it was like I was in his family, too, instead of the one *I* came from. To Barney, family was the most important thing in the world. His mother taught him that. I didn't really understand, but I liked the idea. The other thing he told me was that he thought the reason Juliana wasn't the big singer she should be was because she didn't believe in herself. I thought he had to be wrong about that.

I wandered back to my desk, and my eyes fell on Dorothy Kilgallen's "Voice of Broadway" column in *The Journal American*. How could this be the same woman? In this column, she glorified the simple joys of The Stork Club's Sunday Morning Rumba Breakfast for parents and their children. Only a few months before, she was ruining Barney's life by using her column to call him a communist.

Barney told me Leon didn't believe in the House Un-American Activities Committee, otherwise known as HUAC, should exist because of the first amendment—it was taking away people's right to have their own thoughts. Leon refused to cooperate, so they sent him to jail. The worst of it was they blamed Barney for his brother. They acted as if Barney *was* Leon, and not himself, with his own mind. People got scared to go to Barney's clubs, and performers who'd known Barney for years were afraid to perform there. Westbrook Pegler, in his column in *The Daily Mirror*, called on Barney to disown his brother, but Barney believed too much in family. Pegler hinted that if Barney didn't disown his brother, then he must be a communist too. Lots of folks agreed with him. What was wrong with everybody?

One day Max came into my office and said, "Al, I don't want you visiting Barney anymore."

"Why?" I asked. "He teaches me things, and he's all alone."

"I know. I feel bad, but—"

"You don't think he really is a communist, do you?"

"No. It's—self-preservation." He tried to smile. "You're not to contact him in any way. Don't call him on the phone, or send him a telegram."

"I can't even say good-bye?"

"No."

"But if all his friends desert him now—Max, nobody would ever think you're a ..." I whispered, "communist."

"We can't take that chance. We need to stay on the right side of the columnists. We have other secrets that can't get out. The columnists are our bread and butter. They feed the cooks, and the waiters, and the bathroom ladies, and you. We need them."

"But you said Barney was a good person for me to know, and now I know him, and you ... that's not right!"

He jumped up. "This isn't about right and wrong, dammit! If you want to keep working here, you *can't* see Barney again."

"Is that an order? Or a threat?"

"Not an idle one. I can't lose this club. I couldn't go through that again. You have to choose. The Mt. Olympus *is* me, all the 'me' I have." He walked out.

I flopped back into my chair. I wanted to at least explain to Barney, but I couldn't betray Max. If only I could see Barney once ... but what if Max found out? Or a columnist?

For the next few weeks, I had horrid dreams of the columns and Greek statues of the Mt. Olympus crumbling and falling into the swimming pool. In one dream, I saw Barney coming toward me, walking blindly through a mist. He held a lantern to light his way, but it shed no light. "Al, where are you?" he cried out. He walked by me, not knowing I was right there. The columns turned into Max, bleeding.

I heard Barney was losing lots of money. He rarely had customers anymore, but that was okay because performers wouldn't perform for him any more. They wanted to, but they were afraid they'd ruin their own careers. Then one day, at the beginning of the month, he sold his clubs and disappeared.

I picked up my copy of *Billboard* lying on the chair. I cleared a space on my desk and opened it to the back page. I ran my hand over the expensive full-page ad, pulling its significance into my own body. It read: "Bloodied, But Unbowed."—Barney Josephson.

Chapter 12

February 1949

"AL?" MAX STUCK his head into my office as I was thumbing through *The Journal* and *The Mirror*. I was making sure Franklin Dodge, our PR man, was doing his job—getting us mentions, but not the wrong kind. "Mind if I come in?"

"…No." I hesitated, because it sounded like something was eating him, and he was gonna hit me with a surprise I didn't want. He sauntered in with a pose of, 'I have nothing better to do today,' which was never the case. His Galois was already lit and stuck in the holder.

"I mean I wouldn't want to disturb you," he said.

"That never bothered you before."

"I see you're reading the dailies. Good girl."

"What do you really want to say?"

"May I sit down?"

"Since when do you ask?"

"Well, I think I've been rude to you, and I want to correct that. You're growing up to be a fine young lady. One any man would—"

"No. Sit."

"Al, after what happened to Barney Josephson, you *have* to consider—"

"What happened to Barney has nothing to do with me. And he wasn't a Communist. His brother was. One who *quit* the party back in '35. This lady here." I slapped the *American Journal.* "This Dorothy Kilgallen, saying that Barney's mixed race policy was a communist plot while her own husband runs around getting young girls pregnant and then dumping them."

"Al!" He ran to shut the door. "My God, she's a powerful woman! Anyone around here could be working for her."

"Why doesn't she clean up her own house before she goes around—"

"If she heard you talking like that she would be all over us. She is very sensitive about her husband's indiscretions."

"Indiscretions? That's what you call them?"

"Please, Al, you've got to get this. Without these columnists' good favor the Mt. Olympus will die just like the two Café Societies did."

"Barney's clubs didn't die. They were murdered."

"Perhaps, but you can't say these things, not even to me. You're scaring me to death. This brings me back to your getting married." He inhaled a long stream of smoke. "Franklin asked me to talk you into it. He knows his PR, that's why we pay him all that money, and he thinks we were lucky Barney had so much to dig into it distracted them away from us."

"Our good luck is based on the bad things that happened to Barney? That's horrible."

"I didn't say that. I simply meant we were lucky they didn't go after us and find—you know. We may not always be so lucky. I was damn scared during those months. I still am. Franklin feels it'd be safer for everyone if you were married."

"Everyone in this whole club's safety depends on me getting married?"

"I wouldn't put it that way. But it would certainly make our investment more secure."

"And Virginia and Shirl think this?"

"I didn't actually ask *them*, but Franklin—"

"This is only coming from Franklin? Tell him to go out and do his job. There's nothing in this weeks' papers about us. He's blaming our not getting coverage on me so you don't fire him. There's something sleazy about that man."

"Of course, there is. He's in PR."

"I wouldn't know what to do with a man."

"You don't have to do *anything* with him. Only—live with him. You could have separate bedrooms. Separate living rooms. Kitchens! Even separate apartments. You need the license that tells the world you're not 'funny.'"

"I'm not 'funny!' But no columnist would put something like that in a newspaper. Their editor wouldn't let them."

"They put it between the lines. I don't want them picking on you. This life is not right for a young girl. Don't you want children like other girls?"

"No. I've never wanted them. There's some part missing in me, but dang-it, our whole dang business can't stand or fall on whether I get married on not. Can we stop talking about this?"

"Uh …" He turned in his chair and seemed to be looking past the window in my office door. "Sure … it's … there's someone—"

"No. Tell me you don't have someone out there for me to meet."

"Of course not." He pulled open the door. "See? No one." He stood with his hand in back of him, shooing away the "someone" who wasn't there. "Would I do that without your permission?" He closed the door.

"Yes."

"He's a friend of mine."

"Oh, Max."

"You don't have to meet him if you don't want to."

"Good. Tell him I'm sorry for his trouble."

"His name is Bartholomew Montadeus Honeywell the Fourth."

"Don't you know anybody with a normal name, Maxwell Philbert Harlington the Third?"

"He comes from a good family. With money. That'd be good for your future security."

A young man, about my height, who I suspected was Bartholomew was jumping up and down, and waving at me through the small window in my closed door. I waved back, smiling through gritted teeth. "Please, Max, do something."

"I'll get rid of him, but think about it. This nightclub life is hard and ugly and … well, you're a girl—I know you're plenty tough for a girl, but I think you're going to need certain things that this life can't … You should have someone to take care of you."

"Him?" I pointed. Bartholomew was still jumping up and down waving.

Max ran out my door, grabbed Bartholmew by the elbow pulling him away, yelling, "What's the matter with you?"

Chapter 13

January - April 1949

I SAT AT the counter of Hector's Cafeteria finishing up one of Hector's famous cream puffs, my thoughts on … who else? Juliana. Almost every night, I'd climb into bed and imagine her lying next to me. Then I'd … you know. It was the only way to keep her with me. But when it was over, I'd feel a hole in my stomach that I tried to fix by imagining Juliana taking bows at the Copa, and throwing me kisses from the stage 'cause I was the one who got her there.

I looked down to see a brochure from City College on the floor with a dusty shoe print. I heard Juliana saying, "You're the college type." I picked it up.

Back then, I had no idea what she'd meant, but now I wondered; if I went to college, would I learn enough about business to make Juliana into a star faster? *She* almost went to college.

Max was all for it. He thought I'd learn modern business methods. I planned on studying business and music, but girls at City College were only allowed to major in Education. I wasn't interested in being a teacher, but Max told me to do it anyway. He said, "An education is something no one can take away from you." So in January, 1949, I registered as an Education major, one course: Music Appreciation.

I never got to know many of the other students 'cause I was always running from class back to the club, but when the *Kinsey Report on Sexual Behavior in the Human Male* came out, I had to stay and listen to what students were saying. I was hurrying to get back to the club to get ready for my shift, but as I passed the benches and trees in the quadrangle, I heard a group of students talking about the book. Right out in the quadrangle! I stopped to listen. A student in a suit and tie, his jacket buttoned tightly over his belly announced to the other men and the one girl, "I think the book is enlightening. It's about time we're getting a glimpse into the dark world of sexuality …"

"Maybe it's dark for you—" the girl said.

"The book on women hasn't come out yet," the guy shot back. "You don't get an opinion."

"Try and stop me."

"Other people's sexual practices," a Negro with glasses, standing near a tree announced, "that's what the book is about. Kinsey is making peeping toms of us all."

"You're afraid," the girl said, "people will find out you're one of those ten percent of men who are homos."

"Don't be disgusting," the second Negro man sitting on the bench near the fat man said.

I'd never heard anyone speak so openly about sex, especially not in mixed company. And the book even spoke of homosexuals! No books ever did that.

* * *

One April afternoon, I arrived early for my Music Appreciation class. I'd heard from some classmates that they were planning a sit-down strike to protest religious and racial bias on campus. I wasn't sure what a sit-down strike was, but the issue seemed important. The Chairman of the Romance Language Department had refused to give the Ward Medal for proficiency in French to a Jewish student who'd earned it. Another professor in charge of assigning students to dorm rooms was segregating white students from Negroes. Jeepers, even the army had been desegregated since July.

As soon as I walked through the main gate, the girl with thick glasses I'd seen in the quadrangle a few days ago jumped off the Shepherd Hall steps and pushed a sign into my hand—"Jim Crow Must Go"—and I joined the others who were walking back and forth in a line carrying posters.

Suddenly, the sound of sirens and police were everywhere. Their megaphones ordered us to disperse. "It's our *constitutional* right to assemble and protest," we shouted back at them. "We shall not be moved."

The cops grabbed students, handcuffing them and dragging them to paddy wagons. *The business! I can't get arrested.* I ran, stumbling over bodies on the ground, as cops were hitting them with clubs. I had to get out. Out! I pushed against arms, backs, stomachs. Smack! Something hit me. Legs, fists everywhere. Dull screams like distant howls. Run! Where? Pushing bodies. Go. Go. I was whisked out of the crowd of pressing elbows and billy clubs. Mindlessly running. A man holding my arm, running with me. We passed beyond the school gates and down the sidewalk. Blares of sirens screaming by us. Running, running, slowing. Leaning against a telephone pole catching my breath. "Gosh, what happened?" I asked between gulps of air.

"You're bleeding, and your dress is torn," my unknown companion said. I felt the blood dripping down the side of my face. "What happened?"

"The cops went nuts," the young man with the curly, dark hair standing before me said. He looked to be around my age, twenty-six or so. He wore a rumpled white shirt, no tie, and brown, baggy corduroy pants.

"I'm Aaron Martin Buckman."

"Aaron," I mumbled like I was reciting an old Sunday school lesson. "Brother to Moses. Helped Moses speak to Pharoah."

"Are you Jewish?"

"No."

"I thought only Jews talked Torah right after almost being stomped to death."

"When I was a kid, I read the Bible twice. Sometimes things from it pop out of me at odd times."

"Why twice?"

"I was looking for a loophole."

"A loophole for what?"

Then it dawned on me that *he* was probably Jewish. I couldn't tell him I was looking for a loophole for the Jews so they'd get into Heaven even though they didn't believe in Christ. It would sound so … I mean, the guy saved my life. "Nothing, Aaron," was my lame response.

"Call me Marty. Being Aaron is too much responsibility. Who are you?"

"Al, uh, Alice. Huffman. Thank you for getting me out of that." I had no idea what we were talking about. I started to shake, and I wanted to get back downtown to people I knew.

"Your first war?"

"Is that what that was?"

"Arresting college kids? Some of them aren't more than eighteen. I think I should take you to the emergency room to get your head bandaged."

"I gotta work."

He held his folded handkerchief against my forehead. "What kinda work?"

"Oh … waitress." I wasn't sure why I lied, but it seemed like the right thing to do. "How about you?"

"Student. Strange to be a student at my age."

"GI Bill?"

"Yup. How about we get a bandage on your head and go get coffee?"

"Can't. Work. Remember?"

"Just testing."

"Testing what?" The last thing I needed was to get involved with another man. If I were Catholic, I'd have to do about a thousand years in purgatory to make up for my sins against Danny and Henry. I gave him back his handkerchief. "I think it's stopping."

"Tell me," he whispered, "are you ...? What I mean is—I was wondering, if you—"

"What?"

He looked up the street and down and whispered, "Are you—a, well ... you know."

"No, I don't."

"No?" He took a deep breath. "'Cause sometimes, I kinda feel—alone here. At school. So, I thought maybe you were a ... too."

"A what?"

"Well, a ..." he spat the word, "communist."

"No! Heavens. Why would you think that? Are you?"

"I might be." He ran back toward the campus.

* * *

A communist, a communist, I repeated to myself as I hung from the porcelain strap in the crowded downtown IRT. A short, round woman jabbed me in the ribs with a mop handle. How could he be a red commie? He was nice to me. Well, he did say "might be." How could a person "might be" a communist? I wished that lady would quit jabbing me. I was gonna punch her soon. I looked with envy at the people sitting peacefully on the red cushioned seats in front of me. Aren't you either a communist or you're not? Maybe he was trying to capture me, and make me like him. That's what they do.

My mind shot back to a smoky bar, Chumley's. Four kids from the potato fields of Long Island. My best girlfriend, Aggie, told us, "They try to turn you into what they are, so you can never be normal again." But when she said that, she didn't mean communists. "Lady, will you please stop ..."

"I'm sorry. It's hard to balance." That's when I saw she was pregnant, and I felt two feet tall. A man sitting in one of the cushioned seats hid his face behind his newspaper. "Hey!" I barked at him.

He sheepishly got up, doffed his hat, and gave her his seat.

By the time I pushed my way down Forty-Second Street through the crowds into the Mt. Olympus, I was a shaking mess. Shaking from my first sit-down strike with the police turning into monsters, and shaking with the thought of the man who saved me who *might* be a communist. Luckily, the Mt. Olympus wasn't open for business yet.

"Al, what happened?" Virginia Sales came running. She sat me at one of the tables and whispered, "Did someone beat you up for being a gay girl?"

"I'm not a gay girl," I whispered back.

"Oh, that's right. I keep forgetting." She ran to the kitchen for ice.

Everything inside me came unloosed, and I started to bawl. "Sit-down strike. At the school and—"

"What's a sit-down strike?" she called to me.

"The students closed down the classes and ..." I rocked back and forth, "the police came ..."

"I would think so." Virginia hurried back into the main room with a dishcloth filled with ice cubes, and held it to my forehead. "Students can't simply decide to stop classes. It would be chaos. I hope you won't get involved in something like that again."

"Have you ever known a communist?"

"Good gracious, no. They're evil people. Does your school let them in?"

"The papers called Barney Josephson one. He didn't seem evil to me. Did you know he was helping his brother, Leon, start a housing development like Levittown; only Barney and Leon's place was gonna let Negroes in too. That sounds like something good, so how could they be communists? Did you know that Leon was involved in a plot to kill Hitler way back in '35?"

"Oh, my."

I remembered my friend Dickie, who came to the city to be a dancer. It was the one thing he wanted more than anything in the whole world. He came home from the war with a bad wound that killed his dream. If Leon had killed Hitler, then dear, sweet Dickie, who'd never hurt anyone, would be dancing on Broadway now.

"Barney said after that, our government started following Leon around; but our government wouldn't follow around a private citizen, would they, Virginia?"

"I should say not."

"Besides, why would the government bother Leon for something that happened back in '35? HUAC didn't even exist then. But Barney said I was too young to know that things never start at the time when you first see them; they start much earlier, when you *can't* see them. Does that sound right to you?"

"I don't know," Virginia said, upset. "You're asking me too many questions. Hold still and keep this ice on."

"Where's Max?" I asked.

"He found a boy on the corner, and you know—"

"You didn't stop him?" I jumped, up and the ice pack fell to the floor. "We open in a few hours!"

"Stopping Max from that would be like trying to stop a moving truck with a pigeon feather."

"He can't do that anymore, and not right before we open."

I ran outside and found one of his many boyfriends strutting down Forty-Second Street in a leather jacket, no shirt, his chest gloriously on display. "Hey, Little Boy," I called, running after him. "Where's Max?"

"How should I know? He's nothing but a score to me. I don't keep track of Maxie's social calendar."

"Like heck you don't. How would you even buy lunch without Max's 'patronage?' Give."

"I know where he is." A voice came from near my ankle. I looked down to see the Vet with no legs sitting in his wagon, his back leaned up against a dumpster. He held out a cup.

"Where?" I jumped onto my knees.

"It's gonna cost ya, girl," the grizzled man, old before his time, said. He smelled of stale tobacco and number 2.

I reached into the pocket of my skirt, pulled out a nickel, and dropped it into his cup. "Where?"

"Come on, Sister. You can do better than that. I'm a Vet. I lost my legs for you."

I found a dime in the bottom of my purse and dropped that in. "That's it. There's no more. Tell me quick, or I'm gonna start thinking you're taking me for a ride."

He grinned, revealing a row of rotten upper teeth and no lowers. "Your boyfriend's at The Astor Hotel bar."

His laugh followed me down the street and clung to me as I squeezed through the pressing crowds. I dashed into the hotel and into the bar. "Max!" I yelled as if he were about to jump off a roof. Well, he was. If Shirl found out … The whole bar of mostly men in suits stared at me.

I threw my shoulders back and strode over to Max, sitting on a stool in his suit and tie, one hand gripping his fedora, the other wrapped around a Manhattan.

"What are you doing?" Max asked.

"We open in an hour. What are *you* doing?"

"Having a drink."

"You can do that at the Mt. Olympus, but you don't drink while you're working. That's the first thing you taught me."

He took a sip from his glass. "Cute. The one directly across from me on the other side of the bar. The blond. Don't look! I don't want him to know I'm interested. But what do you think?"

"Max, you can't do this. All your money, all your dreams will go down the sewer if you don't pay attention to business." Mine too, I thought.

"You're doing pretty good running things."

"I can't run the club by myself. I don't have your knowledge or experience."

"I can't find him," he said, looking into his glass. "I've contacted the war department and the VA. No one will tell me a thing."

"You've been trying to find the man you fell in love with in the army?"

"Scott Elkins."

"You never told me."

"I didn't want you to know what a sap I am."

I rubbed the back of his hand lying on the bar.

"I didn't want to ask too many questions. They may figure it out—what we were to each other—and slap him with a blue discharge, too, if he's still in the service. I thought of calling the Chamber of Commerce of his town, but I can't remember his town's name. Armpit, West Virginia or something. West Virginia." He sighed. "How could *I* have fallen for a kid from West Virginia? You think I should get a private detective?"

I wrapped my hand around his. "Come on. Let's go home."

"Home?" He smiled.

"Well …"

He squeezed my hand. "Home."

Chapter 14

April 1948

IT TURNED OUT Aaron Martin Buckman was in my Music Appreciation class. I'd never noticed him, but he noticed me.

"Did you read what the *New York Times* said about our strike?" Marty asked when we walked through the quadrangle. He wore wide-legged corduroy pants and a corduroy jacket with patches on the elbows, no tie. "They said it was caused by communist agitators?"

"Yeah, I read that. But *I* wasn't a communist agitator."

"Neither was anyone."

"No?" I stared at him.

"Oh, that. I'm not a communist."

"You're not?" I thought this might be a trick to take over my mind.

"No. I think there was another question I wanted to ask you, but then the communist thing came out."

"What other question?"

"Uh … thought maybe we might have something in common."

"Like what?"

"You can't think of anything?"

"No."

"Oh. I think if the communists are fighting for the little guys, like Jews, Negroes, and the working class, and even calling for equality between the sexes—"

"Really?"

"Really. It might not be such a bad thing."

I'd never heard anyone say anything good about communists before. I thought I'd better be careful around this guy. "What's your major?" A safe question.

"Theater."

"I used to act." It slipped out, and I wished I could pull it back.

"No kidding. Professionally?"

"I was on Broadway once." Was I bragging? Telling him this could lead him to my other life. A place I didn't want him to be.

"I'm impressed."

"Don't be. The show closed in eight days. But I did do a lot of radio drama and radio commercials. That's all in the past."

"Why?"

"I'm living another life now."

"As a waitress? That doesn't sound so—"

"As a student."

"It seems like you could make a lot more money doing radio commercials than waiting tables, and some actors are getting jobs on TV. I heard they're paying twenty-five dollars for a fifteen-minute show. That's got to beat waiting tables."

Was he trying to capture me?

"Well, you should, at least," he continued, "try out for *Of Thee I Sing* that they're doing here in the fall. I'm going to."

"Break a leg. My acting days are over. These days I …"

"Yes?"

"Wait tables and go to school."

"Hey, do you like music? Dancing? A friend of mine told me about this place where Mabel Mercer appears regularly. Don't you love her? She's my favorite nightclub singer. I don't know when she's gonna be there again, but when she is, you wanna go with me? The place is called, uh … uh …" He snapped his fingers. "Yes! Max's Mt. Olympus."

"I'm gonna be busy."

Chapter 15

August 1949

SOME NIGHTS, I'D run home before the eight o'clock show to do my schoolwork and eat. I'd eat these new frozen meals that came out called TV dinners; you were sposed to eat them in front of your TV, but I still didn't have one of those. I was glad to hide my head in a textbook or work sixteen hours in the club. Anything to drown out my longing for her. I'd begun to think I'd never make her into a star. What did I know about that? Maybe we'd never be together.

One warm August afternoon in 1949, a boy on a bicycle pulled up in front of Max's Mt. Olympus as I was unlocking the door. My arms were filled with groceries I planned to take home when I eventually went there. "Miss Huffman?" the boy said, jumping off his bicycle.

"Yes?"

"This is for you." He handed me a lavender envelope and ran back to his bike.

"Wait." I rummaged through my purse while balancing oranges, Wonder Bread, and three cans of Green Giant peas. "I'll give you—"

"No. That's been taken care of. She said not to take anything from you." He hopped on his bike and was gone.

She? I fumbled with the keys, and they fell to the ground. *She?* I bent to pick them up, and an orange fell out of the bag and rolled toward the sidewalk. I dashed after it and another fell out. *She. She.* To hell with the oranges. I let them roll away, found the right key, and opened the door.

I flipped on the light and threw down my bundles. The envelope smelled of her perfume. I slid out the letter with her flowing handwriting. Broad circles and loops. I pictured her sitting at her desk in her room, her fountain pen floating over the thin lavender notepaper. She'd never use the ballpoint I got her at the end of the war when Gimbels started selling them. I almost didn't care what it said.

My lungs were bursting with excitement from merely seeing those feminine circles and curlicues. It read:

Al, come see me tomorrow. My place. We'll be alone.
Juliana.

Chapter 16

SHE LIFTED THE tray that held our tea glasses and sugar cubes from the counter. "I'll take it," I said, leading the way from the kitchenette to the couch and placing the tray on the coffee table. It'd been a long time since we'd sat in her parlor drinking Turkish tea from the little hand-blown glasses the Sultan's son gave her mother decades ago.

She didn't approve of what I was wearing. I could tell as soon as she greeted me at the door. A hint of 'how could you go out like that' lingering briefly in her eyes. Maybe I wore my dark jacket with the heavy black skirt because I knew she'd hate it. Maybe I wore my hair, plastered down to the sides of my head with bobby pins, more severely than I ever really wore it because I knew it *wouldn't* attract her. Maybe I wanted to show her that *I* was an independent career woman. Maybe I wanted to show her how much I *didn't* need her.

We sat on her couch sipping our tea, not talking. It was like we'd forgotten how to talk to each other. Four years is a long span in romance-time. I never knew how long until I sat on her couch, counting the painfully slow *tick-tocks* of the clock on her mantel. My eyes wandered aimlessly about the room, wondering why she'd asked me to come.

Her curtains were burnt orange now, not green. The slipcovers on the furniture were now colored with swirls of brown and orange, and the lampshades had been changed to fit the room. The portrait of her mother-in-law, framed and severe, still hung on the wall near the window.

Sun poured through the shades, growing hotter with each ticking moment of that damn clock. I looked at her sitting there in that airy green and white dress, one luscious leg crossed over the other. She had only sandals on her feet. Each toenail perfectly painted a pale, coral red with her lips painted to match. And there I sat in those ugly clothes, as if I was wearing a suit of armor. Her fingernails were rounded and had grown beyond the pads of her fingers. Could that mean she wasn't seeing any girls? *And* she wasn't wearing her wedding band.

"A television!" I gracelessly climbed over the coffee table, hiking my skirt above my knees, to get a closer look. "I don't know anyone who actually *owns*

PassWords

Kyle >
Karl slow 05

Blake >
five slow 42

one of these." Words were tumbling out of me fast. "Of course, I'm working all the time, so I don't visit many people in their homes. Most people I see at the club, so—"

"Are you all right, Al?"

"Splendid!" I said with too much cheer. "As a matter of fact, I think I'll get myself a TV next week."

"Then the rumor is true?"

"What rumor?"

"That you're part owner in the Mt. Olympus."

"I do all right. It makes a nice piece of furniture, doesn't it? A Motorola. I was thinking about getting a G.E." I had never thought about getting a TV, but if *she* could have one, so could I. "And it's got an AM/FM radio on the side. Where's the antenna?"

"It's built-in. Why don't you sit down over here?"

"Built-in, huh? That's modern."

"Come. Sit."

"Okay." I climbed back over the coffee table, knowing that was driving her nuts. "I like the new curtains you put up." She knew I could care less about curtains.

"Yes." She took a sip from her glass. "Part of our new look."

"*Our?* You mean, both you *and* Richard decided on the color? How does that work? Did you show him swatches and he nodded yes or no? Or did you drag him to Bloomies? Tell me, Jule, how did you and *Richard* do it?" I was yelling at her. I didn't expect to do that.

"Al, what's the matter?"

"Nothing. Sorry. I've been putting in a lot of hours at the club. And I've been taking classes at City College like you suggested. Do you remember suggesting that?"

"Uh, well—"

"You don't, do you?"

"Well, I think—"

"We were in your bedroom, and you told me I was the college type. What type is that, Jule? Huh?"

"Well, you were always smart and—"

"Do you still have your own bedroom?"

I jumped over the coffee table and pushed open the door to her room. "I see you haven't changed a thing in *this* room. You know, I used to think of this room as *our* room, but it never really was, was it? Tell me Jule, does he sneak in here while you're sleeping and stick it in you? Or do you tip-toe down the hall to the other room so he can stick it in you there? I know! He drags you by the hair and—"

"Stop it. I don't know what's the matter with you, but I don't deserve to be spoken to in that manner."

"You don't, huh? Well, I stopped going to your rehearsals because it was too hard watching him kiss you, putting his arm around you. Right out in public. Did you notice I wasn't there anymore?"

"Of course, but what did you expect me to do? He's my—"

"*Husband.* I know. *He's* allowed to do that. Right in front of everybody, he can kiss you on the cheek, even on the lips if it's not too long and there's no *tongue* involved, and everyone thinks it's so damn sweet. *I* want to kiss you, goddammit." I banged my fist on the mantel.

"Then why are you standing over there, yelling at me? Come here."

"I want to kiss you in the street. Now. Let's go."

"Stop talking silly."

"We can't ever do that, can we? We can't hold hands or kiss in public because of what people will *think* we are. What are we, Jule? What are we that we can't do that?"

"What we do is illegal. Haven't you read in the newspapers about the police arresting men *and* women who go into those bars? The last thing I need is to be arrested for …"

I ran to sit beside her. I'd never seen her scared before. "Easy, hon." I took her hand in mine and kissed it. "Don't worry. I won't sneak up behind you in public and give you a peck on the cheek. I'll save up all my pecks for the really good stuff behind closed doors. Right now, I've got a whole lot of pecks saved up. It's been a long time."

"Yes, it has."

"Why didn't you contact me?"

"I did. A few years ago, I invited you for Sunday brunch."

"With him. How did you think I could …?"

"Why did you disappear?"

"I didn't. I've always been a few blocks away. I couldn't take it—you and him. But you never called me to tell me when he wasn't around."

"I couldn't."

"I know. You don't chase after your women. Yet you contacted me now. Why?"

"Business."

"Business? That's all?"

She put her glass on the coffee table and leaned close to kiss me, but stopped. "Uh, can we first …?"

She pulled the bobby pins from my hair. "You look like an old-maid librarian who got lost in the stacks." She fluffed out my hair. "We can work on the styling later."

She kissed me, and I kissed her back. Her lips on mine were like coming home. We sat on the couch, and kissed and kissed, and it was oh, so much more than a peck, and it was oh, such delight to have her lips and her tongue against mine again. She could have asked anything of me and I would've done it.

"I'm worried about Richard," she said when we paused from our kissing.

"Oh, swell. I'm sitting here kissing you, and you're worried about Richard."

"I'm beginning to think maybe everyone was right. Maybe he doesn't know what he's doing. Could you come to my rehearsal Monday, and tell me what you think?"

"Why would you trust me to advise you?"

"You're managing Max's Mt. Olympus. You work with talent all the time. You're getting your experience with the master."

"Why don't you call Max? Max is the one to advise you. I'm still learning." This was happening too soon. I wasn't ready.

"You'll come on Monday. Won't you?"

"You are such an enigma."

"I'm a what? Your vocabulary is certainly benefiting from college."

"It means—"

"I know what it means." She smiled.

"Oh, I'm sorry. I didn't mean to sound—"

"Like a show off?"

"Pedantic."

"You don't have to use all your new vocabulary in one afternoon. You'll come Monday?"

"It's hard seeing you with him."

"I know, but you'll come, won't you? Because I ask you to?"

"Jule …" I whined.

"You know, Richard is gone for the weekend."

"He is?"

"Won't be back until Sunday night, late."

"Juliana, you're manipulating me."

"And I'm doing a magnificent job, aren't I? Come. I have a surprise for you."

I leaned on the doorsill of her bedroom while she stood on tiptoe, pulling a package from the shelf. She laid it on the bed. "Open it."

I undid the paper that was taped around the box. The box said, "Electric Spot Reducer." I opened it, and inside was a strange round thing with a metal top sitting over a rubber cup. It had a black handle and looked like something that belonged in a Flash Gordon movie.

"What is it?"

"I saw it advertised in *Confidential Magazine*, not a great source, I admit, but lately, I've been concerned I was putting on a little around the hips. It's supposed to help you reduce in certain areas."

"Come now, you look great."

"And I'm in show business and have to think about those things. So, I put it on and—let me show you." She plugged it in and turned on the switch. The thing whirred and buzzed. I hopped off the bed. "My goodness, what is it?" I crept back toward it. "That thing helps you lose weight? How? Where do you put it?"

"Sit down."

"I don't know …"

"Sit. You'll see."

I sat down on the bed, keeping my distance from the thing.

"A little closer," Juliana said.

I slid closer.

"Now, stay there a minute."

I did as she said while she sat opposite me, making us into two bookends around the buzzing, whirring, out-of-space thing. "Well?" she said.

"What? Oh! Oh, my. Oh, my …"

"Yes." She laughed. "The first time I used it, I had three orgasms, one right after the other. Richard wasn't home. Take off your underthings. I'll show you."

"You want to put that where? No, I don't think—" I backed up.

"Think how much fun it'll be for the two of us? Richard would never understand or let me use it."

76

"Really?" I jumped up and tore off my stockings, girdle, and underpants. So did she. We laughed and kissed. The thing still buzzed on the bed. We looked down at it.

"Shall we give it a go?" she asked.

Chapter 17

MY MOOD WAS lighter than it had been in a long time. I practically flew down the street toward the Carnegie rehearsal studio Richard rented.

Juliana and I spent the most spectacular weekend together. I called Max and told him something important came up, and I couldn't do my shifts at the club. He interpreted that to mean I had to study, and he always supported that. Guilt seeped into my stomach. I didn't like not being honest with him, but it wasn't *me* who said I had to study.

We cooked and ate meals together. Well, *Juliana* cooked. I set the table. We laughed more than I think I'd laughed in four years, and I wore rolled-up dungarees all weekend.

I tried to find out what she didn't like about how Richard was managing her, but she only said, "Come see. Give your unbiased opinion."

Unbiased? Didn't she know I'd do anything to push Richard out of her life?

Friday night, when she was on top of me using her fingers, her tongue, and that vibrating thing, I made— "The Big Mistake." I was going up, up, up toward my climax, becoming lost in her hair, her mouth, and her breasts … At the highest, deepest moment I yelled, "I love you, I love you, Juliana!" As soon as I said it, I knew I'd doomed myself. Instantly, she removed all stimulation and slid off me. I came crashing down.

She didn't say a word, only pulled on her robe and stepped into the parlor. I scurried out of bed and stood in the doorway as she took one of Richard's cigarettes from the gold case that lay on the coffee table.

"Jule, you don't smoke."

"Sometimes, I do." She flicked the lighter at the tip. "Sometimes, I need to."

"It was a reflex. I haven't been with you in four years. It slipped out."

"Surely you've been with someone during all that time." She blew out a stream of smoke.

"No."

"No?" She turned toward me. "Four years? Four years, Al. No. You're giving me too much responsibility." She stamped the cigarette out in the ashtray. "I can't have that."

"I'm not giving you *any* responsibility. Let's go back to bed."

We did, and the rest of the weekend went fine, like my big mistake had never happened. Except—I wondered who *she'd* slept with during my four years of abstinence. Had she meant Richard? Thinking it was him was somehow easier to take. But I didn't think that's who she meant.

It was a beautiful, sunny day, already warm; it'd be sweltering by noon. When I entered the Carnegie Studio, Juliana was on a low stage singing, and Johnny was playing the piano. Richard sat in the front row, moving his head to the music, thoroughly enjoying himself. I took a seat in the back. Juliana was singing and moving like Carmen Miranda. It was awful. I wanted to cover my eyes with my hands. Thank God, she wasn't wearing the outfit.

Richard turned around, saw me, and waved. I nodded.

"No, Richard!" Juliana shouted. "I am not doing this. You are not going to make a fool of me."

"But Julie." Richard stood. "This will get you into the Copa. The Spaniards are all the rage this year."

"Carmen Miranda is Portuguese."

"She is?"

"Brazilian," Johnny said, taking a drink from the glass on top of the piano.

"Portuguese," Juliana shot back. "Look it up." Then she turned back to her real target. "I've had it, Richard. I'm not going to do this anymore. I'm done. Finished. You're an idiot." She stomped off the stage through a back door.

"Wait. We can fix this," Richard called, bounding onto the stage, his small stature requiring a little hop. He waited, his arm poised in the air, but Juliana did not come back. "Johnny," he said, turning toward the piano. "It wasn't that bad, was it?"

Johnny shook his head sadly and took another sip from his glass. He started playing some melancholy tune I'd never heard before.

"Richard," I walked toward him.

"Alice." He grabbed his jacket from the back of his chair and slipped it over his wrinkled, sweat-stained shirt, then tightened his tie. "You see how she gets? How can she expect to get anywhere when she acts like that? You're in this business. Did you think it was bad?" His slicked-back, dark hair was coming loose from whatever he'd slicked it with, and sliding onto his brow.

"Well ..." I should tell him it was horrible and get her away from this no-talent oaf. "Richard, Juliana's her own person. She's not someone who should be doing another singer's material."

"That's what all the singers do. Check *Bill Board*. Perry Como and Russ Morgan both have a hit with "Forever and Ever," and a few years ago there were three versions of—"

"Yes, but Juliana has her own special style. You have to help her get that out so it's clear to her audience that she's *not* like those others doing different versions of the same song. *She's* unique. That's what has to come across to the audience."

Richard took a pack of Marlboros from his inside pocket and shook one loose. "That seems pretty risky."

"It is. Playing with risk is the only way Juliana will be a success."

"What should I do?" He pulled the cigarette from the pack with his teeth. "I don't know what to do, Al." The cigarette wiggled up and down as he spoke. "I think she's beginning to sense I'm in over my head. Don't tell her I am. I love her so much, and if I lost her ... I'm a good businessman. I don't want you thinking I planned on taking her for a ride when I offered to manage her career. If we were talking real estate, stocks, bonds, mortgages I'm the best." He lit the cigarette and blew out a stream of smoke over my head. "I figured show business is a business. How different could it be? But ... she's such a passionate woman." His face got instantly red. "I mean about her singing. I want to give her what she wants, but I don't know what to do."

"Maybe I can come up with something."

"You think so? Hey, let me take you for a cup of coffee. We'll talk. No. Dinner. At the Oak Room. That's in the Plaza. Expensive."

"I know where it is, Richard. You don't need to spend money on me. I need time to think."

"Sure. Take your time. But not too long. How long do you think you'll need?"

"I don't know."

"I know you're busy. I've read about you working with Max Harlington at the Mt. Olympus in the papers. Being a career woman must take a lot of time, but would you ... talk to her? Now? She's pretty upset. I'm afraid she's going to walk out on our partnership. Tell her I can fix this. That I'm not such a bad guy. She'll listen to you. She respects your opinion."

Richard just asked me to save his 'partnership?' Which one? The marriage or the business? This was my chance to be rid of him forever … "I'll talk to her," I said.

He grabbed my hand in two of his and shook it vigorously. "Thank you. Thank you." He was so sincere.

As soon as I walked through the backstage door I heard Juliana singing, a capella, "O Mio Babbino."

I leaned against the wall, listening. The vibrations of her voice seeped inside me. I hadn't heard her sing opera in a long time. I closed my eyes to feel her more deeply. *I* could be her manager. I could tell her Richard doesn't know anything. But I didn't know enough yet to manage her *whole* career. I didn't have enough contacts or money. Richard didn't know anything, but he did have money. Lots of it. And he knew people with money. This will take a lot of money. *And* he was a man.

I followed the sound of her song, and it led me to a small room. I stood in the doorway, listening. She looked so alone standing in the middle of that barren room, with only one chair pushed up against the wall. I had no idea what she was saying, but my heart split open with the sounds of passion and love exploding out of her. I wanted to enfold her in my arms and take her pain into my own body, but I knew she'd never allow it.

She turned and, seeing me, instantly stopped singing.

"Gosh, no. Don't stop," I cried out.

She smiled without saying what I knew she was thinking. That was what I'd said Saturday night in bed.

"Well?" she asked.

"Shirl thinks that's the kind of music you should be making your living with."

"Shirl doesn't know what it takes."

"She told me a few years back that she knows people who could help you."

"Nobody starts a career like that at my age. I'll be lucky to get the nightclub career going. What am I going to do, Al? I need to sing and I need an audience to hear me."

"You have an audience. People come to your shows."

"A huge audience in important clubs, not the dinky clubs I've been playing. My mother would be so disappointed in me. It's bad enough I didn't go into opera like she wanted, or continue my studies at the Conservetoire de Paris, and bad enough I ran away to the States at sixteen to sing in dives. Left her alone. Didn't protect her from … What would she think if she knew how far I didn't get? And—what if I've made such a huge mistake that I can never … Al, I promised … a long time ago when I learned of her death, I promised …"

She always talked about her mother's death as if it were by some natural cause, instead of …

"I wasn't a good daughter to her—wild, unthinking. You should've seen her when I performed on stage. She'd sit in the front row on the edge of her seat, mouthing the words I sang like she was up on that stage with me. In a way, she was. She had a beautiful voice. When she was young, she sang opera in Paris and Milan, and the stage-door Johnnies would line up to kiss her hand. Only, *her* stage-door Johnnies were princes, and dukes, and the sons of earls. She gave it all up for me, and I've squandered her gift, and I don't know how I'll live if …"

I thought she might actually cry. I hurried toward her, but she put a hand up. "No."

I stopped. "I won't. I wish …" I could see in her eyes she didn't want to hear what I wished, so I let my wish sink back into my heart. "Don't worry. Richard and I are going to talk. We'll figure something out."

"*You're* going to work with Richard?"

"I guess so."

"You don't mind?"

"Of course I mind. But you're going to be the star you were meant to be, and I'm going to do whatever it takes to make that happen. There's a couple of things I want."

"Anything."

"First, you and Richard have to listen to me. *Really* listen. And do what I say."

"Fine."

"Make sure you both don't forget that. And—"

"You want a fee, a percentage? Of course. We can—"

"I haven't thought that far ahead yet. What I want is …" I was breathing too fast. "There's something I have to say to you."

"Say it."

"And I don't want to hear any of your cockamamie theories about why I can't or why I shouldn't."

"What is it?"

"I—Just a minute." I walked back to close the door.

"My goodness, what—"

I exhaled the words on a breath and closed my eyes. "I'm in love with you."

I opened my eyes. I couldn't read anything on her face. "Okay, you didn't fall over or turn into a pillar of salt. That's a start. I'm in love with you in all the ways I'm not supposed to be; I'm in love with you in all the ways you say I can't be."

Her lips moved to speak. I raised my hand. "Don't say anything. I need to say it out loud, and I need you to hear it. I may say it again sometime. I will never say it front of other people, and you don't have to say anything back. All you have to do is listen to it. Do we have a deal?"

She took in a deep, uncomfortable breath. "All right. If that's you want."

"Good. I'll get started."

Chapter 18

IT WAS NOON as I jaunted down the street toward the Mt. Olympus, floating like a Macy's Thanksgiving Day balloon. I'd said it right to her. It wasn't an accident, or a "reflex" that slipped out in a moment of passion. It'd been building for years, and now I'd said it right to her face. I'm in love with you, Juliana. In love with you.

I practically slid down the center carpet into the main dining room of the club, then turned to go into Max's office.

"Where have you been?" Max asked. "You're usually here early."

"I was here. Then I went out." Shirl and Mercy sat near Max's desk. "Did I miss some meeting I didn't know about?"

"Impromptu. Sit. Shirl and I have been discussing—"

"Where's Virginia?" I asked. "If we're having a business meeting shouldn't she be here?"

"She's a woman."

"Excuse me?" Shirl said.

"You know what I mean. Virginia has no head for business. Sit, Al. I've been going over our numbers, and we've been down for the last few months on Tuesdays at 8 p.m. I'm worried."

"That's not exactly bankruptcy," Shirl said. "Are the other times up? Is it only Tuesday at eight?"

"I know it's strange, but we're too new to absorb even a slight shortfall. Not this early in the game," Max said. "We've got to figure out why this is happening and fix it."

"It sounds serious," I said, concerned that I'd be out of work and out of a dream.

"It is," Max said.

"Not that serious," Shirl said. "Don't scare the kid."

"Of course your business is off at that time," Mercy confidently announced.

We swiveled in our seats toward her. Mercy never had an opinion at business meetings; she came to keep Shirl company. "Nobody's gonna come here Tuesday at eight," she said matter-of-factly. "Everyone's home watching Milton Berle."

"Oh, come now," Max said. "*Everyone?*"

"Haven't you seen that show? Uncle Milty is like a religion to some people. Didn't you read this week's *Newsweek* and *Time?*"

Now everyone swiveled toward me. "Well …" I said, trying to shrink. I didn't want to tell them I'd spent the weekend with Juliana. "They're probably on my desk under a pile of dailies, weeklies, and monthlies I haven't gotten to yet."

"Milton Berle is on the cover of *both* at the same time," Mercy said. "Not even a president has done that. They're calling him Mr. Television."

"Al, you should know this," Max told me.

"I don't own a TV."

"Get one. Today. Here. Take this." Max handed me some large bills. "The club will pay. And read those articles. I want a full report. Then we'll meet again to discuss what to do." He stood, ready to leave his office.

Mercy broke into peels of laughter and we all stared at her. Gasping for air she said, "You mean you've never seen Milton Berle in a dress?"

"We know lots of men who wear dresses," Shirl said. "It's not that funny." She got up and signaled Mercy to follow her out of the room.

"Max, can I talk to you?" I asked.

He unbuttoned his suit jacket and sat behind his desk, swiveling his chair toward me. "Have a seat."

"I can't. I have to pace. I need your help." I sat down.

"Are you in trouble?"

"I have an idea, and I need you to help me."

"Shoot."

"What?"

"Tell me the idea."

"Oh."

He pushed a cigarette into the holder and lit it.

"I want to manage—Don't say no before you've heard me out."

"Okay. You want to manage what?"

"Juliana."

"No."

"Max."

"I can't let you do it. You don't know enough to manage *anyone* by yourself, and Juliana is *way* over your head."

"I know."

"Well, then?"

"She's not over *your* head."

"Are you out of your mind? You know how I feel about Juliana."

"No, actually, I don't. I know the two of you haven't spoken in years."

"She's trouble. There's no way I'm going to manage her."

"Oh, she wouldn't let you. She feels the same way about you."

"Of all the damn nerve. After all I did for her."

"Richard has to be her manager, but he's an idiot."

"Bingo. You have the makings of a great manager."

"He's going to ruin her career, and I can't let that happen, but I don't know enough about the business yet. I don't know enough people to make the right calls, and Richard's a man. People would rather do business with a man. He also has some contacts through his bank. Money people. So his involvement could be useful, but not till her act is right. That's where you and I come in. Please help me to help her."

"Let me get this straight. You want *me* to help you help Richard help Juliana?"

"Yeah."

"That's nuts."

"I know, but say you'll do it anyway."

"She chose Richard over me. It was her choice. Why should I now help to make *him* look good in her eyes?"

"Because I'm asking you to."

"You know I have plans for you, kid. I want you to run the new place all by yourself. Take over the entire operation."

"Yes! Yes!"

"I was even thinking of having you take a look at a few new singers I've been hearing about. See if you want to manage any of them. Get your feet wet."

"Yes!"

"This work with Juliana could distract you from building a solid, lucrative career."

"It won't. Please Max."

"Aren't you worried that, besides Richard, there are other girls? I've heard rumors about her and that French girl."

"Margaritte."

"That might be the name. And then there was this other person, a he/she."

"Andy."

"Maybe. I don't know what she'd be doing with a man-woman. What do you do with one of those?"

"People make up stories about beautiful women. That doesn't mean she's … Besides, I'm going to keep her so busy with her career, which is more important to her than Richard, me, or any other girl, she won't have time to even *think* of anyone else. The only girl she's going to see day in and day out will be me. So? Will you help me?"

"Quite an interesting plan you've got there."

He leaned way back in his chair, his two hands pressed against each other and held to his lips. He was silent for so long, I wanted to jump over the desk and choke him.

"She needs her own material. I've looked in on a few rehearsals from time to time. That jerk has her singing songs that everyone sings. Stupid move."

"Where can I get her new material?"

"She needs her own composer. Someone fresh, exciting. Maybe unknown." He got up and rummaged through a file. "Give her these three songs. Her accompanist, Johnny, wrote them."

I took the sheet music into my hands. "He did? Why didn't he say he could write for her? He's there listening to that fiasco every day."

"He's drunk. If you can keep him off the sauce, he can write her some terrific songs, but she still needs a better act. I haven't thought about *that* in years—"

"*I* have. When I get something on paper I'll show you."

"If you can sharpen up her act—hire a good musical director—and she does the material you're holding, I can set her up with some career-moving visible gigs. But that act better be good. I'll be putting my recently revived reputation on the line."

"It won't be good, Max; it'll be great." If only I was as confident as I sounded.

"Then, if all goes well, she gets some great reviews, in a year or so she'll be playing the Copa." Max sighed. "It should have happened long ago. She'd better not find out that I have anything to do with this."

"She'll think Richard did most of it."

"Don't you want her to know that it's mostly you?"

"Yeah. But she'd still be stuck with Richard, and if she's forced to face what a dope he is, she'll feel ashamed for the choice she made. That would affect her career. Juliana takes her whole self up on that stage." I couldn't tell Max that I knew Juliana would divorce Richard once I make her a star.

"You're right," Max said. "She does takes all of herself on stage. I'm glad you know it. Get everything in writing. Here, take this." He handed me a card. "This is my lawyer. Have him draw up the papers, and be sure he includes your percentage."

"I can't take money from Juliana."

"You darn well better. This is business. Don't go soft on me now, kid. You call him. Make it all legal and contractual."

"Okay, okay."

I held the new music tightly to my chest. My dream was gonna happen. "Max, why are you doing this for her?" I asked.

"I'm *not* doing it for her," he said. "Now quit wasting time, and go make Juliana a star."

Chapter 19

"YOU THINK THEY'LL be here soon?" I couldn't believe Virginia was as excited as me. We leaned over the balcony outside my Milligan Place apartment, waiting. A slight breeze before the day's August heat ruffled our skirts.

"They said noon," I told her. "It's almost that now. It feels like Christmas night waiting for Santa when I was a kid. You know, I never even wanted one, but when Max told me I *had* to get one ... You don't have one yet, do you?"

"I have no use for a television set. What would I do with it?"

"Watch it."

"I like listening to my concert records on the Victrola in the evening, but it's thrilling you're getting one. I've only passed by them in Klein's radio section, but I never actually watched a whole program."

"*You* shop at Klein's?"

"Even *I* can appreciate a good bargain."

"Oh. Well, you'll watch mine."

"Could I? Oh, you. You're never home."

"Max says I have to watch it, so now it's part of my job. Juliana has one!"

"Well, I would expect *her* to have one. Where'd you buy yours?"

"Leonard's Radio Store down on Radio Row. Oh, look! They're coming."

I waved my arms at the truck as it navigated through the gate I'd left open. The two guys living in the apartment next to mine, NYU students, ran onto the balcony with us. They wore dark slacks with white shirts, open at the collar. "You getting a TV?" Harold asked.

"Yes!" I said proudly, like I'd accomplished something important.

"Jeepers, a TV!" Philip said, "I can't wait to finish school so I can get one, too. What kind did you get?"

"An RCA!"

"Oh, they're good," Harold said.

"How big?" Philip asked.

"Sixteen inches! As big as a magazine page, the man in the store said."

"A sixteen-inch screen!" Philip jumped up. "That's enormous! You are so lucky. Can I come over and watch it sometime?"

"Sure. Both of you. Bring your girls. We'll make a party of it."

The truck driver did some fancy maneuvering around the cement bench and the little tree, stopping in front of the stairs that led up to my apartment.

"Al," Virginia squealed. "You're getting a TV! A TV!"

The deliverymen waved as they jumped out of the truck. "Which one of youse is Alice Huffman?"

"That's me! I'll be right down."

"Sit tight, hon. We gonna bring it up to youse. By duh by, I'm Dan and dis here's my partner, Mickey."

We waved at the two smiling men with big shoulders. "I love dis job," I heard Dan say to Mickey. "Folks are always glad to see us."

They threw open the back doors of the truck and slid my TV down a wood plank onto a dollie.

"Oh, Al, it's so big," Virginia exclaimed. "It's going to make a beautiful piece of furniture."

"And it has Golden Throat," I told her. "That's why I got an RCA instead of a Dumont."

"Really?" Virginia sounded impressed. "What's Golden Throat?"

"I don't know, but it sounded important."

The men were pulling my TV toward the stairs.

"Al!" The two girls who lived in the third apartment down, a secretary and an elementary school teacher, came hurrying out to the balcony, their dresses swishing around their calves. "You got a TV! How pretty."

"Isn't it?" Virginia said.

"The cabinet is made of Maplewood," I told them. "Modern."

The men pulled and pushed my TV up the stairs, onto the balcony, and into my apartment with my neighbors following. Virginia and I had to squeeze by everybody to get into the living room. Once inside, the neighbors watched from the doorsill.

"So, where ya wan' it?" Dan asked.

"Next to that window across from the couch."

They rolled the TV to where I directed and bent to unwrap it from its casings.

"Oh, Al," Virginia exclaimed, as the TV was revealed. "It's simply gorgeous!"

"It is, it is," came the chorus of my neighbors pressing against the open door.

"I have a lovely old lamp that will look perfect on top of it," Virginia said. "It's an antique. Used to belong to my grandmother. Let me give it to you."

"I can't accept something like that."

"Please take it. I want to help you celebrate your new TV."

"Well—I've never had an antique before."

"And now you do. I'm sure you want to be alone with your TV, so I'll go."

"No. I want you to be with me for my first time. Let's watch it now."

"Could we?" Virginia absolutely glowed with excitement.

"Why not? It's mine." I ran toward it, my hand ready to turn one of the knobs. "Is this the right one?" I asked Dan.

"Don't touch dat!" He sounded like the voice of Oz.

I jumped back, wondering if Dan had stopped me from blowing us all up.

"Ya can't go round grabbin' at knobs. Dis is a complex piece of machin'ry," Dan explained. "Youse ain't been taught prop'ly to operate her, yet. Now, sit yerselves down while I splain the intricacies of operatin' yer new TV."

"I'll wait for ya out in the truck, Dan," Mickey said. "Looks like yer gonna have yer hands filled up with dem. Good a'ternoon, ladies." He nodded in our direction. "Excuse me," he said to the neighbors who still pressed against my door. "Youse can't stay here. Alice needs to think." He herded the neighbors out of the doorway and closed the door.

"Would you like me to go too, Dan?" Virginia asked.

"Ya can stay if ya wanna, but ya gotta sit quiet."

"Of course."

Virginia and I sat dutifully on the couch.

"Youse can follow along with dis here manual." Dan handed us a thick book, opened to the page where we would begin. He stood by the TV and patted the top of it with his hand. "Dis here baby is no toy. Ya gotta respect her. Dis knob here—" He touched one of the round dials. "Dis is yer On-Off Sound button. Ya turn it halfway like dis, and wait fifteen to twenty seconds while it's warmin' up. While yer waitin' for dat ya pulls out the Selector Light here and dat begins yer 'lumination. Then ya come over here to dis dial, the Station Selector. Dis one ya turn to the number of da channel ya wanna watch."

"It seems awfully complicated," Virginia said.

"It is."

"Now dis is your antenna. A vital piece of yer equipment. Ya use it fer adjustin' yer pitcher. If ya don't get dis set right on top of yer TV, you ain't gonna get nothing but fuzz. Why don't we put it on? Ya ready?"

Virginia and I sat at the edge on the couch, breathless.

Dan smiled and waved his hand over one of the buttons, pretending like he was going to press it, but he didn't. The suspense was killing me. Finally, he pushed it, and light came from the screen. We waited. I was going to watch a TV show from my very own TV set! A screen full of white speckles came on. "What's that?" I asked.

"Oh, dat means nuttin's on."

"Nothing's on?" Virginia and I said, disappointed.

"Dere ain't so many shows on durin' da day. Most stations got shows on from 7 p.m. to 11 p.m. at night. You're gonna like dem."

"I work at night," I said.

"Oh. Well, uh …" He looked at his watch. "I know. Dere's a show startin' right about …" He turned the selector knob. "Yeah, dis is it." A man dressed like a train engineer sat on a log with a girl of about nine. "My kids love dis one. It's called 'Mr. I-Magination.' You see dis train guy here? He takes kids on make-believe journeys."

It wasn't a terribly interesting program. It had cardboard trees and paper mache bridges, but it was a still a TV show on my very own TV set. We didn't watch long, 'cause Dan went on to teach us about what to do if the picture rolled in a horizontal direction, or what to do if the picture got streaks in a vertical direction, or what to do if the picture got double and triple images on top of each other.

After a while, I wanted Dan to be done. My head was getting too filled up with images of static and rolling pictures. At last, he said, "Well, dat seems to be it. Da rest is up to youse."

I walked him to the door. "Thanks, Dan. You've been very informative and—"

"Of course," he said, standing in the doorway. "If she blows a tube, or sumpin' serious like dat, Leonard's Radio is a phone call away."

"Thanks, Dan."

I almost got him out the door when he turned back. "You blow a tube and we come over and put in a new one."

"That's nice of you. Good-bye." I gave him a gentle shove.

"Unless, of course, it gotta go to da shop. Dat might be some days. Maybe even a week." He chuckled to himself. "Dat darn near kills some customers. Can't stand bein' away from deir TV. Oh, but yours is brand spankin' new, so dat's a long time aways."

"That's good," I said, pushing him out the door.

"My goodness, that man can talk," Virginia said.

"Only doing his job. I spose. But Virginia, *I* own a TV! Me! Just like Juliana."

"Yes. Her."

"We gotta watch something," I said.

"But there's nothing on but that Mr. I-Magination."

"That's pretty boring."

We sat on the couch admiring the blank screen.

Chapter 20

MAX STILL SEARCHED for Scott, the boy he fell for while he was in the army. He actually hired an honest-to-goodness real private detective like Humphrey Bogart in the *Maltese Falcon*, but he still hadn't found him.

I began work on Juliana's career. After making my preliminary plans and talking them over with Max, I met with Richard for afternoon tea at the Palm Court. I would've rather met over a cup of diluted coffee and a greasy cheese sandwich at Hector's—would've wasted less time—but Richard needed an elaborately expensive setting where he was served elaborately expensive food to concentrate. We ate scones and were allowed to choose from a variety of specialty teas from around the world. I wore my usual suit jacket and skirt, but I had my hair done up with a few curls, making it less severe than usual.

"Richard, I want to make sure you understand that Juliana still thinks of you as her manager."

"Thank you for that, Al." He placed his napkin on his lap. "I don't know how to express my gratitude to you. You want a car?"

"No, Richard, I don't want a car. I want you to listen to me."

"Of course."

Our scones arrived on a silver tray. Richard took one.

"I'm the one who's going to be calling the shots," I said. "I'm going to tell you what needs to be done, what personnel needs to be hired, what contacts need to be made, and what money needs to be brought in. I expect you to follow my directions."

"What am *I* in charge of?" Richard leaned forward eagerly, taking a big bite from his scone.

"You're in charge of making sure Johnny doesn't drink. If he does, you come and tell me right away."

"Wait." He reached into his inside pocket. "Let me get this down." He took out a leather billfold, removed a piece of paper and a pencil, and scribbled on the paper. "What else?"

"That's it."

"But—"

"Basically, all you have to remember is that I'm the one who is really in charge, but you're going to get the credit."

"That doesn't sound manly."

"That's how it has to be, or else, I can't go further with this. And Juliana will probably leave you."

"It's that serious?"

"Yes. So, tell me now. Are you going to follow my instructions or not?"

"Anything for my Julie. You're the one with the experience in this business, but could I make one suggestion?"

"What?"

"Have you ever thought of wearing, well, something more feminine? *I* don't mind, but I'm sure you'd like to get married someday, and dressed like that, well—"

"Our meeting is over." I threw a twenty-dollar bill[3] on the table and walked out.

---

3 Twenty dollars had the same spending power as $204.60 does today.

Chapter 21

AT THE END of the month, I called a meeting with Juliana, Richard, Johnny, and Stan Devenbach, a well-known musical director. Stan was coming at a high cost that I had convinced Richard to pay.

I rushed in to join the men and Juliana who were already seated around a long table, my folder under my arm. The men stood as I entered, and they sat when I did. We huddled together, sweating into our Coca-Cola bottles on the hottest afternoon in August. The windows were high up and opened only a few inches. The ceiling fans did their best to slosh through the humidity.

I wore my women's suit jacket and skirt and kept the jacket on. If the men had to sit in that room in their jackets, so would I. I was determined to make them forget my age and my sex; they had to see me as competent. *I* had to see me as competent, but as I took my place at the head of the table, I wasn't at all sure of what I was doing. Only Juliana looked cool and comfortable in her striped, multicolored, cotton shirtwaist dress with a flair. She smiled at the men and they smiled back.

Richard pulled on the lapel of his jacket. "Ladies?" he asked.

"Yes, please," Juliana said, indicating to the men that they could remove their jackets. Only Stan didn't remove his.

I wasn't sure where I fit in this dichotomy, but I used it as my opportunity to remove my own jacket. Sweat stains clung to the men's shirts, which was to be expected. Expected in men, *not* in women. I wondered if I was showing the same marks and should replace my jacket to hide them. What were the rules for being a woman in a man's business? I hated being distracted by things like sweat stains. The men weren't.

As I was about to begin, Johnny left the table to play the piano. We turned to look at him. "Johnny," I called, "we're ready to begin now."

"You start." He ran his fingers down the keys. "You don't need me."

"Yes, we do," I said.

"No, you don't." He ran his fingers back up the keys.

"I'll talk to him," Juliana said, starting to rise.

"No," I said. "I'll go." I put my folder under my arm and walked across the floor. I had to bring him back with me, or the return trip would be a long one, indeed. The group's respect for me would melt into the summer heat.

"Hey, Johnny," I said, standing next to the piano. "We're having a meeting and we need you there."

"No, you don't." He began playing a melancholy tune I didn't recognize.

"Of course we do. You've been working with Juliana for years. She counts on you."

"Then why are *you* standing here and not her?"

"She was going to come, but *I'm* in charge now."

"So, you're my big boss now, huh? And where do *I* fit into your plan, big boss? The piano player? I've been directing Juliana for years, but now I see I'm out 'cause you got yourself a big shot director, and you didn't even have the guts to tell me, Big Boss."

"Stan has Broadway musical theater credits, so I thought—"

"You wanted the best and I'm not it? How do you know what's best? You're a kid."

I could feel the sweat dripping down my sides as the room got hotter. I didn't hear talking, so they must be waiting for me to do something. I wished Max was with me. He'd know what to do. "I'm older than I look. I'm twenty-six. And I may not know as much as you, Johnny, but I know these songs are good." I slipped Johnny's songs out of the folder. "I want to use them in Juliana's new act."

Johnny took the sheet music into his hands. "Where'd you get these?"

"Does that matter? I got them. I want more. I want you to do the musical arrangement for Juliana's whole act: some your songs, some old favorites, some modern pop and showtunes. So yes—I do need you."

"You want to use *my* music. No kidding?"

"No kidding. Now, are you going to walk back over this floor with me so those people staring at us don't walk out?"

He grinned. "I had you going, didn't I? You were scared, kiddo. Thought I'd leave you flat."

"Yeah, Johnny, I was scared. And I don't ever want to be that scared again. You think you can deliver that music?"

"In my sleep. Let's get this party going."

I didn't think it was a good time to mention his drinking.

Back at the table, I started breathing again. "Here's the gist of what we're doing," I said. "Johnny's arranging the music, Stan's directing the singing and dancing, and Richard, we need you to bring in the money, and—you can work with Stan and me on hiring the new male dancers."

"Why do we need new male dancers?" Juliana asked. "Riley and Warren are my friends. I don't want to dump them."

"Don't. Keep them as friends. But for the act, we need new dancers because—I guess there isn't any nice way to say this—"

Johnny grinned. "They're fairies, Jule."

"Well, I was trying to come up with something a *little* nicer," I said.

"You don't mean they're—homos?" Richard asked in sincere shock. "But I've had them in my home. I've introduced them to my nieces. They can't be degenerates. My wife would never associate with homosexuals."

"I had no idea, Richard," Juliana said. "Really? Are they?" She looked at me for confirmation.

I had to look down at my notes so I didn't laugh. "No. I don't think they're like that. They're just a little too—*sensitive* for the act. We need to hire a couple of rough and tumble dancers. The new act is going to be about—I don't know how to say this in mixed company, so I'll just say it—sex."

"Al, mind how you speak in front of my wife," Richard exclaimed.

"Shhh, Richard," Juliana said, patting his arm. "I've heard the word before. Listen."

I looked away from Juliana so I could continue. "Juliana is going to be seductive with the audience, the men. She needs to wear long gowns that hug her body, sometimes slits on the side, plunging necklines."

"Ooh, I like this," Juliana said.

"I don't," Richard said.

"We need to hire a top-notch costume designer," I continued. "There needs to be a subtle tease to everything she does. The way she moves, dances, sings, but nothing openly sexual. Sensuous. Seductive. Secretive."

"You're pretty good with those S's," Johnny said. "Maybe you should use them in the PR campaign."

"Maybe," I said, rolling the idea around in my head.

"I don't like putting my wife's body on display like that," Richard said.

"She needs roses."

"Roses, not violets?" Juliana asked.

"…No, roses." I couldn't believe she said that in front of everyone. Violets were secret love flowers between women. "Roses are for flirting with men. Maybe use them to touch men's faces."

"Hmm, interesting," she said.

"But she also needs to relate to the wives and girlfriends. It would be deadly to alienate them. They're the ones who drag the guys to the show. Maybe she could leave a rose or two for a woman to show it's a game that women play. Stan, you can fine-tune it."

Stan nodded over his notebook where he busily jotted notes.

"Besides dancing with our male dancers," I continued. "She'll dance with a few men in the audience."

"Definitely not," Richard said. "I cannot allow my wife to flaunt herself to strange men and—"

Stan held his glasses in his hand and leaned into the table. "It's good, Alice. We keep it subtle. It's all about what 'might' happen, but never actually does. We create a fantasy around Juliana."

"Yes," I said.

"No," Richard said. "What if one of those men grabs her, tries to hurt her?"

"All the clubs have bouncers," Stan replaced his glasses and sat back.

I looked over at Juliana. "It's worth a try," she said.

I had hoped for more enthusiasm from her.

"What?" Richard was aghast. "You're my wife. Your reputation—"

A crash of thunder exploded into the room, shaking the windows, followed by a flash of yellow and blue light.

"Phew, that was close." Johnny laughed.

I gripped my chair seat. Everything had gone so well. Why did this have to happen now? Now, I was about to make a fool … Another crash, louder than the first. Memories of the lightning that had pierced the radio, then burst into flames when I was twelve flooded me. I had to restrain myself from crawling under the table. The men rushed to the windows.

"We're going to have a heck of a downpour in a few minutes," Richard said.

"Maybe it'll cool everything off," Stan said, standing.

Only Jule still sat at the table with me. I stood up. I had to move, go somewhere. I walked toward the wall near the door. Another crash and I clung to the molding around the doorway. Jule rushed over to me.

"Don't let them see me," I whispered to her. "Please don't let them see me like this."

"Hey, is Al all right?" Richard inquired.

"She's fine. A dramatic ending to a dramatic meeting. Sound effects and all."

Johnny led the group of men toward us. "So that's it? We're done for now? Let's go downstairs and stand under the awning and watch the rain. Then we can take a cab downtown to McSorley's for a beer. What'd ya say, girls?"

"Certainly," Juliana said, "except for the fact that McSorley's doesn't admit women."

"You're right." Johnny snapped his fingers. "I forgot."

"As if you, of all people, forgot that," Juliana said.

"Let's go some place where the girls can go," Richard suggested. "How about the Starlight Lounge? It's right around the corner."

"Not me," Stan said, checking his pocket watch. "I have to get home to the little woman before she sends for the Pinkertons." He picked up his briefcase and swung a closed umbrella out in front of him like a cane; he was the only one of us who had thought to bring an umbrella.

"We'll catch up with you later," Juliana said.

"You sure Al is okay?" Richard asked.

I must have looked strange hanging onto the doorway like I was trying to keep the wall from falling down.

"Fine. Al and I are going to talk."

"Oh, girl talk," Richard said. "That could go on for hours. Yakitty Yak. Let's go, Johnny. We can down a few brews before they get there." He threw his arms around Juliana and kissed her on the cheek. "Don't be too long, dear, and be sure to walk in between the drops."

As the men were exiting into the hallway, there was another crash of thunder. I dug my fingers deeper into the molding. "You can go," I told Juliana. "I'm okay."

"Oh, yes, you look fine." Juliana laughed. "I can wait."

"I feel like a jerk. I'm supposed to be big-time, hiring big people, dealing with contracts and large sums of money, and a little thunder and lightning turns me into this quivering—"

There was another crash, followed by a series of loud rumbles and then blinking colors. "Oh, damn." My fingers gripped harder. "I don't want you to lose faith in me. That I can't manage your career, because I can."

"After today, I have no doubt," she said.

"Thanks. You want a drink. You don't have to stay here. I'll come soon."

"I'm going to stay here until that racket stops. I wish I could hold you."

"I wish you could too." I tried to laugh.

She peered around the door into the hallway. A few men stepped off the elevator, shaking umbrellas. Their footsteps were heavy as they stamped the water from their shoes. "What a downpour," I heard one say.

"I can't," Juliana said. "But I *am* here. You aren't alone this time."

"I know."

Chapter 22

"NO, YOU CAN'T do it that way," Stan Devenbach, our musical director said, shaking his head. "It's flat."

"I do not sing 'flat,'" Juliana said, indignant. "I happen to have perfect pitch. How dare you say that to me? Al, get him out of here, or I may do something you'll regret."

Stan turned toward me as I approached the stage. "I will not put up with these fits of temper, Alice." His lips were a straight line of contained anger. Stan knew his business; he'd been at it for more than twenty years, but he tended to be pretty straight-laced. He expected everyone to do things his way, no questions. Sometimes we called him "The Professor" because he peered at us through thick-lensed glasses, wore a bow tie, and rarely removed his jacket no matter how warm it got in the rehearsal studio. Johnny could use some colorful language, so Stan was constantly reprimanding him. Stan had a quiet little wife he hurried home to after every rehearsal. He never went out for drinks and conversation with the rest of us.

"I don't think Stan meant it the way you're taking it," I said, hurrying to avoid a major riff.

"We don't need him, Al. Johnny has been directing me for years."

I wanted to say, "And look where *that's* gotten you," but since Johnny was sitting at the piano, staring at me, waiting for my response, I only smiled. "Johnny is busy writing your music, and he's doing a splendid job. Splendid, Johnny." I nodded at him, and he nodded back. "I'm sure we can work this out."

I walked over to Stan and guided him toward the doorway. "Stan, I know what you mean. Let me talk to her about it. I think I can fix it. Give me a little time alone with her."

"Alice, we do not have time for these tantrums, and the way she was singing that song—"

"I know. It's almost lunchtime. Why don't you and Johnny have a bite, and—"

"I will not go anywhere with that foul-mouthed 'musician,'" he said, musician the way some people said, "homosexual." He marched to his chair and picked up his briefcase. "I will return in one half-hour, Alice, not one minute less or more. She'd better be ready to do it correctly. I'm a busy man. Remember our agreement." He walked stiffly out the door.

"I spose you want me to go, too," Johnny said, rising.

"Do you mind?" I asked in my humblest voice.

"Of course I do," Johnny said. "But for Juliana—anything." He blew her a kiss, grabbed his cap and walked out.

Juliana sat on a high stool in the center of the stage, one foot propped against the bottom rung, the other crossed over it at the ankle. She wore a sleeveless, light-blue blouse with a navy-blue pencil skirt.

"What did he mean 'remember our agreement?' What agreement?"

"Contractual stuff."

"I can't work with that man," she said. "Did you hear him? Calling *me* flat. Never." She stood and lifted the water glass from the top of the piano.

"I don't think he meant musically." I paused, concerned she'd now turn her venom on me. "I think he meant *emotionally.*"

"Well, of all the nerve." She slammed the water glass back down without taking a sip. "*I* know how to deliver a song, *and* I can knock an audience on its rear end."

"Yes. When the song has a humorous slant. Or when the song's sexy with a sexy beat and it let's you flirt and dance—there's nothing like you. The whole audience feels the charge."

"*But?*"

"But you seem to have trouble going full-throttle on some of the ballads. That's why there's only a couple in your act."

"Oh, really? You think I can't sing ballads, so you've cut them down to cover my *retardation*? Who the hell do you think you are? You're a kid from the country or, what are they calling it these days, 'the suburbs.' You didn't know a thing about this business until a few years ago, and now you think you're some kind of expert."

"I don't think I'm much of an expert on anything. Except your career and how to make it happen. That I *do* know about, and you have to listen to me. We have a deal. So pay attention."

She walked to the stool and sat down. "Say something. Make it brilliant."

She was not the kind of woman who took instructions easily. "From that stool, sing 'O, Mio Babbino Caro.'"

"Now?"

"Now."

"It's opera. It has nothing to do with this show."

"Sing it."

"From here? With no accompaniment? Do you have any idea how difficult that is?"

"No. But you can do it. I've heard you. Begin."

I sat down in a front row seat while she grumbled under her breath, I think calling me names. Juliana sat silently, her head bowed. Then, she raised her head and lifted the song from the stage floor into her body, letting herself *become* the song. Watching this transformation made it hard for me to hold onto my professional pose. As the sounds poured out of her, the child inside me jumped up and down, my mouth hung open, and my heart fell on the floor. When she finished, she took one look at me and laughed. "If all my audiences were like you, I wouldn't need to eat, sleep, or have sex. I'd just sing."

I swallowed, stood, and tugged on the edge of my jacket. "Jule, what you did just now, you have to do with your ballads; you have to put all of yourself into them."

She sat down on the stool. "You don't know what you're asking."

"No, I don't. Tell me why you can put all of yourself into an aria, but not when you sing a ballad or a love song."

"I—can't explain it."

"But you know you're not doing it."

"Of course I know!" she shouted, jumping up. "Am I finished? My career's over. Is that it?"

"Don't be silly. You *can* do it. I've heard you." I looked around the room. The doors were closed. "That time you sang, 'My Romance' to me," I whispered. "And then, you—kissed me for the first time. Do it like that."

"Don't ask me to do that."

"Why?"

"Because—you were this innocent kid looking at me like I held the secret to the universe. You were sweet, and open, and ... Don't make me talk about this."

"You're afraid of showing raw emotion in front of people, aren't you?"

"Of course not. I've been singing in front of people since I was three."

"Embarrassed then. Is that why you didn't pursue opera professionally? You were afraid of the nakedness?"

"I'm not afraid of nakedness. That's you."

"Wrong metaphor. Right idea. Sing '(I Love You) For Sentimental Reasons' right to me. Look at me and sing it. Sing it with the same intensity that you sang 'O Mio Babbino.'"

"Don't ask for that."

"What's different? They're both emotional."

"One, in 'Babbino,' you don't know what the words mean, and two, it's about a girl telling her father she's going to run away with her boyfriend."

"That's it? Gosh, for something that sounds that beautiful I'd expect the words to mean something grander. Like something about heaven or God."

"She's extremely passionate about it, threatening to throw herself off a bridge. It's hard to explain in English."

"It's being personal that embarrasses you, isn't it?"

"Will you stop saying that? Nothing embarrasses me."

"Not true. You're embarrassed when you have to stand there and be *emotionally* naked. That's it. You're embarrassed right now at having to listen to me talk about it."

"Stop psychoanalyzing me."

"I wouldn't know how to do that."

"Everybody's doing it these days."

"Quit changing the subject. I want you to stand on that stage and sing '(I Love You) For Sentimental Reasons' with the same depth of feeling you gave to 'O Mio Babbino.' Prove that you're not embarrassed. Sing to me, Jule."

I sat down in the front row again.

"You love doing this to me, don't you?"

I grinned. "Only a little."

She stomped her way back to the stool and broke into a silly dance step.

"No fooling around. Do it seriously."

She stood in front of the stool, her head down for a long time. The silence grew heavy with my tension. She opened her mouth, looking not quite at me, but close enough, and sang. I fixed my eyes on her to make her as uncomfortable as possible. It wasn't so easy for me either to look at her straight-on while she sang a love song.

She stepped down from the stage one white, high-heeled shoe after the other in delicate little steps. She walked toward me as she sang, a challenge in her eyes, and stopped only when she was so close to me that I could feel the soft material of the edge of her skirt against my knee. It was a duel, and she had no intention of losing. She sang with such feeling, almost looking right at me, that

I wiggled in my seat. My eyes scanned the room to be sure no one had slipped in to see whatever we were—I imagined her bending over to kiss me, and I would have accepted that kiss even in that public place. The last line still vibrated over my head when she said, "Did that meet with your approval, Miss Huffman?"

Before I could melt at her feet, clapping came from behind me. It was Stan.

Chapter 23

I KEPT UP my work at the Mt. Olympus while preparing for the opening of Max's new place, The Haven, on 52nd and Fifth. We were headed for Swing Street! Down the block from our new building was "21" and Jimmy Ryan's; another few blocks away was the Copa. The Mt. Olympus was doing so well that Max was going to keep both open with me as sole manager of The Haven. *And* I was going to get my own cabaret and liquor licenses. *My* name on both!

There were plenty of women who owned bars, but a woman in full charge of a Cabaret? Well, *I* didn't know any. But me! So I was happy, really happy, but—the darkness—it was always there, and sometimes there was a knife in the air and my mother slashing at her arms and at me. I had to stop thinking of all that. It was happening. My dream was coming. I had every reason to be happy. She couldn't hurt me anymore, but there were times when I wasn't so sure. *Especially* when I was happy.

While Max was dealing with designers and carpenters, and spending a fortune making The Haven ready, he had me going to dives to look at unknowns who might become another client for me to manage. I think he hoped I'd find someone who would take up so much of my time, I'd drop Juliana, but there was no chance of that. I was young. I could live on three hours of sleep, Nedick's hot dogs, coke, and the occasional brandy.

Whenever I went out to the clubs, Bart would pick me up at my Milligan Place apartment like it was a normal date. Yes, he was *that* Bart—Bartholomew Montadeus Honeywell the Fourth, who Max tried to get me to marry in '48. Bart became a necessity. Max paid him to escort me on my nightly hunts for a new client, since I couldn't enter a club without a masculine appendage dangling from my arm.

Bartholomew was about my height, short for a man, but his striking good looks, platinum blond hair, and slender physique made up for his short stature. He wore white pants and a white suit jacket over a white shirt and white tie. All that white showed off his pronounced tan. I was sure his dimpled smile drove men wild.

Bart and I had gone twice to The Number One Club at 1 Fifth Avenue, not far from my apartment, for the Monday Night Amateur Show. The

Number One was one of the few clubs that didn't expect me to arrive in a formal gown. It was a pretty casual place, so Max dressed me in a simple flower print with only a slight flare. It was sleeveless in consideration of the eighty-degree heat. I think not having to dress up was what convinced me this place harbored hidden genius despite the not-so-hot "talent" I'd seen so far.

"Shall I retrieve us a bit of libation?" Bart asked as we sat sandwiched among four tables of rowdy drinkers.

"A Tom Collins for me. I hope they at least have that."

What passed for a stage was a grand piano wedged between two poles. A square piece of wood on the floor between the poles was the stage.

Bart placed a bottle of beer in front of me, no glass. "That's all they had." He sat down, pressing one leg delicately over the other. He twirled his white loafer at the gentleman with the petite mustache across from us, sitting at his own tiny table. "Look, Bart," I said. "You can't be running off like last week and leaving me to sit here alone."

"I assure you, my dear," he gestured with all five of his carefully-manicured fingers, "it was never my intention to cause you any anxious fright last week. I merely met an old acquaintance. However, for our sojourn tonight, I shall remain glued to your side."

I sighed. "Not that close. Sit there. And no more 'acquaintances.'" Last week, the "acquaintance" was the bartender. This week, he turned his dimpled smile toward the mustached gentleman. Normals were delightfully blind to these flirtations occurring around them all the time.

The lights went black. No warning. A young blonde girl slunk out onto that ridiculous stage in a clinging blue gown that no designer had designed. She glided in a circle of blue light as someone in the dark played a horn better than I'd ever heard it played in the big clubs. She sang "Blues in the Night." Sultry. Sexy. She sang right through the audience's chatter until they finally had to shut up and listen to her. She was a white girl singing the blues like a colored girl. I could barely stay in my seat. What a find. I had to represent her!

She only sang the one song and then slithered off. "Bart, I'm going backstage," I whispered as the next act was setting up.

"Oh?" He looked at me hopefully.

"Yes, you can go talk to that guy over there. *Don't* leave without me."

I slid in and out of the tiny tables of people talking, ignoring the act that was on stage. It was good to be free of Bart, but I wondered if I was breaking some rule. Was I sposed to bring him into the dressing room with me? I didn't know how to be a career woman, and I didn't think to ask Max about that. Barney told me not to sit on my instincts, so I plowed ahead despite feeling like everyone was watching me.

I took a breath and stood straight, pretending I knew what I was doing. I walked through the darkened hallway. A woman leaning on the wall, smoking a cigarette, directed me toward the backstage door. "Thattaway, honey."

Inside, under a few bright, bare light bulbs, was a room packed with entertainment hopefuls in various states of undress, crowding around a long make-up table.

"Yeah, you wan' sumpin', lady?" an old baldheaded man in suspenders sitting near the door asked, as he sucked on a cigar.

It must've have been 110 degrees in that room, and with all those sweating bodies, the smell almost knocked me over.

"The girl—she sang, 'Blues' …" Trying to hold my breath and talk at the same time wasn't so easy. "…in the Night.'"

"Hey, kids," the old man yelled, gesturing with his soggy cigar, "which a youse done, 'Blues in da Night?'"

"Da's me," the young blonde called, pulling a slip down over her small breasts. "Ya wan' sumpin'?"

"Dis here lady wants sumpin'. Make it snappy. She ain't got all day. She's dressed nice."

The girl stepped past a leggy dancer who was pulling on a nylon stocking. "Ya wan' sumpin', lady?" she asked me.

"You're the girl who sang 'Blues in the Night?'" I tried to hide my shock. Or was that disappointment? I was expecting a sophisticated …

"Yeah, dat's me. So's ya like it?" Her voice had the same nasal quality as Judy Holiday in *Born Yesterday.* She tightened one of the straps on her slip.

"Yes, I did. Very much. And I wanted to talk to you about representation." I handed her my card—wondering if I should get the hell out of there. What would Max do?

"Hey, you! Don't goes talkin' to *her,*" a young colored man, barely eighteen, in a sleeveless undershirt shouted. He climbed over chairs and bodies to get to us. "Don't be flauntin' yerself like some two-bit ho'." He pressed a dress into her hands. "Ain't I learned ya nuttin. Ya covers yerself up when ya talkin' to the public."

She started to slip into the red and blue-striped dress.

"Ya wanna hire her?" the young man asked. "She does bahmitzvahs, weddin's, birthdays. Even funerals if ya gots the cash. But ya gots to fix it wit' me first." He pointed a thumb at his chest. "I's her manager."

"You're this young woman's manager?"

"I sure is and she don't come cheap. You gots a old man round here somewheres? I ain't negotiatin' with no female."

"I think your friend and I should talk," I said to him, then turned to her. "Did you look at the card I gave you?"

The girl looked down at the card in her hand. "Jesus gawd, LeRoy, get a damn load of dis. She's wit' Max Harlin'ton. My gawd, dis could be my shot."

"Yeah, and she could be a screwball. Sorry, lady, *I's* her manager. She don't need nobody else."

"Uh, could you tell me your name?" I asked the girl.

"Oh, yeah. I'm Connie and dis here's LeRoy. He's my special someone, if ya know what I mean. I'm his goil."

"Don't be tellin' her that. This are business. That all she gots to know 'bout."

"Pleased to meet you, Connie. I'm Alice Huffman. And LeRoy." I nodded at him and took out my date book. "Connie, why don't we make a date to meet at the Mt. Olympus? Bring some of your material."

"Hey!" LeRoy squawked. "You can't comes in here and steals away my client. Don't ya know nuttin' 'bout ethics? I gotta come wit' her."

I wasn't sure what to do with him, and I wasn't even sure I still wanted Connie. I wished I could crawl into Max's lap.

"Then, you and Connie have a contract?" I asked.

"Hell, no! We ain't got no contract," Connie answered. "Quit yer catterwallin' LeRoy. Dis here lady could maybe give me my start. She works with Max Harlin'ton! 'Sides, we only gonna tawk. Righty, dighty, Miss Huffman?"

"No. I want to hear you sing, too. You don't have to worry about hiring an accompanist, though. We have someone at the Mt. Olympus who can—"

"*I* plays for her! Piano, horn, drums, you name it. Where she go, I goes."

I turned to Connie. "How about we say tomorrow, noon." I flipped to the page in my date book, balancing it on my knee. "So that's Connie … Connie what?"

"Lingus."

"Excuse me?" I looked up from my date book. "Your name is uh—Connie Lingus?"

"Yeah!" LeRoy said. "You wanna make sumpin' outta it?"

"Stop, LeRoy." Connie said. "Lotsa folks make fun of my name. It ain't no never mind."

I tried to smile. What had I gotten myself into? "Well," Big smile. "Names can be changed, can't they?"

"See Con? She gonna change ya and ball up all our plans." His arms flailed around his body. "That's what they does."

Connie put her arms around his head, stopping his aimless movement. She kissed his neck. "No, baby, she ain't gonna change nuttin'. I ain't gonna let her. You always worrying 'bout stuff that don't never happen. He does that, Miss Huffman. It takes me to stop him from doin' dat. You know how men are."

LeRoy put his thin brown arms around her and pulled her close. "She gonna do somethin' to you, Sweet Pea. That what they does. Stick by me. I love ya how ya is."

"LeRoy and I got plans, Miss Huffman. He gotta stay in my plans. Ya know what I mean?"

"Of course. But Connie, could we speak a moment outside? Privately."

"No!" LeRoy shouted, stepping in front of Connie. "Ya can't take her. She mines." He spun around and grabbed Connie by her shoulders. "Con, I knows about life. You barely grown, but me, I knows things so ya gotta listen. She gonna do things to your head. That's what they does. They ball up everything in your head, so ya can't hardly think no more. What'd I tell you 'bout them?"

"It's up to you, Connie. But is LeRoy in charge of everything you do? You can't think for yourself?" I knew exactly what I was doing, and I wasn't at all pleased to be doing it. "I don't know that I'd want to represent someone who didn't have her own mind."

"Don't be listenin' to her crap, Con. She gonna ball up everythin' in your head. That's what they does."

"I sure as hell *can* t'ink for myself," Connie said firmly, stepping away from LeRoy. "I'm only gonna go out and tawk wit' her a minute, honey. Dat's all."

"See what she doin'? Changin' you. That's what they does. Don't goes, baby. Don't goes out there wit' her. There ain't no good out there. There ain't no us out there. You ain't never comin' back."

"I ain't got no shoes on. 'Course I'm comin back."

As we stepped through the door I heard LeRoy crying out, "No, Connie, you ain't comin' back. You ain't. That's what they—"

I closed the door as we walked into the hallway. Connie opened her purse and took out a used gum wrapper, opened it, unwrapped the old gum, and plopped it into her mouth.

"Connie, how badly do you want this? How badly do you want to be a star?"

"You can make me a star?"

"I think so. A lot's gonna depend on you because it's gonna take a lot of work and a lot of sacrifice. What I need to know is if you can sing on Tuesday the way you sang tonight."

"Sure can. I been singin' since I was four, Miz Huffman. My father taught me practic'lly 'fore I could talk."

"Then are you willing to make the necessary sacrifices?"

"You betcha."

"I'm going to speak to you frankly, woman-to-woman 'cause I know you're smart. How far do you think a hopeful like yourself would get in show business with a colored business manager?"

"Uh ... but we been together for three years." Tears swelled her eyes. "He sticks up for me. We're in love."

"Let me ask you this. How far do you think a white performer would get in this business with a colored boyfriend?"

"But ..."

"You think about it. I don't want to influence you." *Like hell I didn't.* "I'll leave Tuesday noon open. Don't show up if you're not prepared to make the *necessary* sacrifices."

I left her in the hallway with a thin stream of tears smearing black streaks down her face. I left her with a choice to make, but I knew what her choice would be. No talent like that was going to sit quietly inside of her. Still—I didn't sleep too well that night, or many nights afterward.

Chapter 24

September 1949

ALL OVER THE city, all over the country—the world too, I guess—we were glued to our Sunday *New York Times*. Richard, Juliana, Johnny, and I were having brunch at the Peacock Restaurant in the Waldorf Astoria on Richard's dime that was considerably more than a dime—but he sure owed us a good time after yesterday's rehearsal.

Johnny had been playing the intro for "Put the Blame on Mame," and Juliana came out dancing and singing in a black leotard and tights. Richard jumped out of his seat and ran up on stage with Juliana's bathrobe in his arms. "Cover yourself!" he yelled, trying to drape the robe over her shoulders.

"Richard!" Juliana pushed him away. "I'm rehearsing."

Stan approached the stage, as always, wearing his three-piece suit. He removed his thick glasses. "Mr. Styles, what do you expect her to wear to rehearse a number like this? She has to move. For the actual show, she'll be fully covered in an appropriate-length dress. Now, if you would be so kind as to leave the stage. We have a great deal of work to accomplish today."

"Well, uh … I guess." Richard reluctantly hopped down from the low stage, caressing Juliana's bathrobe. "Sorry, fellas. Sorry, Johnny."

Johnny nodded.

We got through that song okay, despite Richard squirming around in his chair. But, gosh, she did look good, and I kind of wanted to throw a robe around her myself. I mean, Johnny was looking at her with those eyes men get.

Then we set up for the "If I Were the Only Girl in the World" number. This was the song that Stan had chosen for her to dance with men in the audience. He had Spatz and Wallace, our dancers, two brothers who came from a family of Vaudevillians, sit at a couple of tables down front and pretend to be audience members.

Juliana had changed into a simple navy-blue day dress. Her voice was in top form, and it was the kind of song she could have fun with, so we all sat there falling in love with her again. But when she stepped down from the stage and reached out for Spatz, taking him into her arms and flirting with him, Richard got squirmy in his seat again. I held onto his arm and shook my head no. He reached into his suit jacket pocket and took out a pack of Marlboros. He shook so bad he couldn't get the cigarette out of the pack, so I took one out for him and put it in his mouth. He couldn't connect his lighter with the cigarette, so I lit it for him.

I watched her from the corner of my eye while keeping Richard busy with his cigarette. Juliana, her arms around Spatz, sang right into his face. It was extremely romantic. As the song came to an end she kissed him on the cheek. Richard jumped up. "No. Definitely not. Julie, you cannot flaunt yourself in front of these men."

"Richard, stop it," Juliana said with contained anger. "This is no place for your insane jealousy. This is the act."

"Easy, Juliana," Stan said, walking toward her. "We can't have you getting upset."

"But Stan," Richard whined.

Stan turned toward him. "That's Mr. Devenbach to you, Mr. Styles. And now, Mr. Styles, please sit. Quietly."

As Richard slunk back into his chair, the messenger I was expecting ran in. "Here it is, Al."

I took the envelope from him and pressed a coin into his hands, sending him happily off. "That it?" Stan asked.

"Yup." I handed the envelope to Stan. He slid out the sheet music and let his eyes scan over it. "Okay," Stan said, handing the music to Juliana. "Look at the second verse."

As her eyes scanned the page, a grin formed on her face. "Phew. Yes!"

"Johnny, play the intro, please," Stan said.

"Whatever you say, boss."

"Don't call me boss."

He grinned at Stan as he ran his fingers over the keys, playing the intro to "Bewitched, Bothered, and Bewildered."

She sang the first verse of that song, drawing me in. I had to get closer to the sounds, to be surrounded by them. I struggled to ignore Richard, who was stabbing a pencil into one of his hands. He got through the first verse without drawing blood, but the second verse ... Well—when she sang, "And worship the trousers that cling to him," his face contorted into such a burning radish that it looked like it was going to explode. Then she sang, "Horizontally speaking, he's at his very best," and Richard flew out of his seat, fists raised. "No! No!" Juliana pushed through to "…Thank God, I can be oversexed again."

"You've changed the words," Richard yelled. "Julie, you can't sing those filthy words. Put the real words back! I've heard that song on the radio and I *know* those words are—"

"These are the words Hart wrote," I told him. "They were the ones Vivienne Segal sung on Broadway."

"Lorenz was my dear friend," Stan added. "May God rest his soul. And of course, the words he wrote cannot be sung on the radio, *but* they can be sung in a cabaret. Al convinced me that we owe Larry this honor."

"But Doris Day and Helen Forrest don't sing it that way on their records. No one will ever record it."

"We're trying to break new ground," I told him. "We want to do something entirely new with Juliana."

"By letting her sing filth? Julie, tell them you won't."

"These words are perfect for me, Richard. Go home."

"An excellent idea," Stan said in his usual calm manner. "Mr. Styles, go home. You cannot continue to interrupt my rehearsal. Please leave. Now."

"*I'm* paying for this."

"And we are all grateful to you. Aren't we, everybody?"

We said things like, "Sure are. Thanks, Richard," and so on.

"But I …" Richard said. "She's my …"

"Unless you would rather *I* left …" Stan pulled on the cuffs of one sleeve, then the other.

"No!" Juliana cried out. "Richard, go!"

"Well?" Stan crossed his arms over his chest.

"I'm sorry, Stan," Juliana said. "This is all so unprofessional. Richard, you have to go."

"But I'm your husband!"

"You are. And we don't need any husbands here. We do need the musical director."

"But I'm your manager."

"Yes. And my manager doesn't need to be here, either. My musical director does. I'll see you at home tonight, darling."

He looked around the room for support, but found none. He marched toward the door.

"Oh and Mr. Styles," Stan called before Richard could get through the door. "You shall never again enter any of my rehearsals. I appreciate your cooperation. Thank you." He turned back to us. "We can proceed now."

To make it up to us, after he and Juliana went to church, Richard brought us to the Peacock for a leisurely brunch. We didn't expect the *Sunday Times*, usually a favorite brunch activity, to so thoroughly upset our appetites. Shivers of fear rippled up my arms. "I can't believe it," Johnny said. "They're not supposed to be as smart as us. Everyone said they couldn't do it."

"Well, they did it," Richard said softly, taking a sip of his Mimosa. "They did it."

Juliana sat quietly in her breezy-cool dress, her dark hair tumbling loose around her face, her gaze looked far away. What was going on in her mind?

I pushed my eggs Benedict aside and looked down at my paper. I read the words over again to myself. "We have evidence," Truman told the press, "that within recent weeks, an atomic explosion occurred in the U.S.S.R. ..."

The Russians had the bomb.

Chapter 25

October 1949

OVER THE NEXT few months, we engaged in a nonstop flurry of activity. Nothing like constant movement to take your mind off possible world destruction. But it was always there—the awareness. Everything was the same and nothing was. We always knew that one stroke of Stalin's mentally-deranged, Soviet Union finger could exterminate us all like scurrying little bugs. Best not to dwell on it too much.

I was going to take the fall semester off from school, but when I casually mentioned it to Max, he blew up. To appease him, I registered for one course. I thought a scene-study class might be easier than something theoretical—no exams to cram for, but I was wrong. I was constantly taking the subway uptown to rehearse some scene I had to present to the class, and then dashing back downtown to manage the club and Juliana's career. But I had to admit I liked being back at the acting. Acting at school gave me more gratification than it had when I was considered a so-called professional. The scenes I read were from plays I cared about, not the lame radio junk I used to get paid for, like: "For a wash that's whiter than white, brighter than bright ..." Jeepers! The Russians have the bomb, for criminy's sake.

I was two people. There was me, the college student, who went to school in shirtwaist dresses and flare skirts and occasionally stayed up late in bars having deep conversations about the world. And there was the old-maid career woman me, who wore business suits and clunky heals and rushed to the club to hire a bouncer or rehearse a line of scantily-clad chorus girls.

All throughout October, Johnny feverishly wrote new songs for Juliana's act. As soon as he finished one, Juliana was learning it, and Stan and I were working it into the show. Johnny hated it when I suddenly threw on my coat to go uptown to rehearse. "Not *that* again," he'd complain. "You can actually get a degree in acting? What kind of a Mickey Mouse school *is* that? And at your age? You must be a fossil over there."

He was wrong. With so many veterans going to school on the GI Bill, lots of students were my age. Mostly men, though. Women who were qualified for Veterans Benefits didn't come to City. Maybe they didn't want to be teachers.

Johnny, Stan, and I were also pulling together songs we hoped would be Juliana's first 33 rpm LP microgroove album. LPs were so new that Max thought maybe we should stick with two songs for a 78 rpm, but from the talk I was hearing in the music department at school, it was clear that the new microgrooves were the way to go; they would put Juliana ahead of the rest. Max agreed, happy I was learning the latest in the business. Convincing Richard was harder, but I prevailed.

We hired Juliana a new vocal coach, the best from Max's best-of-the-best list. Of course, she didn't know her coach came from Max. I made the contact and Richard forked over the money. Juliana was thrilled with how the act was shaping up, and I reveled in seeing her so happy. Of course, she and I didn't get to be alone with each other very often. I kept telling myself that someday all this would be behind us, and we'd have plenty of time together.

Max recommended a photographer, and the most gorgeous, glamorous pictures of her were taken. Maybe too glamorous for my taste. Juliana had a natural beauty that didn't require a lot of makeup or special lighting. It came from a quiet confidence in her beauty that emanated from the inside of her. Max approved the photos, so we put them on posters around town under the logo, "Sensuous. Seductive. Secretive."

She was booked to play The Onyx in early November. My anxiety rose. This would be Juliana's biggest gig since I started managing her. Juliana seemed unfazed throughout the last-minute preparations. That is, until the *Newsweek* article came out.

She was resting in the alcove off to the side of the rehearsal space at Carnegie Studios, eating her lunch of lime Jell-O. She was always on a diet, which worried me; she had a perfect hourglass shape. If she changed that, she'd be harder to book. I walked over to where she sat in a white straight-backed chair, reading a magazine.

"Johnny finished another song," I told her, leaning on the opposite wall. "Stan and I thought you might want to try it out this afternoon. See if we can fit it into the act."

She didn't stir from her reading, only shook her head. "Why are they doing this?"

"Doing what? What are you reading?"

I looked over her shoulder and saw the title in bold letters.

"QUEER PEOPLE."

"What magazine is that?" Holding her place, she flipped the cover toward me.

"*Newsweek*? Why would they …? Are they even allowed to print words like that?" My heart thundered, and a shiver ran through me.

"Apparently. Read the rest. They use *all* the words."

I read the article to myself over her shoulder.

"The sex pervert, whether a homosexual, an exhibitionist, or even a dangerous sadist, is often regarded merely as a 'queer' person who never hurts anyone but himself. Then the mangled form of some victim focuses public attention on the degenerate's work, and newspaper headlines flare for days over accounts, and feature articles packed with sensational details of the most dastardly and horrifying crimes."

"'Homosexual.' It's right there in print," I said. "I thought quality magazines and newspapers couldn't use that word, that their editors wouldn't let them, but there it is."

"The world's changing. I feel it more everyday."

I took a deep breath. I had to calm down for her sake. I knew none of this applied to me. My feelings were only for Jule. No other woman ever … well, there was Marta the Jewish girl, but that was meaningless kid stuff, so that didn't count. But why was my heart pounding over a simple little article? "Jule, this doesn't have anything to do with you," I whispered, trying to believe what I said. I looked over at Stan and Johnny, sitting near the far wall behind the post, eating. Johnny, of course, knew about Jule, and maybe Stan did too, but no one ever talked about it.

"Oh, yes, it does have to do with me." She stood, rolling up the magazine tightly in her two hands.

"They mean the guys."

"Oh, do they? And I suppose they meant 'the guys' when a group of girls chased me and a friend through the woods and beat us up so badly we spent weeks in the hospital."

"Oh, my God. When?"

"I was young. It was nothing. But believe me, Al, in their minds, we are all rolled up into one perverted, degenerate …" She coughed like she was going to choke or be sick.

"Easy." I went to put my arms around her.

"No," she coughed out, pushing me away. "Please."

"Tell me."

"It was nothing. I shouldn't have brought it up; it's only the article. I was a child." She spoke as if it had happened to someone else. "After the beating, they visited me in the hospital, and threatened to … My mother came to the hospital every day and doted on me. I made up a story about some elusive gang of boys, because if I told her what really happened, those girls would've told her the truth about me. For a year, they had me running errands for them."

"You? I can't picture you … I'm sorry."

"Disappointed?"

"Uh … no …" I was.

"One afternoon, the leader of the bunch ordered me on my knees to wash her shoes with my tongue. I punched her in the face. She went down. Hard."

"I knew it! I knew *you'd* never—"

"The others ran away scared, and I was expelled. When Mother got over her anger, she found another boarding school. How about that? You like that story better?"

"Isn't that what happened?"

She grabbed her purse. "I've got to go."

"Go? Where? We have a rehearsal."

"Tell Stan I'll be back in an hour." She threw the magazine to the floor. "I have to go to mass."

Chapter 26

"PICK UP YOUR cue!" Marty yelled at me. We met in a diner not far from the school. Marty's army buddy, Moshe Steinman, was there to rehearse the scene too.

We sat at a round Formica table, bright red, while the jukebox played Vic Damone singing I didn't know what. His sound was so boring, I couldn't tell what it was. The boys were finishing up their eggs. I couldn't eat.

"Take it easy," Moshe said, sipping his coffee from a thick mug. "You shouldn't talk to a girl like that. It's disrespectful."

"Yeah!" I shot back at Marty.

"Nuts to that. *She's* already been on Broadway," Marty told Moshe.

"You have?" Moshe sounded impressed.

I wished I hadn't told Marty that. Too much expectation.

"But *I* haven't," Marty continued, "and I don't expect you to get in my way." He waved an unlit cigarette at me. "Come on, Al." And snapped his fingers in front of my glazed eyes. "Get with it."

He didn't know I'd only had two hours' sleep. The coffee wasn't helping, and I couldn't look at the leftover egg on their plates. His face and voice softened as he lit his cigarette. "I didn't mean to yell, but this is important to me. I've got plans and I'm starting late."

"You're right," I said. "I haven't been putting in the time."

"What've you got to do?" he asked. "You're only taking one course and waiting on tables. Don't you care about your future?"

"Yeah, Marty, I do." My own anger seeped through.

"Marty," Moshe said. "Don't speak to her like that. Soon she'll get good sense, get married, have babies, and forget all this career nonsense. It's a phase. Something lots of girls go through."

"Oh, do we?" There went my ally.

Moshe always wore a dark suit jacket, often too small for him, and a bow tie, with a yarmulke on his head. Marty looked rumpled, dressed in his baggy corduroy pants and his tweed jacket with the patches on the elbows. He kept his tie folded in his pocket.

"Let's go to my apartment." Marty's chair scraped along the floor as he got up. "Less distraction. We need to move around if we're going to get this scene right."

"We can't," Moshe said, nodding at me but addressing Marty. "It wouldn't be right."

"Alice doesn't care about things like that," Marty said. "She's not like a regular girl." He sprinted toward the door ahead of Moshe and me.

What did that mean?

* * *

Marty's apartment was a one-and-a-half on 129th and Lenox, in a fourth-floor walk-up. I stood in the hallway looking in through the open door. "Well?" Marty said, "Aren't you coming in?"

"I don't know." My insides were a jungle of heartbeats. "I can't just go in there. Alone. With you."

"Oh, come on. We're friends. We're going to rehearse. What do you think I'm going to do? Attack you?"

"No. But—I've never been in a man's apartment alone before." Well, there had been Max, but somehow, he didn't count. I whispered, "What will people think?"

"Nothing, if you hurry up in here," he whispered back, grabbing my arm and pulling me inside; he shut the door. "There. You're in and I haven't done anything to you. Yet." He growled in my face and I jumped back. He laughed. "I promise; you're safe with me. Here, I've got something to relax you."

He took a small book off a makeshift bookshelf and handed it to me. "See how small it is? That one's *Ariel*, the whole biography of Shelly in one tiny book. They were small like that so soldiers could carry them in their pockets. They didn't cut any words out; they just shrunk the whole thing down."

I felt the book lying in the palm of my hand. Marty was right. Just being close to a book *was* relaxing.

Marty's poverty, or lack of interest in material possessions, was apparent from the décor: two wooden milk crates for sitting, an overstuffed chair with the stuffing coming out, and no rug. He had the type of bed that disappeared into the wall.

I looked over at his homemade bookshelf. "Wow, so many books." I went to the shelf that held the tiny ones. "Gosh, you must have hundreds of these."

"My mom used to send them to me."

I took one in my hand. It opened backwards. It was a Jewish prayer book. It had Hebrew on one side of the page and the equivalent English on the other. In the very back of the book, that was really the front, in blue ink, it read: "Don't forget to say your prayers. Mom" A warm feeling drifted through my body.

"Those books made the war easier to take."

I put the book back on the shelf. "That must've been awful, fighting a war. I can't even imagine it."

"Good. You shouldn't. You're a girl. Your job is to look pretty."

I turned to stare at him.

"What?"

"Nothing."

He sat on the edge of the arm of the overstuffed chair. "I'm sorry Mosh wouldn't come up. He thought I was damaging your reputation, and he didn't want to be a party to that."

"He might be right."

"Nah. He's just a religious guy. He wasn't, you know, before the war. Now, he's trying to find himself as a Jew."

"It was terrible what they … The pictures … What they did … It was awful. Did you, uh … did you have any family?"

"They were all my family, every single one." He sighed. "Let's rehearse that scene."

"I'm sorry if I said anything wrong. I don't know what to say to you. It's all too huge for words."

"That's why it's better to rehearse."

* * *

As Marty and I arranged the student desks into a makeshift stage in the unoccupied classroom, Moshe stood in the doorway scowling at me. "Come in, Mosh," Marty said.

He shuffled in, still staring at me. "Drop it," Marty said, shaking Moshe's shoulder.

"What's the matter?" I asked.

"It's nothing," Marty said. "It's—Look, I'm gonna tell her. Mosh thought you didn't respect yourself by coming into my apartment." He grabbed Moshe's shoulders and shook him. "Cut it out. She's my friend. It's a new time. The war changed everything."

"Not the rules of common decency," Moshe said, looking at me. "No amount of time will change that. Because of the war and *everything* that happened, we must cling tighter to morality, not throw it away."

My own guilt bubbled up.

"Okay, you said what you had to say." Marty released him and pushed another desk into our makeshift set. "Forget it. She didn't do anything."

Somehow, I'd become one of those little badminton feather-things that gets batted back and forth over the net. What *I* thought or felt didn't seem to matter.

"I bet she didn't do anything," Moshe said.

"Hey, wait a minute," I said. "I'm here, you know, and I don't like what you said. I don't go around doing what you think I go around doing. I thought you were a nice guy."

"And *I* thought you were a decent girl, not one of those—"

"That's it, Marty. I'm not staying here for this." I grabbed my hat, coat, and purse and rushed out the door.

"Damn you, Moshe," I heard Marty say behind me. "I wanna rehearse, dammit! I'm not gonna get a bad grade because of you." He came alongside me in the hall. "He doesn't mean it. It's that religion of his."

"Isn't his religion your religion too?"

"Sorta. I'm pretty loose about my beliefs. I don't go in for most of the rigmarole. I don't mean rigmarole. I respect the folks that follow tradition. It's just that for me, well—I do Yom Kippur to make my mother happy, but even she's less religious since my father walked out when I was ten. Come on, Alice. Let's rehearse. You don't want to fail your midterm, do you? Ignore him; that's what I do."

"But Marty, don't you see? He might be right. I did go into your apartment."

"We rehearsed. That's all. Come on."

We got through rehearsal. When we presented the scene in class the next evening, we were a hit, and received A's for our effort. "We need to go to a club and celebrate," Marty said, walking between Moshe and me toward the quadrangle. "No excuses, Alice, call in sick. Mosh, you were terrific too. Come with us."

Moshe, pouting, walked ahead of us into the quad. Marty dashed after him. "Do you have to be this way?" Moshe stopped, and the two of them talked.

"Look, Marty," I called. "You and Moshe go. I have work." I was about to leave when suddenly, they were laughing. I stopped. I didn't think Moshe was capable of laughing.

Marty walked toward me. "Moshe decided not to go so you and I can—" Suddenly, Moshe was on Marty's back, his arms around his throat. He tossed Marty to the ground near my feet. I jumped back. Marty threw Moshe off him, and the two pounded their fists into each other's faces.

Two big guys strolling down the walk with their girls ran into the scene and grabbed Marty and Moshe off each other. Once they were dusted off, I looked into their bleeding faces and said, "I'm not going anywhere with either of you. You're both certifiable." I headed toward the gate.

From behind me I heard Moshe say, "So I guess that means you and I can go somewhere. Huh, Marty?"

Chapter 27

November 1949

JULE RECOVERED FROM her panic over the article, but the calm she'd exhibited in October evaporated. I wished she'd tell me more about what had happened at school. She didn't seem like the kind of person anyone would beat up. Although she pretended she was fine, she wasn't for the whole week before she opened at The Onyx. I made her lots of hot Turkish tea and hired her a private yoga teacher. By opening night, she was completely certifiable and had no energy to pretend she wasn't. I sat with her in her dressing room, trying to get her to do her yoga breathing exercises, convincing her she wasn't going to fail, and keeping Richard out; he made us both a wreck.

"I can't do it, Al! I can't." She paced frenetically back and forth in the dressing room while I leaned against the make-up table.

"Of course you can." I laughed, hoping to lighten her mood. "You have to. There's an audience out there waiting for you."

"Send them away."

"You know we can't do that."

"This is your fault, you know. You got me into this. I am such a disappointment. A disappointment to you, to Shirl, to—"

"You're not. Look at me." I held her by the shoulders to stop all that frantic activity. "Your mother is looking down on us right now, and she is so proud. You are *not* disappointing her. You are fulfilling her. She's going to be here tonight, helping you, loving you, and bursting her buttons."

"Do you truly believe that?"

"Tonight, I do."

"Then you're more nuts than I am, *but*—I'll do it. For Mother."

And she did.

I know it was my imagination, but when she started in on her first song, I swear I saw some filmy … Ridiculous. Cigarette smoke. And yet—something deep inside me wanted to believe she was there, and was maybe even looking down on me, too, pleased with what I was doing for her little girl.

The reviews were glowing. The critics especially liked her rendition of "Girls Were Made to Take Care of Boys." *The New York Times* called it "sweet." Many adjectives could be applied to Juliana, but "sweet" was not one of them; we had to be doing something wrong. I campaigned to have the song cut, but Stan wouldn't hear of it. The real success of the evening, though, was her dancing with guys from the audience and singing, "If I Were the Only Girl in the World."

The last guy she took up on stage was horribly shy and stared at her. She led him through the foxtrot while she ran a red rose over his face, played with his hair and winked at him. At the end of the song she kissed him on the cheek and walked him back to his wife or girlfriend sitting with their friends at the table, laughing. Applause exploded as soon as she got back on stage. "Memorable," The *Herald* called it. Walter Winchell on the radio said, "Item: Songbird Juliana at The Onyx will fly away with your heart." After those reviews, Joe Helbeck called Richard, who passed the phone to me; Joe wanted to extend Juliana's contract from a week to three months. Richard negotiated a hefty increase.

* * *

Richard and I waited for a seat at the bar in between shows one night. The place was packed. Waiters were running everywhere, carrying trays of drinks, the bartenders sliding orders down the bar as fast as they could make them.

"Interviews," I said. We took our drinks and squeezed onto two stools that had been vacated. "We need to set up some interviews in national magazines. Do you know anyone who can help us?"

"Can I get you another sidecar?"

"No. Tell me. Is there anyone you can contact to get this going? I'm hiring a full-time publicist tomorrow—*not* Franklin Dodge. He's creepy. But we should milk your contacts as much as possible."

"Well, I have a friend who's a big shot at *Life*. Is that the sort of thing you mean?"

"Richard, I could kiss you. Do you think you could get him to set something up?"

"He owes me a few favors. I advised him to buy a couple of stocks that are now tripling. I'll call him tomorrow."

"Now I absolutely love you."

He looked down, embarrassed. "Uh, Al, I want to tell you how grateful I am for all you've done for us."

"Us? Oh, us."

"Helping Juliana get her career on the right track saved our marriage. Not that she'd ever divorce me."

"What?"

"Our religion doesn't permit divorce."

"Yeah, I know, but some Catholics must get divorced."

"Bad ones. The ones that get excommunicated. That would kill Juliana."

"It would?" A cold chill ran up my back.

"She loves our religion. To be separated from it would be worse than death for her."

"But she could still be Catholic *and* divorced."

"Not in the truest sense. She'd never again be able to partake of the Holy Eucharist, and you know how serious that would be."

"Uh, I guess."

"Not being permitted to take the Holy Eucharist," Richard explained, "would be the same as being pushed from the bosom of Holy Mother Church."

What was he saying? "Then she could be something else. Some other religion."

Richard chuckled. "You obviously don't know Juliana very well. There is only the one true church, and Juliana knows it. Nothing could ever substitute for that in Juliana's heart."

Richard continued to talk, but I couldn't make out his words. I kept thinking how I'd done all of this for Juliana so that one day I'd be rid of *him*, but ... *Never?*

"I was afraid she'd leave me," Richard was saying, "and live a separate life like her mother and father did ..."

Yes, she could do that. Hope.

"...We were always arguing. But we're much closer now, all because of you."

"Because of me? How nice." I took a few swallows of my drink.

"I hope someday," Richard went on, "to return the favor. I don't want to interfere, but don't you think you should start seriously considering marriage?"

I took another sip of my drink. "I'm married to my career, Richard." After he'd bashed in my guts, the last thing I wanted to talk to him about was marriage.

"But it must be such a lonely life."

"No. Not lonely at all." Leave me alone before I punch you.

"I'm going to start looking for you. In my travels, I meet lots of nice, young fellows with promising business careers."

"How is Johnny coming along with his drinking?" I asked. "Or should I say his *not* drinking?"

"Good. I rarely see him take a drop. Sometimes, a few of us fellows go down to McSorley's and he'll have a beer, but I don't think you could call that drinking."

Chapter 28

January 1950

"AL, IT'S SO good to see you. Just a minute. Let me give Bertha my coat." Virginia stood near the hatcheck booth, sliding her fox fur down her arms and smiling at Bertha, our new girl. "I suppose it's terrible of me to stand here without an escort, but I'm sure Max will be along soon."

The lights were a warm glow, set for pre-show dining. I hadn't had time to change out of my schoolmarm outfit. All wrong for an evening at the club, but I was the boss when Max wasn't around, so I could get away with it. The orchestra played a medley of the top Billboard hits from December and January.

"Allow *me*, madam," Moose Mantelli said, helping Virginia slide her coat off the rest of the way. His stomach pushed against the buttons of his tuxedo. He still wore his pork pie hat.

"Well, thank you, Mr.—? Mr.—?" Virginia said.

Jimmy the Crusher stood behind Moose, holding his fedora in his hand. He whipped Moose's hat off his head with his left hand, keeping his thumbless right hand hidden in his pocket.

"Mantelli. Moose Mantelli. Very pleased to be serviceable to you, Madam." He draped Virginia's coat over his arm and put out his stubby fingers. "And who may I say I am having this comodious pleasure of making an acquaintance with?"

"Oh." Virginia giggled and took his hand. I wondered if she knew who or what Moose was. "Virginia Sales."

"I'm most appreciated to be in the presence of such a lovely lady."

I don't think Virginia noticed his eyes exploring her body. She did look lovely in her Dior New Look blue silk dress that hugged her form and then flared out around her knees and calves. "Well, thank you, Mr. ... uh, Mr. Moose? Oh no, that's not right, uh ..."

"Mr. Moose comin' outta the likes o' you suits me fine, Miss Sales." He winked at her. "Might I escort your beauteous self to your table?"

"Well, I'm with my friend, Miss Alice Huffman."

"Al's yer friend? Me and Al go way back, don't we, Al?" He hit me on the back so hard I almost fell over. "Well, youse two ladies go right along. I'm gonna look out fer yer coat, Miss Sales." He turned to the hatcheck girl, "Hey, Bert'a, take this will ya?" and threw it over the poor girl's head.

"Miss Sales …" he called after us, taking Virginia's gloved hand between his two.

"Yes?" she said.

"If you need anyt'in', and I mean—*anyt'in'*, you come and tell ol' Moose."

Virginia looked suddenly shy, and that infernal giggle popped out of her again. "Well, thank you. Mr. Moose."

I led Virginia to a table I'd reserved for the two of us down front. It was Virginia's birthday and Max wanted to do something special for her. I suggested to him it might be nicer to take her to dinner at the Oak Room, and then to the hit *Death of a Salesman* at the Morosco. A show at the Mt. Olympus wasn't special for her, but Max was busy with plans for the new club and said he couldn't get away even for a few hours. Not even for her birthday.

"I haven't seen you in months," Virginia said as she took off her navy-blue gloves and laid them on the table.

"Virginia." I leaned forward. "You know who that guy is, don't you?"

"No. Who?"

"Moose Mantelli."

"He told me *that* himself."

"He's a mobster. Good friends with Frank Costello."

"How thrilling. I think he liked me. Don't you?"

"He was flirting with you."

"Do you really think so?"

"And you were flirting back."

"Oh, no. Well maybe a little. I mean, when a girl reaches a certain age and a gentleman shows a modicum of interest, you can't stomp on his foot."

Rudolfo, the headwaiter, stood at our table at attention in his black tuxedo. "Miss Huffman, Miss Sales, good evening." He put two menus in front of us. "Would you like a cocktail to start?"

"None for me, Rudy," I said. "I'm still on."

"I'll have a glass of the house wine with dinner," Virginia said. "And I know what I want, so you can take this menu. I practically have it memorized. Bring me the steak tartar with fresh greens."

"And you can bring me a couple of Henri's fried oysters," I told Rudy.

"That's all you're having? You should eat more. Keep up your strength."

"It's plenty."

"Have you heard from Tommie?"

"Nice letter last week."

"Me too. Imagine! Our Tommie, in Hollywood! In my letter, he was complaining that RKO hadn't lined up a script for him yet. My goodness, it's only been a month. He can be impatient. I told him I was sure they'd use him soon. In the meantime, he should seek out the best teacher and study. Oh, did you read that article about Senator McCarthy saying there are two hundred and five Communists in our very own government! Two hundred and five!"

"Yeah, I read that, but I don't know if I believe it. That's an awful lot."

"I hope you're right. It gives me the willies. So, tell me what you've been doing. I never see you anymore."

"I've been doing everything, helping Max run this place, and getting the new place ready for the March opening, and then there's school, and I've just started managing a new singer."

"My goodness, that's too much for one person."

"I love it. Except …"

"Yes?"

"I rarely get to see Juliana alone. I see her almost every day, but we're never together. Did you know that if Catholics get a divorce they get kicked out of their religion?"

"Yes. I think it's a stupid rule in some ways. I mean, people do make mistakes. Still, divorce is an awful thing. No religion approves of it, but they go to extremes. You know what they say about divorced women."

"Yeah. That they're loose."

"Exactly. I'd never want any part of that. Of course, I'm not married, so I may never have to concern myself with it."

"What have you been up to?" I asked, feeling like a lead ball sat in my stomach. Forever. I'm stuck with him forever.

"Well, the good news is Max decided to stop looking for that man, Scott, he met in the army. Didn't he tell you?"

"No. We never have time to talk."

"I thought he would never stop thinking about him. Every time I saw him he'd either tell me about the latest lead he *thought* he had on Scott—he'd be elated—or how the last lead led to nothing, and he'd be blue and I'd have to perk him up. I'm not very good at perking people up. Especially Max when he's mourning the loss of a man. But at last, he's decided to forget him. He's going to put all his attention on building the new club. That's what he told me, and he hasn't mentioned Scott in a month. And now this."

"Now, what?"

"Inviting me here to celebrate my birthday. He's never done that before."

She didn't know she should be expecting much more.

"We've been closer than ever, lately," she continued. "Of course, it wasn't me who told him it was my birthday. I wouldn't want to remind him about my age, but my mother ..."

"How *is* your mother these days? Max told me she's been, well, difficult."

"Difficult? That's one word for it. She scares me. Back in the spring, she was selling off some of my father's art collection. She let valuable pieces go for a song, like the Monet. My father loved that painting. When I saw it was gone, I cried. She hired a dealer who I'm sure took advantage of her, buying her lesser artists at high prices. Probably pocketing a handsome commission.

"I don't want to sound greedy, but that's my inheritance she's throwing away. I have the trust fund from my father, but it's small compared to what I'll inherit once she ... Oh, that's an awful thing to say. I suggested she speak to Max—he knows art and has invested in some good pieces. That's what kept him from completely going under when his first club closed. Well, she said, 'I won't do business with your ... 'pimp.' She said that word right out loud. She's always been a little, well, testy, but never crass. So improper. Where is her dignity? After all, she *is* a Sales. The terrible things she says to people. Not only to me. The other day, she called her oldest, dearest friend on the telephone and accused her of sneaking into our home through the second floor window to spy on her. Al, the woman is seventy-nine years old!"

A laugh popped out of me, but I hurried to swallow it.

"Oh, you can laugh. I did. Before I cried. Sometimes, a few minutes after Nola clears away her luncheon or dinner dishes, she yells at Nola to bring her food, accusing the poor woman of starving her. I thought it couldn't get any worse, but ... sometimes she stares at me and asks me where Virginia is. I'm standing right there, Al, but she doesn't believe me. I'm afraid to leave her alone. One day, she was out in the neighborhood and got lost. She *couldn't* find her way home. A policeman brought her. She's lived in our neighborhood for fifty years! Oh, but Max comes over sometimes to help. To entertain her. And since she can't remember who he is, she enjoys him. A few times he helped me to ... well, to ..." she whispered, "She messes herself sometimes, but Max takes it in stride. He said it's much easier to deal with than the war. Oh, he's such a dear man, and I depend on him. And now that he's stopped looking for Scott … You know, it reminds me of the time when I was about to have my uh— well, you know, my child, Joan. How helpful he was. And—loving. I wonder what's keeping him."

"He'll be along soon. The Swing Street club keeps him pretty busy with the contractors."

The assistant waiters in white jackets laid our food on the table in front of us.

"We've gotten much closer since he stopped looking for Scott. It's sad that he couldn't find a boy he cared for, but he has lots of boys who love him."

"Maybe he was hoping for a special someone to share his life with."

"He can share his life with me."

"Virginia, I know he cares for you, but— "

"What?" she said, with a challenge in her voice.

How dare I stomp on her fantasy? "Nothing."

Rudy checked to be certain the waiters in white jackets had done everything correctly, then wished us, "Bon Appetit." He snapped his fingers, and they were all quickly gone.

"I almost forgot." Virginia opened her handbag. "I brought you a copy of …" She pulled out a thin pamphlet. "I got it at the post office. I know you have no time for extra reading …" She handed me a copy of 'Survival Under Atomic Attack.' "…but this is important."

Sweat gathered around my waist as I opened the booklet to the section called, "What Are Your Chances?" It read:

"Even if you have only a second's warning, there is one important thing you can do to save yourself: Fall on your face."

"Really? That would work? I mean, the radiation—"

"That's nothing. The Japanese have gotten over that fine. Read the pamphlet, and do what it says. The Soviets are inhuman devils. We must be prepared."

The house lights faded as the stage lights came up. The orchestra rose from a lower, unseen deck and appeared behind a fountain shaped like a man and a woman in togas, pouring water from a bucket into the shallow pool.

"Where *is* that man?" Virginia whispered. She turned in her seat to scan the room before the light had completely disappeared. Jimmy the Crusher was taking his seat next to Moose Mantelli who was sitting ringside with the boys at Frank Costello's table. The light highlighted that face for a few moments. He seemed to be looking at me, but it was hard to tell for sure with the way his face was half-melted. Moose waved his fingers at Virginia and Virginia waved back as The Maxines filled the stage with their song, elaborate headdresses, and high-kicking legs.

Max joined us as the Maxines made their grand exit, shaking their rear ends at the pool.

Chapter 29

March 1950

CONNIE LINGUS, WHOSE name was now the more delightful—if I do say so myself—Lili Donovan, and the accompanist I'd gotten for her were rehearsing, "After You've Gone." That was the number she'd be doing for the opening of The Haven. The lights were the flat daylight type, none of the magic that took over the night when the Mt. Olympus was open. From the side windows, I could see snow falling in big flakes. Only a few hours to go before the dinner show. I hurried about, checking on the chef and making sure the assistant waiters were dressed in their crispest best—white shirts, black ties, and white tuxedo jackets. I had to send one man to the back room for a fresh shirt, and I had a talk with Dave, our head checker, who was *supposed* to inspect each waiter for cleanliness.

I'd gotten a call from Jules Podell at the Copa, and we'd scheduled a time to meet. It was unfolding exactly as Max had said it would. *And* as I had dreamt it. I had never lived a dream-come-true before, but it looked like I was about to. I hadn't told Juliana about Jules Podell yet. I didn't want to add more pressure. Besides the show at The Onyx, she was flying out to Chicago six nights a week to do the late show at the Chez Paree. Again, the reviews were glowing. The *Life Magazine* interview was due out in a couple days.

I looked at the time. "Oh, damn. I promised Max I'd call Walter's agent tonight." This was the Walter Liberace who had walked out on Madame Spivy when Jule, Shirl, and I were at Spivy's Roof during the war. He'd recently become plain ol' Liberace. Max left me a note to book him for the Mt. Olympus early in the new year, while he was over at The Haven supervising the movers bringing in the red leather banquettes.

I ran toward my office to make the call when I saw ... him. He sat at a table that hadn't been set yet, with only a white tablecloth and an ashtray. Someone must've left the front door unlocked. I walked around the table to see his face, but I knew who he was before I got there. "You're him, aren't you?"

He looked up at me with dark, questioning eyes, then, stood. "Ma'am?"

"Sit," I said, pulling out a chair and sitting opposite him. "You're Scott."

"Scott Elkins, ma'am."

"From Armpit, West Virginia."

"Sorry?"

"Oh. That's a joke between, uh—"

"The name of my town is Pickle Paw, ma'am, and I'm proud of it."

"Of course you are." Well, he didn't have much of a sense of humor. He spoke with a slight West Virginian accent and wore a navy-blue suit and tie. He must've been twenty-five, from my calculations. Yes, Max did like them young. Eleven years younger than himself. There was a subtle femininity about him that was quiet and pleasant, not something the straights would notice. Something in the way he used his hands. A delicate touching of his dark hair to be sure it hadn't slipped away from its Vitalis. His dark eyes, too. Penetrating, questioning like a girl's. These were the eyes that Max had fallen in love with in a bombed-out bar in Palermo.

"Max's been looking everywhere for you."

"Is Maxwell here, ma'am?"

"Maxwell? You call him …? Uh, he's at his other place right now. The new one he's opening. The Haven. I'll call him. I know he'll come right over."

"Don't disturb him, ma'am." He started to rise. "I shouldn't have come."

"No, wait, don't go." I got up to stop him. "He wants to see you."

He remained standing as if on a precipice between returning to some other life and beginning something new. "Let me get you something," I said. "It's kind of early for a drink, but it'd be okay if that's what you want. Do you?"

"I don't drink, ma'am."

"You don't?" This was too much. Max had fallen in love with a man who couldn't possibly be more unlike him.

"How about a cup of coffee? Or tea? I have a friend who thinks tea cures just about anything."

"Coffee would be fine, ma'am."

"I'll be right with you. But could you please not call me ma'am?"

"I don't know if I can do that, ma'am, uh, I mean … Ya see, that was the way I was raised, ma—"

"My name's Alice. How about calling me that?" I figured it was too soon to tell him about 'Al.'

"Thank you, Alice. I surely will try."

I hurried to ask a waiter to bring him a cup of coffee, while I ran to my office to call Max. He wasn't in. I left a message with one of the decorators to find Max and get him over to the Mt. Olympus pronto. Then I ran back to Scott. I was afraid he'd bolt if I didn't keep an eye on him. "So, Max and you were army buddies during the war."

He stared into his cup before picking it up, then wrapped those feminine fingers around it. "Yes. It was all difficult." He sipped from the cup and placed it back in its saucer. Every gesture cautiously deliberate. "I guess Maxwell told you. He was very kind to me. I'd never been so far away from home before."

"Max thinks you're quite special."

He grinned for the first time. "Not so special. Only a West Virginia boy with a grandma to take care of who doesn't know what he's doing."

"How *is* your grandma?"

"Grandma's aces. I miss her. I've been working in Washington DC at the State Department. I was only a low-level accountant, but it was paying the bills, and I could send her a little money to help out."

"Has something happened? You said 'was.'"

"Uh …" His eyes darted about the room. His fingers stroked the tabletop.

"Look, Scott, I'm good friends with Max. I know you and Max were close. I also know that Max is a—" I whispered, "—homosexual."

"He told you about me?"

"Yes, but it's okay."

"You mean, you know I'm like him?"

"I'm glad Max found someone to care about. Most of my friends are like that. I'm not, but I care about my friends, so I don't mind that they are. You can talk to me. What happened in Washington?"

"I quit. There are frightening things happening there." He looked around as if afraid someone could be listening. "They're firing people suspected of," he whispered, "homosexualism. They're saying sexual perversion and communism go together, so for the sake of the country … Do you think that's true? They say inverts are emotionally unstable with a weak moral character, so that makes them more likely to join the communists and plot to overthrow our government. Do *you* think so?"

"No. Who's saying those ridiculous things?"

"Everyone in Washington. It's almost the only thing they talk about these days. I couldn't go home to Grandma yet. I thought maybe Maxwell could give me some advice, since he knows about being one of those."

"You've known all along Max has been looking for you, haven't you?"

"Yes, ma'am, I mean, Alice."

"Al. That's what my friends call me."

"Why?"

"It's my name. You didn't let yourself be found. Did you?"

"Miss Al, I care a great deal for Maxwell, but I was very afraid to see him again. Afraid I'd fall into a sinkhole of sin."

"A sinkhole of sin?" Oh, this was too much.

Max walked in. My look of anticipation cued Scott, and he turned in his chair, gripping the back, rising. Max seemed to stop breathing. "Scott. Is it really you?"

"Scott and I have been having a nice talk, and now, I think you should take him into your office and continue that talk. Don't you, Max? I have some work to do around town, and I won't be back for a few hours."

"Won't you come into my office?" Max said, leading the way. Scott followed. I told Lili and her accompanist and the waiters to take off the next couple hours.

I was locking the door on my way out when Virginia appeared. She wore a flower-print dress with a thin, white-fringed wool shawl wrapped around her shoulders. "Al."

"Virginia," I croaked. "What are *you* doing here?"

"Looking for Max. I went to The Haven, but they said he'd dashed over here. I'm cooking him dinner at his place, and I wanted to make sure spaghetti and meatballs was all right. Not terribly exotic, but Max has amazingly prosaic tastes for such a worldly man."

"…Why don't you call him?"

"Because I'm here. Is he in there?"

"Uh …" Should I lie? It wasn't like Virginia was his real fiancée. She had to know this was going to happen sometime. But *I* didn't want to be the one to tell her.

"Well?" she asked. "Is he in there?"

"Yes and no."

"You mean he's with a man. Let me in. I'll wait for him at one of the tables till he's finished."

"Uh, Virginia, it's—Scott."

The sound of her heels hitting the pavement as she walked away reverberated in my ears for days.

Chapter 30

THE DAY FOR the opening of The Haven came, and Max sent me to a special hairdresser. The finest, of course. When I emerged from the beauty salon, all coiffed and buffed, my hair didn't look much different. Short to my neck with tight curls. I'd told Francois he better not give me one of those powder-puff styles. I think I scared him. It could've been my fist pointing at his new nose.

Max had me fitted for a navy-blue, strapless, floor-length gown with a New Look flair. I'd never worn strapless before, so I worried I'd step on the hem and pull the whole dang thing off what Juliana called my "boyish body." That would not make a good impression at the opening of Max's new Swing Street club, but it might get the headlines Max wanted.

Max wore his black tie and tails, and as usual, looked dapper; his Rhett Butler mustache neatly trimmed. He'd even flown down to Florida for a week to get a tan for the occasion. Men and women in formal clothes arrived in limousines and strolled up the red carpet where Max and I stood waiting to greet them. He was my escort. Journalists and photographers recorded the moments.

One early arrival was Mayor O'Dwyer with his new wife, the sexy fashion model Sloan Simpson. The crowds parted as Agnes de Mille, who'd been the choreographer for last year's hit, *Gentlemen Prefer Blondes,* stepped out of her limo. She was a longtime friend of Max's. While they were talking, I shook Iva Wither's hand, who had played Julie Jordan in *Carousel* and was getting ready to open the same show in London, in June. "Miss Withers," I said, "I really enjoyed watching you work."

"Oh? You saw *Carousel?*"

"Yes, of course. You were wonderful."

"Which night were you there?"

"I'm not sure. It was three years ago."

"I did have a good night that night, didn't I?" She laughed, and I laughed with her.

Lots of Broadway show people, chorus boys and girls, milled about, hoping to be noticed by someone, anyone. Virginia Sales arrived on the arm of Scott

Elkins, an unexpected pairing. As the two stepped out of Virginia's limo, a flash of memory shot into my mind. June 1941. Six months before the war that few expected, or wanted, I walked along a street like this with the kids I'd grown up with: Danny, Aggie and Dickie. Almost ten years ago. How excited we'd been to see all those limos. Now, it was almost mundane to me, and I had no idea where Aggie, Dickie, and Danny were. I was the most unlikely of our group to still be in the business, but I think I was the only one who was. Occasionally, I'd check *Variety*, but I never saw their names, not even in bit parts.

Virginia looked more beautiful than usual with her hair up in that new, feathered, allure style. Her dress was a black rayon-faille that both clung to her body and fell in drapes around it. She wore a string of pearls with matching earrings. Scott looked handsome in his black tuxedo and homburg, his overcoat hanging open.

Bertha, the hatcheck girl, took Virginia's mink coat and Scott's hat and topcoat. The maitre'd directed them to their seats, and I instructed him to have the waiter bring their drinks on the house.

When I turned back around, I noticed Bertha leaning against the hatcheck booth, staring at me. She was a hefty girl with a broad smile. Her clothing was usually drab, but for this night, she wore an off-the-shoulder, beige gown with a huge cloth flower tacked to the center of her rather large breasts. She quickly busied herself counting tickets when she saw I'd caught her. It wasn't the first time.

A young piano player played ambient music on the cavernous stage that had small balconies at various levels up the sides. For a hefty price, wealthy patrons could be served their meals on those small balconies and be seen throughout the whole performance.

On the main floor, tables and chairs made of the finest oak surrounded the large dance floor on three sides. The red leather banquettes hugging the edges of the room were of the softest leather. Upstairs, there was a smoking lounge where men could go and be men and talk business. No women were permitted up there. This venture set Max back quite a sum, and I'd invested in it myself. We hoped to start breathing again in a few months.

"Al," Max whispered into my ear. "Over there by the bar, talking to Mae West and Liberace. Next to Franklin Dodge. The woman in the dress that blinks under the lights. That's Dorothy Kilgallen."

I jolted backwards.

He wrapped his arm around mine, pulling me forward. "I'm going to introduce you. I want you to get friendly with her. Ask her to lunch."

"After what she did to Barney Josephson?"

"And if you don't smile at her and be your sweetest-self, she'll do the same thing to us, and we'll end up on the dole. You have a new client who's counting on you, and Juliana is opening at the Copa in May. You need this woman. Loyalty to Barney will get you a place on the bread line. Now, come. Plaster a phony smile on your mug, and let's get to work." He demonstrated with his own wide grin. "That's what I like to see," he said as I grinned back. "All part of the job."

As we approached the creamy-white bar that sat a little to the left—made all the more prominent by the deep-red rug that covered The Haven's floor—I saw Dorothy Kilgallen smiling in her sequined, deep-blue, New Look gown. She had a small hat perched on top of her head, and tight brown curls hugging the nape of her neck.

As we drew close, I remembered what she had written about Canada Lee, the famous colored actor, who'd been on Broadway starring in all the colored productions during the war. Brooks Atkinson, the critic, said he was the best Negro actor America ever had. A few years back, he even played a white man in white make-up. But *she* accused him of kissing a white woman in Café Society, Uptown, and *that* somehow proved Canada and Barney were communists.

"Dorothy," Max said brightly, "I want you to meet my assistant, Alice Huffman. No, let me correct that. At the Mt. Olympus, she was my assistant. Over here at The Haven, she is the manager, full charge."

"A pleasure, Miss Kilgallen," I said as our gloved hands met. "I love reading your column, and I wouldn't miss your radio program. They both let us know what's really happening behind the scenes."

"It's a pleasure to finally meet you, too, Miss Huffman. I've heard so much about you."

My stomach jumped. *What? What?*

"Have you met my husband, the actor, Richard Kollman?" She dragged him away from the bar, where he hung onto the edge. He seemed already to have begun celebrating. He saluted me and went back to caressing the bar.

"I saw Juliana's show at the Onyx. Quite impressed."

"And yet you didn't mention her in your column."

"All in due time, Miss Huffman. She's new. I'm waiting."

"Waiting till she's a star? Aren't you afraid of missing your chance to discover her?"

"A star? That's a tall order. She may have to wait in line."

"Juliana doesn't wait in line for anyone. Be sure to catch her show at the Copa in May. You'll see what I mean."

"I see. Then it must be true what they say. *You* are Juliana's manager."

"I have no idea who 'they' are, but it's all the work of Richard Styles. *He's* her manager. I'm merely a fan."

"Richard Styles, hm? I don't think I know him. No matter, you and I must have lunch. And soon. I think we have a lot to talk about. Take my card." She reached into her purse. "Call my secretary. She'll set something up."

"Al!" Walter called out.

"Excuse me, Miss Kilgallen." She nodded and turned to talk with Max who was getting a drink at the bar.

Walter Liberace stood at the bar, flirting with Franklin Dodge while holding hands with Mae West. He'd been a big hit in the Las Vegas clubs, which made him filthy rich, I'd heard. And always anxious to stand out. I guess that explained the pink tuxedo.

"Hi there, Walt. I mean, Liberace."

"Hello, Al, and of course you know my date, Miss Mae West, the lovely."

"The lovely what, handsome?" Miss West said, shaking one of those treacherous hips. "Do you mean me or ... you?" Everyone laughed at her perfect imitation of herself. Walter—uh—Liberace merely smiled. They pecked at each other's lips.

"All right," Franklin Dodge said, doing a little dance and waving his hands over his head. "Everyone look casual, but face this way." He snapped his fingers two times. "Smile, Love Bunnies!" We were bombarded by a blast of flash.

As we blinked away the yellow spots, Walter Winchell and his wife stepped up to the bar.

"Walter," Max said, "you remember Miss Alice Huffman. Now, you say some nice things about her in your column tomorrow. She's going to make a big splash in this nightclub world."

"A splash, huh?" Mr. Winchell said, taking a drag from his cigarette, then shaking my hand. I couldn't believe I was shaking Walter Winchell's hand. I wished my father could see me. "We'll see about that. I've never heard of a woman running a nightclub." He turned to his wife. "You dear?"

She shook her head no.

"Well, *I* think it's wonderful," Miss Kilgallen said. "We're entering a new world, Walter. You'd better watch yourself. We girls might take over."

"Hmph," Mr. Winchell said, shaking his bald head.

"Don't worry about mentioning *me* in your column, Mr. Winchell," I said. "I've been managing Lili Donovan, who's opening tonight for Mable Mercer. I'm sure you're going to want to talk about *her* in your column. And in May, Juliana."

"We'll see." He took his wife's elbow and yanked her toward his table. My stomach knotted. As he walked away I remembered that I should've gotten his card, asked him to lunch. A woman couldn't ask a man to lunch. Could she? With his wife right there?

"Dorothy," Max said to Miss Kilgallen as he drew in smoke through his cigarette holder. "You must come to the Mt. Olympus next week to see the new show. Our headliner will be quite a surprise."

"Maxwell, don't leave me in suspense. Who?"

"That's a secret," he whispered, then winked.

"Oh, Maxwell, you are too cruel." She pouted.

As Max guided me away from the bar, I asked. "Who's going to be our new headliner at the Mt. Olympus?"

"I don't know yet. I'll catch Dorothy's column tomorrow and find out."

I slipped from Max's grasp. Everyone seemed to be seated, waiting to be served. This was my chance for a moment alone. I was headed toward the exit when ... "Hey, you don't belong in here." The voice of our bouncer, Joey, boomed above the clatter from behind the bar. "Delivery boys ain't 'lowed to come through the main dining room. Go out and take the back door."

"Hey!" LeRoy, Lili's colored boyfriend/ex-manager, shouted back. "I ain't no deliv'ry boy, man. I's a musician! And a customer." He puffed out his chest. "See? I even wore a tie for ya'lls shindig. I ain't no slob. I knows things."

Oh, gosh he'd even worn a nice gray suit, and still he wasn't dressed right. I hurried over to the bar. *What to do? What to do?* My eyes quickly scanned the dining room. It was crowded with well-dressed men and women mingling about. It didn't look like they'd noticed what was going on by the bar. Yet. I didn't see Max anywhere.

"You be talkin to a arteest, man. That what I is," LeRoy continued, strutting near the bar. Bar customers stared. Some took their drinks and slipped away. "And I's here on accounta my old lady's singin' tonight jes' the way *I* learned her."

"'Less you talkin' about Miss Mable Mercer," Joey said, "and you better *not* be talkin' bout that grand lady, we don't got no colored girl singers here tonight, so buzz off 'fore I throw ya out on your keester."

LeRoy hopped up on a bar stool, daring Joey to do something.

Joey grabbed him around the chest, pinning his arms to his sides, and yanked him off the stool. "You ain't stayin' here, nigger, disturbing these nice—"

"Uh, no, Joey," I said, too quietly. "Maybe you shouldn't uh—"

"You!" LeRoy said to me, pushing against Joey's thick arms. "Call off your goon, will ya?"

"Al, you know this jungle bunny?" Joey asked.

"Please don't call him that."

"Oh, we got ourselves a real New Dealer here, and we's sposed to lay right down 'n kiss her damn feet. Look, you! Tonight's Con's big night. I jes' wanna sit and listen. So's I can sees she's doin' what *I* learned her and you hasn't gone and messed her up. I ain't gonna spoil your—hey, baby!"

I spun around. Lili was hurrying toward us. *Oh, God, no.* I ran to her before she could reach LeRoy. "Lili, you can't see him."

"But he's feelin all hurt inside and depressed. I ain't gonna jus' leave him like dat."

"You hear how you're talking? All the time you spent in elocution classes, and one look at LeRoy and it's all gone. He's the last thing you need if you still want the career that's sposed to start tonight. Do you still want that?"

"Yeah! I mean, yes, but ..." She looked come-hither and innocent at the same time in her slender, black-velvet dress with the upraised, satin collar.

"Go back. I'll take care of it."

"Ya won't let Joey hurt him?"

"No. Turn around and go backstage."

She nodded and left.

"Hey, baby!" LeRoy cried out from some deep inner place; Joey's thick arms were still wrapped around his skinny body.

"What's going on, Al?" Max came over. "Who's the Negro?"

"A friend of Lili's. He wants to hear her sing."

"Oh, Jesus, tonight? We're loaded down with celebrities and columnists."

"What do I do, Max?"

"He's not even dressed." Max reached into his inside pocket and pulled out a business card. He scribbled something on the back. "Give him this. It'll admit him and a date—*not* Lili, a colored girl—the very next time Lili appears here. When's that going to be?"

"If all goes well tonight, next month."

"I wrote Harold's number on the card, so he can rent a tux on me. Maybe it's time we did follow Barney's lead. I don't know. Here."

"Don't *you* want to give it to him?"

"Oh, no. He's not going to like this, and *you're* the manager."

Max walked away, and I stepped toward LeRoy, trying to look confident. I don't think Miss Viola Cramden, my old acting teacher, would've been proud of how I was playing my part. Max was right. LeRoy wasn't at all happy with our second-rate handout solution. "You white folks figger you gots answers for everything, doncha? But ya'll see. Ya'll see." His eyes were as cold as daggers aimed at my heart. He grabbed Max's card from my hand and did a little curtsy. "Oh, thank ya missus. I jes' don' knows what I woulda done wit'out the likes of you." He tap-danced over to Bertha to pick up his fedora and sauntered out of the club, doffing his hat to the couple who were entering.

After that, I really *had* to go outside and be by myself. The March night was cold. A whole sky full of stars shone down on me as I stood there shivering, clutching my arms around my bare shoulders. I could hear the faint sound of the orchestra playing "Do the Hucklebuck."

I couldn't really see the stars. I just wanted to, so I imagined how they'd look up there if I *could* see them. The glare from the neon lights was in the way. I remembered how it was when I stood in my backyard in Huntington and looked up at the sky and the stars would be there looking down at me like protectors; they were always there. Different in winter than in summer. But always there. That was long before I knew anything about homosexualism, inversion, perversion, or colored men who wanted to kill me.

Juliana was in Chicago performing at the Empire Room. It was because of *me* she was there. I'm not responsible for how the world is. Of course it's not fair, but I can't *make* it fair. If I try, they'll go for me, so there's nothing I can do. And yet—I don't belong here either, in this world of expensive gowns and jewelry. If Max didn't dress me, they'd never let *me* in … Juliana, I miss you so very much. I could see her standing there wearing her burgundy velvet evening gown with the white opera gloves. My vision was so clear, I could almost reach my hand out and …

That morning's headline read: "Perverts Fleeing State Department." Ever since they announced the State Department had fired ninety-one homosexuals, there were more articles every day that talked about how homosexuals were dangerous to the country. Not me. I'm not that. I was about to duck back inside when I found Scott standing beside me. "What are you doing out here?" Scott asked. "You must be freezing."

"I am. I was going back in."

"Maxwell wants me to move into the apartment next to him. He said he'd pay."

"Don't you want to?"

"I couldn't do something like that." He took off his jacket. "Here, put this around you. What would people think?"

"This is New York City. Nobody has to know."

"What would I be? His mistress?"

"He wouldn't think of you like that. He wants to be close to you, and he can afford nice things."

"Am I a nice 'thing' for him to afford? I'm sorry, Al; I know he doesn't think of me that way. I don't think I can live like … Friends in Washington keep writing and telling me they're firing and arresting and—"

"Easy, Scott. It's not happening here."

"It's not? Then what was that raid on the Third Street Bar last week? They arrested those people. One guy I know lost his teaching job because of that."

"You're not going to get arrested. You don't go to those bars. You don't even drink. It could be fun to live near Max, and let him take you to nice places. He'd never let you get arrested."

"I don't like breaking the law. That's not how my family raised me. I wouldn't know what to say to my grandma."

I pulled his coat tighter around my shoulders. "Lots of homosexuals live in the city and have family in other places, and they don't tell them. You don't have to tell her."

"Then I could never see her, 'cause as soon as she saw me she'd know."

"Oh, come on. How would she know a thing like that?"

"She wouldn't know specifically what it was, but she'd know I was lying. I couldn't face her. I've been going to a doctor. Don't tell Maxwell."

"What kind of doctor?"

"A psychoanalyst. He says he can cure me."

"Really?"

"I don't want Maxwell to know. He might think I don't care about him, and I do. It's what we do—you know, Maxwell and me—it's against God. If this doctor cured me, I could still be friends with him, but in a manly way. Maxwell thinks this disease isn't a disease. He thinks it's the way we're born. Have you ever heard anything so queer?"

I sighed. "Scott, I'd like to help you, but I don't know what makes anyone like that. I don't think I'm one. I only have those feelings for Juliana. I've never felt that way for any other girl, so I don't think it applies to me." An image of the Jewish girl whizzed through my brain.

"You know, they got a law in DC," Scott said. "I've heard it referred to as the 'Sex Pervert Law.' It says they can confine sex perverts to St. Elizabeth's Mental Hospital for treatment for as long as they want. That's why I left. My mother—well, she spent some time in one of those places. It was awful."

"My mother, too. I think it made her worse."

"I know. My mother was sad. Being treated like that wasn't going to make her happy. When she found God, that made her happy."

"My mother never found God. Only demons, devils, and me, her biggest demon."

"We better get inside," he said. "If we don't hurry, they're going to start talking about *us*."

"Now, that might be a good thing." I laughed as we slipped back through the door.

Virginia and Max were having an animated and, I suspected, angry talk that stopped as soon as Scott and I got back. Virginia took a few big gulps from her vodka stinger and slammed it onto the table as we sat down.

I sat beside her as the waiters put out our appetizers. Mine was the *pate de fois gras*. Scott joined us with a shrimp cocktail. The orchestra played bebop, and some patrons were dancing.

Max stood to address Mrs. Murryfield, who had arrived. Mrs. Murryfield was a heavy woman weighed down with jewelry and three chins. "Mrs. Murryfield, how nice to see you again," Max said, charm oozing out of every pore. "Come. Sit next to me."

"Max, you dirty dog." She giggled. "Kissy kiss?" She leaned a fuzzy cheek in Max's direction, and he kissed it.

Mrs. Murryfield was one of Max's early financial supporters, and he didn't want to lose her. She was a widow living on a substantial inheritance from Mr. Murryfield, so Max volunteered to find her an escort. He had sent his car to pick her up, but he couldn't find Bart—the escort. As long as Max paid attention to her, though, Mrs. Murryfield didn't seem to mind.

"Irving," Max said, hopping from his seat and hurrying toward a smiling middle-aged man with receding gray hair.

"Hello there, Max."

"Glad you could make it." Max vigorously shook the man's hand.

"I told you if I were in town I wouldn't miss your opening. Oh, I want to introduce you to ..." From behind him he pulled a squat little woman with a hairdo straight out of the thirties—finger waves with a dang part in the middle. "Mrs. Ives."

"Charmed," Max said with a slight bow. "I'd be pleased if you both join us at my table."

Max led the way. "I want you all to meet Senator and Mrs. Ives."

Scott and the other men stood until Max had gotten Mrs. Ives seated.

We all said hello, introducing ourselves as the senator and his wife busied themselves with cocktail forks and napkins.

"Well, Irving, tell us," Max said as he sat down. "How are things in Washington?"

"Never a dull moment. I've been appointed to a most interesting subcommittee."

His wife shook her head at him.

"You're right, dear. Not appropriate dinner table conversation. Lovely décor you have here, Max." He bit into his *pate de fois gras*.

Mrs. Murryfield said, "Oh please, Senator, do tell us about the committee. How exciting to hear directly from the horse's mouth, so to speak, what's happening in Washington. The newspapers get more exciting every day. Oh, I love that Senator McCarthy. *He's* going to keep this country safe from those commies. Have you met him?"

"Yes, I have," the senator said.

Mrs. Murryfield swooned.

"As a matter of fact, Senator McCarthy and I often have a cocktail together after a long day of government." He was enjoying her admiration.

"Do you?" Mrs. Murryfield said. "Thrilling. You simply must tell us everything."

"Well, as matter of fact, it's because of him that I'm on this new subcommittee."

"Tell us, tell us." She clapped her chubby fingers together.

"It's a committee to investigate the employment of ..." He looked around as if a spy might be hiding under the table, then whispered, "...homosexuals and other sexual perverts in government. I hope that doesn't shock you."

She giggled. "We're all grown-ups here. Tell us more."

Max pushed a cigarette into its holder and flicked his lighter.

"Well there seems to be little factual information about homosexualism," the senator continued, "So we're planning an investigative study to—"

"Irving," Mrs. Ives said. "Do you think you should speak those unpleasant words in mixed company?"

"I don't mind," Mrs. Murryfield eagerly said. "We must learn how to protect ourselves from those monsters. Your husband is doing important work. Does anyone object to hearing frank language about the senator's work?"

Virginia was too busy sipping another vodka stinger and staring off into space to pay attention to any of it. Scott, with a look of terror, stared into his shrimp cocktail as if expecting one of them to jump up and bite his nose.

I said, "Uh, well, uh ..." I took a sip of my wine and then another.

Max glared.

Mrs. Murryfield clapped her pudgy hands together. "You see? No one minds. Please, Senator, continue."

"Well," the senator began. "Most of what we know about homosexuals comes from scientific studies, and, of course, the police have had a great deal of experience with them as criminals, but no one has given thought to the personnel problem—and believe me—this *is* a problem. How can we have such people working in our government agencies? Everyone agrees they are security risks."

"Then why do the study?" Max asked.

"What?" the senator asked, puzzled that someone would dare interrupt.

"Why spend tax payer dollars on an investigation if you already know the answer?"

"Of course, we have to do the study."

"My point is, Senator, if you're going to do an investigation, shouldn't you do it *before* you decide what the answer will be? Perhaps homosexuals are *not* security risks."

I dropped my fork, and it clattered to the floor. The whole table, even Virginia, stared at Max. I couldn't believe he was confronting this man. We had two nightclubs at stake. If this guy figured out about Max, he'd close both clubs down immediately, that night. All he had to do was get one of the beat cops outside to arrest us. I pictured thousands of our dollars drifting down the sewer. Scott held his cocktail fork frozen in mid-air. A waiter handed me a clean fork. Our reputations destroyed! Tomorrow's headline: "Max Hartwell and Alice Huffman Arrested for Homosexualism." That would be especially cruel to me, since I wasn't one. My career over. No money. Living in a cardboard box on the Bowery. Juliana gone. Why was Max doing this? My hand lost its grip; the fork fell again.

"Maybe they're *not* moral weaklings," Max continued.

"Of course they are," he whispered. "Look at what they do."

"What do they do, Senator?" Max asked.

"Yes, what? What?" Mrs Murryfield asked eagerly.

"Really, Max, isn't that going a bit too far?"

"What do they do that makes them *security* risks, Senator?"

"Oh. They can be bribed. The commies will threaten to tell about their sick lives. Who wouldn't give in to pressure like that? And these homos could be anywhere. They're hard to detect. Which makes them perfect spies for the other side. We're learning that some of them can even look like anyone else. That's why the study's important. We need to know how to recognize them. Dig them out before they've ruined our country. They could be sitting right here next to you, and you wouldn't know it."

"Really?" Max said.

We all stared—afraid to breathe.

"I got carried away. I didn't mean any of you … Forgive me. I was speaking metaphorically. They belong to secret cults and try to recruit others to their debauchery. That's why we must yank them out into the open. And soon. Before they pollute our institutions. Like the army. Did you know we've even found them there?"

"Have you?" Max said with exaggerated surprise.

"Oh, but don't worry; we got rid of them."

"How nice," Max said.

"This is so exciting," Mrs Murryfield said. "To hear two intelligent men having such an illuminating discussion."

I was about to faint. Scott was still staring at his untouched shrimp. Virginia ordered another vodka stinger.

"But, please," the senator began again, "don't think I don't sympathize with these mentally deranged people, because I do. I'm not heartless like some other congressmen I could name. No. I pity them. Many can't help themselves.

It's like being a—well, a pyromaniac who can't help starting a fire. As much as you may feel for the poor pyromaniac's plight, would you allow him to run free through our schools and government offices? Of course not. It's quite the same with homosexuals. We can't hire people whose behavior violates all moral codes of acceptable conduct. This *pate de fois gras* is delicious, Max. Isn't it, dear?" he said to Mrs. Ives.

Mrs. Ives nodded at her husband with a small smile.

"You've certainly hired a splendid chef," the senator said.

"You compare homosexuals to pyromaniacs?" Max returned, the rolling boil under his words about to explode all over the table. I raised my eyebrows at him, trying to get him to drop it.

"I'm no poet," the senator continued, chuckling, "but I think that was a particularly apt metaphor."

"Do you?" Max inhaled smoke deeply as he stared at the senator. I held my breath, hoping he wouldn't say one more thing. He let the smoke seep through his lips. "Well, here's what I think …"

Scott dropped his fork.

I stared at Max, sending him thought messages.

The senator said, "I'm eager to hear your point of view."

"Yes, yes," Mrs. Murryfield said.

"*I* think … that …" He looked at Scott, then Virginia, then me, all staring at him, holding one collective breath. "That … you are right," Max choked out. "Now, if you'll excuse me," he said, rising. "I have a great many guests to greet."

"Of course," the senator said. "We all understand."

Throughout the evening, Max was up and down, talking to reviewers, food critics, Mayor O'Dwyer and his wife. Periodically, he'd introduce me to people. I met as many columnists as I could—talking up Juliana and Lili. Senator Ives and his wife spent much of the evening dancing, and I was relieved not to be around them. Moose Mantelli came with his latest girlfriend, but I noticed him giving Virginia the eye. Jimmy the Crusher came alone, as usual.

As the night wore on and we finished our dinner, Virginia looked more agitated, and I never saw her without a glass in her hand. "Are you all right?" I asked her.

"Yes. Fine. Don't I look it?" Her words came out sharp, sarcastic, unlike her. "Waiter. Hey waiter, another vodka stinger."

"Maybe you should slow down," I tentatively said to her. "You're not used to drinking like this."

"Who are you to tell me how much *I* should drink? Max!" she called out. "Hey, Max, honey. Dance with me, will ya?"

Scott leaned over to her. "He's kind of busy, but *I'll* dance with you, Virginia." He rose.

"You? You think you can handle a *real* woman, you fairy?"

Scott's face showed that Virginia's arrow hit him just where she was aiming.

"I'm going, Al," Scott said. "Tell Maxwell I'll call him in the morning."

I ran after him. "Scott, she doesn't know what she's saying. She's had too much to drink. Stay. Max wants you here."

"She's right; that's what I am." He handed his ticket to Bertha. "I have to walk." He grabbed his overcoat and homburg from Bertha and dropped a coin in her jar before he marched out the door.

I looked back at Bertha, and she was staring at me, again. "What? What?"

"Oh! I'm sorry." She disappeared behind her racks of coats.

"Good. He's gone," Virginia said when I got back to the table. Tears were inching down her face.

"I know this is hard for you, Virginia. Is there anything I can do?"

"Would you come with me to the lady's room? I want to fix my make-up."

"Let's go."

She was handling the liquor better than I thought. She walked by herself with only a few stumbles.

I stood beside her while she looked in the gold-framed mirror in the lady's lounge, her hands pressing heavily against the onyx sink. "I'm losing him for good this time, Al." I noticed Angie, the colored bathroom attendant, busying herself with dusting the pink lounge chair, and trying to become invisible. "Uh, Angie, maybe now would be a good time for your break."

"Yessum," Angie said, hurrying out.

"Losing Max? Virginia, you never had him."

"These past five years have been wonderful. He came back from the war so changed. We even talked about marriage."

"You did?"

"I don't mind his boys. Many are real gentlemen. Polite. Respectful. A person could build a life around that, don't you think?"

"Maybe you could. I couldn't."

"You share Juliana with Richard. How is that different from Max and me?"

"You better get done before someone comes in, or Max comes looking for you."

"He won't come looking for me. Never again. Not with—*Scott*. This one is different. Max is in love this time. I can't compete with that. Will you look at my face? I'm getting old, Al. Forty-three. Does it show?"

"You don't look old. You look beautiful."

"Spoken like a woman to another woman." She turned and leaned against the sink, cocking a hip at me. "Do you truly think I'm beautiful?"

"Yes."

"Show me what you do."

"What I do? I don't understand."

"What you do with Juliana. Teach me. Kiss me." She slid along the sink, getting closer.

"It's not something you need to know."

"Like this?" she asked, touching the bodice of my dress. "Do you feel this?"

"Of course I feel it."

"No, I mean do you *feel* it."

"Come on, Virginia, let's stop this."

"Kiss me."

"Virginia, you're straight. What kind of a straight woman would you be if you went around kissing—"

She kissed me, full-mouth and tongue; her hand reached into my gown and inside my bra, and the sensation ran all the way down to my toes. "Love me," she begged. "I need to be loved. Please."

This was crazy. I pushed myself away from her. "Okay." Doorstop under the door. I was determined this woman would feel physical love. Even if it were only for a few seconds, she would have that memory. I threw my arm around her, pulling her flush against my body.

Before I could kiss her, her lips were all over mine. I ran my hands over her breasts and tried to move her to the lounge chair. We missed the chair and slipped onto the shiny onyx floor. I crawled on top of her. Not so easy with all those crinolines we wore. I pushed my hand under her dress, past the garter belt (thank God it wasn't a girdle) and into her underpants. I was going to give this to her. She would have the memory of love shooting through her whole body.

Suddenly my breathing sped up. Oh, God, no, this is for her, not, not ... Oh, God, oh, God. She climaxed just as there was a loud knocking on the door.

Oh, no. I didn't want to rush her afterglow, but those knocks were angry, and if they broke through ... I mean, the Manager of Max Harlington's new exclusive club found on the bathroom floor with her hand up ...? I took my hand out. It wasn't the kind of headline Max wanted, and Kilgallen and Winchell were out there. "You okay?" I whispered.

"Yes." Tears rolled down her face.

"I don't want to rush you, but there are some angry women outside that door who want very much to get in here."

"Huh? Oh! Yes!" She jumped up.

We dusted and straightened ourselves. I washed my hands while she tucked a few strands of her hair that had come undone back under their bobby pins.

We avoided each other's eyes in the mirror. Now that it was over, it all seemed rather embarrassing, and we still had to unlock the door and face those women who were going to be awful sore.

I tugged my dress back over my breasts and made sure it was in place. "Ready?" I asked Virginia. "Maybe we should pretend you were sick, and I was helping you."

"You want me to act?" Virginia was thrilled. "I haven't acted in ages. Yes! Yes!"

I led the way through a line of squawking women. Virginia leaned heavily on my shoulder, the back of her hand placed on her forehead moaning loudly. "Oh! Oh! I'm so ill. So ill! Illness wracks my fevered brow."

I hurried Virginia to the main dining room before she gave a curtain speech.

Lili was singing, "After You've Gone." I should have been back stage with her before she went on, comforting her, especially after what happened with LeRoy, but instead I was in the restroom doing—well ... Lili looked good up there. A real professional. Suddenly, Kilgallen and Winchell and all the rest were important to me, too.

I walked toward my table. Max, who stood in the corner listening to Lili, nodded at me. He was pleased. Mabel Mercer's pianist replaced the pianist playing for Lili. Mabel Mercer joined Lili for the last verse. Wow! What a duo! Then Lili slipped from the stage, and Mabel Mercer sang, "It's All Right."

Virginia, already seated, looked at me shyly and whispered, "Thank you, Al."

"Uh, yeah," A blush crawled up my face. I picked up the linen napkin I'd thrown down on my seat when I went off with her. I was about to sit when it struck me like a lead ball dropping on top of my head. I'd been with a woman who wasn't Juliana, and I liked it.

Chapter 31

April 1950

A SINKING IN my stomach stuck to me each day as I moved into the office at The Haven. Even Kilgallen's and Winchell's glowing reviews of Lili's performance could not shut up the conversations that battled in my head. I worked on memorizing the monologue I had to deliver as my final assignment for my class. Lady MacBeth's "Out Damn Spot." I wished I'd chosen something less guilt-ridden. "You didn't have an orgasm," one voice said, "so it didn't count as 'being with a woman.'" Then the other voice would say, "But I've heard some butches never have orgasms." Maybe I was a butch, like Shirl said. Then the first voice would say, "But I did it for Virginia's sake. I was doing her a kindness." Followed finally by, "Oh, yeah, you were a regular Girl Scout crawling around in Virginia's underpants."

I distracted myself with preparation for Juliana's opening at the Copa. For days, I only saw her at a distance while she rehearsed. I set up interviews and photo sessions. Still, the voices nagged me. I couldn't shut the damn things up.

Maybe I *was* a "butch." Nah. Juliana was usually on top; *she* must be the butch. Juliana didn't look like any butch I'd ever seen, and sometimes I was on top, and there were other times we'd be side by side. So, what was that?

I didn't have any desire for a repeat performance with Virginia, but that little tryst on the lady's room floor took away a safety I'd clung to for years. Juliana was no longer the only woman I'd been with. I was one of those perverts mothers warned their daughters about.

It was late afternoon. I'd finished my class about making a cheerful bulletin board for first graders. Dull. I headed for the school library to find a book on what I was. I wandered up the steps, trying to look nonchalant, not a care in the world, ho-hum. I swung my arms back and forth, flashing a dopey smile at the librarian and heading for the card catalogue. I looked around, making sure no one was about to peek over my shoulder and see what I was looking up. The library wasn't crowded, only a few students sitting at tables poring over their books.

My hands shook when I reached for the drawer. I slid it out. My fingers touched the cards, moving toward HO—B ... hobo, hobnob ... skipped some ... HO—C ... hockey ... skipped more ... HO—L ... hold-up, hollandaise sauce (recipes for), holly (Christmas, types of) holsters, holy days. Big breath. Here goes. My fingers touched "HO—M."

"Hi, there," a voice whispered in my ear.

"What!" I shoved the drawer closed and jumped back, my heart bursting out of my chest. It was Marty. "What are you doing sneaking up on a person like that?"

"Shh," the librarian said.

"I didn't sneak up on you," he whispered. "Are you all right?"

"Fine! I was—"

"Guess what? I got the lead in the spring play. Gabey in *On the Town*."

"You did?" We bounced into each other's arms, jumping up and down.

"Shh," the librarian said.

"Let's go outside," Marty suggested. "Oh. Did you want to finish your research, first?"

"Not important."

As soon as we left the library, Marty took off his tie and stuffed it in his jacket pocket.

* * *

"You got a piano," I exclaimed when I walked into Marty's apartment behind him.

"My mother and Aunt got it for me. It's used and it keeps going out of tune, but it's mine." He hugged it as he sat down on the bench. The sheet music for *On the Town* was open to "Lonely Town." I leaned over his shoulder to study the words.

"It's what's *under* the words that I'm having trouble with, the feelings. Since you have experience, I thought ... I've never been *that* lonely."

"No, you wouldn't know, would you?" Moshe said, coming out of the kitchen sucking on an orange Popsicle. He leaned against the doorway molding, his too-small jacket open, his bow tie crooked. "You weren't expecting *me*, were you?"

"No. I wasn't."

"I'm Marty's roommate now." Again, that sound of victory.

"Really?" I said.

"No. Not really," Marty said. "He's staying here till he finds his own place. Moshe, stop looking so dramatic. Alice is only here to help me work on this piece."

"I bet that's all she's here for. I only know of one kinda girl that goes into men's apartments—"

"Stop it," Marty scolded. "She's here to help me because *she's* been on Broadway."

"So, I've heard, and heard, and heard," he said rhythmically, moving toward the door. "And heard, and heard ..." He slid into the hallway and pounded down the steps. "And heard, and heard, and heard ..."

"You let him move in here, after he beat you up in the quadrangle?"

"He didn't beat me up. I held my own."

"I don't care who won. Why is he here?"

"His parents kicked him out. They can't stand how religious he's become, and *they're* religious. What was I sposed to do? Leave him out in the street? He wasn't always like this. The war ... it did something to him."

"You were in the war, and you don't act like that."

"Things don't bother me the way they do him. He's terribly sensitive."

"Oh, yeah, I can see how 'sensitive' he is."

"He is. We both went to Bronx Science High, but he didn't have any friends."

"I can't imagine why."

"The school was wrong for him. He'd rather write poetry than do science. I don't think he's written one poem since the war.

"You care about him a lot, don't you?" I said.

"He's an army buddy. I mean, we grew up together, but in the army you ... Well, your buddies are—they're, uh ... He's a buddy. Come on. Help me with my song." He played a chord and sang.

* * *

Later, I went back to the library. My heart pounding, I searched the card catalog—nothing. Then I thumbed through the stacks, but again, nothing. How could we be such a burden to the world, and, yet, in the library we didn't even exist? As I was about to leave, I saw a list of reserved books, the books the librarian kept on the shelves behind her desk. I requested the one titled *Textbook of Abnormal Psychology.*

I sat with the book at one of the tables and pored over the Table of Contents—nothing. I was about to give up when I thought to take a quick look at the index. I found it! It was listed under "Disorders of the Amatory Desire." The writer called homosexuality "undesirable," but if you only did it once in a while it wasn't abnormal.

That's good, I thought. Still, he said, once you started doing it, it was easy to get the habit, and that *was* abnormal. There was no cure.

Juliana and I didn't do it often, so maybe we didn't have the habit. Of course we did. We only didn't do it much because we didn't see each other much, or Richard was in the room. If I could, I'd do it with her every day.

Chapter 32

I RECLINED IN my office chair at The Haven, my feet propped up on an open drawer, sipping my tea, trying to look relaxed. All pretense. I had hundreds of things to do. My desk was piled with papers to be read, but I wanted to quiet the churning inside me. How could I have been alive for twenty-seven years and not known I was this thing I was?

I'd never fit in anywhere, but now? Guilt flooded me like a broken spigot. But guilt about what? Juliana? The best part of me? Virginia? Such a good soul. Then what? I had no answer. Only the vague feeling that in some way I was tainted.

I held my breath as I picked up the *New York Times* and read "Perverts Called Government Peril."

"Will they never stop this?" I punched the article with my fist over and over. *"Stop it! Stop it!"*

* * *

I stood in the middle of the empty room of The Haven—staring into space as the voices battled in my head.

"Al, are you all right?" Scott said from behind me.

I turned. "Fine."

"I finished up the books." Max had made Scott our accountant. He stood in his shirtsleeves, tie loose, putting on his jacket. "I was going to get a cup of coffee. You want to join me?"

"Can't. I have to pick up some new publicity photos."

"Okay. See you later."

"Wait, Scott. Yes. I *would* like to have coffee with you." I ran toward my office. "Wait. I'll get my coat. Do you mind making a side trip for the pictures?"

"That's fine." He put on his hat. "I'll meet you out front."

When I opened my office door I found Bertha, the hatcheck girl, standing at my desk. "Bertha, what are you doing here?"

"Dusting." She held up a feather duster. "Haven't you noticed how clean your office has been? I come in here and tidy up every day before I'm on, but only when you're not here. I wouldn't want to bother you."

"Why?"

"Because you're an important person."

"Not really, but why are you dusting my office? We have cleaning staff for that."

"Oh. I didn't know."

"Haven't you seen them every day before we open?"

"I want to help you. I'll finish this up for today and find something else to do. This came." She reached for a large envelope that lay on my desk.

"Hatcheck girls don't bring the mail in either." I took the envelope from her.

"Yes, of course." She hurried from my office.

I supposed I was being hard on her, but she gave me the creeps. There was no return address on the envelope. I remembered Scott waiting in front of the building, so I grabbed my hat and coat, tucked the envelope under my arm, and ran to meet him.

As we walked down Forty-second, I asked, "How's your psychoanalysis going? Oh, is it okay to ask that? I don't mean to pry." The barkers were out in full force, yelling for customers to come into their stores for the sales.

"That's okay," Scott said. "I think it's going good. Maybe …"

We pushed through a crowd trying to get into Hector's Cafeteria and the Claridge Hotel. The sidewalks were choking with bodies bumping into each other, winter coats making our girth swell. In amongst the exhaust from cars and taxis, I could smell the perfume of the women passing by. Sometimes, I'd get a wiff of the chestnuts the vendors roasted on the corner. The crowds were so thick on the sidewalks, I almost stumbled over the legless Vet in the wagon. "What? Ya effin' blind?" he yelled up at me. Taxis honked and darted in and out of traffic. Buses and cars squealed so loud, I thought for sure someone was going to careen into someone, but they didn't.

"Maybe we can talk about it over coffee," Scott continued, his protective arm around me so I didn't get swallowed by the masses. "You know the Starlight Lounge?"

"Yes. Haven't been there in awhile, but I know it."

"They have a good piano player. Want to go there?"

"Sure. Let's take the bus."

We hopped onto a green and white city bus and took it up to Fifty-Seventh. "Wait here," I said outside the Carnegie building. "I'll be right down."

When I entered the studio, Johnny was playing one of his new love tunes. He'd been turning out songs like crazy for the new act. Juliana leaned against the piano, totally lost in her song. She wore her pale-green day dress with the slight flare and matching pale-green heels.

Richard came up to me. "Beautiful, huh?"

"Oh, yeah." I swooned. "I mean the song." Catching myself. "The song's beautiful."

"What do you think of these?" He held his lit cigarette between his teeth and handed me a brown envelope. "They're the proofs for the new publicity photos. I want to see which ones you want to use."

While I slid them out, Juliana smiled at me and waved, but continued to sing. I was Cock Robin with an arrow shooting through my heart. I finished sliding out the eight-by-tens. They were of Juliana in a blue Army Nurse Corp uniform, only she didn't look like any Army Nurse I'd ever seen. A few of them focused on her breasts, the tie undone, the buttons of her blouse unbuttoned to the center of her chest, showing her cleavage. Others were leg shots, where she was showing more leg than an Army Nurse would have dared show during the war.

"I don't know, Richard."

"It hit me a couple weeks ago that she was in the war. She's a genuine war heroine; she was right on the front lines."

"But she wasn't a nurse; she was a singer, and the war was serious business. Do you really think we should use it like this? I mean, look at how much skin she's showing."

"Yeah, that kind of bothered me too, but you were the one who said we had to make Juliana's act, uh—pardon me—sexy, but keep it subtle. This is gonna work. Look at Marlene Dietrich. The war's working for her."

I put the photos away. I had to discuss this with Max.

Juliana was singing "Manhattan." I waved good-bye, but she was busy flirting with Johnny. Ouch. I hurried down in the elevator to Scott.

We walked around the corner to the Starlight. The lighting was soft, and there were cushioned seats. Only a few patrons were scattered about at different tables, and one couple huddled over a beer at the bar, speaking in hushed tones. The piano player played "Embraceable You."

As we entered, Scott took off his hat, and we followed the waitress toward the lounge. He stood by the table, listening to the piano player. "He's good," I said. "And cute."

"I didn't notice *that*."

"I bet you didn't."

"Well, uh—what's that you got there?" he asked as he helped me off with my coat.

"These are photos, and this came in the mail today. No return address."

"Mysterious."

I opened the "mysterious" envelope and pulled out a folded newspaper. The *Long Islander*. "Gosh, it's been ages since I've seen this. I wonder who—" I shook the envelope to see if a card fell out. Nothing. "This paper is important in Long Island. Stories about the locals. Who's getting married, buying a house, graduating, just died. Of course, I may not know anyone anymore. It's so built up with Levittown and the other developments going up where the potato fields used to be."

The waitress came over. "What can I bring you?"

"Did you want something to eat?" Scott asked.

"No, but I'd rather have tea instead of coffee."

"One coffee, one tea," Scott said to the waitress, then turned to me. "Let's see it."

"You'll be bored."

"We have a paper like that in Pickle Paw. *The Independent*. Put out by one guy in a dusty office on Main Street. All the local gossip he can fit into four pages. It looks like your town is doing better than that."

"Walt Whitman founded it in Huntington where I was born. He used to walk around delivering his paper and talking to customers, and then the next week he'd print the gossip he'd heard the week before."

"I don't think I'd talk to a guy like that. So, what's it got to say?"

The piano player burst into something wild and hot with lots of up and down riffs. It was impossible not to look up from the paper and listen. Scott used our table as a piano and played along with the kid.

"You play?" I asked.

"A little."

"I'm surprised. You don't seem like, well—"

"Like the type? I'm not. I said a little."

A middle-aged man walked over to the piano and pointed a finger at the boy, and he instantly switched to "Tea for Two."

"Let's see that paper," Scott said.

I opened the paper flat on the table and was instantly awash in nostalgia, wondering which of my old friends sent it. I was hoping it'd been Aggie, wanting to be friends again. Stupid of me to tell her about my feelings for Juliana. The ads were for places I knew: Smiley's, the local gas station where Dad had worked, Walker's General Store.

"Oh, here's something," I said. "Emily Weller had her third child. I knew her in high school and, and ..." Suddenly, tears.

"What's the matter?" Scott asked.

"Could I miss them? I haven't seen my parents in nine years."

"Gosh, why?"

"A fight on my wedding day. My husband-to-be walked into the room when Juliana and I were kissing."

"That's not good."

"That pretty much ended my wedding. The last time I talked to my mother she was on the phone yelling that I was a—I hate this word—a queer."

"Your own mother called you that?"

"Yeah, so I haven't seen them since."

"Maybe if you got into psychoanalysis you'd get cured. Then you could make it up with them."

"You think I'm one of them?"

"Well, the way you feel about Juliana—"

"I should go to a doctor and be cured of loving her?"

"You can still love her, but not *that* way."

"Oh, no, look at this." My eyes scanned a small notice with a high school picture of a girl I didn't know. There was a penciled circle around her face.

"What?"

"Danny. A boy I grew up with. He lived next door to me. He's getting married." I had a strong suspicion that it was my mother who sent this paper to say, 'I told you so,' but maybe it was Danny.

"That sounds good, so why the 'oh, no?'"

"He was my beau when I first came to the city and then Max ... forget it."

"I know Maxwell had a rambunctious past."

"That's one way of putting it. Danny and Max had a brief fling. Then Danny joined the army. I saw him right after the war. He'd fallen in love with a soldier. He was thinking about getting to know him better; he was a little scared about it, but I really thought he was going to do it."

"But he's getting married, instead? Don't you see? He's cured."

"Is he?"

"Yeah. And if *he's* cured, it means a cure is possible. You should have a drink to celebrate. I don't drink myself, but it seems like someone should drink to this news. What'd you say his name was?"

"Danny."

"Danny. My hero. Is wine okay, or did you want something else?"

"Wine's fine."

Scott picked up the drink menu. "Uh, the only wine they have is this, uh, Louis Jadot beauj, uh oh, I'm never going to pronounce this right."

"We don't have to pronounce it; we, or I, only need to drink it."

"True." Scott signaled the waitress. "Bring us one glass of this," he pointed at the menu, "and I'll take a Coca Cola. That's as strong as I get."

"Scott, if you had a friend who you thought might be … gay, but you weren't absolutely positive. Would you come out and ask?"

"Why would you do that?"

"To have a more honest friendship."

Scott shook his head. "No. You can't ask someone a thing like that. What if you're wrong? It'd be an insult to them, and you could lose your friend, or worse. With it being illegal in New York to hire a homosexual, that person could ruin your future."

"But I'm not one of …" almost came out of my mouth. Then I remembered, I was. "But I wasn't talking about me. I was talking about someone who I thought might be—"

"If you're wrong, that person could get you kicked out of college."

"I guess you're right. Could I show you these pictures?" I asked, eager to change the subject. "Get your opinion."

"Sure. Not that I know anything about show business."

"I want your opinion as someone who served in the war. You see, Juliana entertained the troops on the front lines for a few weeks toward the end of the war, and I wanted to see what you think." I slid a few photos out of the envelope. "So?" I asked.

"I suspect a—normal man would find them … She looks pretty, but you're not asking the most qualified person."

"I have mixed emotions about them. On the one hand, I like looking at them. She looks—'hot.' And that makes *me*—hot. Gosh, I can't believe I said that to you."

"That's okay. I understand."

"You see, even though she and I are kind of working together, we don't get much time—you know, alone, so when I see these pictures, I get … Why am I telling you this?"

"Because I'm your friend."

"That's nice. I don't know that it's such a good idea to use these pictures. They seem to exploit the war. I mean, that was serious business and people lost their lives. You were in it. What do you think?"

He shrugged his shoulders. "I don't see them as so bad. That was a brave thing for her to do, so why not tell people?"

"I guess. Then there's this other part of me. That part doesn't like the idea of having men look at her, and you know, thinking—the things men think."

"That's your sick part. The part of you that thinks you're in competition with men when you can't be. You're a girl. My analyst tells me the reason so many people are becoming perverts these days is because our roles are getting mixed up. He says it's because girls think they can be independent of men, so they act mannish. That makes men lose confidence in their manly role, so they start acting womanish."

"Do you really believe that?"

"I don't know." Scott sighed. "That's what Dr. Snyder says. Can I have one of these pictures? This one. This cleavage one."

"Sure, they're only proofs, but why would you want that?"

"Dr. Snyder says I should look at pictures of women. He suggested French postcards. You know, the kind that shows girls with no clothes on. Guys in the army passed them around. I don't want to look at those kinds of pictures, but this one, it's pretty so—"

"Take it. Don't think anything *really* disgusting about her, okay?"

"If only I could."

We both laughed.

Chapter 33

I SAT AT my desk sipping my hot, morning tea; only it was mid-afternoon, and the tea was tepid. My desk was piled high with the usual precariously-balanced newspapers. I placed my teacup on the desk and carefully slid *The New York Times* from the bottom of the stack. I got past the first page, and the second, on my way to "Arts & Leisure," but was stopped by the headline on the third page: "Federal Vigilance on Perverts Asked." Couldn't there be one day without these articles? We were only a few days away from Juliana's opening. What if people found out about us? How awful to be thought of as sick, an unnatural thing, with no right to exist. I'd never work again. I remembered my father back during the depression. How ashamed he'd been that he could find no work.

Through my office window I saw Shirl walk by, and I threw open the door. "Shirl!"

She spun around and looked at me strangely. "Is there an emergency?"

"No. Well, maybe. No. Could I talk to you a minute?"

She stepped into my office and sat in the chair at the side of my desk. "This is a switch," she smiled. "Me in *your* office. I like watching you grow."

"Shirl, I—realized I'm a—a ..."

"You have me in suspense."

"It's hard to say—about yourself—uh, homosexual." I pushed the word out.

"Uh, Al? I thought we had this conversation years ago, and we established that then."

"No. *You* established it. I didn't think it applied to me. I know that sounds nuts with me being certifiable for Juliana, but I thought if it were only one girl then I wasn't really ... I've been with another girl."

"Wonderful."

"No, it's not. It means that I'm one of those people the papers talk about."

"You always were. Just because they're talking about us now hasn't changed anything. Are there any possibilities with this new girl?"

"No. She's straight."

"Oh, Al, stay away from straight girls. They have their little experimental fling, step on your heart, and then go running back to the men. But still, this is good. It means I can introduce you to some—"

"I don't want to meet anyone. I want to know about what I am and why I'm this way. Maybe I need a doctor. Have you ever gone to one of those?"

"I don't want some doctor telling me who to love."

"But how does it happen?"

"We're different. Is it so terrible to be different?"

"Yes! It's terrible when people think you're dangerous and they have to stay away from you because you might do something awful to them. Are there any books?"

"The only books I know will tell you you're sick. I don't think you need to read them. No. Wait. There is one. It's been banned in England. They came close to doing that here, but they didn't succeed. Still, you need to be cautious about who sees you reading it."

"Banned?"

"The courts called it obscene. I'm not sure what I think about it, certainly not obscene, but lots of women find it useful. It's a little too tragic for my tastes, but Mercy loved it. Bawled all the way through it, which is how she decides if a book is good or not. I'll bring it to you tomorrow."

"What is it?"

"*The Well of Loneliness.*"

* * *

Next day, Shirl brought me a brown paper package. Inside was a copy of *The Well of Loneliness*, which was further wrapped in a plain brown wrapper. When I peeled back the paper, I found a card from Mercy that read: "I'm so happy you've decided to read this. When you're finished, come for tea and we'll talk."

I was too busy with Juliana's opening to read it. No time for this book. I had a pile of work, and I promised Marty I'd go to his play, so … I opened to the first page and went on to the second, the third, the next and the next. Finally, when it was time to set up The Haven for the first show, I called Max and asked him to send someone over from the Mt. Olympus to cover for me. I took a cab back to my apartment and read all night, not stopping for Marty's play at school—I'd go on the weekend—and into the morning. By mid-afternoon of the next day, I closed the back cover and took a cab to Shirl and Mercy's.

* * *

"Al, you look terrible," Shirl said, when I showed up at her door.

"I've been up all night. I came to see Mercy. Is she here?"

Mercy peered around the corner. "Come. We'll go into my sewing room. I just put on a pot of coffee. Oh, you prefer tea, don't you?"

"Coffee's fine. I've been drinking it all night."

Mercy and I sat close together in puffy chairs in her bright yellow sewing room, huddled over our coffee. She wore a blue and white housedress and white ankle socks. She kicked off her penny loafers.

"Merce, how could you have found this book helpful?"

"You didn't like it?"

"The main character, Stephen, says that people like us have male souls. Do you feel like that?"

"I don't, but I think Shirl has a male soul. Didn't you find it romantic and …" she whispered, "…sexy?"

"Not really."

"That first woman. Wasn't that affair a little sexy?"

"Yeah, a little, but that woman was so mean to Stephen."

"Yes, but for a while it was a passionate friendship." She giggled.

"But that ending—"

"You didn't think it was romantic? It shows the inverts' greater capacity for suffering."

"If I'm one of those, I don't want a greater capacity for suffering. I don't want to suffer at all."

"But you sacrifice yourself."

"No, I don't."

"You stick by Juliana no matter what, help her with her career even though you know she'll never leave Richard. What would you call that?"

"Mentally deranged. It's how the doctors say we are."

"Oh, come now, you're not mentally deranged. You're a romantic in love. Like me, like Stephen."

"Mercy, in this book, these inverts are called freaks. Stephen cries out to God; it's right here. I put a slip of paper in the page to mark the place." I opened the book, slid my finger down the page and read aloud. "'Acknowledge us, oh God, before the whole world. Give us the right to our existence.' I don't want to be a freak, someone who even has to beg God to be acknowledged. Did you see that movie, *Freaks*?"

"Yes. And it was horrifying that people had to live so deformed with other people laughing at them, but remember, the point of that movie was that it was the *normal* people who turned out to be the true freaks. Maybe there *is* a parallel to us."

"Do you think you're a freak because you love Shirl?"

"Well—maybe a little, if I get right down to it. It's not the way most girls behave. Is it?"

"No, but—"

"I love Shirl. I'd have it no other way, but sometimes, when I go to Philadelphia to visit my mother, I wish Shirl could be there with me. When my father died, I had to do everything alone. I had to take the bus to mourn with my family alone. Shirl couldn't stand beside me and hold my tears or God bless my mother, or kiss my sister on the forehead. She couldn't call me on the phone, because my relatives would've hung up on her. Yes, there are times I've wished Shirl was my honest-to-goodness, born male husband, and I wish every day I didn't have to pretend to my family she doesn't exist. I was raised to be someone's wife, someone's mother. I darn Shirl's socks, cook her meals, keep her house clean, and I love every minute of it, but ..." Tears suddenly slipped down Mercy's face.

"You wish you weren't ...? "

"Oh, no. I love who I am. I love my life with Shirl. It's—I'd like a child, that's all, and this life can never give me that. But I've never loved a man. Shirl is all the man I ever want."

"Mercy, I'm so confused. And—scared of myself."

"Why?"

"I've never said this to anyone before, but ... for a long time, I didn't even dare think it, but ..." I whispered, "I have a lot of maleness in me."

"I know."

"You do?"

"Of course. So?"

"I always feel like I'm trying to hide it, but it keeps jumping out, and I have to stuff it back inside me, because if I let it out I'll be a freak. Still, I don't think I'm like Stephen, but I have these dreams. They scare me 'cause ... I think I might turn into ... When I was little, I wanted to be a boy so bad."

I took a deep breath. Was I really going to tell her this? She sat there looking gentle with the softest smile, ready to receive anything I said. I had to take this chance. "I used to run out of the house some days and walk around the block, and ask God to turn me into a boy. I was convinced there had been some mistake in Heaven, and I figured since God loved me—I mean, gee, someone had to, and they told me He did in Sunday school—He wouldn't want me to be miserable for my whole life—so He'd miraculously turn me into a boy, like I was sposed to be.

One day I'd wake up and be a boy and—truly happy. Of course that never happened, but when I was around twelve I started having these dreams. I thought maybe God had finally decided to do it, or He was going to do it half-way and make a fool of me." I took a sip of my now-cold coffee and looked away. "I dreamed I grew a beard in the night. It felt so real, in the morning I had to touch my face to make sure it hadn't happened. I still have that dream on and off, and it still scares me. It's the maleness in me, I suppose. What if Juliana sees it?"

"She probably has, and that's why she keeps you around."

"What?"

"We all love you the way you are. Whether you have a male soul, or something else, doesn't matter. It's a dream. It's what you're doing when you're awake that matters. And on that note, if you didn't like that book, I have another one for you." She bounced up and slid in her stocking feet to a small bookcase. "Try this. It's from France, recently translated into English."

I held the small paperback and read the title, *Women's Barracks*. "It's about people like us?" I asked.

Mercy smiled. "It's good to hear you say you're one of us." She kissed me on the forehead.

Chapter 34

May 1950

MARTY BURST INTO the auditorium, chorus girls dripping from both arms. "Alice!" He shook off the girls and threw his arms around me. "You came!"

"Wouldn't have missed it."

"You've got to come with us."

"Where?"

Taking my hand, he pulled me up the aisle. "We're going out to celebrate."

"No. They're *your* friends. I'll be an outsider."

Still pulling me along, "Two outsiders on the town. It'll be fun. You'll be my date."

Moshe leaned against the wall near the exit, pouting. He wore his usual suit that was too short for his arms and his yarmulke. He held his fedora in his hand by its brim.

I slid my arm out of Marty's. "You go."

"Don't let *him* bother you." He pulled my arm back around his. Cast and crew gathered around us, hitting him on the back. A few girls kissed him. I got pushed up against Moshe—"Oh, excuse me"—and together we watched Marty play-fight with some guys.

Marty pulled away from his fans and threw his arms around Moshe and me. "Let's go."

The whole crowd, many who had already started drinking, ended up outside the Washington Gate, where we hailed cabs. A light mist fell. I was shoved into the back seat of a cab, and when I turned my head to see who sat next to me, it was Moshe, not Marty.

On my other side, a girl I didn't know sat on her beau's lap. They kissed each other with open mouths, seemingly unaware that their passion was making their arms and legs knock into me. When I slid over to give them more room, I almost ended up on Moshe's lap. He gave me a venomous look. I slid back toward them.

Moshe and I sat with our hands pressed neatly into our laps, his caressing the brim of his hat, while we pretended not to see the man trying to get his hand under the girl's skirt. She giggled and swatted him away without separating her lips from his.

"So—Moshe. He was good, wasn't he?" I thought a little conversation might ease our awkward situation.

"He was okay." He stared out the window. The driver turned on the wipers, and I listened to them swish-swish across the window as the mist turned into a drizzle.

"I thought he was very alive on that stage."

"Maybe." Still staring out the window. "But he should be doing the classics, not this musical theater nonsense."

"Marty never told me he wanted to be that type of actor."

"No. He wouldn't." Again, the sound of victory.

"Well—how have *you* been?" I asked.

"And I'm sure *that's* a sincere question. So, you're his date for the evening."

"Do I look like his date? He's not even here. I'm really no threat to you."

His head whipped around to face me. "What's *that* supposed to mean?"

"Nothing. I didn't mean anything." I was more than a little afraid. "I'm sorry." How could I make such a mistake in front of straights? Okay, they weren't paying attention to us. But still, if they heard me, they could report it and get us both kicked out of school. A chill ran through my body.

The cab pulled up to the curb, and Marty yanked open the door. "Come on."

The couple crawled onto the running board, the man on all fours, the girl on his back. They fell onto the sidewalk, laughing. Moshe grabbed my shoulder, pulling me back toward him like he wanted to hit me. "I don't know what you *think* you know, but you don't know anything. It's not true."

"I know."

I sidled out of the car. The drizzle had turned into rain. I was surrounded by the blinking neon lights of Swing Street. The Street! I can't be here with them. The Haven must be a little … I looked up at the awning to my right. *Birdland! I can't go in there.*

Marty grabbed my arm. "Hurry. You'll be drenched." He took his tie out of his pocket and hung it around his neck. He marched me past Tony the doorman and signaled Moshe to follow us. I kept my head down, so Tony didn't see me. Marty and Moshe took off their hats.

The place was dimly lit in a glowing red. We walked down the carpeted steps toward the hatcheck girl. In the distance, I could see the main room with patrons clustering around little round tables. I slid my hat to the side of my face so Trudy didn't see me.

"Isn't it all too wonderful?" Marty said as we drew closer to hatcheck. "Let me take your coats. I'll give these to the girl and get the tickets."

Marty came back waving the tickets, and we walked down the steps to our table. Marty looked up at the birdcages hanging from the ceiling, each one with a little bird inside. "I read about this, but gosh, he really does have birds everywhere."

"And over there. By the bar." I pointed to a large cage. "A talking mynah bird."

"How'd you know it talks?"

"Oh." *Damn.* "They all talk. Don't they?"

"I don't know, do they?"

We stepped into the main room and were led to our table. To our left, men were squashed around the bar.

Moshe sat opposite me, looking as sullen as ever. Customers took their seats and waiters hurried to serve them.

"So, I have news," Marty announced. "I got an acting job. I haven't even graduated yet."

"Tell us!" I said.

"TV. Only a small part in a fifteen-minute show. For Autolite Theater."

"I know them. I once did a radio bit on their show."

"So much in common," Moshe whispered.

I decided not to give him the dirty look that was trying to crawl onto my face.

"Marty, you're gonna be on *my* TV, in *my* living room."

"If you look fast."

The waiter came over, "Drinks? Hey, Al, how are you?"

"Fine," I said softly to the caramel-complexioned waiter, keeping my eyes on my drink menu. "I'll have—"

"A side car, right?"

"Uh, Manhattan."

"Really? But you always …"

I wiggled my eyebrows at him, hoping he'd catch my drift.

"What'll you gentlemen have?"

Marty ordered a dry martini, which seemed right for him, but when Moshe, who I expected to order something like chocolate milk, ordered a dry martini too, that *was* a surprise.

Lou dashed off, and I looked up to see Marty and Moshe staring at me.

"Well?" Marty said.

"What?"

"How is it you know our waiter, and he knows what you drink?"

"Oh, well, he must've mixed me up with someone else."

"No, he knew you," Marty said. "He called you Al. Why'd he call you that?"

"I don't know."

"Come on, *Al.* What was that about, *Al?*"

"We've worked together."

"Where do you work, exactly? I always thought it was in some little diner, but if you know *him* and he knows your drink, you must work in a fancy place like a nightclub."

"Kinda."

"You're a cigarette girl, aren't you?" Moshe hissed. "See? I told you she's nothing, but a—"

"Don't finish that," Marty and I said at the same time.

"Which nightclub do you work in?" Marty asked.

"The Master of Ceremonies. They're going to start."

Pee Wee Marquette stood on the stage in his little tuxedo. He was a midget who announced the shows. The musicians had to treat him kindly, or the next time they did a show at Birdland he'd mispronounce their name in an embarrassing way.

The lights came up on a huge stage, revealing a full orchestra with the Charlie Bird Quintet downstage. Last year, to attract teenagers to the Mt. Olympus—they were calling older kids teenagers now—Max put in a pre-show bebop dance hour. For the opening, Charlie Parker played a few of his bebop songs. It attracted a huge crowd, and ever since then, "teenagers" were finding their way to the Mt. Olympus. Charlie "Bird" Parker became our regular special guest.

As the music played, Lou ran by, dropping off our drinks. Moshe swallowed down his in a couple gulps and ordered another. My listening of the music was erratic because all I could think of was that Shakespeare quote about the tangled web that chokes you when you're deceiving people. When the music stopped and the musicians left the stage for a break, Moshe said, in between sloppy gulps of martini, "She cavorts with musicians, Marty. That means narcotics, and drunken orgies, and—"

Charlie Parker came over to our table. "Hey, Al!" He held out his thick brown hand for me to shake. "I thought that was you sitting there, but I had to come over and be sure. How ya doing?"

"Good. Bird, your new show is terrific. I love the addition of the strings. No other jazz musician would do that."

"Well, I'm not any ol' jazz musician."

"No, you're not. I want you to meet my friends, Aaron Martin Buchman, and this is Moshe Steinman."

"Hi, fellas," Bird said to two fans whose mouths hung open. "Hey, Lou." Bird signaled our waiter. "Another round of drinks here. On the house." He winked at me and disappeared into the roomful of fans.

"Holy Smoke!" Marty said. "You actually know him. You called him Bird."

"I bet she's a drug addict," Moshe said.

"Shut up," Marty said. "And don't tell *me* you didn't get a thrill out of meeting *Bird* after all the hours we've spent listening to his records. Spill it, *Al*. How is it you're buddies with "Bird?"

"Yeah," Moshe said, his head swaying. While Marty and I were nursing our second drink, Moshe had finished his third, and was waving down Lou for another.

"Marty, I'm a student when I'm at school. That's all I want to be."

"Instead of a whore?" Moshe drawled.

"Okay. That's it." I got up and sped toward the exit, pushing customers out of my way, forgetting my coat. Marty caught up with me under the awning outside. The steady rain was a persistent drumbeat against the canvas above our heads.

"Alice, wait. Your coat." He handed it to me without helping me into it. He rarely followed the ordinary rules for men and women, so I put my own coat on. "He's been drinking. He doesn't know what he's saying."

"He knows exactly what he's saying because it's what he thinks. Look, Marty, at the school I'm a student. Your mother expected you to go to college; she encouraged you, and if it hadn't been for the war you would've gone years ago. I never in my wildest imagination thought of myself as a college student, but that's what I seem to be. And some days I even fit in. I don't want to lose that by—by ..."

"Telling me who you really are?"

"I suppose."

"I think I know a lot more about you than you realize."

"Like what?" I crossed my arms over my chest.

"Like ..." He looked out toward the street. Cars whooshed through puddles, reflections of colored lights sparkled in the water running down the street. "Like ... gosh, this is hard to say. Alice, you're ..." Despite the two of us being the only people standing under the awning—Tony must have gone off somewhere for a smoke—Marty stepped closer to me and whispered, "You're ..." And swallowed. "You're gay, aren't you?"

A cold chill shot through my body, and "No!" with great outrage almost flew out of my mouth, but then I stopped it. I'd never had to acknowledge this thing out loud beyond Shirl and Mercy, but now it was the school ... "Yes. And you are too."

We both sighed.

"I'm glad that's out," he said. "I've known about you since the beginning."

"When you asked if I was a communist."

"Yeah." He laughed. "Dumb."

"I think after a while I got it, but I was afraid to get it."

"I feel safe around you," Marty said. "It's not like that with other people. Those things they say about us in the papers ... There are others like us at the school, some in the cast, but trying to find out for sure is treacherous. I get a suspicion, but what if I'm wrong? It'll ruin my future career. There are ways of telling on the street and in subways, but at the school ..."

"There are?"

"Code words. And that's really for sex."

"You do that with strangers in subways? How?"

"In the bathroom. But my point is, I don't want to take that chance at school."

"You do that with strangers in subway bathrooms?"

"Yes, and if you keep repeating it I'm going to feel guilty, and it's the one thing I don't feel guilty about. Let me get Moshe in a cab, and you and me'll go some place and talk. I want to know about you and Charlie Parker. You really know him, wow."

We walked back into the place, squeezing through the people overflowing the bar, and made our way to Moshe, whose head was on the table; his hand gripped his half-filled glass. "Where's the waiter? I've got to pay the bill," Marty said.

"You take care of Moshe. I'll get this." I took a few bills from my purse.

"Well, look at you. We *definitely* need to talk. I *know* waitresses don't get paid like that."

Marty scooped Moshe up into his arms, while I gave the bills to Lou. As Marty dragged Moshe toward the hatcheck girl, Moshe's head fell back and his yarmulke fell off. I picked it up while Marty stuffed him into his coat.

Marty dragged him into the damp air. The rain was once again only a drizzle. The air seemed to revive him, and he raised his head from Marty's shoulder. "What's going on?"

"Taxi! Hey, Taxi!" Marty called out, shaking his hand in the air to flag a cab. Who knew where Tony had gone off to? A couple of green and yellow-checkered cabs with their flags up slid into the curb, and Marty yanked open the door of one of them. He dropped Moshe inside and gave the address to the driver. "Don't go till you see him go inside. I'm giving you something extra for that." He handed the driver money.

As Marty slid back out of the cab, Moshe's eyes got wide. "Hey! Aren't you coming, too?"

"No. Alice and I are gonna talk. You go home and sleep."

"He dropped this." I handed Marty the yarmulke.

"I'm coming too," Moshe said, sticking his leg out of the car. "You're not getting rid of me that easy." He pushed his foot against the running board and grabbed Marty's coat, trying to get out.

"Put your yarmulke on,"—Marty put it on his head—"and go home and pray. You need it."

Moshe continued to push against Marty's body and got his second leg out of the car onto the running board. "Cut it out, Mosh, you're in no condition—"

Moshe wrapped his arms around Marty's chest in a killer-wrestler move. Or was that a hug? "Don't leave me." He started to cry.

"Stop, you're crushing me."

"Look, buddy," the hack said, "your dough ain't coverin' all night. Get in or out."

"Oh, hell, Moshe. I'm sorry, Alice, I better get him home. We'll go out another time. Next week? I wanna hear about you and Charlie Parker."

Chapter 35

I HESITATED AT the top of the steps. The basement door had only the number 181 on it. Strange not to be hidden under the shadow of the Second Avenue El. They'd taken it down during the war because it shut out the light. Soon they'd be building the Second Avenue subway. I stood only a few blocks from The Christian Ladies of Hope House, my first home in the city. The boarders of Hope House were long gone, the building in a bad state of disrepair. The Third Avenue El squealed in the distance. There was talk they'd be taking that down too, soon.

I wore my Dior New Look white sleeveless dress with a butterfly pattern and a flare skirt, the hemline at my lower calf. My hat had a wide brim and was made to look like woven straw.

This place catered pretty much to the same crowd as we did: big shot bankers, celebrities, Wall Streeters, mobsters, and tourists. Folks with money to spend. But it wasn't *really* like our place at all.

It was dark inside, lit only by flickering candles. On the stage, a bright light shone on chorus boys, dressed like chorus girls, singing and swishing to "That's My Fella" from *Up in Central Park,* a Broadway hit in '45. The audience laughed at their femininity as they sang about their "man." My eyes adjusted to the dim light, and I noticed the rich Wedgewood blue and white walls. At the bar, I saw straight men and gay boys leaning over their drinks; some of the gay boys had their arms around each other. Didn't they know sitting like that made them part of the entertainment whether they wanted to be or not?

"Hey, Al!" Marty called from the bar, running to me, a drink in hand. He wore his too-big corduroy pants with his tie hanging crookedly around his neck.

A woman in a tuxedo approached us. "May I show you to a table, sir?"

"Yeah. Thanks," Marty said. "In the back, please." We followed our hostess. "Isn't this place great? One of the guys from the cast brought me here a few weeks ago. He figured out about me." We sat at a round table.

"The most famous fag joint in town," I said.

"Al!"

"I'm only quoting *USA Confidential.*"

"Be happy. This is a place for us."

"This place isn't for us. It's a place for straights to come and laugh at *us*. When I first came to the city, I went with my friends from the Island to the Life Cafeteria on Seventh Avenue."

"I know the place."

"We stood with our faces pressed against their large windows, making fun of the homos inside as if we were at the zoo. Now, *I'm* one of those homos in the zoo."

"Stop. The talent here is the best."

"If they wanted to perform at the Copa or Jimmy Ryan's, could they?"

"Well … no."

"And if a girl showed up who wasn't an entertainer or a waiter, but was wearing a tuxedo, would they let her in?"

"Of course not. What's your point?"

"It's not a place for *us*. It's a place for *them*."

"Boy, you sure know how to bring a fella down. There *are* places for us. Lots of them. More since the war."

"You mean the ones where people get arrested?"

"Come on, Al, lighten up."

"I'm sorry. I'm not used to being …" I whispered, "…gay. It's new to me and a little scary. I have a career I care about, and someone could come along and—"

"Tell me about that. Your career. What do you do?"

"You're right. This place *is* nice. Can you get me a drink first?"

Marty signaled the waiter or waitress—I didn't know which was the right word—but it was another girl in a tuxedo. Everyone waiting on tables were girls in tuxedos. "What can I get ya, doll?" our waiter said, directly to me.

"You want dinner?" Marty asked.

"No. A Coca-Cola."

"Not something stronger?"

"I have to get back to work."

"One coke," Marty said to our waitress, who was smiling at me. "I'll need a refresher on this. A very dry martini, hold the olive."

She took Marty's glass as she gave me a wink and left our table.

"You certainly made an impression on her."

"How did she know I was like her? I'm sitting with you. You could be my boyfriend; so how'd she know?"

"I don't know. What difference does it make? Tell me about your career."

A woman in a tuxedo sang on stage, her deep-black hair slicked back off her forehead. She sang into the mic like she was making love to it. It was Vic Damone's hit, "You're Breaking My Heart." A small jazzband composed of female and male impersonators backed her up.

Marty waved a hand in front of my eyes. "Hello? Oh. Andy. Yeah. She's a beauty. She sings here two or three times a month when she's in town. She's one of the stars of the place. Really brings in the ladies."

"Andy," I mumbled. "I knew I'd seen her before."

Andy took a few steps toward the edge of the stage, smiling and winking at the ladies in the audience. I stamped down the quick surge of hormones that shot through my body. Juliana's Christmas party. I had never met anyone like Andy before that party. A girl who *really* looked like a man. Shirl told me that Andy was a he-she.

"Have I lost you?" Marty asked.

"I used to know her. It was a long time ago. I was thinking if she was a real man, I could get her a real career."

"She *has* a real career. She makes a fortune in tips here."

"Really? From straights?"

"They love her. But what do *you* do?"

"Look, Marty, I—do something I love. For a while it looked like I was never going to find that something, but … I don't want to lose it."

"And I don't want to lose my shot at being a matinee idol, either. Come on, Al, you know me. I'd never tell."

I took a deep breath. "Okay … I manage Max Harlington's The Haven, and I'm also a talent manager."

"I can look and sound like Andy!" Marty hurried to say.

"Oh, you," I laughed.

"After I get some Broadway experience, I'm planning on going to Hollywood to make my big splash," Marty said. "You have any Hollywood connections?"

"I might."

"Oh? Mysterious. You and I need to do some serious talking."

Andy left the stage to thunderous applause. A line of chorus boys impersonating chorus girls danced onto the stage in pink and purple chiffon, balancing feathered headresses. One of the girl-boys stepped forward to sing "Doin' What Comes Natur'lly," from *Annie Get Your Gun.* The audience went into hysterics.

Marty pulled a cigarette from his shirt pocket and cupped his hand around it. "Want some of this?"

"Is that what I think it is?" I whispered. "Put it away. Don't I have enough worries?"

He slid it back into his pocket. "You don't need to go all temperance on me. Everyone here does it. But not in the open. You hang out with musicians, certainly you must've—"

"Never."

"You're kidding? Why?"

"When I was a kid, my church showed us a movie, *Reefer Madness*. Ever seen it?"

"Never heard of it."

"It's a church movie. It showed people going crazy because they were addicted to marijuana."

"You don't believe that."

"Not anymore, but my church scared the beejeebus out of me, so I can't. Sorry."

Our waiter put our drinks down and dropped a card in front of me. She winked before she left.

"Well, well," Marty said. "She's sure interested in you. What does it say?"

I picked the card up. "She wants to meet me when she gets off at 2 a.m."

"Going?"

"No."

"Why not? You have a special 'friend'?"

"Sort of. I guess."

"I can't believe my luck."

"*Your* luck?"

"Meeting you that day at the sit-down strike. Do you know Mabel Mercer?"

"Somewhat. To say hello. We're not buddies."

"I love her. When she sings I want to lay down at her feet. Introduce me."

"No."

"I thought we were friends."

"Yes, and since we're friends, I'm hoping you understand that I can't introduce Mabel to every hopeful—"

"You call her Mabel?" He went limp and stretched the upper part of his body onto the table. "Now, I'm in love with you." He popped back up. "I'm not *every* hopeful, but I'm not going to take that personally because I'm going to change your mind."

A woman sitting at a table near the stage screamed. "She's a man! She's a man!" She jumped up, stomping her feet as if trying to avoid a rat. "That woman is a man! Get me out of there, Herbert! Get me out of here."

"Yes, dear." The two squeezed past tables and rushed by the bar.

"You didn't tell me it was *that* kind of place," the woman squawked.

"I thought you might enjoy something a little different." Herbert hunched his head down into his shoulders, trying to become invisible.

They slipped out the door, and the audience and performers laughed before going on with the show.

"I've heard that happens at least once a month," Marty said. "Look! Over there. That cute guy by the door. I wonder if he's a friend of Dorothy."

"Who's Dorothy?"

"I'll explain later. Yes! He's headed toward the bar. He's sitting … at the end. I think … I'm not sure."

"Do you want to go and ask?"

"No. I'm with you. I'll go over there later. Tell me more. You run The Haven *and* you manage talent. Who?"

"Right now, Juliana and a newcomer, Lili Donovan."

"You manage Juliana?! Oh, gosh. I saw her at The Onyx. She is one powerful singer."

"Yes she is. She's opening at the Copa next month. Her big moment and mine. I hope."

"I can't ask you to meet her. Can I?"

"Why don't you get a date. A *girl*. I'll reserve you a couple of complimentary tickets."

He grabbed my hand and kissed it.

The line of chorus girls had been replaced with a solo female impersonator who slinked onto the stage looking like Mae West. She sang "A Guy What Takes His Time" in a white fur wrapped around her neck, big boobs pressed against a shiny top. At times she looked like she was about to have a girlie orgasm right on stage.

The door opened and a horde of tourists with cameras and large satchels poured in. This place was known for dropping off four or five bus loads of tourists every night. The tuxedoed girls scurried about seating them.

"So where's your other half?" I asked.

"My 'other half'? What's that sposed to mean?"

"Did I say something wrong? How's Moshe?"

"Okay. He moved back with his parents. Promised them to stop sounding like Moses on Mt. Sinai condemning the Israelites to forty years in the wilderness."

"Actually, it wasn't Moses who did that; it was God."

"I forgot you're some kind of Torah scholar."

"Don't you miss him?"

"It's what's best for him. To be with his parents."

"And you don't mind not having your lover with you?"

"My lover? Good God, where did you get a ridiculous idea like that? Moshe's not gay."

"He's not?"

"Jeeze, no. For a guy with all that religion in his head to be gay, well, that would just about kill him."

"That's what I thought was happening."

"No. We had a thing in a fox hole, but lots of guys did that. We were scared and needed to count on each other. Lots of straights did it, too. That's not common knowledge, but, you know ... It didn't mean anything. Well, it *did*. But not what the shrinks would think. No, it's the war and thoughts of the holocaust and trying to be a good Jew that's got him down. He dwells on the hate. Bastard Nazis. You know, they didn't only wipe out whole populations of our people. That's horrible enough, but even people who didn't have any relatives involved—they took away any sense of safety in the world. Trust.

"Before it all happened, there were lots of jerks who hated us just for being Jewish, but you learned to handle that. But this—how do you learn to handle something like this? There's no book to read. The Torah or the Talmud won't give any answers. So how do we continue to live in this world? How do we go to our jobs, to our schools, to the theater, out to dinner with friends, laugh, knowing that there is this horrible force in the world that can tear us apart bit by bit? How do we live knowing that?"

"That's pretty much how I feel about being gay in the world," I said.

"I know what you mean."

"It terrifies me, Marty. I can't be like Max and Shirl, and tell the world to go to hell. I've never fit in anywhere, but lately, as manager of The Haven and as the one running Juliana's career, I belonged somewhere and I belonged to something. Juliana's voice is special, so bringing her to the public means I'm doing something that matters. Another Juliana won't come around for a long time. But now? I know that one wrong person finding out about me could end everything. So, Marty, how *do* you do it? Continue to live in the world, go to school, rehearsals, dream of the future while you know there's this horrible force out there that wants to destroy you? How do you do it, Marty?"

"You just do it. You do it because you have to. There isn't any other way. That's the only answer I've come up with. Somehow, you have to keep doing it. You have to become better than you ever thought you could be. You have to *insist* on finding the joy in this life, and not be consumed by the hatred. Because if you're consumed, if you do miss out on the joy that exists in this world, they win. They've suceeded in destroying you. Oh, God, look who walked in. Adonis in a Brooks Brothers suit."

"What about the cute guy at the end of the bar?"

"Who?" He ran toward the door.

I turned in my seat, watching him go. When I swiveled back around, I found Andy, her seat back facing me, her legs thrown to either side of the chair as if he were straddling a horse. She lit a Camel. "I have another set to do," he said. "Wait for me. I'll walk you home."

Her eyes shaded by dark brows, the hair equally dark, slicked back from her forehead. She was beautiful, no, handsome, no … I couldn't open my mouth to answer. What did you say to this kind of—of person?

"You're a little bit of a thing." Andy smiled, puffing on her cigarette. "You shouldn't be walking those dark streets alone. Juliana'd never forgive me if I didn't take care of you."

"I'm not a thing, and I walk 'those dark streets alone' all the time."

"A modern woman." He touched his index finger to the back of my hand. A surge of heat shot through the center of my body, and she smiled like she knew.

She slid from her chair, and with a steady, confident gait headed toward the stage. The audience cheered. He dropped his cigarette on the floor and stomped on it. A girl in an aisle seat scurried to pick it up. Andy mounted the stage and sat on a stool, adjusting his bow tie, nodding at the orchestra of men dressed as women and women dressed as men, and began to sing "Time After Time." Her gaze passed from one eager-faced girl to the next. One time, I thought she winked at me. It was hard not to listen to her. I took a deep breath and left.

Chapter 36

ABOUT A WEEK before Juliana's opening at the Copa, I snuck into a rehearsal that was in progress. Since Stan had barred Richard for being annoying, rehersals consisted of Stan, Johnny, Juliana, Becky, the costume mistress' intern, Jake, the stage manager, and the two male dancers, Spatz and Wallace.

When I took my seat in the back, Juliana was singing "They Can't Take That Away from Me." All the extra hours she'd spent working on ballads with her coach certainly were paying off. She wore a blue chiffon dress with a flare skirt and stepped around the stage on stilettos with complete grace and poise. The subtle sway of her hips made her maddeningly sexy. I figured what she was doing to me was a pretty good gauge of what she'd do to the men in the audience at the Copa.

"Okay," Stan said with one loud clap of his hands as Juliana finished. "All men out. Except me, of course. Take an early lunch. Juliana you'll have lunch with me later in the afternoon. All right?"

"I will cherish every moment I am alone with you, Stan." She winked.

"Yes, well …" Stan was completely embarrassed. He had no sense of humor, and Juliana loved taking advantage of that. "I want to rehearse the on-stage costume change now."

"What?" I jumped out my seat.

"Did you have something to say?" Stan asked.

I took a deep breath, regaining my composure. "Can I speak to you a minute?"

"One minute; that's all." He turned to Johnny and Juliana. "Rehearse the finale, you two. What is it, Al?"

"We never talked about an *on-stage* costume change."

"You told me to enhance your idea. That's what I'm doing."

"It's supposed to be subtle. She's not supposed to be naked up there."

"There'll be a screen and a girl in the back to help her. It's a quick costume change. You saw the plans."

"I didn't know the changes were to happen on stage. I thought you meant an intermission."

"The intermission is *after* her act. She's not big enough to have two slots. "

"Yet."

"We'll see, won't we? The intermission is *after* Juliana because the audience is waiting for the great comedian, Joey Adams. He is the true star of the evening. Let's have a little humility. I assure you, all the costume changes will be tastefully done. Can we proceed now?"

"I guess."

"All right," he announced. "While we're working on the timing, I want the men out. Jake, put that screen up before you go."

"Sure thing," Jake called.

"This won't take long. Therefore, gentlemen, return in *one* hour."

"Who plays while she's changing?" Johnny asked.

"At this moment, we're only rehearsing the actions. This afternoon we'll do it with music."

"But still …" Johnny protested.

He wants to peep at her.

"I don't mind," Juliana said, "if the men stay."

Sure, prance around in your birthday suit for the men.

"No," Stan said. "The men have to go."

"This is ridiculous," Johnny said, heading toward the door, one hand pulling out a pack of Chesterfields from his pants' pocket. "We're show people." He lit the cigarette. "We don't care about this stuff." He turned back to Juliana. "Hey, Juliana! You wouldn't mind me seeing you in the all-together, would ya, dear?"

Juliana called back, "I would relish it, sweetie." She cocked a hip at him.

Johnny wolf-whistled as he spun around and smashed his beat-up old newsboy cap down on his head. He whistled all the way out the door, and I knew he was seeing dirty pictures of her in his mind. How could she encourage a thing like that?

"Close the door behind you," Stan called out. "And don't be late, you."

"Becky," Stan called to the wardrobe mistress' intern. "On stage."

Becky was a young girl with blond waves hanging down to her shoulders like Lizbeth Scott. Only, she *wasn't* like Lizbeth Scott, who was in lots of noir films. No, Becky had plopped a dang blue bow on top of her head. Lizbeth Scott would *never* do that. I bet Becky thought that bow made her look real cute. She couldn't have been more than nineteen. She wore a polka dot dress with a scoop neckline and a button-down front. Yeah, I bet that Becky thought she looked so *sweet*. And that name! Becky. Straight out of Tom Sawyer.

"Becky, make sure you have the dress for the second half of the act behind the screen," Stan directed. "You'll have to make yourself tiny, so nobody sees you. You're going to be back there until the curtain goes down. It won't be comfortable."

"I can make myself as little as you want, Mr. Devenbach. This is show business; we all have to sacrifice."

Oh, brother. So sweet. Juliana was a sucker for 'sweet.'

"Don't worry about Becky," Juliana said, tapping Becky's shoulder. "She's a real trouper. Aren't you, honey?"

"With you helping me," Becky said.

Batting her eyelashes at Juliana. Jeepers!

"When Juliana finishes the song 'Girls Were Made to Take Care of Boys,' she'll go behind the screen," Stan explained. "Go ahead, Juliana."

Juliana sidled behind the screen.

"Here, she's going to deliver some patter to the audience."

"Patter, patter," Juliana said.

"As soon as Juliana starts talking to the audience, you start undoing her zipper."

I moved closer to the stage, my arms across my chest. She was just going to stand there and let that kid unzip her?

"Okay, go ahead," Stan said.

Juliana waved her hands and made up nonsense words, pretending to talk to the audience while Becky tugged at the zipper; it wouldn't budge. Juliana laughed. "Oh, Stan, this isn't going so smoothly up here."

"Well, what's wrong with it?"

"I don't know, Mr. Devenbach," Becky said, "but I can't budge it."

"Don't rip it. That's an expensive dress. There must be some way to get it down."

"You want to come up here and help, Stan?" Juliana said.

"No. No," Stan's voice was filled with anxiety. "Uh, Al, why don't you, uh …"

"Yes, Al, why don't you, uh …" Juliana grinned at me.

The room suddenly got warmer as I marched up on stage.

"You see, Miss Huffman, it won't—"

"Oh, *please*. Call me Al. I'm not *that* old, you know."

"Two years older than I was when I first met *you*," Juliana said, her eyes taunting my suspicions.

Juliana lifted her left arm so I could get at the zipper; it came down easily. "There. That's how you do it."

"I'm sorry, Mr. Devenbach. Miss, I mean, Al, did it. I don't know why it wouldn't work for me."

"Don't worry about it, Becky," Juliana said. "Al has more experience with zippers than you do. Ask Al to show you." Juliana pulled the zipper back up.

Juliana was doing this on purpose. The smell of her perfume, her luscious body right there, and I had to show this twerp how to undress her.

"You *must* know how to do this," I said to Becky. "You wear dresses, too."

"It's not the same as doing it to someone else."

"No, it's not, Al," Juliana agreed. "*You* know that."

"Hold it here," I said, "so it doesn't buckle when you pull it down with the other hand." I pulled the zipper down, and for a second Juliana and I locked eyes. I looked away first.

"Let me try," Becky said. I pulled the zipper up, and Becky slid it back down.

"Okay, Mr. Devenbach," Becky announced. "It's down."

"At last," Stan sighed. "Take it off her. Al, get out of there."

"You have to do this in one movement," Stan told Becky. "Quick. Pull the dress down to her feet, Juliana steps out, keeping up the patter. Al, you're writing that for her, aren't you?

"You think I can't write my own patter?" Juliana complained.

"You have to have the second dress ready for Juliana to step into," Stan continued. "Then pull it up her body so Juliana can put her arms in."

I started pacing as Becky pulled Juliana's dress down. I could't believe she was allowing this. I was sure she was sleeping with that kid.

A crash. The screen was on top of Juliana and Juliana on top of Becky, both laughing so hard they couldn't get up.

Stan held a hand over his eyes. "Al, could you please … up there."

"Stan," I said, heading toward the stage, "You can't allow Juliana to go up on stage nearly naked with just a screen."

"Nearly naked?" Juliana crawled out from under the screen and stood up. "What's this?" She held her arms out to show she was wearing a full-length beige slip, slit on the side, mid-calf length.

"Oh, please, no," Stan said, looking at her only a moment.

"Stan, can I speak with my *assistant* manager?"

"Yes, of course, but put something on."

Juliana grabbed her robe lying on a chair at the back of the stage and signaled me to follow her to the alcove. "What's the matter with you?"

Under the slip, I could see the outline of her one-piece, long line, bra-girdle combination with nylons attached. "As your manager," I said, trying to concentrate. "I don't think you should do this."

"You're not my manager. Richard is," she said, slipping into her robe.

"And you think *he'd* approve of this?"

"Once we get the kinks out it'll work fine, but *you're* acting like *you're* my husband, and I already have one of those. I definitely don't need another, so stop it."

"Are you sleeping with that girl?" I whispered.

"What girl?"

"Becky, the oh-so-*sweet*. Geesh, that name."

"She's a kid. I don't sleep with kids."

"*I* was a kid."

"And so was I—practically—at the time. I can't do this with you now. We have a rehearsal. The pressure of this opening is softening your brain. Be—have. We're ready, Stan."

I set up the screen again, but I was mad. I sat in the back, mumbling, "How dare she speak to me like I'm a child. If it hadn't been for me ..."

"Let's slow this down," Stan said. "If we practice each movement separately before putting it together, it'll work."

It finally came together, and Juliana was dressed in the second costume; it was a more glamorous black dress with a slit up to the top of her right thigh.

As we finished, the men started drifting back in from lunch. All except Johnny.

"Where's Johnny?" Stan asked.

"Haven't seen him," Wallace said. "We all went for a bite at Child's, but Johnny didn't come with us."

"I can't afford to lose time waiting for that prima donna. We'll work without him. Dancers on stage."

"We're going to dance without music?" Spatz complained.

"What choice do we have with our piano player AWOL? Again. Juliana can go over the more complicated moves."

Juliana was about to slip into Spatz's arms when Johnny walked in, and we got back to a proper rehearsal.

Chapter 37

May 1950

THE DAY FOR Juliana's opening arrived, and I hopped out of bed in time to hear the milkman outside my door, which meant I'd gotten about two hours' sleep. This was Juliana's big moment, the moment that could bring her everything she ever wanted, the moment I'd been dreaming about for years.

I imagined Juliana throughout the day, driving Richard nuts with her opening night anxiety. But oh, how I wished it was me she was driving nuts.

I had given Richard the task of keeping her away from newspapers. I thought it was a good way to keep him busy, and if he succeeded it would work in our favor. All the papers were filled with stories about how sex perverts and moral degenerates were weakening the country.

The Veterans of Foreign Wars blamed "homosexuals" for China becoming a communist country. It seemed there wasn't anything we couldn't be blamed for, but I sure didn't want Juliana worrying about that stuff now that her big day was here. I planned on getting to the Copa early to get rid of any newspapers I found lying around, and to sit with her in her dressing room.

I spent all morning on the phone, running The Haven, setting up acts for the next few months, and making sure Juliana got extra time in the morning with the orchestra.

I had a two o'clock appointment at the hairdresser, and then I was going to dash home to put on my gown and get over to the Copa. I picked up the phone to order flowers for Juliana from Richard and me, when Virginia poked her head into the office. "Hello there."

I'd been avoiding her for a month and a half, ever since our "incident" in the lady's room, but now she was standing at my door with a big smile. She didn't seem to feel the same embarrassment at seeing me that I experienced at seeing her. "Hi, I'd love to talk, but I have to make a call and then I'm dashing off to the hairdresser. Will I see you there tonight?"

"No. Not after what that woman did to Max. I am certainly not going to sit in that audience and—"

"You *know* what happened between Juliana and Max?" I lowered the phone back into its cradle.

"Of course. I was there."

"You were *there*? Then something specific happened? Not just that Juliana chose Richard over Max to manage her?"

"Oh, that's only something Max says to cover up. There's more to it than that."

"Really? Come in. Sit down. Tell me."

"I really shouldn't, but since it's you." She closed the door and sidled into the chair next to my desk. She seemed to be fluttering her eyelashes at me, but maybe that was the light hurting her eyes. "Max was in love with her," Virginia said.

"Max likes boys."

"True. But in her case, he made an exception. I've spent years trying to figure out how she became his exception. I think I know now. In her own way, she *is* a boy."

"Oh, come now. Have you seen how she looks or watched the way she moves?"

"I've done nothing but. Yes, she's very feminine, but so are the boys Max chooses. Look at Scott; the delicate way he uses his hands. When Juliana and Max worked together, they would get each other ... how do I say this politely?"

"I think you and I have gone way beyond 'polite.'"

She giggled. "Yes, we have, haven't we? Well, the two of them would get each other—excited. I'd be sitting right there watching the rehearsal. I went to all the rehearsals back then. I took notes for Max. He counted on me. But when the two of them got going, it was like I'd turned into a statue. They didn't care how they acted in front of me. Touching each other. It was disgusting. As if I weren't even there. I think she may have even ..." She leaned toward me, her hand pressed to one side of her mouth as if reporting on a communist plot. "Well, this she didn't do in front of me, thank heaven, but I think she did that thing with her mouth that low-class women do to men. The woman hasn't a moral fiber in her whole immoral body. I'm sorry. I know you think a lot of her, so I don't mean to criticize, but—"

"What happened?" I squinted at my watch as my time ticked away. Nine years waiting for this story was long enough.

"They couldn't."

"They couldn't what?"

"They couldn't finish. They would get excited, but there was never any culmination. Because of what they both are, I suppose."

"How do you know this?"

"I told you. I was there."

"Where?"

"There. Where they were."

"What?"

"I arrived at Max's apartment in the early afternoon. It was Sunday. Back then, I would make brunch for Max and his new boyfriend. Every Sunday he had a new one. It was fun, the three of us sitting in the kitchen drinking orange juice, eating eggs almandine, Max's favorite. It takes quite awhile to make, you know. Lots of ingredients, chopping and stirring, but I didn't mind."

"Maybe you should have."

"Oh, don't be silly. Well, this one day, I was in the kitchen pouring when I heard shouting. I naturally thought he was with one of his boys, but *she* was in there with him. In his bedroom," she whispered. "The little floozy. Oh, I'm sorry, Al."

"It's okay. What happened?"

"They were shouting at each other. I don't know if I can tell you what they said. I don't use that kind of language. But they were mad at each other because—each one wasn't doing what the other wanted." She leaned close and whispered, "Sexually."

"And?"

"How could she act that way? Wanting him to do things *her* way? I would never do that. Who cares about the sex? She had *him*. He loved her, and she threw it away for sex? There's something wrong with that woman. She wasn't even married to Richard at the time. She could've had Max, but instead she stomped into the living room with her robe hanging open; she was completely naked underneath.

"She grabbed her shoe from under the couch and threw it at Max. Luckily, he ducked in time. He grabbed her into his arms and threw her onto the couch. He was naked too, but I didn't mind that. He held her arms above her head, and she shouted at him, 'Do it! For Christsakes, do *something*.' He stared at her a minute and then said, 'I can't,' and marched back into his room and slammed the door. He didn't come out for a very long time. I convinced him to give me her clothes so she could leave. I guess that's the story."

"And you gave her breakfast, didn't you?"

"It would've gone to waste, but we didn't talk, and she left right after."

"They completely stopped working together because they couldn't have sex with each other? That's nuts."

"No. They kept working together, but they'd get so excited around each other and there would never be a culmination, so they'd get angry and spend the rest of rehearsal yelling. It completely blocked their creativity, so finally they gave up."

"But Max blames Richard for stealing Juliana away from him."

"Richard came along with an offer at the right time. He promised to back Juliana's career, to be her manager, to make things happen for her, but only if she married him. Without that, he wasn't going to do anything for her. I think she also wanted to throw it in Max's face that she was getting married. I was glad she was getting out of his life. I can't understand what a smart girl like you sees in her. A man I understand. Those breasts, but you …"

"Don't knock the power of breasts. I'm rather fond of them myself."

"Do you like mine?"

"Uh … sure, yeah, gosh, look at the time. My appointment! I'm going to be late." I gathered up my coat in my arms. "Why would you ask me a question like that?"

"Because I want to do it with you again," Virginia said, blocking my way.

The phone rang. "Hold that thought. Or better still, *don't* hold that thought." I picked up the phone. "What? Oh, damn. No. Stay there. I'll be right over."

"What is it? Can I help you?"

"That's sweet of you, Virginia, but no. Virginia, I want you to take this time to reflect upon the fact that you're straight. Okay? Gotta go."

She grabbed my arm. "Are you making light of my feelings?"

"No. I didn't mean to do that. I'm rushed."

"You know, I gave a very special part of myself to you that night."

"On the lady's room floor? Look, we'll talk. Later. After the opening."

I charged out the door, putting on my coat as I went. I ran all the way to the studio and tapped my foot waiting for the damn elevator. I burst into the studio. Richard stood over Johnny, who was curled up on the floor.

"I can't do a thing with him," Richard said, hurrying over to me, his shirt all wrinkled, no jacket, his hair flying. "Look at him. He's completely snockered."

I threw my coat on a chair and leaned over Johnny. "Hey, Johnny? Johnny."

Johnny looked up at me like he wasn't quite sure who I was. "Al? Hi. I'm not so bad," he slurred. "I can play blin—blind, uh, that thing that goes over your eyes." He pushed himself up, but his legs folded under him, and he fell backward the way only a drunk can.

"Okay, think, think," I told myself, pacing. "Where's Stan?" I asked Richard.

"Stan? Stan?" Richard looked at me vaguely.

"Stan, you idiot. The director."

"He quit."

"What?

"He walked out last night. Johnny's been drinking off and on for the last couple of days. Stan said he couldn't put his name on this disaster. He has a reputation."

"And a contract!" With an escape clause, I remembered. Since Juliana was not well-known, giving him that was the only way I could get him. "Why didn't you call me?"

"Well, you've done so much. I thought I could handle this myself. I mean, we're finished rehearsing. I never expected Johnny to do this and for Stan to—"

"*Always* expect the unexpected." I wasn't sure where that came from, but I suspected it was Max from one of our many discussions. "You should've told me the very first time Johnny got drunk. Stan should've gotten a replacement."

"But it's Johnny's music, and Juliana feels safe with him. They've known each other for—"

"A phone. I need a phone."

"Over here." He directed me to a small office near the studio. "Work on sobering him up, in case we're stuck. Send out for buckets of coffee. Juliana. Does she know about this yet?"

"No. She's home resting."

"Good. Make sure she doesn't hear a word about it until it's fixed. Home? By herself? That's not good."

"She's not alone. Her friend Margaritte is with her."

"Margaritte?"

"You met her at our New Year's Party in '44. She and Juliana sang opera together as children in Italy. They're close friends."

I knew exactly who Margaritte was, and I could not have that thought right then. "Go tend to Johnny." I dialed quickly. "Is Max there? Oh, no. When will he be in? No, he can't call me back. I don't know where I'll be. Tell him I'm looking for him."

I ran out to Richard, who was yelling at Johnny. "Richard, *you* have contacts. Would any of them know a good accompanist, or musical director, or both?"

"My contacts are in banking, publishing, and public relations, but I have met a few Broadway people at some ritzy parties."

"Call them. We're going to turn this around. I have to check my wheeldex."

I ran from the studio into the street and grabbed a cab to the Mt. Olympus. I dashed inside hoping Max had shown up, but he still wasn't there. I settled myself behind Max's desk and started calling from his wheeldex, since it had more names than mine. I rescheduled my appointment for my hair for 4 p.m.—not an easy thing to do at Pierre's. It required serious groveling.

I called one professional accompanist after another using Max's name. Everyone on Max's A-list was already committed to gigs around the city and the country. They told me to keep them in mind for another time; they'd love to work with Juliana. I was building my connections in the business, which would be terrific for the future, but not so hot for my immediate need. I couldn't go into Max's B-list. Juliana would have a fit.

This was the biggest day of our lives, and it was about to go splat in our faces. No! I would not let that happen. Juliana was going to be a star. Tonight! I'll see to that. Where the hell was Max?

Scott walked in. "Want to get a cup of coffee?" he asked.

"Are you certifiable?" I screamed at him. Scott backed up. "Oh, Scott, I'm sorry. Things are such a mess. Do you know where Max is?"

"No. We haven't spoken for a few days."

"Coffee! That's it!"

"You *do* want coffee?"

"No. That boy in the lounge. He was one-helluva piano player. Bring him here."

"Why would he come here with me?"

"Because you're gonna offer him a job at the Copa, and if you have to, you're gonna flirt with him."

"I can't flirt. The Bible—"

"Says *nothing* about flirting. I know. I read it twice. Now, hurry up. He needs to learn the music for tonight."

"Uh." Scott stood there, looking down at the rug.

"Scott? This is an emergency."

"I—had a piano scholarship to Julliard," he whispered. "I only went for a year, but I could coach the boy if you like."

"No. You could play it tonight."

"It's not proper music for a Christian man to play, but since you're in a jam and you're a friend, I could help the boy learn the music in time."

"I'm not going to argue religion with you now. Go get him, and bring him to the studio."

Scott dashed out as I rushed back into Max's office to answer the phone. "No, Richard," I said into Max's phone. "Not yet. Tell her in an hour when you send for the car. Scott's bringing over a piano player to learn the music. They should be there in a half-hour. You mustn't get hysterical around her. This kid can do it, and she needs to know you believe that. I'm heading to the hairdresser, then I'll be right over. I can trust you with this, can't I? Remember. Calm. Be very calm when you talk to her."

Virginia had moved from The Haven to the Mt. Olympus and seemed to be following me around. Even *she* couldn't locate Max. I bumped into her as I dashed out of Max's office, heading toward the kitchen. "Oh, sorry," I said, a little annoyed.

"You look so busy," Virginia returned. "And I'm doing nothing. Can't I help you with *something*?"

"Could you sit out here somewhere?" I pulled out a chair from under one of the tables. "Here. I don't want to trip on you."

Sitting, Virginia whined, "I feel useless."

When I turned around, I saw Bertha leaning against the wall, staring at me. "Bertha, what are *you* doing here? Aren't you supposed to be at The Haven?"

She hopped to attention as soon I spoke. "Not for a few hours. I thought you might need me here."

"Yes." I hurried toward her with my key, "Could you …?" Then, a new thought. A quick about-face. "Virginia, do you really want to help me?"

"Yes. Please."

"I can help you," Bertha begged. "Let me. *Please.*"

"Virginia, here is the key to my apartment, and take the key to my office. Could you pick up my gown?"

"Let me do it," Bertha wailed. "I'm sure Miss Sales is busy." She grabbed for the keys, and they fell from my hand onto the rug. "Oh. I'm sorry, Al. I didn't mean ..."

I bent and picked up the keys. "No harm done." I handed them to Virginia. "It's the navy-blue one with the sequins; it's hanging on the back of the closet door. Under the bed are my shoes and purse. Bring them to Carnegie Rehearsal Studios, Room Number 502."

Virginia cupped the keys in her hands as if I'd handed her a precious amulet. "Thank you. Thank you so much for this." She sashayed out the door, her rear end bobbing back and forth like she was wagging her tail. I think that was for me. And, well, Virginia *did* have a nice rear.

"I would've done it for you," Bertha said, on the verge of tears. "I wanted to help you."

"Another time."

* * *

"How's it going?" I asked Richard as I burst into the studio.

"I'm going to sue that director," he said. "I know just the lawyers who can—"

"The only way we could get Stan was if we added the escape clause he took. Look at the bottom of his contract."

"Did you get a new director? Julie won't feel safe if there's no musical director. Who's directing?"

"Me."

"You? But ..."

I walked over to Scott, who stood behind the young man seated at the piano. "Can he handle it?"

"This music's easy. Right, Peter?"

"Sure."

"Peter, do you have a tux?" I asked.

"Nope," he said, starting to play. "Where would I get one of those? Hey, can I invite my mother to this?"

"Your mother? Of course. I'll put a complimentary ticket for her at the entrance under your name."

"Gee, that's swell." He smiled a big smile and cut into the music.

"Richard, see to it Peter gets a rented tux at Harold's, and put a comp ticket for his mother at the front."

"I'll get right on it."

"Did you send the car around for Juliana?"

"Yes, she should be here any minute."

"How did she sound when you told her?"

"Well …"

"That's what I was afraid of."

* * *

Juliana paced, breathing too fast, alternating between pressing her two fists into the wall and wrapping her arms around her chest. "You know how old that kid is?" Juliana asked.

"No," I said, "have some tea. It'll be good for your nerves."

"Seventeen. A child."

"Oh, God, I hope we're not breaking any laws."

"What?" Juliana squawked.

"We're not! Sit down. Here. Tea. Good for your throat."

"If you think my voice is going to work tonight you must believe in Santa Claus, too. I swear, I'm going to get Johnny for this."

I put an arm around her shoulders and guided her to a chair. "Sit. You'll be magnificent tonight. That kid is good, and you know it."

"If he's so good, why is Scott hovering over him?"

"Doing a little precautionary tutoring. Nothing to worry about."

"If he can tutor the kid, why doesn't he play it himself? I'd rather have a grown-up playing for me."

"It's a religion thing, nothing for you to worry about."

I guided the cup of tea to Juliana's lips. "Hmm, that's good," she said. "What is it?"

"Peppermint with a little honey. The best thing for your throat. You'll have a little more after you've done the yoga breathing you learned. Come on. Deep breath." I breathed in and out, and she breathed with me. "That's right." Her breath took on a rhythmic peacefulness, and a calmness came over me too.

Then Richard burst through the door. "Julie."

I dashed to the door and pushed him back out. "Shh! Not now!"

"But she got all these flowers," Richard whispered, pushing back on the door.

"Later," I whispered, managing to get the door closed and locked.

"What did he want?" Juliana asked, standing to tie her robe tighter around her waist. She wore the Japanese kimono, white with wisps of pink and yellow tulips, languid on green stalks. I loved her in that.

"To wish you well. Come, sit down."

"I can't breathe like that; it makes me nervous. How did I ever let you talk me into this? Haven't you been reading what the papers are saying?"

"What papers?" I reorganized her make-up on the vanity.

"*The New York Times, The Post, the Herald, The Journal,* do you need me to go on? I know you and Richard have been trying to keep me from reading a damn newspaper, and it's been damn annoying finding my *Times* lining the cage of the canary Richard bought for the express purpose of having it do its business on *my* newspaper. This morning, he completely terrorized the paperboy by appearing at the door in a rubber Dracula mask. But the paperboy and I go way back. He saw to it I got my paper. I know what they're saying, Al."

"Nobody would ever suspect you. This is New York, not Washington, or boarding school."

There was a knock. Juliana stared at the door. "Send whomever away. I can't talk to anyone. I may never talk to anyone again."

I went to the door. It was Shirl. I whispered, "She doesn't want to see anyone right now, but Shirl, she's talking crazy, and—"

"Al, I can hear you," Juliana said. "Let Shirl in."

"Shirl, you're wearing a skirt!" I exclaimed as she stepped inside.

"I do own one, you know. Only one. It's for Juliana's big opening at the Copa. I wouldn't miss this."

Shirl wore a long, heavy, flannel navy-blue skirt with a mannish white blouse open at the collar and a dark suit jacket. She carried a large black satchel. "Sweetheart, how are you?" She hurried over to Juliana.

"Shoot me. Please."

"Stop talking silly, and sit down. Everything's going to be fine." Shirl put her thick hands on Juliana's shoulders and guided her across the room, sitting her down on the divan across from the make-up table. "Now, rest. Mercy's downstairs waiting for me. We didn't want too many people in here. We're going up to the bar to get a drink before the show. Juliana, you're going to be stupendous. *I* know it, and *you* know it. It's going to happen! We've waited a long time for this. We reserved a table down front, so if you start feeling like you're going to falter, remember, Mercy and I are right there cheering you on, and we love you." She kissed her cheek, then hurried back to the door, signaling me to follow.

I stepped into the hallway with her and closed the door. A stagehand ran by yelling, "Where are the roses? Somebody get me the damn roses."

"Ice box in the back," I yelled.

"Look, hon," Shirl said, "she looks stiffer than she usually does before a show."

"I don't understand what happened," I said. "She used to be so calm before her shows, and then that one article and she's a wreck."

"It's not the article. She always gets like this. You never saw it before because you weren't close to it. She can sing for her friends, the hangers-on who 'oo and ah' about how wonderful she is, but she rarely tests herself like you're making her do. She can be great, truly great. I've seen it. But that mother of hers …"

"Her mother? What does she have to do with it?"

"Julie is always trying to please her and coming up short. Pleasing a dead mother is difficult, and those articles, on top of everything, don't help. Her mother *and* her religion don't approve of who she is. *You* help her to have faith in herself, and she'll give you a great performance. But you've got to get her to relax, or she could blow the chance of lifetime. And *that* could be the end of her."

She reached into her satchel and pulled out a cardboard box. "I ordered this for Mercy from the Sears and Roebuck Catalogue. Mercy can get tense some days. It came in the mail today. I'll send for another one for Mercy tomorrow. Right now, Juliana needs it more. Consider it an opening-night gift."

I took the box into my two hands. The cover said "Sears Massager." There was a drawing of a woman with some kind of machine on her hand, massaging her head. "What is it?"

"The instructions are inside. Tell Juliana to put it on her shoulders. No, better—*you* put it on her shoulders, and her back. She holds her breath when she gets like this, and she won't be able to sing properly if she does that. Hurry. You don't have much time."

Shirl scurried away. I slipped back into Juliana's dressing room with the box. She sat frozen on the divan.

"Were you and Shirl out there talking about how I'm going to fall on my face tonight?"

"Of course not. Shirl gave you something to help."

I opened the box and took out this metal thing with an electric cord. "What is it?" Juliana asked.

"It's a massager. It's supposed to relax you."

"Well, if it can do that, it'll be like a miracle elixir."

I plugged it into the outlet. "Lay face down on the divan."

"Are you going to saw me in half with that thing?"

"Lay down. I'm going to relax the muscles in your shoulders and back." I turned the pages of the instruction manual, skimming as she lay down. "Untie your robe, so I can get to your back. Now, it says I put my hand through these straps."

Juliana undid her robe-tie as I held the massager above her, reading. I sat on the divan beside her and pulled her robe down to a little below her waist with my free hand. All she wore was a pair of lacy-white underpants. Such a lovely back. I ran my hand down her back to her waist, and then I moved past the waistband of her underpants. "Uh, Al, now is not the time."

I took my hand away. "Sure, I know. I was getting you ready."

"Ready for what?" She laughed.

I threw the instructions open on the floor so I could refer to them. I flipped the switch on the massager, and it hummed as it shook my hand. "This feels strange."

"As long as it works," Juliana said.

I put my vibrating fingers on Juliana's shoulders. She sighed, "Oh, yes." So, I figured it must be working.

I moved my hand from her shoulders to her back and down her back. "Uh, Al," she said.

"Huh?" I slid my hand with the massager attached down to her waist.

"Al!" she squealed and flipped over onto her back. "You won't believe what …" She pushed her underpants down to her thighs. "Al, please, more. Put it between my legs."

"What?"

"Please. Hurry. Get those vibrating fingers on my clit."

"But you said now wasn't the time."

"Funny, how time flies. Hurry." I pulled her underpants all the way off her and put my shaking hand between her legs. Her back arched, and her breathing came in wild spurts. Her fingers dug into the sides of the divan. I looked over at the door. Did I lock that? Her breathing sped up. I couldn't check right then, but what if …? She was gonna climax. What if someone heard? As her breathing went faster I looked around for something to stuff in her mouth. Her robe was stuck under her body, couldn't pull that into her mouth. The throw rug on the floor was disgusting. She was about to go off into ecstasy. What? What could I …? I put my mouth on top of hers. She threw her arms around me and crushed me into her as I took her scream into me. Then she went limp, and her arms slid off me.

I turned the new toy off.

She breathed evenly now, her forearms over her eyes. Then she laughed. I laughed with her. "Does Shirl know what that thing does?" she asked.

"I don't know."

"Do we have to give it back?"

"No, she said it was your opening-night gift."

That made her laugh more. "Some gift. I owe you a very nice surprise," she said as her laughter slowed. "It's better than the out-of-space thing."

"Impossible."

She lay there on the divan with her arms over her eyes. I pulled her robe out from under her and threw the ends over the front of her lower body.

"You better get ready, Jule."

"What if I can't sing those love songs?" she asked matter-of-factly, eyes closed. "What if I fail?"

"You won't," I said.

"How do you know?"

"I won't let you."

She smiled and sought out my hand. We held hands and stayed like that, quiet, not speaking, for long, lovely minutes.

* * *

Richard was already seated at a back table he'd reserved for us when I left Juliana in her dressing room. The place was famous for creating a South American aura with its Latin and tropical décor. Paper mache palm trees with silk coconuts decorated the room, which was packed with people finishing their dinners.

The Copa had the same capacity as the Mt. Olympus, 400 people. The Haven inched a little past that number, and also had a few smaller rooms for more intimate shows.

It was almost 8 p.m. It wouldn't be long now. When I arrived at the table, Richard stood and pulled out my chair.

"Rehearsal went well, didn't it?" he said as he pushed my chair in. "Despite everything."

"Yes. I think so."

"I want this so much for her," Richard said, choking his cloth napkin.

"I do too."

"I know you do. You've been aces. You know, Al, I love her so much it hurts. Does that sound strange?"

"No."

"Do you want to order dinner now?"

"I can't eat."

"Me, either." He lit a cigarette. "How about a drink?"

"That I *can* do."

He ordered a sidecar for me and a martini for himself.

As the house lights lowered and the stage lights came up, I thought my heart would stop. We had to sit through the dancing and singing numbers of The World Famous Copa Girls and then an up-and-coming male singer who made a big splash in L.A.

Then it happened. The lights came up and there she was, center stage. A black and white lace dress, spreading wide around her legs, her breasts formed into two luscious half-globes peeking out from a low-cut bodice.

Richard gripped my hand under the table with his fingers crossed. Before she even opened her mouth, I knew—by the way she stood; the way her eyes were taking in the audience with a slight come-hither look, this was it. She was going all the way. And from the moment she opened her mouth, and her heart, to sing "Coax Me A Little Bit," the audience was hers. Her hips moved to the sexy Latin beat while she flirted with the men in the front row. She owned that audience as much as she owned that stage, and Pete, the piano player, and the orchestra, and Richard, and me.

I watched as the men in the audience leaned toward the stage as if they wanted to reach out and touch her. A waiter delivering a tray of drinks while staring at her stumbled, and the drinks went flying. The audience laughed. They knew. Juliana said, "Easy Mario." Without missing a beat.

Next, she sang a romantic ballad Johnny wrote for her. My body tensed. Oh, God, please. Midway through I began to relax. "Thanks," I said to whoever listened to desperate prayers. I leaned over to Richard and whispered, "I'm going to get those flowers and cards into her dressing room."

Richard whispered back, "No, you sit. I'll go."

She sang, she danced, she joked; she flirted with Peter and made fun of his age. I got up to stand near the side tables to watch the audience. The change into her second costume behind the screen went smoothly. She teased the audience with quick glances of her naked calves. One guy loosened his tie and mopped his forehead with his handkerchief. His lady-friend punched him in the arm, then they both laughed. It was working. When Juliana came around the screen wearing the silky black dress that clung to her body, one leg peering out of the slit, the audience jumped out of their seats with cheers. And when she began "Put the Blame on Mame," the whole room pulsated.

She went on to sing Johnny's upbeat tempos and a few well-known tunes, but her best numbers were Johnny's slow, slinky, romantic ballads. She was the first performer to sing so many original songs. If the critics didn't tear us apart for breaking with tradition, we'd be making history.

Throughout the show, she was completely Juliana, the Juliana I'd fallen in love with the very first night I saw her, when Max brought four goofy country kids to their first nightclub.

And, of course, the audience was on their feet at the end, begging for an encore. She sang six more numbers before she left the stage.

I was so proud. I fell in love with her all over again.

When I turned to run to her dressing room, I saw Max leaning against the back wall, talking to Jules Podell, the manager of the Copa.

I walked over to them. "Hello, Jules. Max?"

"She was great," Jules said. "Tell Richard to give me a call tomorrow. We want to extend her contract. Talk to you later, Max."

Jules Podell headed toward Juliana's dressing room, where a line was forming.

"You're here," I said to Max.

"I wouldn't have missed it. You look lovely."

"I should. You have impeccable taste."

"I know. I'm sure you'd much rather be wearing a tuxedo, but you don't make a bad-looking woman."

"Where have you been? I called everywhere looking for you. This whole thing almost fell apart."

"I heard. But I knew you could handle whatever came up, and something *always* comes up on opening night. You didn't need me to lean on, so I made myself scarce."

"You mean you disappeared on *purpose*? You didn't have some horrible emergency in Wascaloosca?"

"Time to spread your wings, little one. And it looks like you did a damn good job. *You're* Juliana's manager, not Richard. Why don't you make it official with this extension? Sign the necessary papers, and be done with Richard. Let him be her husband and stay out of it. You don't need him."

"But *she* does. Are you coming to her dressing room to see her?"

"I have a date." Max looked over at Scott who stood a few feet away in his tuxedo, his overcoat in the bend of his arm. "You ready?" Max asked as Scott drew near.

I watched them put on their overcoats and slip out into the cool night air. I wondered how *that* was working.

I heard people laughing and talking as I neared Juliana's dressing room. They were overflowing the doors into the hallway. One of the couples was Marty Buchman and Ruth Goins, his date. He tapped my shoulder as I passed. "You really do this. Manage me, please manage me."

"We'll talk after graduation," I said, with no time to stop.

Flowers, telegrams, and fruit baskets arrived as delivery boys pushed through the crowds to get to her. I squeezed myself into the room past silver fox stoles and mink coats, and the smell of French perfume, too heavily applied onto huge breasts lifting out of gowns many sizes too small, and gloved hands waving programs, and fat-bellied men whose tuxedo jacket buttons were about to pop off, and young men in their Princeton haircuts. The smell of Vitalis mixing with burning cigars and Winstons, Lucky Strikes, and Galoises overpowered the delicate scents of roses and lilies that lined the dressing room.

I listened to the comments. "God, isn't she gorgeous," one young man said to his friend. "Give me five minutes alone with her, please God, I'd die a happy man."

Further down the line a young woman whispered, "How could you? And in public."

Her young man whispered back, "I couldn't help it. It went up. I didn't plan it."

"For *her*. What does that mean about us?"

I plowed through the noisy gaggle to where Juliana stood. She glowed while signing programs and chatting, Richard by her side, his arm around her. Every once in awhile they would peck at each other's lips. The pain in my stomach was in danger of overwhelming me, and I was afraid I would have to leave, but I took a few of Juliana's yoga deep breaths.

Then I remembered—*I did this.* She was signing programs because *I* made that happen. She's not quite a star yet, but ... out of my way, world! I reached into my purse and pulled out my rather tattered program from many years before, and took my place with the others who wagged programs in her face.

I waited while she chatted with these others and while photographers from magazines took pictures of her. She didn't notice me standing there. I'd become invisible. I heard her say to one reporter, "I owe it all to my husband." Richard smiled and said, "Well, it was easy with my wife's talent."

One photographer asked Juliana to kiss Richard for the camera. As she was about to turn her lips to Richard, her eye caught mine. It was only a second but I saw it. A slight trepidation, perhaps. It was hard to know what she felt in that moment, but as their lips were about to touch, I remembered, I could stop this. I was in charge of her career. I was not that kid still pressed up against her dressing room wall, waiting for the glamorous singer to sign my program. "Hey, that's all," I said standing in front of Juliana and Richard. "No more pictures." I turned to Richard. "Richard, tell them no more."

"Thanks guys," he said, moving among them. "No more for now, but come back after the second show."

"Don't ever let them take pictures of you two kissing. Not one," I said to Richard when he got back from escorting the photographers out. "It's not good for her career. Don't overemphasize that she's married. Let guys have their fantasies."

"Fantasies about my wife? You mean," he whispered, "sex fantasies?"

"Not only that, but yes. That's the aura we've been creating since we began."

"I don't like it."

"You don't have to like it. This is *Juliana's* career, and she's the type of performer who inspires sex fantasies."

"Well, thank you, Al," Juliana said.

I looked away from her. "And we need to use that."

"Okay." Richard sighed. "Whatever you think best."

"Can you get these people out of here? Juliana needs to rest. She's got another show at twelve."

"Sure. I'll move them out," Richard said, always amenable. I really wanted to hate him, but he made it impossible. He spread his arms out like big wings, guiding people who were still waving programs toward Juliana. "Okay, folks, no more autographs right now. Juliana needs to rest."

While Richard dealt with the crowd, I, alone, stood in front of Juliana. I suddenly became that scared kid who clung to the wall the first night I met her in person. "Uh … you were good," I said, lamely, looking down at my program.

"What have you got there?" she asked.

"Oh, this. It's the program you wouldn't sign the first night I met you in person. You said you'd sign it when we knew each other better."

"I remember."

"I think we know each other pretty well now."

She smiled and was about to say something when Richard came up to us. "Gals, how about we go upstairs to the lounge and celebrate."

I stared at him, stepping on my moment with her, my heart sinking down to my feet.

"Uh, Richard, we'll be along soon," she said. "Girl talk."

"Sure. You two girls talk." He patted me on the shoulder. "Good job." He brisked out of the room.

Juliana took the program, and dipped her fountain pen into the inkbottle that sat on her dressing table. She kept it poised, her face deep in concentration for what seemed an endless time. I shifted my weight from one foot to the other, waiting.

She sighed. "I can't do this." She held the program out to me.

"I can't write words here. Not the ones you want. I can't do it." She was really upset.

"It's okay." I put my hand on hers. "It's okay."

I took back the program. It would remain forever unsigned.

"Will you let me kiss you, instead?" she asked as she slipped over to the door; I heard the click of the lock. She walked back to where I stood and wrapped her arms around me. She lowered her face to mine and kissed me. She kissed me for a very long time.

Chapter 38

"THOSE WOMEN," I said to Virginia as we sat down at a corner table in Schrafft's for cocktails. "Some of those women in the film. They meant us. Didn't they?"

"Us?" Virginia asked, sliding her gloves off. "Who's us?"

"Me. Those mean women, prisoners and guards, in the picture. They didn't say it, but they meant people like how I am, didn't they?"

I hadn't had much time to think about any of this while I'd worked on Juliana's opening, but now, with that done, it all came flooding back. I'd promised to make time for Virginia, so we went to an afternoon movie. *Caged Women* probably wasn't the best choice, however.

"Yes." Virginia sighed. "I suppose that's what some of those women were. But they weren't *all* mean."

"But the meanest one, the one who tormented that young girl, she was one, wasn't she?"

"Well, she *did* have a boyfriend."

"Lots of us have boyfriends and—husbands to hide behind."

"I thought the movie was a sensitive portrayal of women in trouble and how prison can make them worse."

"You know, they asked Bette Davis to be in that picture, but she said she didn't want to be in any—a dyke movie."

"That's plain ignorance," Virginia said. "It makes me mad that people like that can hurt you. You don't deserve it."

"You're sweet, Virginia, but that's what people think of us. That we're mean, and dangerous, and hurt children."

"They don't know you."

"I like having you as a friend. Uh … as a matter of fact—"

"You don't have to say it. You'd rather be my friend than my—lover."

"I don't want to hurt you."

"I'm fine. I'm sorry I've been pressuring you about that."

"It's okay. You were feeling lost and vulnerable. I understand. It's—"

"Your heart belongs to Juliana."

"Well—"

"And my heart belongs to Max. It's hard to watch him with Scott. Did you know that Scott even cooks?"

"No."

She laughed, but a few tears appeared in her eyes at the same time. She reached in her purse for a handkerchief.

"Why don't we order?"

"Yes." She dabbed at her eyes. "I think I'll have the Schrafft's extra-dry martini. I need it."

I called the waitress over and ordered the Schrafft's Special Manhattan Cocktail, Rye with Italian Vermouth, for myself, and the Martini for Virginia.

Virginia continued, "I wanted to make myself believe I could take a woman lover. It seemed easier, but ..."

"It's *not* easier."

"I guess not with all you've been through with Juliana and the ever-present world's condemnation. I'm glad you're my friend, too. I don't think I've ever had a truly good woman friend before."

"Max feels bad, you know. He doesn't like hurting you."

"I know. And I'm not going to cry anymore." She put her handkerchief back in her purse and snapped it shut. "Besides, Moose Mantelli invited me to have dinner with him this Friday at the Oak Room."

"You wouldn't."

"Why not?"

"Virginia."

"I've heard the rumors about him, but I think they're exaggerated. He's always been a perfect gentleman with me. And *he* likes girls. Oh, don't look so worried. I can take care of myself. Tell me about you."

"But, Virginia ... Moose Mantelli?"

"For Pete's sake, let me have a little fun!" she said sharply. "He makes me feel appreciated. I need to have *some* way of getting over Max."

"Of course, sorry. It's not my business."

"So—tell me about you."

The drinks arrived, and after Virginia's revelation, I welcomed them. "Well, there *is* something I'd like to ask you."

"Yes?"

"What do you know about Margaritte?"

"Margaritte Zimon?" Virginia asked.

"I guess. I've never heard her last name before."

Virginia took a sip of her martini. "I think that's her maiden name, if that woman could ever have been a maiden. She's been married so many times it's hard to know which name is hers. She flits around from country to country and—"

"I know all that. What do you know about Margaritte and—Juliana?"

"I believe they're friends, aren't they?"

"They are, but what *kind* of friends?"

"You're asking me if I think Juliana and Margaritte were lovers?"

"No. I know they were once. I'm asking you if they are now."

Hearing myself say the words out loud was like having a boulder dropping on my chest. Virginia opened her purse, took out her silver cigarette case, and removed an L & M filtered cigarette, her face thoughtful. "Well, I've heard the rumors, of course."

"I don't want rumors. I want facts."

"The only ones who can give you those are Margaritte and Juliana. You know how I feel about Juliana. I hate that she's hurting you. She's using you. Look at all you've done for her. The reviews are stupendous, and she got those reviews because of you."

"Well, she *did* have a little something to do with them."

"Very little. She should spend every waking minute making you feel loved." She gestured with her cigarette. "She *owes* you. The least she could do is dump that husband and be with you."

"I like that idea too, but that's not going to happen. I've grown to accept that Richard's part of my life. I'd rather not think I'm also sharing her with Margaritte."

"Or whomever might strike her fancy."

I took a sip of my drink. "Yeah. So—you don't know anything specific about Juliana and Margaritte?"

"Juliana is discrete. I'll give her that."

"Or faithful to me," I said, a little too harshly. "Well, except for Richard, of course, but I don't count him anymore."

"I heard one rumor I found tantalizing."

"Tell me."

"It's about you."

"Me?"

"This one is ... what's that expression they use? A humdinger."

"I can't imagine what ..." My face dropped. "People haven't found out that I'm ..."

"No, honey, not that," she assured me. "It's about you and a certain someone's *husband*."

"Someone's ...? No. People think *Richard* and I ...?"

Virginia laughed. "Yes! I first heard it at Mr. Pierre's Petite Salon when I got my nails done last week."

"They were really talking about Richard and me?"

"They were talking about it again at the upstairs Copa bar a few nights ago when I went to see *her*. Of course, I set them straight.

I put my hand on her wrist. "You went."

"Only because Max asked me to. I'm surprised he didn't tell you about the rumor."

"Keep it going."

"Al, your reputation. You know what people think of women who ..."

"Better they think I'm a heterosexual home-wrecker than ... that other."

"I see what you mean, but still."

"You don't have to make up stories. Keep them guessing with little hints that it 'might' be true, that you 'might' know something. What a wonderful way to divert them from the truth."

Chapter 39

I WALKED INTO Juliana's dressing room ready to talk to her alone, but when I got there … She sat at the make-up table with her robe only loosely cinched at the waist and her legs crossed, as the robe fell away revealing her thighs. Andy, the popular male impersonator I'd seen at Club 181, sat on the make-up table with her legs propped up on a chair, her tuxedo jacket hanging over its back. Her ruffled white shirt was untucked, with a few of the top buttons undone, the bow tie hung untied around her neck. Juliana laughed as she sat filing her nails. Filing her nails! Why was she doing that?

"Hello," I said, stiffly. "Nice to see you, Andy. Now go."

"Al!" Jule exclaimed. "Don't be rude."

"You've got to get ready."

"She's right," Andy said, taking a puff from the cigarette she held between her thumb and index finger.

I grabbed the cigarette out of her hand. "No smoking around Juliana's throat." I stamped it out in the ashtray Juliana had provided for Andy.

"Al, what are you doing?" Juliana asked.

"No, Julie, she's right. Sorry, Al." She pulled on her jacket and buttoned those unbuttoned blouse buttons I wondered about.

I stuck the clipboard I held in front of Juliana's eyes, but I was paying more attention to Andy tucking in her shirt.

"What?" Juliana asked.

"What, what?" I said, watching Andy bend toward the mirror, tying her bow tie.

"The clipboard. In my face. Am I supposed to do something with it?"

"Oh, yeah. Here." I pointed. "These two songs. I want to switch their order. I think that'll create a greater punch."

"Fine. Tell Pete and the orchestra."

"So, Al," Andy said, extending her hand. "Good seeing you again."

I shook her hand, trying to appear as manly as she and failing badly. It was hard to do in a skirt.

Andy went behind Juliana and kissed her on top of the head. "Well, doll, I'll see you after the show."

With a wave, she whisked out the door.

"You will *not* see her after the show," I said.

"I'll see whomever I please."

"Oh? And why have you decided to destroy your career before it's barely begun?"

"How dare you be rude to a friend of mine."

"Oh, *friend*? What *kind* of friend, Jule? You cannot see her. You've got to know that with your fear of being found out."

"Most people think Andy's a man."

"And what if someone figures it out? What happens to you?"

"Andy is an entertainer. An extremely talented one."

"I know. I caught her act at Club 181."

"I didn't think you went to such clubs."

"I don't. She's very good, and if she were a real man, she would rival Frank Sinatra, but she's not, Jule. She's a girl."

"People expect me to know entertainers. It's nothing unusual. In the early thirties when she was barely a child, the critics were wild for her."

"In the kinds of clubs *you* would never appear in."

"In '34, *Life Magazine* interviewed her about her island. She owns her own island, you know."

"Swell. Times have changed, Jule. Nowadays, *Life* wouldn't sell her a subscription. You can't get away with these things anymore. No one's going to think you're 'artistic' if you consort with people like Andy. They're going to think you're queer."

She jumped up. "Don't EVER call me that. I don't know what's come over you."

"I sweated blood for your career, and I will not let you—"

"Don't use a metaphor like that."

"What metaphor?"

"Sweated blood. It refers to Jesus in the Garden of Gethsemane, who, by the way, had a lot more problems than Andy or my career."

"Swell. Become a nun. You oughta do terrific with that chastity thing. And Jesus *cried* blood; he didn't sweat it."

"Don't make fun of nuns; they're holy women."

I took a deep breath. "Look, Jule, these are dangerous times. I don't know why you've chosen this particular moment, when everything's going your way, to lose your mind, but if you see Andy after the show, the morning papers will announce to the world that you are a pervert, and we will watch the crumbling of your career into tiny little bits. Then you can go sing in one of Andy's 'terribly-gay,' *faggoty-dyke* clubs. I'm telling you, *don't* see her."

"You can't tell me what to do."

"Yes, I can. I'm your manager."

"No, Richard is. You're helping him out."

I took another deep breath. "Where *is* Richard? I doubt he'd be too thrilled about Andy, either. Does he even know about her?"

"Richard flew to Omaha last night. His mother took ill."

"So that's why you're with Andy. You *knew* Richard wouldn't put up with it, but you figured I would. Well, I won't, Jule. I worked too hard to get your name on that Copa marquee. If you let Andy come back here tonight, or I see you anywhere near him, or her, or whatever *it* is, I swear I'll—I'll …"

"You'll what?"

"Don't do it." I slammed down my clipboard on the make-up table and walked out.

I don't know how she got word to Andy, but when the crowds collected outside her door after the show, Andy was not among them.

Chapter 40

June 1950

"NO, RICHARD, DON'T sign anything," I said into my office phone as I shook my cardigan off and turned on the light. The word was out—The Copa was selling Standing Room Only for all of Juliana's shows, and the rumor mill was sizzling. Was it true she was leaving her current agent? "Let the lawyers go over everything," I told Richard. "Bring the list of agents who called, and we'll talk about each one with drinks. But don't, I repeat, don't commit to anything until you, the lawyers, and I have gone over everything. We don't want another guy like the guy she's with now. No imagination. I'll see you tonight. No, I don't want to meet your new young friend from Omaha. Yes, she was great last night. It *is* happening. See you tonight, and please don't bring that guy with you."

I hung up, knowing Richard was gonna bring that guy with him. All month he'd been introducing me to new guys he thought were *perfect* for me. I glanced at one of the papers on my desk. "US Leads the United Nations in a Police Action." I thought the war we were in now, the one the government said wasn't a war, was supposed to be cold. A police action isn't cold; people get killed in police actions. At least it wasn't a war. The phone rang again.

While listening to a would-be producer drone on about how wonderful Juliana would be in a bit part he had in mind for a show he was gonna air in the fall, I stacked the newspapers into a pile, hunting for my mail. No way was I gonna stick her in a TV show after the success she'd had. TV was for comedians. There was a letter from the school. I opened it and pulled out the report. "I'll have her manager get back to you," I told the guy and hung up, staring at my report card. The phone again. "Alice Huffman. No, Richard. I said no. We need to talk first. It's too soon for Broadway."

Max walked in. I waved him into the seat. "Tonight. When I meet you at Child's. We'll start with drinks, then if I'm still talking to you, we'll have dinner. Yes, I'm kidding, but come alone. Those young guys you want me to meet will be headed to Korea soon, anyway."

The paper I'd thrown onto my desk caught Max's eye. He picked it up before I could stop him. "Be there at six. Don't sign anything before we talk." I hung up the phone.

"What's this?" Max asked, his voice stern.

"Didn't anyone ever tell you it's a federal offense to read other people's mail?"

"What is this?"

"I'll take it over. I've been busy. Juliana? The Copa? I didn't go to class much."

"This is not going to happen." He waved my "F" report at me. "You're moving in with me so I can watch you."

"I'm twenty-seven years old. I don't need a father."

"But you should've had one when you first came to the city. Maybe if someone had watched out for you, then you wouldn't have taken up with Juliana. And if that hadn't happened, you'd have a more normal life now, instead of this crazy—"

"I met Juliana because of *you*."

"No, I wouldn't do that to you."

"You invited my friends and me to hear Juliana sing so you could steal my boyfriend."

"*I* did that to you? I did, didn't I? No matter." He pulled out his cigarette holder and pushed in a cigarette. "I saved you from a long life of boring heterosexuality. You have to move in with me. I've never been to a college graduation. I intend to go to yours." He lit his cigarette. "You're getting that degree."

"Yes, Dad. But I don't need it. I have a career that's working out swell. I don't need a college degree to manage talent and run a club."

"For *now* things are going well, but this business is fickle. Maybe, if I'd had a degree when my club went under, I would've had something to fall back on, a way to raise money when I needed to start again. I had nothing when it happened." He pounded his finger on my desk. "You *will* finish that degree. And I like you calling me Dad."

"I'll go to summer school."

"I'm moving out of the Plaza. It's too impersonal. I need something homier. I can hear Hildegarde and Anna arguing all night above me."

"Are they …?" I whispered.

"Of course, but if you tell anyone, you could find yourself bound and gagged in the East River. The Incomparable Hildegarde is the most fiercely secret dyke I've ever met."

"Max! Don't call her that. What a horrible word to use for a friend."

"Al right, all right, I know. Sorry. Anyway, I put down a security payment and two months on a penthouse apartment, a duplex. On East Fifty-third. I'll be rattling around if I have the place to myself. Come live with me."

"Haven't you been rattling around at the Plaza?"

"Yes, and I don't want to rattle anymore. Come live with me, so I can look out for you."

"Are you lonely, Max?"

"I can get any cute young thing into my bed with a flick of my limp wrist." He flipped his wrist.

"Won't I get in your way?"

"It's a huge place. You could have the whole upper floor to yourself. We could both be there for days and never run into each other. Besides …" He looked down and sighed.

"Besides?"

"Look, I'm going to tell you something I wouldn't tell any other soul, so don't go blabbing."

"Cross my heart," I said as I crossed my finger over my heart—"Dad."

"I turn forty next week," he whispered.

"We'll throw you a big party."

"No, you won't! I don't want anyone knowing."

"Wait a minute. How can you be forty? You were twenty-nine when I first met you."

"Was I?"

"That means you should only be thirty-eight."

"I am. To everyone but you. Somehow that age—that other age I told you about—is making me want to build something more substantial. With—someone. Shocks the hell out of me."

"Aren't you still with Scott?"

"Yes and no. There are times when we can spend whole days together and it's pure ecstasy. But then he starts feeling guilty, or he gets a new therapist, and I become a monk. I'm no good at being a monk."

"Maybe if you two lived together—"

"Two men living together?"

"Women do it. Women who are more than roommates. Look at Shirl and Mercy, Hildegarde and Anna. You don't tell anybody."

"You mean, one of us would be the man, and the other would be the girl?" He shook his head. "You know, one time when I was at a party I met these two old guys, and they said they'd been together for forty years. Forty years! Lived together and everything! Like a married couple. I never thought our kind could do that. Have a real life. Forty years! And these guys knew others who lived like them. Scott met a few couples like that in DC. Even pretended they really were married. I can't fathom it—I mean, I always figured being the way I am I'd live alone, going from man to man, and yet, those old guys—there was something nice about it. But I don't know."

"What about Virginia? You two have been engaged for what? Twenty years? Maybe you should marry her for companionship."

"The way I hear it, Virginia thinks quite a lot of you. Never stops singing your praises."

"She told you?"

"Why don't you and she …?"

"Because she's straight, for one. We worked that out a few days ago. We're going to stay friends."

"Really? She told me you made her feel things she'd never felt before. You must be quite the sexual dynamo."

"The poor woman hadn't had any attention in that direction for I don't know how long. Practically anyone who touched her in the right place, and she was gonna … Why am I explaining this to you? Like *you* haven't crawled around a few public restrooms yourself."

"This happened in a public restroom? Shame on you."

"She didn't tell you that part? Oops."

He laughed. "You've come a long way kid. Maybe you and I should get married."

We looked at each other with serious expressions as if we were considering it, then simultaneously burst out laughing so hard our sides hurt.

Virginia walked past my office door. She was weak with laughter too, which was unlike her; she couldn't have heard us through my closed door. Max opened the door, "Virginia. Are you all right?"

"I'm sorry. Did we bother you? Moose keeps me in stitches."

Moose came out of the kitchen eating spaghetti from a large china bowl, tomato sauce dotting his cheeks, chin, and the front of his white shirt. His ample belly drooped over his belt.

"We're engaged!" Virginia announced.

"What?" Max yelled.

I put my hand on his arm. "Be nice. Virginia's in love."

"With that, that …" Catching my drift, he took in a breath. "Virginia, dear." He pretended to be cheerful. "May I see you a moment?"

"Anything you have to say can be said in front of my fiancé."

"Hi there, Max." Moose waved his spaghetti fork at us from the kitchen doorway; he sucked in a long string of tomato-smeared noodle.

"No, Virginia, dear, it can't," Max said with a gritted smile. "Please come in the office."

"I'll leave you two to …" I began, heading for the door. Virginia stormed in, closing the door and trapping me inside.

"You had something to say to me, Max?" Her arms crossed over her chest.

"Are you out of your mind? You're not going to marry that—"

"I am not a school girl whom you can chastise. Am I, Al?"

"Oh. Uh …"

"You must know what kind of man he is," Max continued.

"I most certainly do. The kind that doesn't take me for granted, like *some* people I know."

"He's a racketeer, a criminal! *I* have no choice but to deal with him, but you have no reason to go near him."

"You are so arrogant, thinking you know what's best for everyone."

"This time I do, and you have to listen to me. If you knew what he's probably done, you'd never—"

"I've heard rumors about what he's *probably* done, but I don't pay attention to gossip. If I did, I wouldn't have been with *you* for the past twenty-two years."

"I was never like that."

"No. *He* appreciates me."

"You cannot, under any circumstance, marry that man."

"I'm a grown woman, capable of making my own grown-up decisions. Aren't I, Al?"

"Uh …"

"Why can't I marry him?" she asked us both. "Give me one good reason?"

"I have to explain?" Max shouted. "Well, for one thing, look at him. He's not in your class."

"Snob!" she shot back.

"He's dangerous."

"He's a pussy cat."

"He's involved in illegal activities. You could be hurt. *Please*, Virginia, you mustn't."

She looked at him with sad eyes, a few tears escaping. "But he makes me feel—"

"What? For Pete's sake! What could he possibly make you feel?"

"Max," I said, "why don't you try listening?"

"I'm trying to find out what that goon makes her feel."

"He makes me feel, like—like … Al?"

"Like a woman," I said.

Virginia silently nodded, pressing a handkerchief to her face.

Chapter 41

June 1950

"WE'RE ONLY HERE because Mr. Harlington sent you on a mission." Virginia vigorously shook out her linen napkin and smoothed it over her lap. She took a tiny bite from her chopped chicken tea sandwich. "This lunch is merely part of your job."

Virginia and I sat at a corner table on the top floor of Schrafft's, Fifth Avenue. Despite her mood, she was attractively dressed in a large, lavender hat with a matching feather, a white jacket fitted tightly at the waist, and a dark flaired skirt. Since I was coming from the club, I used that as an excuse for wearing my usual dark suit-jacket and skirt with the chunky heels. "I thought it would be nice to have a little lunch together," I said, in between bites of my peanut butter, chili sauce, and bacon sandwich.

"I haven't seen you in ages and now you call? Why?" she demanded.

"It's only been a couple weeks since we've gotten together."

"Let's be honest, Al. You're only here because Mr. Harlington ordered you."

She was right, but "ordered" seemed a bit strong. He wouldn't let up, always nagging me to talk to her. I kept telling him it wasn't my business, but finally, he convinced me she was in danger, and I knew she wouldn't listen to him so ... "Okay, you're right, but Max is only concerned about you."

"Ha!"

"He is, Virginia. I know he can be clumsy, but he's really afraid you're going to be hurt. First, he told me that Moose is married to a woman in New Jersey. They have three kids. You and he haven't uh ... you know ... Have you?"

"None of your business! And, for your information, Moose told me about his wife in New Jersey. You can tell Mr. Harlington to stick that in his pipe and sit on it.

"Virginia could you stop calling Max 'Mr. Harlington?' It's spooky."

"I cannot. Mr. Harlington and I merely have a formal relationship. And you can tell him Moose is getting a divorce from his wife."

"Moose said that? Really? And you'd marry a divorced man?"

"It's not like I have a line of suitors waiting outside my door."

"You can't marry him because there's no one else right now."

"I'm not. He's a lovely man, and any woman would be proud to—"

"He brings women to the club. Did he tell you that?"

"He's very gregarious. People like him."

"Virginia, these are not Girl Scouts. They wear clingy, sequined dresses and hang on him. *That* I've seen with my own eyes."

"He likes to have fun. What—what women?"

"See? You didn't know about *them*. He brings them around when you're not there. Max thinks they're prostitutes."

"He would, wouldn't he? That's a reflection of his own dirty mind. It's *you* I don't understand. Doing Mr. Harlington's bidding. I suppose you have to do what your boss tells you, so I'll forgive you. Oh, those two colored girls. So sad."

"What?" I asked.

"Sitting at the table over there. They're never going to be waited on."

"Why? They're dressed appropriately. Better than me. At least *they're* wearing hats."

"Schrafft's waitresses don't wait on coloreds."

"Why?"

"It's policy. Those people *do* have restaurants uptown."

"Well, yeah, but if they're shopping in midtown ..." The two Negro women stood and walked down the stairs toward the first floor exit.

"If no one was going to wait on them," I asked, "why did the hostess seat them?"

"I imagine no one wants to say it aloud, so they let them figure it out for themselves. Perhaps they're out-of-town coloreds. You can tell Mr. Maxwell P. Harlington III he can stay out of my life. I am doing fine with my Moose. Mr. Harlington is jealous."

"Maybe, but ..." A new approach. "Did you see James Cagney in *White Heat* last year?"

"It's a gangster picture. I don't go to gangster pictures. They scare me."

"Well, you should. They tell you what those people are like. In that picture, James Cagney was very nice to this girl, and she thought he was a swell guy, until he punched her in the mouth."

"Oh, dear," Virginia said.

I ran my fist through the air. "Socko! Of course, he also found out that she was running around with Big Eddie while he was in prison. That made him plenty sore. Through the whole movie he was always shooting everybody, but then when he found out Big Eddie had shot his mother in the back—"

"How terrible," Virginia said.

"Sure was! Except she was crazy. But James Cagney went crazy, and the G Men had to chase him. Everyone was shooting everybody else." I shaped my hand into a gun. "Pow! Take that copper! Pow!"

Virginia grabbed my fist, "Dear, perhaps, you shouldn't shoot people in Schrafft's."

"Oh." I looked around to see a few women, open-mouthed, staring at me. I smiled at them. "Sorry. But, Virginia, you really should see that picture."

"Heavens, no. Terrifying."

"Virginia," I leaned toward her. "You're dating someone who does those things in real life."

"Oh, stop. Did Max tell you that?"

"No, but that's what mobsters do. Don't they?"

"I haven't a clue. You should give Moose a chance, and stop listening to Mr. Know-It-All. He could learn a few things about how to treat a lady from my Moose. Could we stop talking about Mr. Harlington? I'm getting dyspepsia at the sound of his name. Can you believe they arrested that couple for selling secrets to the communists? Some people are talking about the electric chair. A woman! What a frightening world we live in."

Chapter 42

MARTY AND I walked past the pushcart vendors and the colored men playing dominoes on the sidewalk.

"Their place is up there," Marty said.

Laundry hung from fire escapes, and colored women fanned themselves with newspapers on their front stoops while their children played hopscotch and stickball in the street.

"Hey, I saw you on my TV last week," I said. "You were good."

"Ya liked me? Only a few lines."

"You made a scary Russian spy. As scary as the ones they just caught."

"You think they're scary? They look like ordinary people to me."

"That's what so scary. It's hard to imagine ordinary American citizens doing a thing like that."

"But they aren't ordinary American citizens," Marty said. "They're *Jewish* American citizens. Some people are saying that's why they could do it—betray the country to the Soviets. They say Jews aren't real Americans. I hope they find out they're innocent. Otherwise, it could go bad for the rest of us Jews."

For a few minutes, we walked in silence. What could I say? I didn't even understand what he meant. I'd always been an outsider. I didn't belong anywhere, but that was because of me, not because I belonged to some group.

"You know," he finally said, "I really like working on TV. You have to be one hundred percent on top of your game. An actor can drop a line, and you've gotta jump in and help, or else the show's gonna fail in front of all those people."

"Sounds like theater."

"It is! Only on TV, *thousands* see you drop that line. They're saying TV cables are gonna go clear across the country by '51. You know how many people will see you drop that line, then? The old guys are sticking to nightclubs and Broadway. That means TV is an open field for us young guys. The pay's horrible, but from what I'm hearing, TV's the future, and I wanna be part of it. In the fall, I'm hanging around ad agencies on Madison Avenue. That's who's casting TV, not theater producers.

We passed a row of pickle salesmen. The El rattled in the distance as Marty led the way into the building and up the three flights of stairs to the Steinmans' apartment. It was dark in the stairway, no windows. Marty had been trying for weeks to get me to go to Moshe's for dinner. He wanted me to see the side of his friend that wasn't damaged by war.

Marty stopped mid-climb. "Now, don't be nervous." He wore a fedora, which he never wore, and his tie was neatly tied. *He* was the one who seemed nervous.

"Am I dressed modest enough?" I asked. I wore a dress with a pattern of aqua roses. The hem fell a little below my calves. My light-blue hat was round with a small brim.

"Very nice," Marty assured me. "They're nice people. Not as Orthodox as Moshe was trying to be, merely respectful of tradition." He fiddled with the big bow that hung from the front of my dress. "Moshe's so much better. He's been seeing," he looked around, then leaned close and whispered, "an analyst. His mother's idea. I think it's working." I pulled the bow away from Marty's annoying fingers. "He wants to be nice to you to. Personally, I think he had a crush on you, and that's why he acted so strange."

"I don't think *I'm* the one he had the crush on."

We walked up the rest of the stairs where Mrs. Steinman waited. "Come in." Mrs. Steinman was an attractive woman in her mid-forties. Her blonde hair, that looked dyed, was swept up into a pompadour. "Oh, look at me," she laughed, whisking off her apron. "You must be Alice. Aaron has told us so much about you."

"He has?" I looked at Marty as he took off his hat to reveal a yarmulke underneath.

"We brought you a little something." Marty handed her the bottle of wine we picked up at the corner store.

"You shouldn't have. And you, a poor student. But thank you." She kissed Marty on the cheek. "Oy gevalt, Aaron! You even wore a tie! For us?"

"Anything for my second Mom."

"Welcome to our home, Alice. And Mazel Tov."

She smiled at Marty as he wandered over to the bowl of grapes in the center of the table, popping a few into his mouth. "Though, as you can see, he needs a good woman to teach him manners. I hope you're up to the job." She slapped Marty's hand playfully "Get away from those grapes. Spoil your dinner. Wash your hands."

In the center of their small dining room, a round table was set with two lit candles, plates, glasses, and bread covered with a cloth.

"I want you to meet my husband, Benjamin Steinman."

Mr. Steinman, a tall, square-shouldered man in a gray suit and yarmulke, entered the room, thumbing through his mail.

"Not now, dear," Mrs. Steinman whispered to her husband, taking the mail from him. "It's Shabbos. Come meet Aaron's fiancée."

I shot a quick look at Marty; he studied his shoes.

Mr. Steinman took off his glasses and squinted at me saying to Marty, "So this is the one, huh?"

"Excuse me," Mrs. Steinman said. "I have to check on the chicken." She ran over to the stove.

"Uh, yes," Marty told Mr. Steinman. "I bet that chicken comes straight from your shop. Mr. Steinman owns the finest butcher shop in the neighborhood."

Mr. Steinman said, "Where else would we get our chicken?" He looked at me. "Have you set the date?"

"Date?"

"Not yet, but soon," Marty stepped in. "Right, Alice?"

"Uh ... sure."

"You're getting a good one, you know. We've known Aaron since he played stickball with our Moshe. His mother would bring him over before she went to work. Do you think a shiksa like yourself—"

"Benjamin!" Mrs. Steinman called.

"I'm only joking. No offense, I hope."

"Never you mind, Alice," Mrs. Steinman said. "Mr. Steinman has had a long day. That explains his poor jokes. Why don't you wash up for dinner? Down that hallway."

"Thank you."

Before I'd gotten far, Mrs. Steinman whispered, "Benjamin, how could you? And on Shabbos."

"She's not Jewish, is she? Aaron?"

"Well, maybe sorta ..."

"Benjamin, stop it. Alice is our guest, and you are to treat her as such."

"I don't want Aaron making a mistake. Marriage is a serious step. There are the children to think about."

"*Children?*" I whispered in the hallway.

"... And they must be raised Jewish. None of this half-this, half-that. Not in these times. The children must know who they are. After what our people went through, we need to protect—"

"She's converting," Marty said.

I am?

"We don't need *them* converting," Mr. Steinman said. "We don't need *them* at all. How will a shiksa mother know how to bring up Jewish children?"

"You stop it," Mrs. Steinman said. "Alice will be back soon. She is here to have a pleasant meal and learn a little something about the Jewish people. That's all."

I hurried my hand-washing and charged back into the kitchen. When I turned around, Moshe stood leaning against the molding. His suit fit. No hands dangling miles from his cuffs. His mother, no doubt.

"Come, dear," Mrs. Steinman said, taking Moshe's arm and leading him into the room, like one might do with a blind man. "Say hello to your friends."

"Hey, Mosh!" Marty said with forced joy. "How ya doing, buddy?"

"Good," he said trying to push some life into his voice, but failing.

"You remember Alice," Marty continued.

"Hi, Moshe," I said, afraid he'd call me the Whore of Babylon in front of his parents. He only smiled vacantly.

"Hi, Alice. I'm glad you came."

"Thank you."

"Let's begin," Mrs. Steinman put a lacy white cloth on her head. She and her husband said prayers in Hebrew over the candles, the wine, and the bread.

"Alice, you study at City College like Aaron?" Mrs. Steinman asked once we were seated, eating our borsht soup.

"Yes."

"And you're not worried what too much education will do to your femininity?" Mr. Steinman asked.

"Uh ..."

"Young women have so many new opportunities these days, Benjamin," Mrs. Steinman said pleasantly. "Not at all like when we were young. I think it's exciting."

Mr Steinman shook his head, unconvinced.

"And what degree are you studying for?" Mrs. Steinman asked.

"Education. Primary school."

"How nice. You're going to teach the little ones. Such an important job. Of course, until you get married."

"Yes." I looked over at Marty. He looked down at his plate of food.

"And now you live with your parents?" Mrs. Steinman continued.

"Uh…" I looked over at 'Aaron.' "No."

"She lives in her own apartment," Moshe said. "She's a very independent woman." His voice sounded simply factual, not mean.

"Is she?" Mrs. Steinman said.

Mr. Steinman mumbled, "Independent woman" into his plate of roast chicken.

"Aaron, you've finished another semester. What are your plans for summer?"

"I got hired by a stock company in Maine. I leave on Wednesday."

"A real start on your career," Mrs. Steinman said.

"My Great-Uncle was almost a star in the Yiddish Theater," Mr. Steinman said.

"You'll be gone all summer?" Moshe asked, barely looking up from his untouched food.

"Till mid-August."

"All summer?" Moshe dropped his fork in his plate. "All summer?" he repeated.

"Well, you have yourself a good time," Mr. Steinman said, cutting his meat.

"ALL SUMMER!" Moshe shouted.

"Moshe!" Mrs. Steinman admonished. "Today is Shabbos. Show some respect. Aaron has already told you—"

"All summer!" Moshe lowered his voice, but hit the edge of the table with the palms of his hands. "All summer! All summer," he banged the table again and again.

Mr. Steinman stood. "Stop that. Now!"

Moshe shoved the table harder, and the wine bottle flew at Marty, spewing wine all over his pants. Everyone jumped up. "Moshe!" Mrs. Steinman cried out. "I'm sorry, Aaron, let me get—"

"I love you," Moshe said.

"What?" Mr. Steinman asked.

"Yes, of course, we all love Aaron," Mrs. Steinman said.

"No! I *love* him! I *really* love him." He looked at Marty, "I love you. Kiss me. Hold me again, the way you once did."

"What is this?" Mr. Steinman exclaimed.

"Nothing," Marty said. "It's, uh … nothing."

"It was never nothing," Moshe cried out. "You held me and kissed me. We touched, damn you! I can't stand my life without you. Marty, *please*." Moshe fell to his knees at Marty's feet.

"Moshe, stop this." Marty smiled awkwardly over at Mr. Steinman. "We never … Mrs. Steinman, we never …"

Moshe wrapped his arms around Marty's legs, almost knocking him over. "Don't go."

"Stop it!" Marty said, bending to pull Moshe's arms off his legs. "You and I never …!"

"We did. We loved each other, and it was beautiful. Your penis in me, and—"

"What?" Mr. Steinman exclaimed. "Ruth, go in the other room. You shouldn't hear—"

"Our love wasn't dirty!" Moshe shot at his father. "It was holy!"

"Ruth! Call an ambulance!"

"Mr. Steinman," Marty pleaded, "we never—"

"I can't use the phone. It's Shabbos," Mrs. Steinman said, distressed.

"Do it, Ruth!"

"Alice?" Mrs. Steinman looked at me, helpless. "Would you call an ambulance? The telephone is down the hall."

"Uh—uh …" My eyes whisked over the torn faces about to explode into who-knew-what. "What's the number?"

"On the cover of the telephone book. I wrote it there. St. Sebastian. Next to the telephone."

I ran from the room and made the call. When I got back, Moshe was climbing up Marty's body. "How can you walk away from me? Away from what we did?"

He kissed Marty's face; Marty pushed his head away from him, but not forcefully. Looking at a frozen Mr. Steinman, Marty choked out, "We never did anything like that."

"Please, *please*," Moshe begged, wrapping his arms around Marty's shoulders, running kisses over the side of his face. Marty grabbed a hank of Moshe's hair. "Moshe, stop! We *never* …!" And then looking into Moshe's eyes—"Ah, buddy"—pain carved into his face—he pulled Moshe's head onto his shoulder, and held him in his arms.

"I love you," Moshe whimpered.

"I know, buddy. I know."

"What is this?" Mr. Steinman asked. "Abomination! What did you do to my son? Sodomite!" Mr. Steinman spat the deadly word at Marty. "Hob es in drerd! Sodomite! Sodomite!"

"No, Benjamin," Mrs. Steinman said, "it never happened."

Marty cradled Moshe in his arms. "It's gonna be okay, buddy." He patted his head.

Mr. Steinman paced. "I have no son. My son is dead. My son is dead."

"No, Benjamin, please," Mrs. Steinman pulled on his sleeve, weeping and pleading, "you musn't say that. He is my only. They never ... Aaron told you, they never—"

"I have no son, I have no son."

A handkerchief twisted in her fingers, Mrs. Steinman limped toward Marty. "You didn't. You said you didn't."

"No, Mrs. Steinman, we never—"

She slapped him hard across the face.

The ambulance screamed outside the window, and then the rattle of men rushing up the stairs. Mrs. Steinman ran to the landing and threw open the door. A woman's voice asked, "Ruth, has someone been hurt?"

Mrs. Steinman waved her arms aimlessly, and the ambulance men slid a gurney into the apartment. Before she closed the door, I saw a tightly-packed group of neighbors on the landing, all talking at the same time, trying to get in.

She pointed at Moshe, and the men grabbed him out of Marty's arms. "Come on, kid. Lay down here and—"

When Moshe saw the gurney, he pulled away and backed against the wall. "No!"

"Now, baby," Mrs. Steinman said. "It's only for a little while. Till you're well."

"No, Mom, please don't do this." He ran over to the sink. "I'm not sick."

Mr. Steinman stood by the bookcase with a shawl over his shoulders, mumbling what I thought were probably Jewish prayers. Sometimes he would hit his chest with one of his fists.

"Ma'am," one of the ambulance men said. "Let us get him. We won't hurt him."

Crying into a handkerchief, she nodded her yes.

I began to shake. It was horrible. All of it. Horrible to see this thing; horrible to *be* this thing that I was with Moshe. Anger, fear, hate crashed around the room. And the pain. I had to get out of there. But how? The damn gurney blocked the door.

The two ambulance men backed Moshe into a corner near the stove. He tried to slip out between them, but they grabbed his arms and pushed him to the floor; his yarmulke flew off his head.

"No! Don't hurt him," Marty yelled, tears streaming down his face.

Moshe lifted himself up like he was doing a push-up, but they forced him face-down against the floor again and held him there. His arms and legs flailed, his fists punched at nothing.

Mr. Steinman stopped his praying and took a few tentative steps toward the scene. His prayer shawl slipped from his shoulders.

Mrs. Steinman stood over the scene, crying. "Darling, do what the men say. They want to help you."

The men tried to bend Moshe's arms toward the straight jacket, but he fought against them, kicking.

I remembered my mother on our kitchen floor pleading with *me* when the men came to take her away.

"No, please," Marty begged. "Leave him alone."

"Mommy, don't let them do this," Moshe cried out. "Mommy!"

Shaking, Mrs. Steinman asked, "Can I go in the ambulance with him?"

Still struggling to get the straight jacket on him, one of the men answered, "Sorry. No."

"Mommy, Mommy!" Moshe struggled against their attempt to bind his arms.

My mother screams, her arms tied around her body, "You filthy child won't help your mother." Sounds and pictures roll by me, but I'm not part of it. I'm not here.

Mr. Steinman, silent, pain creasing his face, watched the men.

"Honey," Mrs. Steinman said to her son. "I'll take the subway and wait all night if I have to. I'll make them let me see you."

I'm not here.

"It's Shabbos," Mr. Steinman said, "we can't ride in a—"

"This is my son. I *shall* be at his side."

"We'll take a cab," Mr. Steinman said. "It's faster."

I'm not here.

Like watching a movie, I saw the men secure the last tie around Moshe's waist and fold his arms over his body; he couldn't move, and neither could I. The men in the white clothes lifted him onto the gurney. "Mommy, please," he cried out. "I'll be good."

I'm not here.

"Sweetheart, it's for the best. I'll be there soon." She gently rubbed his forehead, "Gay shluffen, my dear, gay shluffen." She kissed him on the side of his face. "Sleep my child, sleep. Your mother loves you."

His mother wipes his tears with her handkerchief. And Mary stood outside the tomb, weeping. My mother screams. I'm not here.

The men carried Moshe from the apartment. Mrs. Steinman waited at the door, watching them take her son. "Hurry Benjamin, we must go."

"I'm coming. I wanted to get you a sweater, dear. There's a nip in the air."

He dashed from the hallway, the sweater over his arm, passing by Marty and me on his way to the door. He stopped, turned back, and took a few steps toward Marty. "Get out of my home. I never want to see you again. And if you ever, *ever* go near my son or try to contact him in any way, I shall kill you."

Chapter 43

ON THE IND subway line, Marty and I said little to each other. Marty's hair hung down in his eyes, the yarmulke and fedora gone.

I stared ahead at the Civil Defense poster on the wall before me. A man and a woman in helmets, badges on their sleeves; it read: "Alert Today. Alive Tomorrow. Enroll in Civil Defense."

Defense. I tossed the word around in my mind, my body shaking with the rattling of the car. *What does that mean?* Defense. The word seemed foreign.

"Who will be Miss Subways?" the sign next to the Civil Defense poster asked. Five young women pictured in the poster, hoping for my vote, smiled at me.

"For length of service you can depend on: BRASSIERES by Maidenform." The woman posed in her bra like it was normal to appear in public like that. *She'd* qualify. That girl would definitely qualify to be a Mt. Olympus Maxine, or maybe she'd rather work at The Haven as one of Harlington's Honeys. I held out my cupped hand, one eye closed, measuring her breasts to be sure.

"What are you doing?" Marty asked.

"Measuring."

"Measuring what?"

I started to laugh.

"What's so funny?"

I laughed, pointing at the bra lady. "Look, she could be ... Can't you see it?"

"See what?"

I laughed more as tears rolled down my face. "They're going to kill us, you know." I continued to laugh.

"Aw no," he put an arm around me. "Mr. Steinman was upset. He didn't mean—"

"Yes, he did." I was still laughing. "That's what they all want. We're freaks!" I made a funny face. "Everyone wants us dead."

"It's gonna be okay." He drew me into his chest and caressed my head while I wrapped my arms around his shoulders. We got twisted up in each other and stayed that way till the train squealed into West Fourth Street. Marty had to keep going and change at 59th for the IRT. As the door opened, my hand tightened on his arm.

"You want me to walk you home?" he asked. "It's not safe for a girl to be traveling alone at night."

"I do it all the time. I don't need ... Yeah. Walk with me."

He grabbed my wrist and we flew out past the door before it shut behind us. We ran all the way up the steps, out the exit, and across Sixth Avenue. We ran like something was chasing us, and perhaps something was. We sprinted through the Milligan Place gate, past the little tree, up the steps, into my apartment and my bedroom. I pulled the spread, blanket, and sheet down to the end of the bed.

"You get some good rest. It's been a rough night. I'll get going," Marty said.

"No."

"You want me to stay? I could sleep on the couch in the other room."

I stepped out of my shoes and pulled off my dress.

"Al, what are you doing?"

I stood in front of him in my slip. "I don't want to be alone tonight."

"Yeah, but we can't ..."

I put my arms around his neck and kissed him lightly on his lips.

He pulled me into his body. "You know, this isn't going to make us straight."

"I know." I kissed him again.

Chapter 44

July 1951

"AL! AL!" VIRGINIA called through my screen door.

I popped up from my couch, shaking myself awake from a rare nap. "Virginia, come in." I looked at my watch. "I'll get us some iced tea." I headed toward the kitchen, then stopped. "Would you rather a Tom Collins?"

"Maybe for this a Tom Collins is best."

"Coming up." I hurried to make them.

The afternoon sun shone through my window, and a warm breeze ruffled the curtain. "When I found out he was going to have to testify," Virginia called into the kitchen. "I, well ... All I can say is, thank you for letting me come over and watch it on your TV. I never expected anything this important to come out of that box. Oh, how lovely. Grandma's lamp."

"Yeah. Doesn't it look good on top of the TV?"

"Yes, it does. I'm so glad I gave it to you. You know, they could lock him up," she continued. "But he's not a hoodlum. You know that, don't you? Certainly, he's a little rough around the edges, but that's sort of sweet, don't you think?"

"Well ..." I'd never thought of Moose as sweet.

"You know, they're saying Frank secretly owns the Copa Cabana and that Jules Podell is only a ... what did they call him?"

"A front."

"You don't think those kinds of men own the Mt. Olympus or The Haven, do you? I put money into both."

"We all did." I came back into the living room with our drinks. "Max wouldn't let those types invest in our clubs." I put our highballs on the coffee table.

"*Everyone* thought it was Jules who owned the Copa Cabana until these hearings."

"They're so organized," I said. "They've got people across the whole country. All connected. Even in the government. Mayor O'Dwyer, who everybody loved! They said he was connected with this organized crime while he was mayor, and that's why he resigned. O'Dwyer! I voted for him. I knew these guys had something to do with our coin-ops, but …"

"I know Moose has never done anything truly bad. He's too good."

"Virginia," I began cautiously, "are you still planning to marry Moose? Haven't you been engaged for a year?"

"I'm patient. Look how long I waited, pointlessly, for Mr. Harlington. Come see the lovely ring Moose gave me." She held her hand out.

It was a large gold ring with a garishly large diamond. "It's not the kind you usually wear. Your tastes seem to be quietly elegant and this … well …"

"It's a bit gaudy, isn't it?" She hid her hand in the folds of her skirt. "You must consider me a perfect fool, going out with him; I know Mr. Harlington does. Who cares what he thinks? Moose is funny. I wish you'd get to know him better. He says such nice things to me. Not always pronounced correctly, but sincere. Of course, I don't let him take me to local clubs. We go mostly to Long Island."

"None of your friends …?"

"They're society snobs. Not real friends, not like you. They think they're too good for a nightclub anyway, while my true friends are all at the Mt. Olympus and The Haven."

"How's the divorce coming? Is he really getting one?"

"Well … certainly. We don't discuss it much, but I can't continue dating a married man. He knows that. I think."

"You think?"

"I'm lonely. I rarely see Moose, if you want to know. I'm going to spend my life alone, aren't I?" She glanced at her watch. "It's time. Turn it on."

I snapped on the TV and went back to the couch. We heard a gavel knocking against a desk and men talking. The picture rolled and we couldn't see a thing.

"Do something," Virginia pleaded. "He might be on soon. I can't miss it."

I kneeled on the floor in front of the TV, turning one knob, then the other. The rolling slowed.

"All right. That's almost it," Virginia said. "I can see Frank, but …" It started to roll again. "Do something. Hurry!"

"I'm trying, dammit!"

As soon as it was out of my mouth, I wanted to swallow it back down and slap my face. "Virginia, I'm sorry."

"Obviously you don't want me here. I'll go." She picked up her purse and headed for the door.

I jumped up, blocking her exit. "No, please. I do want you here. It's the stress. It's making me ... I'm trying to make you happy, and my TV's going crazy."

"It's working," Virginia hurried back to the couch, her eyes glued to the screen that now had a clear picture. Senator Kefauver sat on a high dais, surrounded by his committee of senators. The camera slid over to a desk with a microphone where a man in a business suit sat. Frank Costello's lawyer. Next to the lawyer, Frank Costello's hands were nervously twisting a handkerchief. That's all we could see of him. I learned from the papers later that Frank's lawyer had arranged for Frank's face not to appear on TV, because his lawyer said, "My client doesn't want to submit himself as a spectacle."

One of the senators asked Frank, "Have you always upheld the constitution and laws of your state and nation?"

We heard Frank say, "I refuse to answer on de groun's dat it might incriminate me."

The senator asked, "Have you ever offered your service to any war effort of this country?"

A long pause, then, "No."

Unless he had a good reason, like my ex-fiancé Henry, who had had polio as a child, there was no excuse for not serving in the war. Frank looked pretty healthy to me.

"Where's Moose?" Virginia wondered out loud.

The senator asked, "Bearing in mind all that you've gained in wealth, what have you done for this country?"

After a pause, he said, "I paid my taxes." The audience laughed. "I ain't answerin' one more question."

The senator yelled, "Get back here, or I'll find you in contempt of court."

"Look, there's Moose!" Virginia squealed, pointing at the screen. "Over on the right. Do you think they're going to call him next?"

"Virginia, don't you understand what happened? Frank walked out. They could send him to jail for that. Our Frank." I had no idea Frank was so sensitive, especially given the kind of work he did.

"The Bench calls to the stand Alberto "Moose" Mantelli."

"His real name is Albert," Virginia said. "Isn't that sweet?"

"You didn't know that?"

"No, did you?"

"I'm not engaged to him." Virginia sat on the edge of my couch. As Moose stood to approach the bench, my TV screen rolled again.

"Make it stop!"

I hurried to the TV, turned knobs, pushed and pulled the antenna.

It came in clear. One of the senators asked Moose, "How long have you been in the Mafia?"

"Whatcha mean?" Moose said, grinning. "Like do I carries a mem'ership card dat says Mafia on it?"

The audience laughed.

Another senator asked, "Do you operate politically, Mr. Mantelli?

Moose said, "Nah. If I done dat, I'd be de mayor."

The audience laughed again. Moose smiled at them, enjoying the attention.

"He's very entertaining, isn't he?" Virginia said. "He can't be guilty of anything."

"Virginia, he's making fun of our government. That's not funny."

"He doesn't mean any harm; he's teasing. That's the way he is. A big tease. Oh, no, it's rolling again. Do something. We're missing it."

"I'm trying. I can't get—"

"I have to see this. What am I going to do?" She lit her L&M.

I hopped up, snapping my fingers. "The Cedar Bar. On University. It's closer than the Whitehorse. We'll go there."

"To a bar? We could be arrested."

"It's not gay. We won't sit at the bar; we'll sit at a table. Lots of women are going into the bars today because the bars are tuning their TVs to the hearings, and not everyone has a TV. The Cedar is closer than the 8th Street Playhouse so … what'd ya think?"

"It's scandalous."

"I know," I grabbed her arm, "let's go."

"Yes, let's."

Chapter 45

August 1951

"RICHARD. SIT. TELL me what she said." I sat at my desk while Richard flew around the room. He had come bursting into my office, tie undone.

"Didn't you read it?"

"I haven't gotten to my papers today. We've got a full house tonight. Mel Torme. I've been going non-stop."

"Then look now! You must have it somewhere in that mess on your desk. How do you stand that?"

"I don't need housekeeping tips from you. Can't you tell me what it said?"

"No." He sat down. "I couldn't get those words passed my lips. What will Juliana think?"

I stood, pulling newspapers from the top of the pile and throwing them on my chair. "For Pete's sakes. Richard, I'm too busy for this. It's the last show, and all I can think of is sleep."

There was a light knock on my door, barely audible. Virginia stuck her head in. "I know you're busy, so I won't keep you. I wanted to say hello. Moose reserved a ringside table for us."

She always seemed to be trying to prove to me (or herself) that Moose really loved her, so I didn't remind her that Moose, Frank, and Jimmy always sat ringside. "That's nice," I said.

"Stop by our table later?"

"Of course."

She closed my door as I slid out my copy of the *Journal American*. I laid it on top and flipped through the pages, looking for Dorothy Kilgallen's column. "Here it is. So what's Dorothy got to say today?" I read aloud, "'The $64 question: What well-known society figure employs a maid who was a German spy during the war?'" I looked at Richard.

"No! I would never do that. I'm a Veteran. Further down."

"Trigger's pregnant? Really?"

"Who?"

"Trigger. Roy Rogers's horse. It says here he—Oh. He must be a she—I always thought Trigger was a boy. Guess not. Anyway, according to Dorothy, *she's* been knitting tiny garments. That's Dorothy's code for pregnant."

"Who cares if Roy Rogers's horse is pregnant?"

"Roy Rogers, I imagine. And the horse."

"Stop making jokes. This is serious. What does the next item say?"

"'The $64 question: What well-known night club manager is seeing the husband of a well-known night club singer?" I took a breath. "Oh, wow."

"Yes," Richard said. "What are we going to do?"

I never expected to actually see it in print. I folded the newspaper and put it back with the others.

"Well? What do we do?" he repeated.

"Nothing."

"What?"

He madly patted his pockets, looking for cigarettes, I suppose.

"What *can* we do? It'll pass."

"Defend ourselves. It's a lie. What if Juliana believes—"

"She won't." I looked through my office door window. "Speak of the devil now."

Richard jumped up, his body rigid. "It's Kilgallen! I'm going out there to give her a piece of my mind."

"You will not." I grabbed his arm. "That'll only make it worse. She hasn't named names. You go out there and confront her, and you'll be confessing, and you can bet *that* will be in tomorrow's column. Calm down. You can't lose your head over these things. Now, I'm going out to greet her and act like I don't care one whit about this bit of gossip because it doesn't apply to me. You go home. This is a game she plays."

"With my life!"

"An unpleasant game, yes, but a game."

For me, this was much easier than for Richard because I knew it could be much worse. I felt a little sorry for him, since he had no idea what a gift this was. I was being certified a genuine heterosexual.

I looked in the mirror that hung on the inside of my closet door and gave my hair a fluff. I straightened the scarf Max told me would do wonders for my little black dress and stepped out of the office. "Well, hello, there, Dottie." She stopped her conversation with Bertha and turned to me. What could Dorothy

Kilgallen possibly have to say to Bertha? Wow, what a snobby thought that was. Big smile. "Dottie, I'm so glad you could come."

Richard tiptoed out from behind me and ran out the door, but not without Dorothy noticing him. "Entertaining, dear?" she asked.

"Business."

"Oh. Business. Is that what they're calling it these days?" Big smile.

I smiled back just as big to keep myself from punching her. "So glad you could make it to Mel's show. I expect this next one to knock some socks off."

She slipped her baby-blue gloves that matched her baby-blue dress into her baby-blue purse. "Well, he can have my socks and any other item of clothing he desires, the little dear. I've been watching him ever since he was kid with the Mel-Tones." She turned to her husband, who stood behind her, waiting patiently. "Have you met my husband?"

"Of course. It's always a treat to have you both in my club."

"Really?" Dorothy said. "And yet, you and I haven't had lunch in quite awhile. Are you avoiding me, dear?"

"Heavens, never. I treasure our times together and your column, dear. You know, Dorothy, I never drink coffee in the morning. I find it too bitter. I read your column, instead."

"...Do you, dear?"

"You are a whiz with a turn of phrase."

"Yes I am. My husband often tells me that. Don't you, my sweet?"

He laid his chin on her shoulder. "Uh huh, snookums."

"My babykins," Dorothy said, patting the side of his face.

"Joseph," I called to the Maitre'd, "show the Kollmars to their table, and bring them a bottle of our finest Cognac on me."

"You remembered?" Dorothy said, as she and her husband followed Joseph to their table.

When I turned to look at Bertha in her hatcheck booth I saw that, again, she was watching me. She quickly busied herself with her tickets. "Have a pleasant evening," I said to her before returning to my office.

She raised her head, a look of shock on her face. "Oh, yes, Miss Huffman, I will. Thank you."

Maybe that was all she needed from me. Some acknowledgment. Had I really been so cold? I would have to correct that.

* * *

The night wound down and I kicked off my shoes, wiggled my stockinged feet as I sat at my desk. My new client, Patsy LaRue, opened for Mel Torme. Despite her name making her sound like a stripper—she refused to change it—her two songs had gone pretty well. We still had some work to do on her act, though. She waved at me as she left for the evening. A sweet kid. Mel Torme and his people left over forty-five minutes ago; the last of the Harlington Honeys were long gone, and I was looking forward to crawling under some sheets.

I slipped on my shoes and went into the next room, where all the magic had been turned off, the lights and pulsating fountains silenced. No music. I always got a small ache in my stomach at this time of night, when almost everyone was gone. It was customary for me to check the room at the end of the night. Sometimes I'd find a few drunken stragglers asleep by the bar, or under it. Joey, our bouncer, would scoop them up and put them out the door facing the IRT. The place was empty now. When I listened deep into the quiet, I could hear Juliana singing on our stage. Soon. Soon I'd make that happen.

"You need me, Al?" Joey called from the hallway.

"No. You go ahead. I'm going to take one more look around and lock up."

I walked over to the stage, stepping around crumbs and papers that littered the rug. I reached the side wall and switched off the work lights. Only the ghost light, with its one naked incandescent bulb, lit the stage now. Shadows of the gods and goddesses loomed large over the floor. As I turned to go, I heard a whimpering sound. From the stage? All the technicians were gone. Or at least that's what I thought. Had a cat gotten caught somewhere? I followed the sound onto the stage, past the gigantic columns, stepping around the pool. I suppose a cat could get stuck in one of those balconies. I headed toward the staircase that led to the first tier. The sound of a moan. Not from the balconies. Backstage? I pushed through the thick curtains that covered the back wall of the stage. Where was the damn light? I fumbled around like a blind man, trying to find my way as the sound got louder. I moved faster, stumbled over musical instruments, bumped into the door where Patsy had changed; it opened.

"Al!" Moose said through the shadows, a bare lightbulb dangling over the bald spot on top of his head. He was pointing a gun at me. The blood in my veins froze as I took in the scene. He sat in a chair, pants open, penis erect. His meaty fist in Virginia's hair, pressing her to her knees between his legs. She moaned.

"Don't do nuttin' stupid, Al," Moose said. "I like ya, but dat ain't gonna get in my way. Yer next."

He pulled Virginia's head back, tightening his grip on her hair. "Now, go, bitch."

"Please," she begged.

He pressed the gun to her cheek. "And no funny business. You bite me an' yer dead."

Still hanging onto a fistful of her hair, he pushed her head down onto him, and whimpering, she took his penis into her mouth.

Moose slumped down in his chair, a dopey look on his face, going deeper toward some euphoria, the gun poised on the arm of the chair. *Is he lost enough? Can I ... what?*

"Faster, bitch," he pushed Virginia's head up and down. "Oh, yeah, gawd, yeah."

My heart banged in my chest. I couldn't move. The navy-blue curtain behind Moose's chair shivered. A flash of metal. Jimmy the Crusher stood there, a hacksaw held over his head. His half-melted face even more ghoulish in the dim light. With one swift blow ... Slam! Onto Moose's wrist. A scream. Blood splattered onto Virginia's face. Jimmy the Crusher sawing. Screaming. Blood and semen. The gun on the ground. I couldn't move. Sawing through flesh, blood, screams ...

I grabbed Virginia's arm and pulled her from the room, throwing my arm around her shoulders. We ran. I didn't stop till we were outside and surrounded by blinking neon, screeching traffic, and a light drizzle. I pulled a couple bucks from inside my bra, and threw my arm up. "Taxi! Taxi!"

We got in the cab, and Virginia curled up into a ball on the seat. I got her up to my living room and onto the couch. She curled up there too, hiding her head under her arms. My blouse on my left side had speckles of blood. "Uh, you want something? Tea? A drink? I only have wine."

Without uncurling herself she whispered, "A toothbrush."

"Sure. I have lots. I always keep extra toothbrushes on hand. In my bathroom, my office, everywhere. I'm a nut about it. But you're not interested in this. Sorry. My bathroom's over here." I put my arms around her and walked her into my bedroom. Her face was splattered with blood. "I have a nightgown you can wear." I opened one of my drawers. "My nightgowns aren't fancy like you must wear. I get them on sale at Woolworths." Her face was blank. I wasn't sure if she could hear my meaningless chatter. I wondered if I should take her to the hospital, but she wasn't hurt.

I left her in the bathroom with three fresh toothbrushes to choose from and a just- washed nightgown. "Ya want me to come in with you and help get that blood off your face?"

She slammed the door. I changed into a nightgown. While I waited for Virginia, I poured two glasses of wine in the living room. I sat in the wooden rocking chair I'd bought recently at a flea market and stared out my window at my little tree. I could only make out its outline, lit by the half-moon in the velvet sky. Is there a God behind all that velvet? A God that cares about us down here stumbling around? A God to comfort Virginia? Something scraped against the inside of my stomach like I'd swallowed a thousand razor blades.

Virginia seemed to be taking an awful long time, thirty-five minutes, forty-five, an hour. A hint of the sun starting to break through the velvet.

I went into my bedroom and stood near the closed bathroom door. "Virginia, are you okay?" What a stupid thing to ask. A flash. *A closed bathroom door. Mom in there, cutting ...* "Virginia!" I yelled, and yanked the door open.

"Don't look at me," she cried, burying her face in her hands, toothpaste dripping from her mouth, down her chin, and over her wrists. The three toothbrushes all had been used and discarded in the sink.

"Virginia," I said, and I almost cried, but I figured that was the last thing she needed from me. I pulled her into my arms, but she pulled away.

"How come I didn't know?" she asked. "*You* knew what he was like. Max knew. But me ... What's wrong with me?"

"Let me wash your face." I filled the bathroom cup with water and held it to her lips. She sipped. "Now, spit." She did. I put a washcloth under the faucet and washed the dried blood mixed with semen and toothpaste from her face and hands. I took a deep breath so I didn't vomit.

I walked her into the room. "You can sleep in my bed. I'll take the couch."

"I'll sleep on the couch. I've already put you out enough."

"I don't mind."

"No!" she shouted, pushing me away. "I *want* to sleep on the couch. Let me do what I want!"

"Okay, sorry."

She walked into the living room under her own steam, and I followed her. "Some wine?" I held out the glass. My whole arm shook as I handed it to her.

She caressed it in her hands and sat on the couch, sipping it. I went back to my rocking chair.

The silence between us made me want to jump out the window and visit my little tree. The pale sunlight of dawn covered the courtyard, and in the distance, I could hear the faint sound of birds greeting the morning. The morning. It was coming again like it always did. "Uh, Virginia, do—you want to talk?"

"No."

"Okay. You're probably exhausted. I'll get you a pillow and cover so you can sleep."

I left to get the bed things. When I got back Virginia, sat in the same place, staring into her empty wine glass.

"Want me to refill that?"

"Please." She held out the glass to me.

I put the empty glass on the coffee table. "I'll fix up your bed first and then I'll get it."

"Now!" She demanded.

"All right." I dropped the bedding on the couch and went for her wine. When I handed it to her she wrapped her fingers around the glass as if it were something precious and drank it down in big gulps.

"If you could stand, I'll make up the bed."

She remained seated, drinking.

"Virginia?"

"I don't need those things. Take them away."

"But if you're going to sleep, you need—"

"Sleep? Do you think I can sleep? That I'll ever sleep again?"

I put the bed things on the coffee table and sat beside her. "Virginia, do you want me to call someone? Someone you can talk to. A relative?"

"No! You won't tell anyone! Please, you mustn't."

"I was thinking you—or me, or—we should—tell Max."

"Never! *Please*, Al."

"Listen a minute. If we don't say anything, Moose could come back to the club. Unless Jimmy killed him. You could see him again. But this time he'll be really mad. If he's still alive. If he isn't, he could have friends who'll look for you."

"I won't come to the club anymore."

"If he wants to find you, he will. He can't be too happy with what Jimmy did. Max should know you're in jeopardy."

"No! He must never know."

* * *

The day after it happened, I got to the club early, long before the cleaners. I hated leaving Virginia alone, but I had to check … In time, she fell asleep, so I left a note with some breakfast things. As I crept backstage, afraid to open that door, visions of what I'd find flooded my brain. I remembered the blood, and Moose's screams, and Jimmy's half-face with no expression. I remembered Virgina sullied with semen and blood, and the fear in her eyes. I pictured finding Moose's severed arm on the floor behind the door. I didn't want to open it. But I had to. Maybe it'd be Moose's whole bloody body. Severed arms, legs? …head?

I opened the door so slowly, I could hear the wood moan and feel my heart almost bursting out of my chest. I closed my eyes and poked my head inside. I forced myself to open one, then the other. Nothing. I took a step into the room, my hand bloodless and tingling from my grip on the doorknob. There was nothing. Not one sign that anything had happened here last night. Not one drop of blood.

Virginia stayed with me one more night and then insisted on going home to that huge mansion. With her mother in a nursing home, she had the place to herself, except for the old English Butler, Ainsworth, who had been with the family since she was a little girl, and Nola, the Irish Maid, whose arthritis made it hard to prepare Virginia's food or clean the house. The next few days after it happened, Virginia didn't contact me, or Max, or anyone at the club. I tried to reach her by phone several times a day, but Ainsworth always picked up. He sounded anxious when he said, "The Madam is occupied. I'll inform her you rang."

She never called me back, and I was plenty worried. I came close to telling Max what happened, but she had been so insistent. I took the bus over and tried to get past Ainsworth, but he was quick to say, "The madam does not wish to be disturbed," before he slammed the door in my face.

* * *

"I hear you've been playing backseat bingo with my husband?" Juliana said, calling from her hotel in Chicago. "How long has this been going on?"

"Juliana, really."

She laughed and then her voice got serious. "What was that item in Kilgallen's column about? Do you think she knows about us and she's using Richard as a ploy? A way to feel things out?"

"I don't think so. You and I never even see each other. How could she guess?"

"I suppose, but the way things are these days, anything can happen, and we have so much to lose."

"I know, but I don't think Dorothy—"

Moose and a young man I'd never seen before passed by my office window. "Uh, Juliana, can I get back to you? Something's come up."

I barely said good-bye before I hung up. I stood in my office doorway, watching Moose and the young man in the sloppy clothes and sloppy hat that he didn't take off as he hopped onto a barstool. Moose had a huge bandage on his right hand. I couldn't tell if the hand had been completely severed or what. I wondered where Jimmy the Crusher was. Had Moose killed him?

Moose slid off his stool and walked over to where I stood, leaving his companion at the bar. "Hi, Al," he said. "How ya doin?"

I pushed past my fear. "I'm doing fine, Moose."

"You tell Virginia I got somethin' special for her, and I wanna give it to her poisonally. Will ya do t'at for me, Al, huh?"

My mouth was so dry I could barely speak. "Leave her alone, Moose."

He laughed, "And t'e likes a you is gonna make me? I have sumfin nice fer you too …" He whistled, and the young kid slid off the stool and jaunted out the club door with him.

Now, I *had* to get Max involved. I hurried back to my office to call him at the Mt. Olympus. "What's this about?" he asked. "I'm busy over here. Handle it yourself. You're capable."

"Not for this."

"Then what is it?"

"I can't talk about it over the phone."

"Okay, okay, I'll get there as soon as I can."

But he didn't get there. Later, at home, in the early morning, I snuck into his room to talk to him, but he wasn't there. The bedspread was still tightly pulled across the bed. I tried reaching him at the Mt. Olympus, but no one had seen him. Now, I was really scared. I wondered if I should call the cops. But what would I tell them?

The next day, Virginia pranced into the club while I was talking to the band. She wore a breezy, flowery dress, all smiles.

"It's a lovely day today," she announced. "Let's have lunch."

My God, what if Moose came in? I pushed her into my office and locked the door. "Virginia, it's not safe for you to be here. I've tried to reach you, but you never return my calls."

"You haven't read yesterday's papers, have you?"

"I did. Theater/nightclub section."

"But not *The Daily News*, page eight."

"What happened?"

She smiled coyly.

"I don't have time for these games," I said, taking my yesterday's *Daily News* from the trashcan and quickly turning to page eight. Headline: "Gangland Killing." There was a picture of a man with a big belly lying on the floor, blood all over his face. A bandaged right hand.

I looked up at Virginia.

She nodded.

I looked back down at the paper.

"Alberto 'Moose' Mantelli, Underboss of the Luciana Crime family, was killed in The Bocavillia Café, in Teaneck, New Jersey yesterday afternoon while eating lunch. A gunman believed to be from his own family entered the eating establishment and showered him with a spray of bullets to his face and head. It was rumored that this was a mercy killing, because it was thought that Mantelli was losing his mind."

Could it have been Jimmy the Crusher?

"I'm free," Virginia said. "Free." She laughed, "Don't you see? I'm free! Free, Al!" Her laughter became wild as she pirouetted around the room like a dancing girl. "Free, free, free!"

"Uh, Virginia?"

"Free! Free!" She screamed, anger pouring out. "I'm free! Can't you hear me? I'm free! Free! Free!"

Max banged against the door, and I hurried to unlock it.

He dashed in. "Virginia, what …?"

Silent tears rolled down her face, "Oh, Max, I have done the most horrible thing." She hid her face behind her fists. "Forgive me. You must forgive me. Forgive me …"

He wrapped his arms around her and looked to me for an explanation; I couldn't explain. "Virginia," he turned back to her. "I'm sure you would never do anything terrible …"

"I did. I did."

Her body folded; she lay on the floor, her head on Max's shoes, her knees held tight against her chest. Max looked to me again to explain. "Uh …" I shrugged my shoulders.

Through the window in my office, I saw Jimmy the Crusher smiling at me.

* * *

Virginia stayed with Max for a few days after the news about Moose came out; she rested on the terrace, enjoying the view and regaining her strength before returning to her mansion. Max helped her to put her mansion on the market. The city quickly bought it as one of the last mansions in that area. They had plans to knock it out down and put in modern apartment buildings.

Virginia took some of the money she would inherit from her mother when she passed and gave it to the butler, Ainsworth, and her old maid, Nola. Ainsworth used it to return home to his native England. Nola found a pleasant old-age rest home in North Carolina that she could now afford with the money Virginia had given her.

Once they were taken care of, Max helped Virginia to move into a cozy, but elegant apartment on Lexington Avenue. It wasn't terribly far from him, so he could stop by every so often to check on her. She was trying to begin anew. At least, that's what she told everyone, but after Moose, she was never quite the same. It was hard to say in what way she was different, but she was quieter, perhaps, more nervous; there was something changed that I couldn't name. She seemed to distance herself from me and Max and from most of the people we knew. It was like she had woven a cocoon around herself, from which she could not wish to emerge.

Chapter 46

THE TIME TO move on came. I decided to take Max up on his offer to live on the top floor of the duplex he'd rented at 53rd and Park at an obscene cost.

Saying good-bye to my old neighborhood was hard. I walked up Eighth Street toward my apartment, passing the Whitney Museum, Nedicks, and Miss Elizabeth Lolly's Tea Shop. Sam's Deli had closed long ago. I missed Sam's cheap salami and cheese heroes, often my lunch during the war. The whole area was crowded now with cars beeping and people shopping; tourists, wide-eyed with the energy that pulsed through the center of that magnificent street. Eighth Street, the heart of the Village, seemed to shout, "I'm alive!"

I pushed through the Milligan Place gate and went up the three flights to my tiny apartment. I kicked away the crushed cigarette butts that lay in front of my door and thought, "That's the last time I'll have to do that."

My living room was as barren as when Aggie and I first arrived in '41. Anything worth saving, which wasn't much, I'd transported to the new apartment myself. The rest went to The Salvation Army.

Standing in the center of the empty room, I listened for the voices and strained to see the shadows of younger selves that had passed by. I stood there listening to the walls breathe, trying to hear our voices. Aggie, Dickie, Danny, and me. There was a time when they meant everything. My whole life was wrapped in and around theirs so tightly that once I thought I would cease to breathe without them. But I didn't.

Still, their sounds must be somewhere in this room. Perhaps deep in the floor boards or behind the painted walls, but … as hard as I listened, I couldn't hear them, couldn't see a thing. We'd all gone on to something else. Certainly, we'd left a trace in each other's lives somewhere, a smoky memory or two, but now, we didn't even know each other. Forever they'd be the kids I used to know from the block.

I stepped over to the window, my footsteps hollow in the empty room. I needed to take one last look at the scrawny tree Aggie was going to bring back to health, but never did because she had to take care of her husband Dickie, who'd been wounded in the war.

I looked out the window at the little tree still growing through the cement. If it could do that, what more could *I* do? I picked up my handbag from the radiator, straightened my pencil skirt, and loosened the Dior scarf around my neck. I took my beige gloves from my handbag and pulled them on. I stopped to look in the mirror I was leaving behind and cocked my hat a little to one side. I had careers to build, my own and Juliana's. I pulled the key from my handbag and bent down to slip it under the mat. I stood in the doorway trying to capture … some past something that … It was impossible. I stepped out the door, closing it behind me.

Chapter 47

September 1951

USUALLY WHEN I had a smidgen of time—and my time only came in smidgens—I would read one of Mercy's lesbian pulp books in my sitting room at the back of my upstairs apartment. Max lived downstairs.

My sitting room in the Park Avenue apartment was filled with the lightness of soft-colored wallpaper in pale green and yellow circles. Max and I were so busy we rarely saw each other. I had my own phone line, and sometimes I called Max to make an appointment to meet him in the living room. Occasionally, Scott would stay over and cook us dinner, and we'd spend the evening drinking wine—Scott would have a coke—and we'd talk. Then Scott and Max would disappear into Max's part of the house, and I wouldn't see them for days. Other times, Scott didn't come around at all. During these "droughts," as Max called them, he would sneak in some good-looking boy for "recreation."

The articles continued. They warned decent, ordinary American citizens to watch out for homosexuals because they were dangerous to American society and must be rooted out of government, teaching, and civil service jobs. Since we were so dangerous, articles and books appeared about how to detect and cure us. Some doctors thought marriage could fix us if we only gave it a chance. But the worst for me was the article that came out in *Coronet Magazine*.

I'd been subscribing to *Coronet* for years. My mother and father had subscribed to it, so I always saw it lying around the house. It had short, fluffy articles on current events, movie stars, stretching your budget, and making your marriage work.

The day was warm, September still clinging on to summer, perfect for an inconsequential read. I relaxed on the balcony in one of the chairs with my feet up on the hassock. Chopin played on the Victrola in the living room, and I kept the French doors ajar to hear it.

I picked up *Coronet,* and the title "The New Moral Menace to Our Youth" shouted at me. It said homosexuality was rapidly increasing and was imposing a threat to the youth of America. "Some male degenerates ... descend through perversions to other forms of depravity such as drug addiction, burglary, sadism, and even murder."

This gentle, innocuous magazine was slitting my throat. All the freedom and silly chances Juliana and I had taken in the forties during the war were gone. Shirl and Mercy knew women who'd completely stopped looking for female partners. They were too scared they'd lose their careers, their friends, and their families. Some women they knew had dashed into marriage with men in an attempt to hide or be cured. Others joined convents. I wondered how *that* was working out.

The tension of the times even showed on Max's face as Scott drew close to him and then retreated. I never dared wear trousers, except behind the walls of my own home.

"What's the matter?" Max asked, leaning on the back of my chair.

"This."

He pulled up a chair next to mine.

"It says," I began. "We're as bad as syphilis."

"Don't take these silly people seriously."

"When did you know you were different?"

"Oh, jeez ..."

"As soon as your Nanny put you in the playpen with the little boy down the street, you headed straight for his diapers?"

"Not that soon, and no Nanny. Just Mom."

"Really? I pictured you with a Nanny. Like Juliana."

"Juliana has me totally out-classed." He reached into his inside pocket and pulled out the silver cigarette case. "I'm a bit of a phony, Al."

"Huh?"

"My mother was a housewife who took in laundry to keep us going. Not very glamorous. Up until I was seven my name wasn't even Maxwell P. Harlington III."

"I knew it! I told Danny that. But what good is knowing now? I can't gloat. What *was* your name?"

"Well, it was—don't tell anyone—Bob Smith."

"Isn't that the name of the guy with the Howdy Doody puppet on TV?"

"Oh, God, is it?"

"I think so. Buffalo Bob Smith."

"Oh, jeez, really? You had me pegged the moment you met me, didn't you?"

"I didn't think your name was Maxwell P. Harlington III because I didn't think *anybody's* name was that."

"My father's name was Maxwell P. Harlington the Second."

"Huh?"

"Don't say "huh," honey. It makes a most unpleasant sound, and obscures your education. He was my *stepfather.* My mother used to do his laundry. Harlington *the Second* was a rich man. I thought of him as my father. I adored him. When he married my mother, he adopted me, and I became Maxwell P. Harlington, the Third, so that *is* my name. But I was always afraid someone would find out I wasn't what that name implied, and then you came along and terrified me. I thought at any moment you were going to announce to the world that I was one big phony."

"But you weren't. You *were* a big time club owner, discoverer of new talent. When I met you you'd fallen on bad times, but you got yourself back up. None of it was a lie."

"Wasn't it? I always feel like I'm lying. My stepfather moved Mother and me into a very impressive house, and I went to the best schools. I don't know that he treated Mother very well, but he was good to me. Whatever I wanted, he gave me. He was grooming me to be the head of some big company like he was, and I would've done anything he wanted. I thought.

"When I was twelve, I got a job taking out the garbage for this dive, a speakeasy we had in the 'bad' part of town where my parents told me never to go. Illegal hooch, singing acts, jugglers, comics. I'm sure it wasn't very good, but I loved the life right away. I didn't need the money. There was this one act—a singer. He must've been fifteen or sixteen, but from my twelve-year-old view, he was a god. He'd wear these grown-up suits and sing sweetly into the microphone and look at me with these big brown eyes. I followed him around, and after a while, I started managing his career. I'd meet owners of sleazy clubs, mob connected, and I'd go right up to them and tell them about this boy— Ricky.

"Then one day, after one of his shows, he came outside where I was waiting. I couldn't see him on stage because I was too young. That night, I watched his act standing on an upside-down garbage pail, looking through a small window. When he came out he was sweaty from giving his all. I don't think either of us knew what was happening, but he grabbed me up in his arms, and I could smell his sweet sweat. And somehow, the grabbing turned into a kiss and then clothes got pulled out of the way, and you know how that goes."

"How long were you with Ricky?"

"Two years. One day, we were up in my room, and my mother happened to come in and we were—you know."

"Oh, no."

"She screamed and ran for my father, who was downstairs reading the evening paper. Ricky was thrown out and blamed for the whole thing, and I was told never to see him again. Of course, that didn't work. We found new places, like the back seats of other people's parked cars."

"Oh, no."

"My options were limited back then. And yes, we got caught, in a beautiful Model T Touring Car, and the cops were called, and we were arrested. We only had to stay one night in jail. The judge gave us a lecture about morality, which, of course, neither of us listened to, and our parents had to come and pay a fine. Ricky's father beat him right in front of the judge. My parents paid the fine, but when I got home, my father wasn't speaking to me. Our relationship was completely broken, and I was devastated."

"Well, you did exchange a couple of letters during the war. Virginia told me."

"He asked me if I was still 'that way' and I told him yes and he wrote back, 'Go to hell.'" Since then, I've had no contact with either of them. My mother always does what my father tells her to. She has to. Who'd want to go back to messing with other people's dirty underwear? What about you? You didn't have any indication before Juliana?"

"Well—that's what I like to tell myself, but ..."

"Oh, tell."

"It's embarrassing."

"Hey, I just finished telling you the true story of Bob Smith of Portland, Oregon; you can share your war stories with me."

"Well, when I was thirteen I made friends with this girl, Marta. She was a Jewish girl who didn't live in our neighborhood, but she went to our school. I'd never met a Jewish person before, so I asked about her religion. Sometimes I'd go over to Marta's house to have dinner, and then one time her mother invited me to stay overnight since we didn't live near each other. We slept in the same bed."

"So you did it with her. Juliana wasn't your first."

"No. I was only thirteen, and not at all like you. We started playing this game. I don't know how it got started, but we kind of dared each other to do certain things. So first, she'd dare me to open a couple of buttons on my pajama top, and then I'd dare her to do the same thing. And then we showed each other our breasts. And then finally—we were excited and scared, so we counted to three and pulled down our pajama bottoms in front of each other. Then we pulled them back up right away, then we pulled them down again and left them down by our ankles a little longer than the first time; it was sort of a game of chicken to see who'd pull them back up first. I'd never experienced such excitement before. We never did anything beyond that or like that again, and we never talked about it.

"Then there was this other time. When I was around fourteen, I went to a park that had an art museum I liked to go to. Heckscher Park. It was closed because with the depression, the town couldn't afford to keep it open, but there was a place at the bottom of the fence that had a section cut out. I wore trousers, so I could crawl under the fence. I read a lot when I was a kid, so I'd go to the park where no one would bother me.

"There was a pond there where I could watch the ducks swim while I read. One day, I was sitting under a tree and these boys came over and made a circle around me; they pointed at me and said things like: 'Is that a girl or a boy?' I became a 'thing,' not a person.

"I didn't know what to say, because I wasn't a boy—I knew that—but 'girl' didn't feel right either. Then one of them pointed at my chest and laughed. 'Oh, look, it's got those things. It must be a girl. Are you a girl?' he asked me.

"I kept quiet, pretending they weren't there until they went away. That's when I realized I didn't know for sure if I was a girl or a boy. I've never told anybody about this before. Even so many years later, it makes me feel— ashamed."

Max put his arm around me. "It's obvious that you're a girl."

"I don't know how I feel about that even now." He squeezed my shoulder and kissed the side of my face.

Chapter 48

"AL," MARTY SAID, as he slid his meatloaf out through the little doors. "I can't believe it," he carried his tray toward a table. "They hired me."

"Who hired you? For what?"

He put his tray down and pulled out a chair for himself, not me. I sat opposite him with my tray. "TV! Aren't you eating?"

"Luncheon engagement with Juliana at Sardi's. I wanted to come and hear your good news. I thought you were already working in TV."

"Small potatoes. This gig is big. The lead. My career is set. My whole damn life is set, and I haven't even graduated yet."

"A whole career can't be determined by one job," I said.

"In TV, it can. I'm going to be seen all the way in California. Thousands of people."

"I thought you wanted to do musical theater."

"I did. Until TV. You've been seeing me in those fifteen-minute dramas?"

"I'm at the club evenings."

"I've been stacking up those little shows, one or two a week, but when I can, I sneak in to watch the sixty and the ninety-minute shows. I've never seen this kind of acting in my life. Total commitment. I've stood in the presence of absolute genius. You've got to make time to see it. Of course, not everything's great, but when it is, it's even better than theater. You're so close to it, you can see every wrinkle of pain, question, doubt in that actor's face. You know what kind of concentration that takes?

"I've been getting to know some terrific actors," Marty continued, "and a lot of them come from the Actors Studio. You know, Marlon Brando came out of there."

"Yes, Marty. I'm in the business too."

"I forgot. I've got an appointment to audition for the Actors Studio next week."

"Good luck. That's prestigious."

"I'm a wreck. I rehearse with this girl from the school every day. It's almost impossible to even get an audition, but these guys I met through TV introduced me to the right people."

"Tell me about your part on TV."

"My show is for General Food Playhouse on CBS."

"Big. I've got Juliana signed to—"

"Have you seen their anthology series?"

"Working."

"Every week they do an adaptation of a novel or a play." He cut off a piece of meatloaf with his fork and ran it through his mashed potatoes. "The one I'm cast in is called "Train to Nowhere" by—by ... I forget. A new writer." He put the meatloaf and mashed potato into his mouth. "The producer, Sal Vincent, said he's gonna get a writer from *Modern Radio and Television* to do a piece on me so I get known. Once you're in with these guys, they keep calling you for other things. My day has come. My mother's over the moon. Oh, no, look at the time! I forgot! Equity. Important union meeting." He ran out, leaving his tray for me to empty.

*　*　*

Juliana was booked into the best clubs in Chicago, Florida, and LA. Sometimes she worked in two states at the same time. She'd do an early show in New York and then board a 10 p.m. flight and arrive on time for a 2 a.m. show in Chicago, which always had a sold-out crowd. There were some clubs still booking a three-show night, so sometimes she did a 4 a.m. gig.

A Broadway producer called, wanting to cast her in the lead of a new musical he was considering, but that fell through. She cut an album that did well on the charts, but didn't get to the very top. I knew that was because she hadn't made a film yet. Richard was always being sent scripts from Hollywood that he passed along to me to discuss with Ben, her agent. Ultimately Juliana went with my opinion—the script isn't right. It was so important we not make any mistakes at this point.

Practically my whole life was Juliana, but I rarely saw her. We communicated by phone, Western Union, or Richard. One of the rare times we met in person was for lunch at Sardi's in April. My idea. We were celebrating the contract she was about to sign to do two cooking shows as a guest of Poppy Cannon, the Can Opener Queen. Juliana didn't even own a can opener; she would never serve her guests canned vegetables, canned tomato sauce, or a cake made from a mix.

She was a genuinely incredible cook, but convenience food was all the rage after the war. Doing these shows would broaden her visibility. And for me, well, it would keep her in town for a couple weeks, which meant I'd see her, but so would Richard. And he would see her more. This lunch was for us. My treat. Imagine, me treating Juliana in Sardi's. If only Mom could see me now.

I reserved a center table where I'd have a good view of her entering. No one could enter a room like Juliana. I gazed at the caricatures of Broadway and Hollywood stars hanging on the walls and imagined that someday Juliana's would hang there too. *I* would see to that. But I couldn't imagine how the artist would possibly take some odd feature of hers and exaggerate it. What odd feature?

Oh jeepers! I was wearing a red dress. I'd forgotten that everything in Sardi's is red or maroon. The walls, the banquettes, the seats, the menus, the awning outside. As I worried about how to get out of my red dress without being noticed, Juliana came through the door, stepping feather-light on Sardi's *maroon* carpet. My heart literally leapt up. She wore a mink jacket over a black linen afternoon dress, and a matching wide brimmed hat sloped over her forehead. The tuxedoed maitre'd met her at the door and led the way. She stepped toward me, her dark hair bouncing around her shoulders. "Well," she said, standing behind the chair, smiling at me. "It's been a while. Hasn't it?"

I couldn't speak. I sat frozen with the vision of her perfect self before me. The maitre'd helped her to remove her coat and guided her into her chair. He bent close to her ear and whispered, "I enjoyed your last show so very much."

"Thank you, Sidney." He bowed and left us. "You look very good, Al. I don't believe I've ever seen you in red before."

"I clash with the room."

She laughed. "I don't think anyone else would ever think to say that. I've missed you." She slid off her gloves, keeping my gaze the whole time. Could there be anything more joyful than to look into her eyes? But, of course, we couldn't touch.

"We don't have much time, do we?"

"Not much. I've been traveling so many months back and forth that Richard has been feeling neglected. He made me promise I'd come right home to him when I got back into town. Of course, he doesn't know I'm already here. Oh, Al, I am so very glad to see you."

My heart danced within me. She never said things like that. I wanted to reach across the table and ... Oh, well. Sitting in her presence had to be enough.

We ordered quickly so we could spend more time talking. Our moments together were too fleeting to waste even one. Anything I had to do back at The

Haven, and there was a lot, I would've gladly crossed off the list to spend one more minute with her. But I didn't have that choice. I ordered the brochette of beef, and Juliana had the Cornish game hen. Watching her weight as usual.

We began with a sparkling burgundy wine. Not having had breakfast, it went straight to my head, and I had visions of her and me—well, you know—so it was hard to concentrate on her funny stories of Chicago and L.A. When she reached across the table for the salt—"Oh, let me," I said. Our hands met for one lovely moment, both holding the shaker; we stayed that way, looking into each other's eyes, forgetting the danger. Then remembering, we quickly let go, and the saltshaker fell, spewing salt all over the table.

Sydney hurried over with a crumber. "Allow me," he said. He'd been watching us. Eyes were always watching Juliana. Probably everyone in the place had seen us drop that saltshaker.

"Thank you, Sidney," I said as he left. We couldn't allow ourselves to forget to be on our guard at all times.

"Did you read this contract?" Juliana asked, taking us back into the real world. She slipped it from her purse and laid it on the table.

"I read all your contracts."

"Then you read the morality clause."

"Oh, that."

"They want me to be 'clean' in my personal life. I can't do anything that would *embarrass* their audience."

"Everyone signs that."

"They can look into my *personal* life, Al."

"They won't. Or they'll find Richard. If you don't sign it, they won't let you do their show. It doesn't mean they think you're, you know ... They don't know about that. They're looking for communists."

"Only communists? I know you're not that naïve."

"You have to sign it, Jule. If you don't, you risk being put in *Red Channels.*"

"I thought that book didn't exist."

"Well, that's what they want us to believe, but I've seen it. It very much does exist. You'd never work again. At least not in TV or film, and you have to break into TV if we're going to push your career to the top. It's hard to say which way the nightclubs are going. These are uncertain times. I'm sorry."

"It's not your fault. It ... I'm not so used to boldly lying, signature and all."

"You're not lying. You're not immoral—exactly."

She smiled and took a pencil from her purse; she licked the end and scrawled her flowing signature at the bottom of the page. "This will get easier, won't it?" She replaced the pencil in her bag. "Lying."

Chapter 49

"IT'S GONE." MARTY paced in front of my settee, looking more disheveled than usual. "I had it, but now it's gone."

He'd just burst in. Scott, I guess had opened the door. Max was at the Mt. Olympus. I had hoped to get some rest before going back to the club for the midnight show. The TV hummed in the background.

"I even thought of quitting school," Marty went on.

"You didn't, though. Did you?"

"No, but yesterday, my life was all set. A week ago, I found out I got into the Actors Studio."

"Congratulations. That's really something. You can build a career on that."

"Yeah, maybe, in the theater, but now this. I was gonna make so much money, I wasn't gonna need school. Salaries have gone way up in TV for the sixty-minute dramas. I'd be making money at something I'm good at, that I love. I was gonna have the perfect life. But now it's gone. How can that be? So fast?"

"This is show business. That's the way this life goes. But, Marty it's one job. Not your whole life."

"I told you, once you're in, you're in, and when you're not ... What happened dammit? I was in." He dropped down onto the couch.

"Did you have words with anybody?"

"No. We were all celebrating in Sal's office a few nights ago. Champagne, caviar, the whole bit. General Foods was in love with me. Couldn't wait to get me on the payroll. All that was left to do was sign the contract. Barbara, the secretary, had to get the final paper work done; she told me to come into the office today and she'd have everything ready to sign. Do you have anything to drink?"

"Wine," I said, getting up. "Want that?"

"If you don't have anything stronger."

"I might have a little scotch. Let me look."

Marty walked back and forth, running his hands through his hair while I went into the kitchen. I could hear Edward R. Murrow's deep voice coming from the box, but I couldn't make out what he was saying. I knew it was about the new hydrogen bomb they were developing, and it was lots worse than the atomic one. I supposed I should've turned it down or off, but I hated missing that show. I poured the last of my scotch into a glass of ice. "Keep talking," I called. "I can hear you."

"This sure is a nice place you got. Must cost a lot of dough."

"Not cheap."

"I went into Sal's office this morning. I had daisies for all the girls."

"That's nice."

"But when I got there, it was like no one knew me. Like I was a stranger. None of the girls said hello, kept working at their desks like I wasn't there."

I came out with the scotch for him and wine for myself.

"Barbara, Sal's secretary, wouldn't look at me." He sipped his scotch. "We always joked together. I gave her the flowers, and she put them on her desk, no vase, no thank you. She called into Sal. He came out. Didn't invite me into his office, didn't pat me on the back like always; then he said—in front of everybody—'Sorry kid, we decided to go with someone else.' God, it was like he punched me in the goddamn gut. I managed to say, 'Why?' He said the sponsor thought some other guy would be a better fit for the role. I looked at Barbara, but she couldn't look at me. A few nights ago, she was sitting on my lap, and I was feeding her cheese and crackers. God, Al, I felt so awful. I'd never felt that awful in my life. I left. What else could I do? My stomach … it was on fire, and I thought I was gonna throw up in the elevator. How could I've been perfect at the beginning of the week, and three days later, I'm out?"

He wrapped his forearms around his middle. "My stomach hurts all the time."

"You should see a doctor."

"Forget doctors!" He yelled. "Why is this happening to me?"

"Not so loud. We don't want the world to know."

"Al, my career, my whole goddamn career was right there in my hands." He held out his cupped hands toward me. "And then, in some horrible second, it was whisked away. For no reason. Do you think someone found out I was gay?"

"Gee, I don't know. Have you been going into the bars or those subway bathrooms?"

"Of course, I have. I'm a guy. Guys want sex. All the time. Do you think someone followed me? What am I gonna do?" He ran a hand through his hair.

"Easy, we don't know that's it, so don't go losing your head. You must've met people you could talk to, find out if that could've—"

"Are you nuts? Nobody talks about that on TV. You gotta be squeaky clean. Oh, God, Al, if that's it, my career's cooked."

"Maybe it's not that. Why don't you call around and see if anyone knows anything? See if any of them have jobs for you."

"I did that. Or tried to. I started this afternoon. No one will take my calls."

"Maybe they were out. You can be impatient, you know. Give them time and—"

"I'm scared, Al. I don't get scared easy, but this is scaring me. If it's because I'm gay, I won't be able to work anywhere. My heart's beating so fast. Al, could you call around? Try to find out something."

"I don't really know TV."

"Just try. That's all I'm asking. I don't know who else to ask."

"Okay," I sighed, "but I can't promise anything. I'm not 'in' with that crowd yet. I'll see what I can do. You know, Marty, it could be nothing. Maybe you're making more of this than it is, being dramatic like you get. I bet someone'll call you this week with a job offer."

The "Star Spangled Banner" boomed from my TV, and Marty jumped up. On the screen, the American flag waved against a background of blue sky like it always did when the station went off the air. Marty stood at attention, saluting. Then, remembering he wasn't in the service any more, joined me in putting his hand over his heart. We stood side by side like that until the song ended and the test pattern came on.

* * *

The next day, in my office, I called Sal, Marty's "almost" producer. The secretary, Barbara, answered. "Hi, Barbara, this is Al Huffman over at the The Haven. Oh, did you like last season's show? I always love hearing that. Let me messenger you over a couple of tickets for the opening of our new show. It starts next Saturday." She was so excited, it sounded like she was jumping up and down in her seat. "Is Sal in?"

"I'm sorry, Al," Barbara said. "I don't like sounding like a busybody, but Sal always needs to know the topic before I put his calls through."

"Sure. The topic is Marty Buchman."

"Oh? Really?" Her voice became distant. "Uh ... you know, Sal stepped out while we were talking. I didn't know you wanted to speak to him, or I would've stopped him."

Why did she think I was calling? "When do you expect him to return?"

"I don't know," she said hurriedly, and hung up.

"Barbara? Barbara?" The phone buzzed in my ear. I replaced the receiver in its cradle. Now *I* was scared. I made another call, and another, and another, but whenever I said the name "Marty Buchman," I got some similar response. Was it because someone had found out he was gay, or could it be something else?

* * *

The man on the other end of the phone told me to meet him at four at Child's. He heard I'd been asking questions about Marty Buchman, and he thought he could help. He told me I had to come alone and sit in the second booth from the counter. He'd arrive in a gray trench coat and a fedora; he'd hang the fedora on the coat rack next to the counter, but he wouldn't remove the coat. I was to wear a red ribbon in my hair. Gosh, I wished he'd come up with a better identifier than that. Me in a ribbon? I ran to Woolworth's to buy one.

There I sat, in the second booth from the counter, my eyes scanning the menu for turkey and mushroom croquettes with a la King Sauce and Potatoes. So specific. But that's what he said to order. Why wasn't the red ribbon enough? I didn't know whether to laugh or get the hell out of there. Was I in the middle of a Grade-B detective picture, or was this guy gonna kill me?

The waitress took my order. Soon after, a man in a gray trench coat and fedora came through the door and hung both the coat and the hat on the rack. *That wasn't right!* He wasn't supposed to hang the coat. He was heading in my direction. Was this a trick?

A man in the booth behind me called, "Sylvester. Here." The mystery man walked past me to join his friend.

I stared at the coat rack. It had been empty when I first entered, but now it had that other man's hat and coat hanging from it. What if my man could't fit his coat on the rack? No, no, my man wasn't going to put his coat on the rack; he was only going to put his hat there. Was that right? Or was it the coat he was gonna hang and not the hat?

Another man in a trench coat and fedora stepped through Child's door. But there was a woman with him—in a trench coat, too. Who the hell was she?

The man hung his hat on the coat rack and said good-bye to the woman. She slipped out of Child's door as he approached my table.

"Is this seat taken?" the man asked, standing at my booth.

I didn't answer him. I wasn't expecting a question.

"Is this seat taken?" he repeated.

"No. Maybe. I don't think so."

He bent over and kissed me on the forehead. "Sorry I'm late, darling." He sat down and signaled for the waitress.

He ordered coffee with milk and a hamburger, bloody.

"You look terrified," he said after the waitress left. "There's nothing to be afraid of. I'm one of the good guys." He held out a leather billfold with a badge: "FBI."

"What? Oh, gosh," I whispered.

"Don't whisper," he whispered back. "That's a sure give-away that we're up to no good," he grinned. "How's the new show coming?"

"Fine. How did you know we're working on a new show? We haven't announced … Oh, you snoop for a living."

He smiled, "I loved your Christmas show at The Haven, Miss Huffman. You're doing a heck of a job over there."

"Thanks. What do you know about—you know."

"Marty Buchman. You can say his name. We still have that much freedom left in this country. The communists haven't taken that away. Yet. But if we're not careful, they're going to take over our beloved country. Only six years ago, we fought a war against fascism so we could stay free. We won that war, or at least, that's what most people believe. But there are forces running wild today, Miss Huffman. Forces that are determined to stomp out our freedom."

The waitress placed my meal in front of me and brought him the coffee.

Lifting his coffee cup, he said, "Please, eat, Miss Huffman. Mine will be along shortly."

"I'm really not hungry. I want to know—"

"But we need to be cautious. Please eat. Enjoy."

I took a bite of food. "Can't we get to the point? Marty was hired, and a few days later, he was out. What do you know about that?"

"I know that he may never work in television again, unless he comes clean."

"Comes clean? What?"

Did he mean 'come clean' about being gay?

He looked over at the people eating in the center of the room. Then turned back to me. "How well do you know our subject?"

"Our subject? You mean Marty? Pretty well."

"Then you know he was recently accepted into the Actors Studio, and last year he did an awful lot of unionizing."

"Is that suddenly illegal?"

"Well, under certain circumstances, these activities could be suspect. The sponsor wants to deliver clean television. Television goes right into American homes. Good, decent American families watch it together. Children watch it. There must be nothing politically muddy."

"Politically ...? Marty's not a communist, if that's what you're getting at." A flash of memory. Marty asking me, 'Are you a communist?' But he didn't mean that; he meant ... Maybe this guy doesn't mean communist either. Maybe it was code for gay, like they're doing in DC.

"You tell Mr. Buchman that when he's ready to talk, we'll receive him with open arms."

"Talk about what?"

"He knows."

The waitress set the hamburger in front of the man. He opened the top of the bun and drowned the burger with ketchup. "Now, if you'll allow me to enjoy this good ol' American hamburger in peace ..."

"What?"

"You're being dismissed. It's all I'm going to say. But be assured that I know things, Miss Huffman. Lots of things. About Buchman. About you. About ... well, let's say it's my business to know people's secrets." He winked, picking up his hamburger; ketchup squished over his fingers. "I suggest you convince Mr. Buchman to talk."

* * *

"Max! Max!" I ran yelling into my Mt. Olympus office, slammed the door, locked it, and paced. Max stood on the other side of the door, knocking on the window. "Well, come in, dammit! Oh!" I hurried to open it. "Sorry, I don't know what I'm doing. Oh, gosh, Max, oh gosh, gosh."

"What are you doing in this office?"

"I had to find you. This guy. He knows about me. Maybe you. I don't know."

"Who knows what? Stop moving around. Take a breath. Now, let's sit down. That's a good girl." He sat opposite me. "Tell me."

I took another breath. "I was trying to help my friend, Marty Buchman. I haven't introduced you to him yet. He was going great guns on TV and then they fired him for no reason. I thought. I had lunch today with a guy and, well, Marty might've been fired for being …" I whispered, "… gay."

"Are you sure?"

"No. The guy didn't come out and say gay. He said, 'communist.' Or— did I say that? I don't know. But we all know communist is code for, you know."

"Sometimes communist means communist."

"I'm not a communist!"

"Who said you were? What are we talking about?"

"Marty got fired from his TV job because he's a communist."

"He is?"

"No. Marty's not a communist; he's gay. But there was this guy—"

"What guy?"

"Pay attention."

"I'm trying."

Marty banged on my door. I pulled it open and threw my arms around his neck. "Oh, Marty, Marty. There's this guy—"

"What guy?"

"FBI."

"Oh, God, what does the FBI want with me?'

"They know about me."

"You? I thought this was about me."

"It is." I paced, trying to collect my thoughts. "Only, he said he knew about me too."

"Knew what about you?" He became aware of Max standing next to my desk and smiled, "Well, hello, there." He thrust his hand out. "Marty Buchman here."

Putting out his hand. "Max Harlington."

"Oh, I've heard so much about you, Mr. Harlington."

"Please. Max."

"Okay, Max. Al didn't tell me you were so handsome."

"Well, that's kind of you to say."

"Guys!" I stomped my feet. "I'm over here having a crisis."

"Oh, yeah," Marty said. "What does finding out about you have to do with me not getting that job?"

"You might have gotten caught up in the blacklisting that's been going on," Max said.

"But I'm not a communist."

"Neither are a lot people who have been accused, but they may think you are."

"So it's not 'cause I'm gay?"

"It's difficult to say."

"What do I do to make this come out all right?"

"You come clean," I told him. "That's what the FBI guy said."

"Come clean? About what? He doesn't want me to admit I'm gay, does he? That would ruin me."

"Instead of guessing," Max said. "I'll get my copy of *Red Channels* and see if you're in it."

Max sprinted from the office and came back with *the* book. "Let's see," he said sitting down. His finger ran over the names as he turned the pages. "No. You're not in here."

Marty expelled a gust of air. "Oh, God, I thought I was done for. Then why …?"

"Let me call an actor friend who really *is* blacklisted, Salem Ludwig. See if he's heard anything."

"I know Salem. A nice older guy. We worked together on a committee at Actor's Equity to get TV to reconsider their rehearsal policy. For a ninety-minute show they expected us to rehearse only an hour and a half. In live theater, Equity allows for sixty hours. We didn't expect *that* much—TV is fast—but we needed to rehearse."

"The FBI guy did mention 'unionizing.'" I said.

"Unionizing? We were trying to give them a good show."

"Let me make this call and see what Salem has to say." Max dialed the number. "Hi Salem, Max Harlington. I wanted to know if you heard anything about Marty Buchman." He told him the things the FBI guy had said. "Really? Thanks." Max hung up and turned around to lean against my desk.

"Well?" Marty asked.

"Salem thinks you may be graylisted."

"What the hell is that?" Marty asked.

"It means they don't have enough on you to list your 'sins' in the book, but they have enough to be suspicious. Working with Equity could be part of it. So could the Actors Studio. Salem heard you got in. He sends congratulations."

"Terrific. I get this big honor and lose my job. You know, Marlon Brando's in that."

"He can get away with a lot more than you can. The Actors Studio evolved out of the ideas of The Group Theatre in the thirties, very liberal, some think communist, which, by the way, is not illegal in this country. The right to think your own thoughts and have your own ideas is a first amendment and, I think, God-given right."

"That's what Leon, Barney's brother said," I told them. "That HUAC had no right to exist because it was policing people's thoughts and beliefs. But now, it's getting even worse."

"Yes. And according to Salem, lots of Actors Studio's members are blacklisted. You're lucky you're only graylisted. Salem told me graylisting is kind of a whispering campaign. One sponsor tells another to watch out for you."

"But I didn't do anything. If the FBI guy already knows about my work at Equity and The Actors Studio, what can I come clean about so I can work in TV?"

"I haven't a clue," Max said.

"But none of this has to do with him being gay?" I asked.

"It's hard to say. I'd be careful with places where cops are likely to be on the prowl. Stay away from subway bathrooms. Don't go home with anyone you don't know."

"I know you," Marty said with a wink.

"This is serious, young man. If they hang a charge of moral perversion on you, your life as you know it is over."

"You mean, I'd have to sell shoes like my father?"

"If you could get that."

Chapter 50

December 1952

AFTER IT FIRST happened, Marty wrote to all the stations and some of the sponsors he knew telling them he hated communism and would never be a communist, but no one responded. Unable to get work, he sunk into a deep depression. It wasn't the money. He still had the GI Bill while he was in school. He felt blocked from doing something he loved; punished without cause. He wondered what "come clean" meant, and how he could do it and be done with this. Occasionally, an FBI guy would follow him down the street or into the subway, always with the same question, "Are you ready to talk?"

"Talk about what?" he'd ask them, and they'd answer, "You know."

He worried what would happen to his career after he graduated. Was he finished? Sometimes, when I'd go over to his apartment to drag him to school, I'd find him still in his pajamas. I was trying to get him some stage work, since Actor's Equity had voted against supporting the black list, but Marty had no professional stage experience and Broadway attendance was down; fewer new shows were going up because audiences were staying home to watch TV. Attendance at the Mt. Olympus and The Haven were being affected by The Box, too, and on especially bad nights, it scared me.

To be close to the entertainment arena, Marty hung around The Haven when he wasn't at school. He'd sit in the back and listen to the show. He got to know all the personnel, like the chefs and waiters, Bertha, the hatcheck girl, Scott. He even made a point of meeting Mabel Mercer when she was booked for one night. Some nights, after the last show, he'd camp out on my floor. I gave him the key to my office so he could come and go as he pleased.

In December of '52, I stomped the snow from my boots and entered The Haven carrying an armload of newspapers to be studied. I stepped over Marty, threw my papers onto my desk and wiggled out of my coat. As I was hanging my scarf on the coat rack, the phone rang. "Al Huffman, here. Yes? Yes! I have someone."

I kicked Marty in the leg. He didn't move.

"Definitely good," I said into the phone. I kicked Marty again. He still didn't move. "You're gonna love him. Can I call you back in two minutes? Don't call anyone else. This guy's terrific."

I hung up the phone and yelled, "Marty, are you dead?"

He squirmed and rubbed his eyes. "Huh? Out drinking last night. Another FBI guy followed me."

"Well, I hope it was a straight bar. Get over to the Broadhurst. Now. You've got an audition for a part in *Pal Joey*. You're a shoe-in."

He jumped to his feet. "What?"

"They need someone right away to play the part of Louis, the tenor in today's matinee. Just a small role. The guy who usually plays Louis and the understudies have the flu. This is your shot."

"A singing part?"

"A few bars. Mostly chorus. It's not stardom, but it's a step or two up the ladder. I want to call the guy back and tell him you'll be there in a half hour."

"Half-hour? Look at me. I'm a mess. I'm not prepared. Yes! Call him."

I made the call while I pulled a fresh toothbrush from one of my drawers. "Here. Never used." I handed him my tooth powder. "Clean up in the Men's Lounge. Max keeps fresh shirts in his other office. I'll get you one."

"Max's shirt? No kidding? You're gonna let me wear …?"

"Down, boy. He's already taken. I'll get you that shirt."

"I'm not warmed up," he said, when I got back with the shirt.

"Warm up on the subway. This is your chance to be on Broadway. Go charm the pants off Max Meth, the Musical Director."

"Yes!" He ran out of my office, then turned back. "I can do this, Al, can't I?"

"Yes! Don't forget your tie."

"In my pocket. You won't be sorry." He ran to the Men's Lounge.

* * *

"I got it! I got it!" Marty yelled into the phone. "They loved me and gave me a contract for the entire run. And besides Louis, I'm gonna be understudying a few other roles!" He cleared his thoat. "Uh, Al?" His voice got soft and humble. "Thanks for this."

"Sure." I was moved by the depth of feeling in his voice.

"I owe you a bouquet of daisies!" he sang out as he hung up.

I sat down with a cup of tea and my newspapers, and glanced at the headline of the *Daily News*. "Ex-GI Becomes Blonde Beauty: Operations Transform Bronx Youth." Another paper read, "Bronx Ex GI Becomes a Woman," and another, "Dear Mum and Dad, Son Wrote, I've Now Become Your Daughter."

I grabbed at the papers, studying the headlines; some slipped to the floor. A man had been made into a woman! Shaking, I turned away so I could breathe, but I had to go back to it. It was like a car wreck I didn't wanna see, but had to. I opened to the middle of the *Times*. Some woman columnist was complaining about the pedestrian traffic sign they put up on the corner of 42nd and Seventh. "We've never had this sign before," she said, "and we don't need it. Why should I listen to a sign telling me when to walk and when not to walk? Before long, they'll have signs blinking 'Don't Walk' at us from every corner, controlling our minds."

I flipped back toward the front, trying to find the page. I found it and read, "George Jorgensen, who served in the army at the end of World War II, went to Copenhagen, Denmark, where he took female hormones and then had a couple of operations to become a woman." I looked up from my reading, my heart pounding. "It really *is* possible," I breathed. I felt my face to be sure no beard had grown there.

Max entered my office without knocking. Panicked, like I'd done something terribly wrong, I hurried to hide the Christine Jorgensen papers. In a dither, I threw them on my chair and sat, crossing my legs.

"Are you all right, Al?"

"Sure. Why wouldn't I be?"

"You're sitting on Christine Jorgensen's face."

"Oh. Uh, well, well ..." I got up and put the newspapers on the desk.

"That's really something," he said. "That they could do that."

"I guess."

"You guess? I'd expect you to be amazed."

"Why?" I asked, defending myself. "Why should *I* be especially amazed?"

"No reason. *I'm* amazed. Medical science sure has come a long way. I think you've been working too hard. You need an assistant. How about we offer Bertha the job?"

I was glad we'd gotten off the topic of Christine Jorgensen. "Yes, to the assistant. No, to Bertha. I can put up with her as a hatcheck girl, but as an assistant? She's always following me around like a lost puppy. Every time I turn around, there she is."

"That doesn't sound like a bad quality in an assistant."

"She seems to be a nice girl, but there's something—sometimes I catch her sweeping the rug outside my office right after the cleaners have vacuumed."

"Why?"

"I haven't a clue. When I ask her why, she says she wants to make me comfortable. But that doesn't make me comfortable at all. And sometimes she leaves a box of chocolates on my desk when there's no special occasion. *And* she keeps dusting my desk when I've asked her not to. I couldn't have her as my assistant. She'd drive me cuckoo. You hire someone. I'm hurrying over to Shirl and Mercy's for a few minutes. Mercy has a new book she wants me to read."

* * *

Mercy met me in the hallway outside their apartment. "This may not be a good time," she said, looking back at her door.

"What's wrong?"

"Shirl doesn't want this getting out, but … she was beat up today."

"Why? Who?" I hurried toward the door. "Is she hurt bad?"

"Banged up some." Mercy followed me to the door. "A few bad bruises, a little blood. She got away before they could do worse."

I leaned against the closed door. "Have you taken her to a doctor?"

"What doctor will see Shirl without telling her she deserved to be beaten up? She wouldn't go, and I didn't have the heart to make her. I'm taking care of her myself."

"Can I see her?"

"Come in. She may not seem herself. She's been getting emotional."

I followed Mercy into the apartment. "Shirl?" Mercy called softly. "I've brought someone to see you. Al."

I entered their parlor behind Mercy. "Why don't you drink some of this tea," Mercy urged, picking up the teacup from the table near Shirl.

"No, Mercy. Please," Shirl said, turning her head away from it. One eye had a black and blue mark that extended down her cheek.

Mercy put the teacup back into its saucer. Shirl wore a long striped nightshirt. She leaned way back into the couch, breathing heavily, a magazine held loosely in her hands.

"Shirl," I whispered. "How are you?"

"What are they doing to us, Al?" Shirl croaked out. She shook her head at the open magazine in her hands. "A genius at the piano. A genius."

I looked at Mercy for some clue to what Shirl was talking about.

"You remember the colored male impersonator Shirl knew in the thirties? The jazz performer?" Mercy explained. "Gladys Bentley?"

"I remember you telling me about her, Shirl. You created quite a picture for me. She wore a white tuxedo and a top hat and flirted with the girls in the audience, white, Negro, gay, straight. Who could forget someone like that?"

A smile creased Shirl's face. "The bravest woman I ever knew. Never afraid to be herself, no matter how many times they carted her off to their pokey. She dressed in men's clothes wherever she went; not only for her act. Didn't matter to her that wearing men's clothes on the street was illegal; that was who Gladys was and she was going to let everyone know it. She'd been dressing masculine since she was a child. She even married a white woman in New Jersey. Big affair. I went. It was a legal marriage too. Not like what Mercy and I have."

"I married you with my heart," Mercy said.

"I know, dear, and that's real enough for me, but Gladys had an honest-to-goodness real NYS marriage license."

"A license?" I asked. "How's that possible?"

"She passed as a man. The clerk didn't question it. She just filled out the license herself. Lots of gays did that in Harlem back in the thirties. Gladys didn't care who knew she was married to that white woman. She yelled it wherever she went. Do you have any idea what kind of courage that took?"

"I think I do, Shirl."

"Well, look what they've done to her." She shook the magazine and sat up straighter, wincing in pain. She read the title, "'I'm a Woman Again.' This trash is supposedly written by Gladys."

Shirl's knuckles were caked with dried blood. "It says here she took female hormones to turn herself into a woman. Why would she think of doing such a thing? What did they do to her? Look at these pictures. Here she's washing the dishes." She held out the magazine for me to see. "That makes her a woman? She should have those hands playing a hot jazz piano. It says she got married to this guy," she pointed to a photo of a Negro man. "What happened to the white woman in New Jersey? What happened to all that bravado and confidence? What happened to Gladys Bentley? Look! They've got her in a dress. What did they do to her? If they can do this to Gladys, what chance to do any of us have?"

276

"The way I heard it, Shirl," Mercy said, "they wouldn't let her work in the clubs if she kept dressing like she used to. She's gonna try doing her act in a dress. She has a sick mother to take care of, so … These are difficult times."

A few tears slid down Shirl's face. "They've killed her. They've murdered her soul."

"Al, you better go," Mercy said. "I'm going to try to put her to bed."

"Sure." I backed up from the scene, shocked at seeing Shirl cry. I remembered Juliana had told me Shirl had been raped in the thirties. This was all too much for one person to go through. No! This was too much for all of us. They had to stop it! We had to make them stop it! We had to … What?

"Take this," Mercy said at the door, handing me a book wrapped in brown paper. "It's just out. *Spring Fire*. It's the beautiful story of two girls in love. Of course, one of the girls ends up in a mental institution in the end, but you can overlook that, can't you?

* * *

When I returned later that afternoon to The Haven, a heaviness in me, Max stood outside my office door. He greeted me with, "I have a surprise for you."

He stepped out of the way, and I saw Bartholomew Montadeus Honeywell, IV dressed in a blue suit and red bow tie standing there. "Hi," he said brightly.

I stood frozen, staring, unable to imagine how Bart Honeywell could be a surprise for *me*.

"Don't you get it?" Max asked. "He's your assistant."

"He is?"

"Yes!" Bart said, with glee. "We're going to be working side by side. Won't that be peachy keen?"

"Oh, yeah. Peachy double keen with ice cream. Max, can I see you a minute?"

Max grabbed his coat from one of the tables where he'd thrown it. "Sorry, no time. Business meeting. You two work things out."

My eyes followed him dashing out the door. I sighed and turned back to Bart, who smiled at me. *I wonder if it's too late to hire Bertha.*

Chapter 51

BART BEGAN WORKING at the club, and he was a big hit. Every night he worked. When he worked. When I could find him. He always wore the sharpest attire—generally wearing a dinner jacket with a formal shirt and bow tie, white or black, for evenings. During the day, which didn't require dressing up, he still wore the latest style—wide-legged trousers with cuffs turned up and tapered double-breasted sport jackets that showed off his waistline. Fat ties. He never wore anything less than the latest, and since his beginning salary wasn't much, I knew he had to have a "side" business going. I was pretty sure that the "side" business was one of two things. I just hoped he wasn't involving The Haven.

He always had a ready grin for everyone who entered The Haven. Women loved him. He flirted with them and made them feel special while making their husbands and boyfriends worry. Dragging their spouses to The Haven, women eagerly wanted to be teased by Bart. His presence certainly was an asset to business. When he was there.

The night Liberace was headlining at The Haven, every table was taken. He was always one of our biggest draws. The ladies loved him. That was something I never could figure out. The place bulged with demanding patrons. It was rumored he was going to star in his own fifteen-minute TV show on NBC in July, which was probably another reason people were clamoring to get tables.

The kinds of wealthy patrons we catered to didn't expect to be kept waiting, or to have anything go wrong. At the last minute, our maitre'd, Joseph, called from the emergency room with a broken leg. The assistant cook was having a hissy on the kitchen floor because the head cook didn't like the way he'd cut the radishes into rosebuds. I needed Bart to help get us through the dinner hour, always the toughest time, and he wasn't to be found. People were squawking, "Where are my mashed potatoes?" and no Bart.

A customer dashed up to me. "My pennies, my pennies! I didn't get my pennies!"

"What?"

"From the cigarette machine! I put in a quarter, but my pack didn't contain the two pennies change. Look!" He pushed an unopened pack of

Chesterfields in my face. "See? There's a tear in the cellophane. Someone stole my pennies!"

I sighed, knowing there'd be more guys shoving cigarette packs in my face. The vending machine guy had swiped the two pennies change again. Where was Bart? I instructed Bertha to make good on the change out of her tip jar and keep a record so I could make it up to her at the end of the night.

"Oh, yes, Al," she said. "I'd do anything for you."

Why did she say things like that? I spun away from her, hurrying into the thick of the room. Then stopped.

Walter Winchell. Center table. Sitting with his entourage of hangers-on. No wife. Damn! When did he come in?

"Walter, how good to see you," I said.

"Of course, it is," he said with that damn air of superiority. If the people back home knew what a snob he was, they wouldn't have been so eager to worship him. "We're waiting for our food, you know."

"I'll have your waiter over here in a jiffy. Rudolfo! Rudolfo!" Max warned me never to allow Walter Winchell to feel less than extremely important.

I leaned on the wall near hatcheck, "Bertha, you didn't happen to see Bart, did you?"

"I saw him go out back a while ago. He was with a customer."

I bounced off the wall and ran past our huge stage, glowing with lights as the Harlington Honeys danced across it. I dashed out the back door into the alley. It was dark and cold. Only moonlight illuminated our trashcans. Then I heard—"Ooh, aah,"—and ran toward the sound. In the dim shadow of neon, I saw Bart. He had his penis in one of our customer's behinds. "Hi," he smiled at me, "I'm a little busy now, but I'll be along in two shakes of a lamb's tail."

Despite being tempted, I said nothing about the metaphor he used.

The customer, upon seeing me, endeavored to pull his shirttail over his rear—I gathered, in the interest of modesty—while continuing the activity. "Oh, Jesus," he said to Bart, "don't stop." And then to me, "You won't tell, will you? Oh, god, I shouldn't be doing this, but—but …"

"Look, Bart, I need you. Finish up and meet me inside. Don't drag this out."

I probably should fire him, I thought as I walked back inside. I can't. I've never fired anyone before. I saw my father slumped over on the porch chair during the depression after he'd been fired. I can't do it. Maybe I could get

Bertha to do it. Boy, would that be an awful passing of the buck. Shame on you, Al. At least I found out Bart wasn't back there selling drugs.

The customer who had been with Bart returned to his seat and gave his wife a big kiss on the cheek. I'm sure he told her he was out sealing an important business deal. She seemed pleased with whatever excuse he gave, and she caressed his hand as the Harlington Honeys did their final kicks. Later that night, I got quite a large tip from the gentleman. The next morning, four-dozen long-stemmed red roses arrived along with a huge box of candy. In the afternoon, it was a gold bracelet. Oh, yeah, this job had its perks.

None of it kept me from thinking about George, uh, Christine Jorgensen. Oh, there were jokes. Lots of jokes. Everywhere. Christine Jorgensen was the number one joke for a while. Everyone had some dirty thoughts about him— her? Along with embarrassing personal questions they wondered about out loud. Things people had never talked about in public before, especially not in mixed company, were now being whispered about right out in the open.

Max, Bart, and I were sitting in my office after the last show when Bart said to Max, "Did they really cut his ..." he looked at me, then back at Max. "You know—did they actually cut it off?"

"I spose," Max said. "But what *I* want to know is what did they do with it? I mean how do you get rid of thing like that?"

The two broke into wild laughter. I sat there with my hands folded in my lap, listening to them. Max looked up at me, his face suddenly red. "I'm sorry Al. I forgot you're not one of the guys. No! I didn't mean that!"

"It's okay," I said. I wasn't sure if was okay or not, but I was finding fewer and fewer things shocking.

Chapter 52

May 1953

"DID YOU READ the latest?" Max asked, coming into my office. He ran a hand through his hair and paced back and forth. "I have friends who work in government jobs."

"Yeah, I read it," I told him.

"It's nuts. They're so scared of us that they make laws against us. When's it gonna end?"

"Well, it's not just us." I picked up *The Times*. "They've got the same law for criminals, alcoholics, and drug addicts."

"Oh, terrific. We're in good company."

Marty burst through the door. "Let's have breakfast, Al. Well, *hello*, Max." He smiled that special smile he reserved for Max. "I didn't expect to find you here at The Haven office. Wanna join us?"

"Not this morning. I'm too upset to eat."

"You haven't read the papers yet, have you?" I asked.

"No. What is it? Broadway closing up shop?"

"Here." I handed Marty *The Times*. "Read about President Eisenhower's Executive Order 1050. It explicitly states that 'sexual perversion' is grounds for banning people from federal jobs."

"Damn, they're really out to do us in, aren't they?"

"People have been getting fired for the mere suspicion of homosexualism for years," Max said. "That's why Scott quit his job in the State Dept a few years ago. Afraid he'd be fired. But this—why did Ike have to make it a law?

"Well—I don't ever want a government job," Marty said. "Yuck. Do you?"

"That's not the point," Max said. "This stuff spreads. How long do you think it'll be before other industries think it's a dandy idea not to hire gays too? The government did it, so why not follow their example? This law puts us all in even greater jeopardy than before. You were in the service; so was I. Well, the country we sacrificed and fought for only eight years ago doesn't want us. We're not citizens any more. None of us." He slammed the paper down on my desk and stormed out.

* * *

"You're where?" I said into my phone later that afternoon. "Okay, okay, stop crying. No, he can't do that. We have a rehearsal now. I'll be right over."

I ran into the main dining room, where the Harlington Honeys, in tights and leotards, sat on the stage or stood around smoking and waiting. "I'll be right back," I said to Sadie Toulouse, our new musical director. She wasn't easy to get, and I didn't want to lose her after all that wining, dining, and groveling.

"I am not used to being kept waiting," she said in her over-done French accent.

"Look, have the girls show you a few of the routines." I told her. "I'll be back in a few seconds. Have a drink to relax you."

"I do not drink when I work," she said, incensed. I dashed out the door and hurried toward the police precinct on 54th. I couldn't believe they'd arrested her. Sally Susie? Could anyone be more down-home innocent than that girl? I didn't have time for the police and their games. We paid them mucho dough to stay out of our lives. We had a new show opening next week, we were way behind schedule, and I had a temperamental musical director who was liable to walk out any minute. I pushed through the heavy precinct doors, and found the sergeant at his desk. "Sergeant Henry, I don't have time for this. I have a show to get up."

"No time for what? What happened?"

"You arrested one of my girls."

"One of yours? Nah, couldn't be. We would never..."

"Sally Susie?"

"*She's* one of yours? Yeah, me and one of my guys was patrolling the area and ..." He whispered, "Al, we picked her up for ... I can't tell you."

"What do you mean you can't tell me?"

"Well ... it's not something anyone should say to a nice girl like yourself."

"Prostitution? Dang it, Henry. That girl just blew in from Oklahoma last week. She doesn't know the first thing about *anything*, let alone prostitution."

"I'm sorry, Al, but we caught her in the 47th Street Diner."

"*And?* I don't recall them passing a law against going into the 47th Street Diner."

"*And* she went from her table where she was sitting alone to another table to talk to another girl who was also alone, and that *is* against the law."

"That law was made for catching prostitutes, not all girls."

"How can anyone know who's who and which is which? Especially when they're in the 47th Street Diner."

"The kid doesn't know anything, so she wanders into a somewhat sleazy diner ..."

"Often frequented by ladies of the evening, begging your pardon."

"I don't have time to debate this with you. I need her. Now. She's not guilty of anything, and you know it."

"There are papers to process and ..."

"Look, Henry. Forget the papers. This is a nice innocent girl from Sweetback, Oklahoma. And I know you're a good guy and wouldn't want to harm the reputation of a girl like that. Haven't you enjoyed those ringside seats I've been giving you and your wife over the past few years?"

"Oh, yes, Al, very much. We'd never be able to afford ..."

"I love making you happy, Henry. Truly. Now, I have to get back to the club and I really need Sally for rehearsal. So why don't you give her a lecture about not going into sleazy diners, as if there were any other kind in this area, and then send her back to me within the hour. How's that?"

"Sure. Of course. Love those Harlington Honeys."

"I know you do. Maybe she'll give you an autograph."

"Yeah?"

I hurried back to the club, and to my shock, Bart was working with Sadie, having the girls show her the Harlington Honeys repertoire. Through my office window I could see a package sitting on my desk. I slipped in through my door. It was here! We all knew it was due out; we'd been waiting five long years and now, finally, it was here. I had put in my order at the 8th Street Bookshop a while ago because I'd anticipated it would be hard to get. I tore off the wrappings and stared at it. *The Kinsey Report on Human Female Sexuality.*

I was right about it being hard to get. The book was flying off the shelves. Everyone was talking about it, especially at my school. It sure blew the lid off some prized notions. And for the first time in public, people started putting the words "women" and "sex" in the same sentence. That kind of open conversation was brand new, but we were all drawn to it. We discovered that quite a few American women weren't as pure as everyone thought.

Critics from all corners came out to tell the world that Kinsey was wrong. Billy Graham on the radio said, "Thank God, we have scores of women who still know how to blush." *The Chicago Tribune* said, "Kinsey is a real menace to society." *Cosmopolitan* had a long article pointing to all the flaws in the research, and ended with an anecdote about a woman holding a baby while she looked adoringly at her husband. The guy completely missed the point of Kinsey's report: Maybe women didn't want to be so holy, maybe they wanted to be human.

Of course, I couldn't talk to anyone at school about the seven percent or the four percent, or whichever number you wanted to choose, depending on the category, of women who were regularly having sex with other women. I couldn't find one article that said anything about that, good or bad. We were so indecent and horrible, Billy Graham, who yelled about every single sin from the largest to the smallest, didn't dare mention us on his radio program. But I couldn't forget Kinsey's numbers, so I pressed them into my heart, knowing there were lots more of us out there somewhere. We only had to find each other.

Chapter 53

"PLEASE COME, JULE," I begged, sitting in her dressing room between shows at The Copa. She was in the middle of another six-month contract. "You're the one who said I should go in the first place. I'm the only one in my family to get a degree. I don't know what I'll do with it, but Max says no one can ever take it away from me."

"He's right. You *are* to be congratulated," Phillippe, her French make-up man, dabbed mascara on her eyelid. "It's a wonderful accomplishment. You should be proud."

"I want *you* to be proud of me."

"I am."

"Please to hold still," Phillippe demanded, switching to the other eye.

"But you won't come. Max has been breaking my back to get this degree for years."

"Al," she tried to interject.

"How can I do this without you?" I whined like a child. If anyone heard me, they'd never have believed that I was the one who had pushed Juliana's and Lili's careers to the top. "Everybody's going to have their family there."

"And you'll have Max, Shirl, Mercy, Scott, and Virginia."

"But they're not you. You're like my family."

"But I'm not your family."

"Ouch."

"Juliana, dear," Phillippe said, applying a coral pink blusher to her cheekbones. "You zimply must stop wiggling, or zis is going to end up on your nose."

"Sorry, dear. Al, why do you make me say things that hurt you? You know I can't go. You know how I feel about being in the same room as Max."

"I can't choose between Max and you. Max has been like a father. He's been looking forward to this for years."

"I'm not asking you to choose. Max *should* be there. Now, can we get back to business?"

"Yeah, I spose."

"Don't look like that. It breaks my heart."

"Obviously, not enough."

"Phillippe please, no more."

"All right, *ma cherie*, but do not blame me if your face to shine like a Christmas bulb under zose harsh lights."

"She looks beautiful and you know it," I told him. "Go."

Phillippe huffed and wiggled his hips at us as he left.

"Here," Juliana said, holding some sheet music toward me. "A young composer sent me this song in the mail. John Wallowitch. Have you heard of him?"

"No," I said, taking the music.

"I like it, but I wanted to see if you thought it'd be right for me."

I put it in my brief case. "I'll look it over. You won't come to my graduation, maybe the most important day of my life next to your big opening, because you wanted to have sex with Max, but couldn't. That's nuts."

"What?"

"Virginia told me what happened."

"Did she?" She sat back in her chair, amused. "I would expect *her* to say something like that. She's been hot for Max for years, so she thinks everyone is."

"So, this whole thing didn't happen over sex?"

"I suppose we entertained those thoughts—for about a minute. What's that got to do with business?"

"But even *you* said it was about that the time I asked you in Schrafft's years ago."

"It got you to shut up about it, didn't it?"

"You made it up? Then what did happen?"

She gave me one of her "I don't want to talk about it" looks. "Max is going to have a party at the Mt. Olympus," I said. "By invitation only. He's closing the place early. It's for my graduation and thirtieth birthday. The most important people in the business will be there. You should be there too."

"On *Richard's* arm?"

"No. It's my birthday."

"I know, but I can't go without an escort, and *you* can't be my escort. We'll have a little celebration later. Just you and me."

"We never have any time together anymore." I flopped down into a chair near the make-up table. "You're always either rehearsing, or recording, on your way to Chicago or LA, or with Richard. I'm always working at the Club or setting up a gig for you or one of my other clients. We never see each other except in some public box with everyone watching us."

"I just said we'd get together, just the two of us, to celebrate your birthday."

"Yeah, and then I won't see you again for six months!"

She slammed a fist on the make-up vanity. "What do you want me to do about it?"

"Nothing! Doesn't matter!"

I grabbed my briefcase just as she was yelling, "You're the one who made me this successful!" I stomped out of the room. As I headed toward the bar, I ran into Richard.

"How's she doing?" he asked.

"Oh, *she's* fine, but *I* need a drink."

"You know, we got an offer for another Broadway show," he said, as we walked toward the bar. "I think we should take this one."

"Talk to me later. After the show."

"You're going into the bar dressed like that?"

I looked down at my suit jacket, skirt, and chunky-heeled shoes. "This is how I always dress."

"I know. But *I* sure wouldn't make a pass at you."

"Who the hell wants you to?" I marched away from him and hoisted myself onto a barstool. "Mike, let me have a sidecar."

"I can't serve you. You know that. Where's you escort? This is a bar. You can't sit here by yourself."

"Look a beer, then. I need a little something to—"

"You know the law better than anyone. If a cop saw me ..."

I could feel the stares. I slid off the stool. Richard sat alone at a table across from the bar. Big sigh. I knew if I wanted a drink, I was going to have to ... I walked over to his table and sat down. "Order me a side car."

Chapter 54

"WHO IS THIS Tommie we're meeting?" Marty asked as we entered the Central Terminal of LaGuardia Airport.

"He's one of Max's old beaux, and he worked with me at the Stage Door Canteen. I first met him in '41 at a Thanksgiving party Max threw in his apartment on MacDougal. When I knocked, Tommie came to the door wearing a hula skirt and feathers. He said, 'Hi, I'm Tommie with an I-E. 'Y' is so boring, don't you think?'"

Marty laughed, "I like him already."

We sat on a wood bench next to the large windows, where we could see the planes taking off and landing. "I was surprised when he said he'd fly from LA to New York for my graduation."

"He must think of a lot you." He lit a cigarette.

"We helped each other during the war. When the army wouldn't take him—he's kind of effeminate, no, he's a lot effeminate, not your type—he'd cover for me at the Canteen when I was becoming certifiable over Juliana. Right after the war, he got cast in the play *Born Yesterday.*"

"He was in *that*? I loved that play. But I don't remember any young—"

"The Assistant Manager."

"Oh, yeah, I remember. The sissy."

"Max told him everyone loves laughing at sissies. That shot Tommie straight to Hollywood. These days, there isn't much call for sissies with what's been going on in Washington, so Hollywood's been trying to build him up as a leading man. They've even changed his name."

"To what?"

"Jack Dash."

"Jack Dash? Hmm. I seem to remember ... I think I saw him in some magazine."

"A couple of months ago, he had a few shots in *Photoplay*. 'Jack Dash: Handsome Bachelor at Home.' That kind of stuff. To test it out."

"And wasn't there something about him dating Debbie Reynolds?"

"The magic of Hollywood. I haven't heard if any of it is working, but if they can turn Liberace into a teenage heartthrob, why not Tommie? Hey, thanks for coming with me today. I've been feeling awful that Juliana won't come to my graduation. It's nice to have a friend here with me. Makes me feel less alone. How are you doing?"

"I'm getting used to TV not being for me. Sorta. I'm not happy about it, but the FBI guy followed me less often when I was in *Pal Joey*. Now, with *Pal Joey* done, no other acting prospects, and graduation here, it's scary. But I don't want to be a drip talking about my problems.

"Well, I just may have something to cheer you up."

"Yeah? What?"

"I recommended you for an industrial musical that Oldsmobile's doing. It's been written for them. With memorable song lyrics like, 'There's no business like Olds business.' You wouldn't be seen publicly, only by Oldsmobile employees, but there are a lot of them, and the money would be phenomenal for both of us."

"Both of us?"

"When I take out my percentage for managing you."

"You're going to manage me? Al, I love you." He grabbed my hand and kissed it all over.

"We can do the paperwork when we get back to my office. I think you should change your name."

"But I like my name."

"I do too, but it's, well …"

"Too Jewish?"

"It's how the world is."

"It's gonna kill my mother."

"I'm sorry."

"I'll make her understand. You and I should come up with something terribly cool."

"I was thinking of Buck Martin."

"Why not Marty Buck? That'd be close to my real name."

"Well, one-syllable first names seem to be working in Hollywood these days. Rock, Tad, Dirk. More masculine."

"Masculine like Jack Dash?"

"Well, with Tommie, it's a stretch, but yeah, that's the idea."

"So, do you think if I changed my name, I'd have a chance in Hollywood?"

"I don't know. Changing your name might give you a whole new career. Of course, you couldn't use the credits you've accumulated so far. That would give it away. But you're on the *graylist*, which isn't even a real thing. It just exists in the minds of certain powerful people. With a new name—who knows, maybe ... It might be easier for me to get you something in TV and flim."

"No kidding?" he said, excitedly.

"I can't promise, but maybe."

"Buck Martin, huh? Buck Martin," Marty repeated his new name, trying it on. "It sounds like a cowboy. I like it."

"Can I ask you something?"

"Anything. I'm all yours."

"Was it always so easy for you to be, you know? Did you always know?"

"I figured it out for sure in the army. All those men." He swooned. "But I had hints before that."

"And it didn't bother you?"

"I was mainly worried about my mother. Ever since my father left us, I always thought it was up to me to watch over her. It would've killed me if she'd rejected me. I told her when I came home on leave."

"What'd she say?"

"She asked me if she should get me a doctor. I said I didn't think so, that I was happy the way I was. She said that was good enough for her. That was the end of it."

"She must be an incredible woman."

"You'll meet her at graduation. Let's celebrate our new 'business' arrangement. I'll get us hotdogs." He bounced out of his seat. Through the window, I saw him buying two hotdogs at the snackbar outside.

"I hope you like mustard." He handed it to me as he sat down. "Juliana's not even coming to your birthday bash?"

"Nah. I know she's right, but ... If she came she'd have to come with Richard, and it would hurt like hell to see the two of them dancing together and ... Damn, I can't stand this life."

"Really? I love it." He leaned back in his chair, enjoying his hot dog. "It's the one thing that keeps me going. I met a whole bunch of new people who are like us in *Pal Joey,* and they took me to the bath houses."

"What's a bath house?"

"Max didn't tell you? I'm sure *he's* been. It's a place you go, well, not you, it's for men. You get a locker and take off your clothes. They give you a bathrobe, but no one covers up very much. You show off your wares to attract attention."

I looked around to be sure no one was close enough to hear. "You know we shouldn't be talking like this in public, but—you mean you do that with a stranger?" I whispered. "I mean, I know Bart ... but you?"

"Lots of good-looking strangers. Sometimes all at the same time. I've never had so much fun in my life. Gay life is the best. Last week, I took a girl to the opera, and while she was in the ladies, I did it with this gorgeous guy in the standing room only section."

"What?"

"All those guys in tuxes standing in the back behind the railing are like us, and well, there are ways. By the time the girl returned, I was ready to go back with her to our balcony seat. There's something exciting about doing it surrounded by that majestic music."

"I'll never understand you gay boys, but sometimes, I envy your freedom. Juliana and I were free once—in the forties, when we had less to lose. I even know what you mean about opera being, well, stimulating."

"Maybe you should try out the women's bars."

"I'm afraid of being arrested."

"Yeah, well, that's something to think about, but I never do. I go to the Astor Hotel Bar alot. It's not really gay, but a lot of gays go there. I've seen Max there some nights. It's a great life, and I owe it all to you."

"To me?"

"You got me that part in *Pal Joey*. Why don't we go outside? Maybe we'll see Tommie's plane come in."

"Do you ever hear from Moshe?" I asked as we were about to step outside. "He's not allowed to contact me, and vice versa. But I heard through mutual friends that they still have him locked up."

"It's been almost three years."

"His parents moved him to a private hospital, and the doctors are trying to cure him. I guess there's no easy cure for getting over me."

"Marty! The man's suffering. It's not a joke."

"I know. Slug me, will ya? I wish they'd let him live his life."

We pushed the door open and stepped outside. The sound of the planes was deafening, and we both had to hang onto our hats so the wind didn't whisk them away.

Marty's wide-legged corduroy pants flapped in the strong breezes. "I think that's him," I called out over a blast of airplane sound. A TWA plane taxied down the runway in the distance. "Come on. Let's go meet him."

We joined others meeting loved ones and stood near the chain-linked fence as workmen rolled the stairs to the plane. The door opened and the passengers filed down the stairs. My stomach bubbled with excitement. "There!" I pointed, as Tommie stepped into the doorway. "That's him."

"You mean that gorgeous blonde with the tan in the charcoal-gray, gabardine, custom-made suit?"

"Yes." I laughed.

"I love a man who knows how to dress."

"You do?" I looked at Marty in his worn-out clothes.

"That doesn't mean *I* want to do it."

One of the workmen opened the gate, and we all poured out. Tommie was making his descent. I yelled, "Tommie!"

He stopped midway, saw me, and held the handrail, striking a pose in his wide-brimmed hat. He laughed and flapped his arms the rest of the way down. "Al! Al!" He threw his arms around me. "Oh, I missed you so! I thought I would perish waiting on that long plane ride till I saw you."

"Oh, gosh, Tommie, it's been ages."

He put his hands on my shoulders. "You look good."

"So do you. All grown up."

"Don't I look famous?" He posed again then broke into laughter.

"Hello?" Marty said. "Remember me?"

"No," Tommie said, "But I'd like to." He extended a wilting hand.

"Tommie, this is my friend Marty Buchman."

"Buck Martin," Marty corrected, deepening his voice and extending his hand.

"Oh, my goodness, young man," Tommie said. "You have a simply marvelous grip."

"Marty, uh, Buck is graduating with me," I told him. "He's also an actor."

"Really?" Tommie cocked a hip in Marty's direction. "It has been an absolutely exhausting trip." He flipped an unlit cigarette into the air, each finger gracefully poised. "Well?"

"Oh." Marty dug into his pants pocket for his lighter and lit Tommie's cigarette.

They seemed to hit it off right away, and as we walked out of the airport— the two of them smoking—I had to run to keep up. "Hey, guys. Don't forget *me*."

Chapter 55

MAX HAD A car pick us up at the Park Avenue apartment. Scott, sitting next to me, asked, "So is Juliana coming today?" Virginia sat in the seat facing us. She smiled vacantly, like she wasn't quite in the same car with us. Ever since, well, … that happened, she often did that. Disappeared inside herself for the briefest moment, and then, in another, she'd be back as if she'd never left.

"No," I answered, staring out the window.

"Did you ask her?"

"Can we not talk about it, Scott?"

"Sure, sorry."

Max sighed and lit the cigarette in his holder.

"Where's Tommie?" Virginia asked, taking out her own cigarette. Max leaned forward to light it.

"He's having breakfast with my friend Marty and his family. Marty and Tommie really hit it off."

"Hit it off?" Max said. "Tommie didn't come home at all last night."

"Didn't you want your family to come to your graduation?" Scott asked. "This seems like the sort of thing a mother and father—"

"Scott, don't push," Max said.

"You *are* my family," I told him.

Scott took my hand in his and squeezed. We drove the rest of the way in silence. Virginia disappeared again. I wondered if anyone noticed but me.

The driver pulled onto the campus, and I directed him to the parking lot.

With my cap and gown in my arms, I left them to join my classmates, who were milling about the grounds of the Lewiston Theater. Marty came running in his cap and gown and threw his arms around me. "Hey, kiddo, we did it. So, put on your gown. Look collegiate."

As I put my arms into the gown, Marty said, "I want you to meet my mother." A thin, pleasant-looking woman with pride bursting out of her paisley shirtwaist dress stood near me. "And this is my kid sister," he said about the young woman holding a baby.

Mrs. Buchman smiled so sweetly that it was easy picturing her wearing an apron in a pastel-colored kitchen, like those magazine ads for Hotpoint. She extended her hand to me, "Alice, I'm glad to meet you at last. Aaron has told me so much about you. I'm pleased he has such a good friend."

Seeing Marty with his sister as she held her baby, her husband making googly sounds at his new child, and Mrs. Buchman—pretty in her light-blue straw hat—made me think of the radio program "Father Knows Best." I took a picture of them to remember what a real family looked liked.

Marty's family left as we lined up for the processional.

"Al," Marty said. "I've got something for you." He reached into the inside pocket of his blue suit. This was the first time I saw Marty wearing an honest-to-goodness suit. And the tie wasn't hanging cockeyed. "Here." He handed me an envelope. I opened it and quickly read the usual pre-printed graduation thoughts—'now, you're going to change the world etc.' I looked up at Marty. "Moshe?"

"How'd you know?

"A feeling."

"I think he wrote a little something inside."

Under Moshe's signature he'd written. "'So sorry. More sorry than you could ever know.' Is he still in the hospital?"

"No. A mutual friend told me his mother got him out four months ago. He's living with distant cousins in Maine who think he's merely neurotic. They don't know about the other or they would never have taken him in. To his father, he's dead, even said Kaddish for him. Oh. That's the prayer for the dead."

"Poor guy."

"Yeah. His mother figures he won't meet anyone like us in Maine. Jams[4] are so blind."

"I guess if they let him out he must be cured, huh?" I asked.

"If that's what you want to think. He should be with us today," he sighed. "You never got to know him—the way he was before the war. Oh, damn, it's starting to feel like a funeral around here. This is a celebration. Come on, let's celebrate."

"Marty, I imagine you're having a party or barbecue or something at your family's place in Queens to celebrate tonight."

"Yeah. Wanna come?"

---

4 In the forties and fifties gays sometimes called straight people "jams." See *Juliana (Volume 1: 1941-1944)* p.363

"Well, that's what I wanted to ask *you*. Max is having a party at the Mt. Olympus. Closed to the public, but he's inviting a lot of big shot people, a lot of people who are—well, they're that way, like us. Lots of celebrities. Theater people and … film and TV, but mostly theater people. It's all really hush hush. Can't have the wrong people getting wind of it. That's be a disaster. I think Tommie's coming."

"Are you inviting *me*?"

"I was wondering if you'd be my escort?"

He threw his arms around me and squeezed as the orchestra began *Pomp and Circumstance*, "I could kiss you. Wait! I will." He lifted me up in his arms and kissed me on the lips.

"Remember, don't tell anyone. A lot of careers are at stake."

"Including mine. I'm not even going to tell my mother."

"Marty, hurry," I said, "You have to march with the B's."

He started walking with the H's. "First you'll come to my place for the barbecue. Then we'll change at one our places—tuxedo, right?—and go to the Mt. Olympus. We'll make a grand entrance."

"Marty, the B's are way up there. They're going to sit soon."

Marty dashed up the center aisle where we, the Class of '53, were entering, and squeezed himself in front of a C. We passed our professors, who lined the aisle, wearing fancy robes of bright colors with gold tassels decorating their caps.

As I marched through the aisle, the audience standing for us, I was so moved I almost cried. It took six years, but now I was glad Max had pushed me. To be a part of this ceremony made it all worth it. I thought briefly of my parents, but then whisked that thought away. I thought of Juliana, but didn't let that spoil this moment, either. I was about to be a college graduate!

We sat through two hours of boring speakers before we had to go up to collect our diplomas. When the dean shook my hand and congratulated me I wrapped my fist around the diploma and remembered Max saying, "No one can ever take this away from you." This was my insurance against a life on the street in a cardboard box begging for a sandwich. I would hang it on the wall of my office. I hadn't expected to feel so proud.

When it was over, cap and gown still on, I pushed my way through the crowds, looking for Max and Scott. I saw girls and young men running into the arms of their mothers and fathers, and I thought, I'm no longer young. It was a new thought, a new realization. I'd turned thirty a week ago, and I was no longer young.

The crowds spilled out onto the grass where proud parents took pictures of their scholar-children.

Scott, Virginia, Shirl, Mercy, and Tommie came hurrying toward me. My gown open, I ran into my friends' arms. Shirl wore her one skirt for me like she had for Juliana's opening. That made me feel special. Mercy was crying. We hugged again.

"Max." He had tears in his eyes as he walked toward me. I reached up to kiss his cheek. "Thank you for pushing me. Dad."

He folded his arms around me, holding me close. When he released me his face was a waterfall and so was mine. That's when I realized how much I loved him and … how much he loved me. I showed him my diploma. "We're going to hang that right over the mantel," he said, wiping his face with his handkerchief.

"I was going to put it in my office, but hanging it over the mantle is even better. I want to get a picture of all of us," I told them.

Max nodded his head to the right and said, "Look."

I followed his nod. There stood Juliana, all dressed up in her navy-blue suit and matching wide-brimmed hat. Was that a vision or really her?

"Go ahead," Max said.

I walked toward her, fearful she'd disappear into the ether. "Hello," she said as I drew close.

"Juliana. Have you been here the whole time?"

"Yes." I walked closer, wanting to throw my arms around her, but of course, I couldn't. There'd be nothing shocking about two women hugging at a graduation ceremony except for the fear in our heads. Oh, hell. I threw my arms around her anyway. Her muscles stiffened, but still she accepted my public hug—for a few moments. Then she stepped away from it.

We stared at each other, not really knowing what to say. She slid off her gloves, "Well," she sighed, averting her eyes from mine. "Nice ceremony."

"Some of those speakers were boring. They must have put you to sleep."

"It was fine." She still wasn't looking at me directly.

"Al," Max said. "Why don't you let me take a picture of the both of you?"

"Do you mind, Jule?" I asked.

"Uh, no."

We stood against a tree, and I put my arm around her waist. She peeled me off her, "Uh, Al, maybe not so …"

"Juliana, really," Max scowled.

"Do you have something you want to say me, Max?"

You could tell by his squished-up face that he had a really good comeback to throw at her, but instead he put on a broad smile. "Nothing, darling. Smile for the camera." He snapped the picture and handed the camera back to me. "Scott and I are going back to set up at the club. Shirl, you and Mercy want a ride?"

"I have my car," Shirl answered.

"What about you, Tommie?"

"I'm gonna catch up with Marty." He gave me a quick hug. "Congratulations, Al. I'll see you, tonight." He sprinted away.

"Al," Shirl said, "why don't you show Juliana around?"

"Do you want me to?" I asked her.

I saw Max nod at her. Then she said, "Certainly. I'd love to see where you've been spending your time."

"First, I want to get a picture of everybody. Come on Max, you stand over there, and Scott and Virginia, next to Juliana—oh I mean—Jule you stand next to Max, uh, no, uh …"

"How about I take a picture of all of *you?*" Juliana suggested, sliding away from the group. "Al, stand over there and put your cap on."

I did as she directed, and Juliana took the picture.

"You two have fun," Max said. "See you later."

Max put an arm around Virginia, "Are you all right?"

"Huh?" She'd been staring into space. She smiled at Max. "Oh, yes, yes, fine."

Scott walked beside Virginia and Max as they headed toward the quad. Shirl and Mercy followed them, making their way toward the parking lot. I had a brief fantasy of Jule and me going to the party together that night. She'd be dressed in a formal gown, I'd be wearing a tuxedo, and we would dance on the roof—no one would stare or say anything mean. It'd be so normal.

"So?" I said. "What do you want to see?"

"What is there to see?"

"This is the Quad. It's a nice place to come study and think."

A boy and girl in graduation gowns passed by holding hands. We started walking. "I have something for you," Juliana said.

"Really?" I jumped up and down, something a thirty-year-old person probably wasn't supposed to do, but I couldn't help it. I was so excited that

Juliana would get me a present that was a real present, not something she said wasn't a present even though I knew it was.

She opened her purse and took out a small box wrapped in birthday paper and a ribbon. "I guess I should've given you this a while ago, but here."

"You wrapped it?"

"I do know how to do that, you know."

"I never figured you'd … You had to think about me while you were—"

"Let's sit down, shall we? You can open it."

As we headed toward the bench, a small group of students came giggling up beside us. "Shh," one of the girls said. "Stop acting like children. Excuse me, are you Juliana?"

We stopped. "Yes," Juliana said.

"We saw your show at the Copa after prom. It was hot!"

Another girl squealed, "Please, would you sign our autograph books?"

"Certainly," Juliana said, but I could tell she was feeling uncomfortable with me standing there.

Once she had signed her name four times and sent them off giggling, she said, "I'm sorry about that, Al."

"What do you think I worked so hard for?"

"I love it after the show in my dressing room. I feel like a queen, then. But in the street … Well, luckily it doesn't happen often in public."

"You're so funny. Nothing much embarrasses you, but something lots of people would be puffed-up with pride about, *that's* what embarrasses you."

"I'm not embarrassed. That's an utterly ridiculous emotion. Excuse me. I know you're prone to it. I simply find it disconcerting when some stranger comes up to me in public."

"Disconcerting? Sounds a lot like embarrassment to me, but if you say it's not, okay. Why don't we sit here?"

We sat on a bench under a leafy tree. I undid the ribbon, wondering what she would pick out for me. She stared straight ahead, not watching me. I opened the box and pushed away the tissue paper. Inside lay a small gold heart pin. "Jule."

"Don't make anything out of it. It's a birthday gift and, I guess, graduation, too. I should get you something else for graduation."

"No, no. This is perfect. It's everything I …" I wanted to cry right there, but I knew I didn't dare. "It's beautiful. I couldn't ask for—for …" The tears were starting to well up.

"Please don't do that," she said.

"I won't. It's really special to me. A heart. Like your heart, maybe?"

"It's your third item of female clothing."

"What?"

"To keep you safe if you ever have occasion to go out in men's clothes."

To keep me safe. She wanted to keep me safe. Aggies' father had said that to Aggie once and I always envied her, but now, Jule—to keep me safe.

"Remember back during the war how we couldn't figure out what the third item was? Bra and underpants were two items of women's clothes if a cop tried to arrest you, but we couldn't come up with that third item. That heart pin could be number three. We thought the world was dangerous back then, but it's ever so much worse now."

We sat in silence, feeling the spring breeze. Across from us, a boy and a girl in open graduation gowns sat on a bench kissing.

"Don't stare," Juliana said, looking down at her hands in her lap. "It's not polite."

"I was thinking—"

"I know what you're thinking. Should we walk?"

"Yeah, sure," I pointed. "Over there was where I had most of my education courses. I hated them, and I don't ever want to be a teacher. There sure are a lot of disadvantages to being female."

"Advantages too."

"Like what?"

"Like feeling lusciously feminine from head to toe."

I laughed, "I do believe you feel like that a lot. But me? I don't think I ever have. Does it bother you to hear me say that?"

"Not if it doesn't bother you. But I don't think it's entirely true. You have delightful feminine swashes to your personality."

"I do?" I paused, trying to take that in. "That building. Up ahead. That's where I took music history and theory. I took as much of that as they'd let me. Oh, and business management. I audited a couple of courses in that, too. And a few drama courses."

"Well-rounded."

We walked quickly across the grounds and came to a large building fashioned after something from Roman days with giant gargoyles. It was empty inside with everyone gone for summer vacation.

"Where are we going?" Juliana asked, suddenly nervous.

"It's over there." I opened the heavy door that led into a huge lecture hall. "Down there," I pointed. "A piano." We walked down the steps that took us past the rows of seats into the well where the professor lectured. "On the final exam, I had to identify different types of music from a few notes the professor played."

"Really? And you could do that?"

"I got an A."

"I'm impressed."

"I'm sure you're not, but I wanted to let you know that I do know something about what I'm doing."

"I'm well aware of that, but I never knew how little I knew about you."

"The acoustics in here are good. Come, see."

"I don't know. We're not supposed to be here, are we?"

"Nobody's around to care."

I led the way down the last of the steps. She seemed to relax when we stood near the piano. "Try it out. See what you think."

"Should I?"

"Yes."

She sat on the bench and let her fingers run up the scale and down again. "Nice." She played one of Johnny's songs. I sat down next to her. "I miss playing. I haven't played in quite a while. You know who is an excellent pianist? Scott. I've listened to him when he's coaching Peter. He's better than Peter."

"You know, Jule, I really appreciate your coming today. It means a lot to me. How did you know where to go? This campus is huge."

She began another piece. "Max called me."

"He did?"

"He told me I'd better get my ass over here. His word, not mine."

"That must've made you mad."

"Yes, but he was right. It wasn't because of Max that I didn't want to come. Max knows this about me, and he said I should I tell you. So here goes. I—always feel this lack in myself. That I didn't continue my education. I went to the finest European schools where I studied music, and I was accepted into the Conservatoire de Paris when I was only sixteen. For opera. My mother was terribly proud. But I was restless for my life to begin so—I quit and came to the states. Threw my opportunity away. It broke her heart. I never got the chance to make it up to her because—well, because ..."

"She—died?" I said.

"Yes. She was—murdered." The color seemed to drain from her face as she said the word, and I was afraid to move. I knew what had happened to her mother because Shirl had told me years ago, but Juliana had never spoken of it before.

She played some chords from *Requiem Pie Jesu.* I loved watching her delicate fingers press against the keys. She stopped. "I don't like thinking about that."

I put my hand on her thigh. "I know."

"Please don't do that."

I removed my hand. "Shirl told me you were very young when you found out that your mother was, uh … your father came to the city to tell you. It must've been very hard for you."

"It wouldn't have happened if I'd been there."

"But, Jule, you were a kid. There was nothing you—"

"My mother and I were close. If I'd been there …" She turned her head away from me, I think because she was afraid she'd cry. "I was only thinking of myself, and she needed me."

"The reason Max and I fought—well, one of the reasons—the last fight—he was really hurt when I told him I was going to marry Richard. He said I wasn't marrying Richard for the sake of my career. He said he could've almost understood that. He said I was marrying Richard because I wanted to hide behind him. I wanted to hide from myself. That seemed ridiculous. Max had run his business into the ground. He had nothing left when I married Richard. I thought Richard could salvage my career, but …" Her fingers ran quickly over the keys. "There may have been a grain of truth to what Max said. Maybe I did want to hide behind Richard, so no one would know—"

"That you're a homosexual?" I whispered.

"Shh, please." She looked around the empty lecture hall. "When I first came to the city, to Harlem, to sing in the clubs, I slept with practically any girl who was willing, and a whole lot were. It was like I'd landed in Paradise. Jeez, it was fun. But I never called it anything. It never needed a name. It was just fun. But now … they label and label."

"So what, you married Richard because you didn't want anyone to know. We're all hiding, if you want to call it that. Even Max doesn't advertise about himself. He won't let me wear a tuxedo to manage The Haven. Bad for business."

"He said I thought marrying Richard would make me straight. There are theories like that, you know. They say marriage can … Well, why wouldn't I want to be straight? Who would choose to live the way we do? In secret, being hated. Oh, how my mother loved her men. You'd think a little of that would've rubbed off on me, but I never understood her feelings or how she let men do the things to her they did. I hoped with Max, but ... You know, for a while I made an effort to be straight in every way. When I first married Richard. I went to their cocktail parties, joined their organizations, went to their lady luncheons. But, Al, those people don't have any fun."

I laughed.

"In the beginning, Richard and I had the most horrible fights. I'd flirt with men, but only at the clubs where I was playing. It was part of the job. Sometimes, it got me another job. Well, I enjoyed it too—the power of it—but it never meant anything. Except, Richard thought it did. Usually, I had my eye on the cute little lady *behind* the guy I was flirting with. Anyway, Max thought I was trying to be straight by marrying Richard, and that's why Max and I fought."

"And now?"

"Now, every day there's another news report or magazine exposé about perverts." I watched her fingers pressing the piano keys. I wished I could touch them and kiss each delicate finger.

"And *now,* I have more to lose than ever. And you know, Miss College Graduate"—she turned to me, a big grin on her face— "that is *your* fault."

"And we're not even at the top yet," I told her.

Chapter 56

"SO TOM," MARTY said, as he forked scrambled egg into his mouth. "Tell us about your adventures in Hollywood."

"That's Tommie," Tommie corrected, "Or Jack Dash, he-man, if you prefer." He swished his filtered Kent through the air.

We sat around the table in the breakfast nook—Marty, Tommie, Max and me—in our bathrobes, except Max who wore his satin smoking jacket—maroon with black trim. It was already after two in the afternoon, but for us, that was the perfect time for breakfast.

I had a ball at my party. Max had invited so many fascinating people, some I already knew and some I *should* know to advance my career. Tallulah Bankhead came with Patsy Kelly. You never saw them together, but everyone knew they were *together*. Mr. Miniaci and his wife, Rose, were there. But to be truthful, Mr. Miniaci was always a charming guest in spite of his line of work and his previous friendship with Moose. Frank Costello couldn't come because he was still locked up for walking out on the Kefauver Hearings.

I was shocked to see Jimmy the Crusher walk in. I hadn't seen him since … well, you know. He even smiled at me. Jimmy didn't smile. Not ever. Maybe that thing his lips were doing wasn't a smile. It could have been a smirk or a grimace. With the fire scars on his upper lip, it was hard to tell. When he slipped the hand that still had a thumb into his coat pocket I froze. A gun?

He lifted out a small box and palmed it; he handed it to me and walked away. I stared at the box gayly wrapped in clown birthday paper sitting in my hand. I looked up to see him watching me from across the room. My heart beat in my throat as I undid the wrappings. Inside lay a silver bracelet, the kind you might put a charm on, but there were no charms. Why would Jimmy give me a present? Do I say thank you? I'd never even spoken to him before. When I looked up from the box to find him, he was gone.

There were lots of Broadway people and a few Hollywood folks who were in town, too. I added more names to my wheeldex, and my name got added to theirs. Broadway and Hollywood people, gay or straight, all knew about these parties. It was one of those open secrets. As long as it didn't get out to the public, we were fine, but if the press started blabbing to Middle America, we'd be ruined. We all knew what had happened to Billy Haines when he'd been caught at the Y in LA with a sailor. Louis B. Mayer tore up his MGM contract and his acting career was pretty much over.

Marty and I danced when he wasn't flirting with Max. I wondered what Scott thought about that.

That party was the best birthday party I ever had in my whole life.

"So Tommie," Marty said, leaning around me. "Come on. Give. What's happening in Hollywood?"

"Here's something juicy. Hasn't hit the wires yet." Tommie said. "Our very own Walter Liberace is taking Cassandra—you know, that London columnist, real name William Connor—to court. Suing him for libel because in his review he implied Libby was—" he whispered for effect, "a homosexual."

"Taking him to court?" I exclaimed. "His career will be ruined."

"That's what I told him," Tommie explained. "But he's convinced he's going to win. He's decided to prove to the whole world that he is as straight as an arrow."

We all laughed. "That's exactly," Marty added, more seriously, "what Oscar Wilde tried to do, and we all know what happened to him."

"What?" Tommie asked.

"You really must read, boy," Marty said. "They sent him to prison. That was in England too. You think it's rough here? Phew, England makes the U.S. look like a walk in the park."

"Oh. Poor Libby. Maybe he'll change his mind," Tommie said. "Enough with the sad faces. What you *really* want is the absolute latest Hollywood gossip." He leaned forward to flick an ash into the clay ashtray made by Virginia's illegitimate daughter. He sat back in his chair, waving his cigarette in the air as he crossed one leg over the other and winked at Marty.

Marty leaned forward, all eagerness.

"Not even Hedda or Louella know this." He paused dramatically while he took a long drag from his Kent.

"What?" Marty could barely stay in his seat.

"Well, this Miss Nancy," Tommie pointed at himself, "is getting married."

"To what?" Marty asked.

"Stop. A girl, of course. I met her at one of George Cukor's Sunday soirées and fell instantly. A sweet little starlet George has been introducing around. Only eighteen. I immediately felt protective."

"A name?" I said.

"Bobby McClaren."

"Well, that will certainly go well with Tommie," Max said.

"That's what I thought. Tommie and Bobby—Bobby and Tommie. It'll look cute on our towels. We want a traditional marriage, something like my parents." One of his hands danced in the air; the other delicately pushed back the hair that had fallen onto his forehead. "We both want children. But enough about me. Al, how are things going with Juliana's career?"

"Moving steady, but she still doesn't have a top ten single. She needs to do a film, but the stuff they send us—"

"I'll ask around," Tommie said. The intercom near the door rang. Tommie jumped up, flapping his hands as if he were likely to take flight. "I'll get it. I'll get it."

He slid on his slippers down the highly polished floor.

Max said, "Tommie deserves to have someone to settle down with. He's been alone for a long time."

Tommie came back waving a cigarette in the air. "It's Bart. The little shit. He's on his way up. He's odd, don't you think?"

"Maybe a little foggy," Max said. "But no odder than anyone sitting here."

"Before I left for LA, I went out with him. A date. One." He held up a finger for emphasis. "I don't know why, but I did not want a repeat engagement. This nancy boy," he pointed a delicate finger at himself, "has the instincts of a real girl. That boy is up to no good. There's something in his eyes. Shifty. Still, he's awfully cute. What's a sister to do?" He sighed as he sat down, carefully arranging his robe so that his shapely legs up to his thigh peeked out. Was that for Marty's benefit?

"I think your instincts are off with this one," Max said.

"Maybe."

The doorbell rang and Marty ran to get it. I heard Bart say, standing in the foyer, "Well, hello there, sweetie, and who are *you?*"

The two men entered the breakfast nook. "I brought genuine New York bagels!" Bart announced as he put the bag on the table. "You must be so deprived out there in that Hollywood wasteland. How ya been, Tom-a-la? Kissy kiss."

They both kissed the air. Then Bart laid out the bagels on top of the bag.

"For Pete's sake, get a tray," Tommie complained, standing to get one.

"So where's the lox and cream cheese?" Marty asked.

"We can put butter on them."

"Butter!" Marty gasped. "There must be a special hell for people who do that."

"I'm full anyway," Tommie said, as he laid the bagels on the silver tray he had retrieved from one of Max's cabinets.

"You can't be full," Bart whined. "I brought them for *you*."

"You can't expect him to eat them without lox and cream cheese," Marty moaned, leaning back in his chair, lighting a cigarette.

"Who *are* you? I've seen you hanging around the club, but who are you?" Bart said.

"I told you. Marty Buchman. No, Buck Martin." He deepened his voice and stood extending his hand. "Howdy, pardner." He sounded like he'd parked his horse out front. "Buck Martin, here. Didn't mean to give ya a hard time about your bagels, pardner."

"You're a Jew, aren't you?"

"What's that supposed to mean?"

"Nothing." Bart smirked.

"If you're referring to my advanced knowledge of bagel eating, then you and I are okay. But if you mean something else then you and I are *not* okay."

"I didn't mean anything. I love the Jews. Some of my bests friends are Jews."

"Name two."

Bart continued. "The Jews are the chosen people. Aren't they?"

"Come on, guys," Max said. "No sense getting upset over bagels."

"I don't think this is about bagels, anymore," Marty said. "Is it, Bart?"

"Stop this now," Tommie said, waving his cigarette through the air. "The Jews went through the worst possible time. What those Nazis did to them was awful. Marty, or any of his people, don't need you putting your three cents into their already difficult lives. So drop it, Bart! I won't put up with it."

"And who are you? Moses?"

"Now you wanna fight me?"

"Heavens, no. I wouldn't want you scratching my eyes out, Miss Nancy."

"You don't get to call me that, so don't."

"Hey, Marty—Buck, I should've brought lox and cream cheese. It was thoughtless of me."

He put out his hand and Marty reluctantly took it. Bart took a seat near Max.

"You won't believe the parties I go to in Hollywood," Tommie said, breaking into the tension. He sat back down at the table.

"Maybe I should head off to Hollywood," Marty said. "Skip Broadway."

"I could introduce you around," Tommie said.

"You could? Maybe I could leave with you next week when you—"

"You have a contract with me," I said.

"I didn't sign anything yet."

"Oh? And you're certain Hollywood is going to embrace you?"

"Oh, that. Just kidding, Al."

"Sure," I said, unconvinced.

"You should get your stage experience first," Tommie said, helping me out. "They're really impressed with that out there. Hey, have any of you heard of the Mattachine Society? It's an organization that was started a few years ago in L.A. by some homosexuals."

"An organization started by homosexuals?" Marty said. "Don't you mean a tea party?"

"It's very hush, hush. No one knows the real names of the members. Someone approached me to join, but I have no interest in cutting my own throat. Hollywood is tough enough without hanging your name on a homophile organization. But still, they put out this magazine I occasonally, *very* carefully, peak at when I find it lying around. They claim to be fighting for the rights of homosexuals."

"The rights of homosexuals?" Bart laughed.

"A bunch of fags claiming their *rights*," Marty laughed. "Rights to what?"

"The right to go into a bar with our own kind and not be terrified of being arrested," Max said. "The right to openly proclaim our love to whomever without having our reputations ruined, or our businesses destroyed. None of that'll ever happen."

"They sound very serious about it, Max," Tommie continued. "One of the magazines I glanced at had a whole list of civil rights they think we should have."

"An organization that's fighting for the rights of homosexuals." Max shook his head. "Poor suckers. The government'll shut them down. But not until they've ruined the lives of the dreamers who dared to hope there could be such rights."

Chapter 57

February 1954

"NICE SUIT," RICHARD said as we sat across from each other one evening at Child's. "It's kind of violet-blue, isn't it?"

"You've seen this jacket before." I took a sip of my tea. "Tell me you didn't sign anything."

"Something's different in how you look today. Maybe it's the hat. Is that new?"

"Richard, stop talking about my clothes. Just tell me you didn't sign anything." A waiter dropped a tray of silverware, and it clanged to the floor.

"This is perfect for her," Richard said, lighting a cigarette. "I don't understand why you're worried."

"She's never done this before. She's never even had an acting lesson. We can't afford a flop at this point in her career."

"She's not going to flop. She's been doing that gourmet cooking show. That's acting."

"No, it's not." The orchestra started up in the other room. A samba.

"Lili Donovan's already done Broadway *twice*, she's signed in Hollywood, and you're doing nothing for Juliana. How do you think that makes Juliana feel?"

"I don't know." A pain stabbed through my stomach. "Is she hurt?"

"What do you expect? You're holding her back."

"Does *she* think that? I'm only doing what I think's best for her."

"You haven't even read this script yet, and already you're against it. Why is that, Al? Do you *want* Juliana's career to grind to a halt?"

"I'm not against this script. I only said I wanted to *read* it before you signed anything."

"So you can say no like you always do."

"I've been talking to some Off-Broadway producers who—"

"Off-Broadway? Jeez, Al, you really *have* lost faith in Julie if you want to stick her in one of those little dead-end shows."

"The Three Penny Opera is not a dead-end show. People are starting to take notice of this Off-Broadway movement. With the right property, at the right time, Juliana could be a part of something brand new. No one knows what's going to happen with Broadway. Prices are going through the roof with audiences staying home watching television. But this new thing might—"

"Juliana belongs in a big Broadway house with a big Broadway audience and *you* know it."

He was right. I knew it as soon as he said it. "Okay, yes, but, Richard, we have to be careful. Look how long it took her to get where she is now. We don't want her to lose that."

"You're playing it too safe."

I wondered if he were right. I wondered if my feelings for Jule were making me protect her too much.

"This is perfect for her." He pushed the script toward me. "You'd see that if you'd give it a chance."

"I'll look it over tonight. Maybe now *is* the right time." I took the script into one of my hands, lifting my coffee cup with the other. *Summer Daffodils.* "Nice title."

Richard flicked an ash into the ashtray. "And titles sell shows."

I turned to the first page. "Summer Daffodils, a drama in three acts. A drama? Richard, it's a drama. Not a musical. She can't do this." I closed the script and pushed it back at him.

"Ben completely agrees with me."

"Sure. He gets his ten percent no matter what happens to Juliana on that stage." I leaned across the table, pointing my words at him like bullets. "Richard, it's not a musical. It's all talking. A drama. Do you have the slightest idea of what New York critics will expect from her? Have you the slightest idea how many will *want* her to fail because she's coming from cabaret? No. She can't do this."

"I already signed the papers."

"What? Whatever possessed you?"

"I'm her manager."

"No. This isn't possible. Why would these producers even want her for this?"

"I talked them into it."

"How?"

"I reminded them about her work on the front during the war and how good that would be for PR. Broadway's hurting right now, and I'm an excellent salesman." He proudly took a puff of his cigarette. "A few months ago, Juliana and I were at the theater and she wondered what it would be like to act in a play. She said she wanted to do it someday. I want to give her whatever she wants."

"You have to give her what is *good* for her; not respond to every whim. That's why you're her manager. To protect her from herself. And you are supposed to listen to me, and do as *I* say. That's our agreement."

"I have a mind of my own, and people respect me in this town. I don't need to check with you about every move I make. I've learned a lot in these last few years."

"Obviously not enough. I'm going to contact these people and try and get her out of this."

"You are not. You're not going to make a fool out of me."

"You did *that* to yourself. Does Juliana know about this? Did she sign papers?"

"I discussed it with her. She didn't need to sign. I did. *I'm* her husband."

"And she didn't call *me?*"

"Why should she? *I'm* her manager."

That hurt. "I need some wine."

"Waiter," Richard called, waving. "Two glasses of wine, please."

"Don't worry, Al. I know you have Juliana's best interest at heart, but she's going to be wonderful in this. She can do anything. Oh, jeez, will you look at those two daffodils over there." His face was creased with disgust. "All dressed up to go dancing, I suppose."

I turned to see two young men in tuxedos moving through the dining room to the back where the orchestra played.

"*Those types,*" Richard continued, "usually don't show up till past midnight. I hope Childs' isn't encouraging them to come at the dinner hour, too. Broadway *must* be going downhill if they're letting the cupcakes in before sunset."

"I've heard the tourists like to come and laugh at the fairies," I said. "They're good for business."

Chapter 58

BACK IN MY office, I went into action. First I called Ben, Juliana's agent. He was happy with the arrangement, especially with the ten percent he'd be getting from the hefty figure he'd negotiated for Juliana.

As I hung up with Ben, Marty called, wanting to know if I had anything for him. He only had a couple months' rent left before he'd be evicted, and he couldn't ask his mother again. I picked up a note that someone—Max?—had left on my desk. "Yeah, I might have something. But you have to be careful with this one," I said into the phone. "It's the lead in Sorell Morton's new one, *Hey There, I'm Here*, with Dame Margaret Dunton. Yeah, I know. Big. Career-maker. They want a newcomer. You fit the description. But Dunton can be hell on her leads. If I refer you, you have an excellent chance. If you do get it, *don't* sleep with her. You wouldn't be the first gay boy she tried to "convert." I'm telling you, don't fall for it, no matter how much pressure she puts on you. I don't have time to go into detail right now, but let me know if you get it, and if you do, we'll meet so I can brief you. Contact your agent right away. Who are you with now? Okay, good. They know what they're doing over there. Have Billy set it up."

I hung up the phone and immediately dialed Juliana. I took a deep breath before speaking. I couldn't be the hurt friend when we spoke. I had to be the businesswoman whose only objective was to save her client from what could be a major career disaster. As soon as I heard her voice, though, the two got mixed up and the hurt friend, lover, or whoever came rushing out like hot liquid spilling all over her. "Jule, why the *hell* didn't you call me about this contract? Dammit."

"Richard told me you approved it. I thought you were too busy to call me."

"Listen to me carefully. I am *never* too busy to talk to you about your career. No. Correct that. I am *never* too busy to talk you about *anything*. Ever. Do you hear me?"

"Is this a bad thing? A mistake? Oh, no, Al."

"It's okay." Now that I'd completely botched this up and made her into a wreck, I had to convince her everything was fine. "It's going to be all right."

"You're sure?"

"Yes. Don't worry."

When I hung up I knew she was worried. Richard and she would fight tonight, and I couldn't be there to calm her because *he*'d be there. The ever-present Richard. My hands shook as I hung up the receiver.

Max poked his head into my office. "Everything okay?"

"Yeah, sure."

"Well, you've got a whole line of girls waiting out here to audition for you. Don't you think you better get started?"

"Oh?" I said, my mind completely filled with worry over Juliana. "Why are you telling me instead of Bart?"

"I didn't see Bart anywhere. Is he in charge of this?"

I grunted and marched into a room of female hopefuls. I was looking to replace a couple of Harlington Honeys who had moved on to bigger and better. Bart was supposed to be running it. He was supposed to pick the most promising girls and set up appointments for them with Sadie, our musical director. But as usual, he was nowhere to be found.

All through the auditions, I couldn't focus on anything other than getting Juliana out of that contract. Then, I'd wondered if maybe I *was* holding her back. It'd been easy to move Lili on. Why hadn't I done that for Jule? Was it some fear of losing her? Lili was easy to put into ingénue roles. Jule's age was against her. There'd been producers who would've put her in those ingénue roles to use her name, but I had to protect her from piranhas like that. At thirty-six, she should be doing leading-lady parts in musical theatre, but she didn't have the experience.

I was down to the last singer; a slender, twenty-year-old blonde. Cute, in a twinkly sort of way, but twinkly singers didn't bring in big spenders. The kid wore a simple, pale-green day dress that buttoned down the front.

She told me her name, which I promptly forgot, because my mind was stuck on getting done with the audition and back to getting Juliana out of that contract. After two hours of listening to girl singers from Kansas, and Nebraska, or wherever the hell they came from, I was growing deaf. This kid would have to be some kind of special for me to notice her.

She introduced me to her accompanist, Lucille Wadwacker. Now, that's a name you *didn't* forget. Lucille was about the same age as the singer, but not as attractive. She wore thick glasses that made her eyes look like they were popping out of her head. And that nose. It was long, thin, and pointed. Something like the wicked witch in *The Wizard of Oz,* but that's where the comparison ended.

Lucille's body wasn't anything like a skinny witch. Lucille had curves that she didn't mind showing off. She wore a dress—two or three sizes too small—splashed with flowers of many types and colors. A daisy spread out over her rear when she bent to pick up some sheet music that slipped out of her arms. Her bodice dipped down low, leaving no doubt that while nature may have cheated her in some areas, it had amply made up for it in others.

The place was empty except for the singer, Lucille, and me. I was steaming about Bart. *Some assistant.* The tables were in disarray, and the waiters and the cooks hadn't come in yet. Lucille sat her daisy-clad rear on the piano seat and spread out her music, ready to play. The singer stood close to the piano and announced that she would sing, "Someone to Watch Over Me." I quietly sighed, *here we go again.* It must've been the twentieth time I'd heard it that day. I slumped down in my chair and squinted at my watch. I'd give her two minutes to thrill me.

She sang with a pleasant voice, but nothing exciting. Like lots of girls I saw, she had possibilities, but no spark. I was about to say, "Thank you, Miss, we'll let you know," when she nodded at Lucille. Lucille jumped into a marimba rhythm, wiggling those treacherous hips while she played "Sway." I sat up straight. The singer opened the bottom buttons of her dress, poked her legs out at me, and sang. I could see where her nylons hooked to her garter belt. She gyrated her hips in time to the music, boring her eyes into mine. This definitely wasn't the way Dean Martin did that song. This girl was all sex.

She stepped down from the stage, gliding toward me, smiling like she wanted to devour me. There was something intimidating, yet alluring about this girl who now definitely had my attention. With hips shaking, she turned her rear toward me and bent to pick up a steak knife a careless waiter had left on the carpet. She waved the knife in the air, swirling around to dance behind me, before beating out the rhythm with the handle on the top of an uncovered wooden table.

I twisted my body around in my chair so I could keep watching. She wasn't wearing any underpants, just that garter belt, and oh yes, this gal was having a memorable affect on me. Not the kind that would land her a job at The Haven, though.

She ran her hands up her body, over her stomach and to her breasts, all the while swaying to the music. When she jabbed at the air with the knife, I started to feel like I should get the hell out of there, but … I was mesmerized. As the song came to an end, she spun around to face me and slammed her spiked heel between my legs. If I hadn't been wearing a skirt to catch the spike, I would've been speared in a very awkward place.

Lucille had stopped playing and left the room. I was alone with this odd, possibly dangerous kid. She slid her foot down my leg and unbuttoned her top dress buttons. She pulled the two sides of the dress apart. I should've stopped her, but as she pulled the dress down to her waist—held on only by a belt—it became clear she wasn't wearing anything other than the garter belt, nylons, and heels. My breath got caught somewhere between my lungs and my throat.

She undid the belt and let the dress fall in a heap around her shoes. She leaned over me, her hands gripping the arms of my chair, her breasts only inches from my mouth. "Make love to me, Al."

"Uh, someone ..." I ridiculously coughed out. I wasn't handling this at all well.

"Don't worry, Al. Lucille won't let anyone in."

"Lucille?"

"She's outside standing guard."

She opened a couple of buttons on my blouse and slipped her hand inside my bra as she kissed my lips.

I *wanted* this girl just then. I wanted to grab her, and touch her, and roll around on the disgustingly unvacuumed carpet with her, but *Lucille is standing guard?* Was all this for a job, or was it some elaborate trap? A picture of me being carted out of the club in handcuffs by the cops shot through my mind. I saw my name in the *Times* and the *Herald*, and even *The Staten Island Advocate,* "Alice Huffman, Manager of Max Harlington's The Haven Arrested in Lesbian Tryst." I saw some government official ripping up my cabaret and liquor licenses, all my clients quitting me, Max firing me, Juliana turning away in shame. I saw myself living on the street, eating out of garbage pails.

"No!" I shouted, yanking her hand out of my bra. "You need to go home now." I stood up and picked up her dress. "Put this on. This is no way to break into show business." I put it in her hands.

She let the dress slip from her fingers. "You think this is for a job? I love you."

She tried to kiss me. I backed away. "You can't love me. You don't know me."

"Haven't you ever heard of loving from afar? I've watched you with Juliana, with Max. You're magnificent. I heard you liked girls—"

"Put this on." I handed her the dress again. "I'm not that way." I backed up more.

She threw the dress over a chair. "Yes, you are." She took a few steps toward me. "But it's all right. So am I."

My body wanted this girl, standing only a few feet away from me, naked except for her heels, garter belt, and stockings. I wanted to forget all good sense and join my parts with her parts, but terror won out. "Go home."

"You don't mean that." She tried to get her hand down the waistband of my skirt.

I grabbed her wrist. "Get dressed. I'm going into my office now. Don't be here when I come back out. I don't want to have to call the cops." I flicked her wrist away from me and marched toward my office.

As I swung open my door to go inside and slam it behind me for effect, she said, "You'll be sorry you treated me this way."

I stood, watching her slip into her dress and throw on her coat. She headed toward the exit, but stopped and glared at me. I thought she was going to make another threat, but she merely stormed out of the club.

I leaned on my open office door, breathing heavily, but not with passion. *Who was that kid?*

I was about to disappear behind my office door when I saw Bertha standing there. "You were wonderful."

"Bertha! What are you doing here? We don't open for hours."

"I fell asleep in the kitchen. I do that sometimes."

"Why?"

"I was sleepy. You were so noble tonight, Miss Huffman. Truly. That girl was a tart. I don't know where on earth she got the idea that you were sick like that, but *I* know you're not."

"That's right, I'm not."

"I know. You're not one of those mental cases. You're a career woman. That's why you're not married. There's nothing wrong with being a career woman. Nothing 'funny' about it."

"No, there isn't. You should go now. The waiters will be in soon to set the tables. You wouldn't want to get underfoot."

Chapter 59

MY FOURTH PHONE call that night uncovered an important secret investor in *Summer Dandelions*—Shirl. Leaving Bart—who finally showed up—in charge, I was about to dash out the door when I saw the paper on top of the pile; *The New York Times* had a review of *Hey There, I'm Here*, Marty's new play.

Marty had left messages for me during previews, but I hadn't had time to get back to him because of trying to get Juliana out of that contract. I'd missed opening night too.

The review extolled the talent of Dame Margaret Dunton. It spoke of the stupendous training English actors and actresses receive compared to our clumsy American actors who stomp mindlessly across the stage. "And speaking of mindless stomping, we have Buck Martin." *Oh, no.* The reviewer felt sorry for the brilliant Dame Margaret suffering through the wooden, squeaky-voiced antics of such a leading man.

I quickly scanned through the rest of the papers, trying to find one good phrase; they all said something similar or worse. Marty must be absolutely prostrate. I knew I should call him, but ... Juliana, that contract ... I reached for the phone, but then—I'll call him tomorrow morning. I pulled on my coat and ran out.

"Wait," Bertha said, leaving her booth and trotting after me. "You can't go out like that."

"Like what?"

"It's cold out. Let me button you up."

I yanked myself away from her and ran out the door.

I arrived at Shirl's house at eleven that night. My hair hung raggedly in front of my eyes. I pushed it back under my hat before ringing Shirl's bell. I couldn't discuss business with Shirl looking like the wreck of the Hesperus.

Shirl came to the door in her striped nightshirt and slippers. "Thanks for seeing me. I know this is unorthodox, coming to your home to discuss business, and at this hour, but like I told you on the phone, it's important."

"Come in. Mercy's put on a pot of coffee. You know, I'm usually in bed by nine-thirty."

"I know. And I know this is a big sacrifice for you, but once you hear—"

"Hi there, Al," Mercy said, tightening her yellow and green flowered robe around her slight frame. "Coffee'll be ready soon. Oh, you prefer tea, don't you?"

"Don't fuss. Coffee'll be fine."

"No fuss. Now, you be nice to Al, Shirl. She wouldn't be here at this hour if it weren't urgent." Shirl lit a cigar.

It hit me. I could've waited till tomorrow. I was here now because *I* hoped to sleep tonight; I hadn't given one thought to Shirl's sleep. With her strict rules for business, I may have blown this for Juliana. I told myself to stay humble, respectful, but not mealy-mouthed.

"I'll get that coffee and tea," Mercy said, dashing toward the kitchen. "And put out that filthy cigar." She stopped to open a window.

"What's so urgent that you roused me to talk business?" Shirl seated herself in her chair.

"Uh …" I couldn't turn into a recalcitrant child. "Juliana. Did you know they cast her in the lead of *Summer Dandelions*, opening in the fall?"

"There's no music."

"I know."

"Why have you come to me with this?"

I took a deep breath, then coughed because of Shirl's cigar.

"You really ought to take care of that cough," Shirl said, taking another puff of her cigar.

"I called in some favors and found out you're heavily invested in this show."

"That's a secret. You've really turned into quite the spy. You don't think Juliana can handle it?"

"Do you?"

"She can be surprising."

I sat on the couch. "In time. After a few acting classes, but now? She's almost on top as a singer. If she failed at this … You know Juliana. And you know New York critics. Other entertainers might ride it out, but Juliana?"

"How did this happen?

"Richard, of course, and Ben. Without talking to me. I could kill them."

"Richard means well."

"He's an asshole."

"Watch your mouth. You were always a sweet girl. You need to keep some of that even as a businesswoman. What do you want me to do?"

Mercy put the coffee and tea on the coffee table. "Don't you two boys stay up too late. Bad for your health. I'm going to bed. Nice seeing you, Al."

"You too, Mercy. Good night."

"Would you consider withdrawing your investment?"

"That would close the show."

"I know."

"I invested in this show to help a gay boy I met at one of the bars. Maybe I could speak to the producer and *threaten* to leave if Juliana does it."

"That might work."

"Talking behind Juliana's back? I'd only do it because *you* think it's best. You understand?"

I took a sip of my tea. "Yes."

"Are you sure you're not going through all this to make Richard look bad in Juliana's eyes?"

Chapter 60

"AL! AL!" I vaguely heard Max's voice piercing through my sleep.

"Huh?" I squinted at the rain smacking my window and hid my head under my pillow. I'd worked till four—an hour ago—so waking up wasn't so easy to do.

"You can't sleep," Max called louder.

I squinted up at him standing over me in his red and black-checkered bathrobe. "What?"

"Get up. He's upset. I don't know what to do."

"Who's upset?"

"Scott. He came home with me tonight."

"That's nice. Have fun." I pulled the covers over my head and fell back to sleep.

"No!" Max wailed. "Pay attention. He's not talking, not moving. I did something to him." He paced back and forth at the bottom of my bed, his leather slippers flapping at his feet.

I forced myself to sit up. "What'd you do to him?"

"I thought I was making love to him, but suddenly he crawled off the bed. He's shaking in the corner of the room. You've gotta help him. I don't know what to do."

"And *I* do?"

"I'll never forgive myself if I hurt him." He ran his fingers through his graying hair. "Do something."

I put on the light and shook my head, trying to bring full consciousness back. I slid out of the covers and walked zombie-like toward my bathroom.

"Where are you going?"

"To brush my teeth."

"There's no time for that. You have to go to him now."

"*You* go to him now. That's who he needs. *I* don't talk to anyone without clean teeth. I'll be right there."

I brushed my teeth in between pulling off my nightgown and pulling on a pair of underpants and some trousers. I ran back to my room to scramble into an old sweater. I didn't bother with a bra. I dashed down the stairs and met Max pacing outside his bedroom door on the other side of the apartment.

"How is he?"

"Just stares. Come in. Oh, he's naked. You've seen naked men before."

"It's something I try not to do, but I suppose I can manage for a friend."

Max walked into the room and sat on the corner of his unmade double bed knitting his fingers together. Scott sat on the floor, his back pressed up against the wall between the closet door and Max's roll-top desk. His knees were pushed against his chest, and his arms covered his head as if he were sheltering himself from enemy fire.

"You see?" Max said. "He stays like that. I haven't been able to get him to talk. He won't get up. What did I do to this poor man?"

"Shh," I said, as I sat on the floor next to Scott.

"Are you okay?" I whispered to him.

"Obviously, he's not." Max jumped up. "Why are you asking him stupid questions?"

"Because I don't know what I'm doing. Go in the living room. Make yourself a drink. I need to think."

"A drink. That's a good idea. A drink." He walked out.

As soon as he was out of the room, Scott looked up at me. "Thanks, Al."

"I don't understand."

"I don't want to hurt him. He's such a good man. But I can't do it."

"Do what?"

"I can't … The sex. He needs that. And I can't."

"But you have before, haven't you?"

"Yeah, but I always suffer after. Inside me." He pointed at his naked chest with only a smattering of hair. "Inside—the pain—the pain of knowing what I did. I have to go." He stood up. "I'm naked!" He put his two hands over his thing. "You shouldn't be in here with me like this." He groped for his robe lying on the bed. "Go!"

"Sure." I got up and stood by the bureau. "I'll be over here if you need—"

"No. Get out of here."

I went into the living room. Max was pacing back and forth in front of the French windows, sipping a glass of sherry. He always kept a bottle of sherry in the living room cabinet. Water ran down the glass windows in wide sheets and bounced against our patio floor. Max, as always, had thought to bring in the plants before the worst of the rain fell. The city skyline blinked red, blue, and green through a prism of water drops.

"Well?" Max said.

"Maybe we should call his psychoanalyst," I suggested.

"He quit. Do you want a glass of sherry?"

"I wouldn't mind."

He poured a glass and handed it to me. "Don't spill it on the rug."

"Only you would turn everyone's life into a nightmare by getting a white rug." I took a nervous sip from my glass as I flexed my toes through the rug's heavenly soft wool. "Maybe that's why he's like this."

"Because of the carpet?"

"No. Because he quit his psychoanalysis. *You* know people. If he didn't like that one, maybe you should get him a new one."

Max leaned back against his shiny patent leather grand piano. "I know some MDs who come into the club regularly. They might be able to recommend someone, but you know, those fellows fill his head with crap against homosexuality. I think it makes him worse. I was glad when he quit. I thought he was ready to accept himself—and us—now this."

Scott stood in the archway dressed in slacks, sports jacket, and tie, holding his fedora. "I'm going now. Sorry I caused so much trouble."

Max straightened up. "You didn't."

"I think I did." He turned to go.

"Go with him," Max whispered to me.

"It's pouring out there."

"All the more reason. He shouldn't go out in this."

"But *I* should? Look how I'm dressed. I'm not even wearing a bra."

"You don't need one."

"Thanks a lot, and you wanted me to do what for you?"

"Hurry. You can grab a couple of umbrellas from the stand in the hall on your way out."

I got downstairs, I dashed out of the elevator, and into the lobby, pulling on a coat to cover my clothes. I ran out the door as the rain splashed over the sides of the awning. "Cab, Miss?" Alfred, the doorman asked.

"No, thanks. Did you see which way a man in a gray sports coat went? No umbrella."

"Mr. Elkins. He's over there, ma'am," Alfred said, pointing.

Scott stood on the other side of the street under an awning. A tiny thread of morning light sparked in the sky, poking through the nighttime darkness. I pushed open one of the umbrellas and waited on the curb as a cab drove by; splashing mud all over the bottom of my brand new coat. Once it passed, I ran over to Scott—afraid he'd run away, but I think he was waiting for me. "What are you doing, Scott?"

"I was going to go home until you decided to follow me."

"Max is worried. Here. He wanted me to give you this umbrella."

He smiled and took it. "That's sweet of him. Such a good person."

"He is. So why …?"

He looked away.

"You want some breakfast?" I asked. "My treat."

"I'll have breakfast with you, but only if *I* pay. I'm still *that* much of a man."

We raised our umbrellas and walked up the wet sidewalk toward the all-night diner a few blocks away. The pale light was expanding in the sky, opening the way for blue.

By the time Scott and I got to the diner, the rain was a mere drizzle, and we were closing our umbrellas. I love the subtle colors of early morning, especially after a rain has washed the sky clean. The colors are delicate and pastel-like as if they were born in a Monet painting. I love the smell of early-morning coffee, and the way the percolator sounds in an all-night diner when the aprons on the waitresses and countermen have started to droop. I love the smell of bacon and eggs and everything becoming possible again, especially at an all-night diner at six in the morning.

Scott sat looking out the window as we sipped our coffee. "You know, Scott, you're not like all the other guys Max has been with. You're special. I think he's in love with you."

He took a sip of his coffee. "Please don't say that. I never asked him to."

"But I think you feel the same."

"I'm trying not to. He asked me to live with him. How can two men live together? Like that? He wants us to try to be—something to each other. He talked about these men who lived together like a man and woman for forty-five years and said that there are more men trying it. I knew men in DC who did that. Some even exchanged rings like it was real, but I couldn't be a part of that. That's a perversion."

"Why did you quit your psychoanalysis? Wasn't it helping?"

"Dr. Brown—"

"Brown? That's a new one."

"A new old one. I go through them fast. Dr. Brown wanted to get me interested in girls like the rest. I even went on a date with a girl a few weeks ago."

"How'd that go?"

"I think I bored the poor girl out of her mind. I didn't know what to say to her. Dr. Brown said I should at least try to hold her hand before the end of the date, and I was going to do it. I promised myself I definitely would, no matter what, do that. But as the night went on, I got scared and I didn't. After that date, Dr. Brown said that even though being with a man was a sickness, it wasn't a terrible one. He said that even Sigmund Freud said there were lots worse things in life than homosexuality."

"You wouldn't know it, the way people have been talking these days."

"He told me about famous men who had been like me, men like Alexander the Great, Oscar Wilde, and Walt Whitman. Their sickness didn't keep them from being great men. He thought, since he and I didn't seem to be getting anywhere with curing my sickness, that maybe I should go with Max, because being alone in the world had to be worse than being homosexual. He said if I could find any love in this world, even if it was with another man, then I should go and enjoy that love—the one that was right in front of me."

"What a fantastic doctor. So why are you upset?"

"I tried. Tonight. To be with Max. To be with him completely. To let myself love him, but I started shaking, and I was terrified. A terror that Max was about to kill me overtook me. I know that sounds crazy, but ... Al, no matter what Dr. Brown says, it's ..." He whispered, "It's a sin. And if I don't atone and stop doing it, I'm going to hell." He sipped his coffee.

"Scott, you know the Bible lots better than me, but when I was a kid I read it twice from cover to cover."

"What for?"

"I was looking for a loophole."

He laughed. "You must've been a very odd child."

"Ask my mother."

"A loophole for what?"

"I had this friend who was Jewish. I met her at school, and I found her really interesting. Like, her family had their Sunday on Friday night, and they ate food I'd never heard of. In Sunday school, they used to tell us that the Jews were going to hell because they didn't believe in Jesus. That didn't sound right to me. I mean, her family was really nice. One time, during the depression, her mother gave me uh, it was called, uh, filtie fish to take home to my family."

"So you read the Bible looking for a loop hole for your friend. That's sweet. Did you find one?"

"I think so. And I think it's a loophole for you too."

"What?"

"Well, the thing that impressed me the most through all those stories of bloodshed, incest, and betrayal was where it says, 'God is love.' I figured that if God is love, that's the loophole for all of us. 'Cause what kind of loving God would throw his kids into a fire no matter what they did?"

Chapter 61

March 1954

"I AM NOT pleased," Shirl said through gritted teeth.

We sat in Shirl's office. I resisted the temptation to slink down in my chair like a little boy who'd been sent to the principal's office. I wanted to plead Shirl's forgiveness, but I dared not. She would never respect me as a businesswoman. I was on shaky ground already.

"I took my money out," Shirl continued, getting out of her chair. She leaned heavily against the front of the desk, her eyes boring into mine. "Every dime. Now, I'm out of what could be a big hit."

"I didn't think they'd be able to raise more money. At least not that fast. How could anyone have known that kid playwright had a rich uncle, one who'd seen Juliana at the Copa and fallen in love with her?"

"*You* should've known."

"Maybe you could get back in. No show is going to turn down a hungry investor."

"After the stink I made about Juliana being cast as the lead? The stink *you* told me to make. I don't put my tail between my legs for anyone."

"I'm sorry, Shirl. Maybe it'll flop."

"Is that what you're hoping?"

"No! Juliana would die. But yes, for you. Maybe. I don't know."

"The thing is probably going to be a smash, and I'm going to be out a fortune. I could smash *you*." She shook a meaty fist in my direction. "The things I said about her—if she ever found out—"

"You didn't tell them she was ..."

"Of course not. I'd never tell them the truth. What kind of friend do you think I am? I did all this because *you* asked me to. Never mix business with friendship." She pressed her fists against her temples. "What was I thinking? I was thinking *you* knew what you were doing. You with the big college education."

"I know."

"Mercy wanted me to invite you over to our place for dinner tonight." She picked up the phone receiver. "Can I tell her you're coming?"

"You still want me in your home?"

"No, but you *are* Mercy's friend."

"I knew *you* long before I met Mercy."

"But I'm not speaking to you. Are you coming or not?"

* * *

I arrived at Shirl and Mercy's door that night in my very best men's suit, especially tailored for me by Juliana's tailor: gray with a gray and red striped tie. I rarely dressed like this, but I thought it might help me to get myself back in Shirl's good graces. I draped my trench coat over it so as not to be someone's target. I carried a bouquet of daisies, Mercy's favorite. I had to make things right.

"Al," Mercy exclaimed when she opened the door. She wore an airy blue chiffon dress that floated around her ankles as she moved. "Come in. I was so happy when Shirl told me you could come. I've been cooking all day, so I hope you're hungry."

"You shouldn't have gone to all that trouble for me. Oh, here. These are for you."

"My favorite. How thoughtful." She caressed them to her breast. "Let me take your coat. Shirl is finishing up some work in the other room. I'll tell her you're here." She spun around, heading out of the room, my coat over her shoulder; then she quickly spun back. "Don't you look nice? So dapper. I swear, if I weren't attached ..." She clicked her tongue and winked at me as she bounced out of the room.

I undid my suit jacket buttons and sat on the couch, staring at the theater books Shirl had lined up on the shelves against the opposite wall.

"What's next?" Shirl said from behind me. I turned as she came into the room, wearing her usual navy-blue suit and tie. She must have hundreds of those hanging in her closet.

I stood. "Next?"

"Juliana's going to be in *Summer Dandelions,* like it or not. What's next on your agenda for her?"

"I got her an acting coach. She's going to be working with him every day till they open. The cast had their first table read last week, and I didn't get any desperate calls from the director or her, so I'm hopeful. Today, the director was going to have them up and moving around." I held up two crossed fingers.

Shirl nodded, holding up her own two crossed fingers. Mercy poked her head in. "Dinner's ready, so you boys get a move on it. Shirl, did you wash your hands?"

"Yes, Mother, all clean. See?" She held up her hands for inspection.

"Al, you can wash up on your way to the dining room. You've been on that filthy subway."

"Yes, ma'am."

After washing my hands, I found Shirl in the dining room. Mercy carried two heavy silver trays of food from the kitchen. I ran to help her. "You sit. I've got it. I used to carry more than this when I was a waitress at Lindy's."

"But I don't mind helping."

"Sit," Shirl said. "We don't put our guests to work."

Hesitantly, I sat.

I'd never been invited into Shirl's dining room before. Under the current awkward circumstances, it seemed strange I was being afforded the honor now. The room had one long mahogany table in the center with mahogany cabinets lining the walls on either side. A weighty, masculine look. Shirl sat at the head of the table. On the wall above her head was a gilded portrait of a man from a different time, maybe the fifteenth or sixteenth century.

"I see you're looking at Queen Christina."

"Queen? That's a picture of a woman? Garbo played her. I like this real picture better than the way Garbo looked."

"Me, too. Christina was a homosexual."

"But in the movie, she gives up her throne for the *man* she loves."

"Don't go to Hollywood for your history, or to college, either. They didn't teach you anything very important, did they?"

"I guess not." I smiled at the thought that a professor would even use the word homosexual in a college classroom. He'd be fired.

"She gave up her throne," Shirl continued, "because she refused to marry when the nobles told her she must. She found the very idea of marriage repulsive; she knew she would never have an heir, so she thought it best for her country if she abdicated. She had a special woman friend, Ebba, who she wrote letters of great devotion to. Historians explain this away by telling us that Ebba was married, so of course her relationship with the Queen could not have been 'unnatural.' But you and I both know that marriage to a man does not mean a woman can't be gay."

"Has Juliana seen this picture?"

"Of course. She's eaten in this dining room many times. I have a book I can lend you on Christina. You have to read between very many lines to get to the true story, but it might be fun for you. A glass of Merlot?" She held up the bottle. "A friend brought it from Paris. We simply cannot get a decent wine in the states."

"Let me give it a try."

The phone rang. Shirl had telephone extensions in every room of the house. We both stared at the black phone sitting on top of the cabinet across from the table.

"Don't you dare," Mercy said. "We are civilized beings. We do not interrupt our meals for telephones."

"Yes, Mother," Shirl said, giving me a look.

I knew we were both wondering if it were Juliana. It continued to ring, demanding our attention.

"This wine is delicious," I said, trying to ignore the sound of the ringing.

"What do you think of the new things we're going to need to get onto the subway?" Mercy asked. "What are they calling them?"

"Tokens," I said.

"What's wrong with putting a dime in the slot?" Shirl said. "It's been like that since the subway began. If it's not broken, don't fix it."

"No, we used to put a *nickel* in the slot," Mercy corrected. "After the war they raised it to a dime because of inflation. Now they need to raise it to fifteen cents to support the growing system. People can't stand there putting in a dime and a nickel. It would take too long."

"Fifteen cents[5] is outrageous!" Shirl said. "Have you seen the state of those cushions lately?"

"I heard they're going to take them out," I said, "since they're getting ripped up."

"Sure. Charge more and make our ride even more uncomfortable than it is now."

"You don't like change," Mercy giggled. "You should've heard her, Al, when they changed our phones to direct dial."

---

5 15 cents in 1953 has the same spending power as $1.35 in 2017

"My business depends on the telephone. I didn't have time to stop what I was doing to learn that new dial nonsense."

"Who was the one who went to the special class the city gave?"

"Even now, I still don't like dialing on my own," Shirl grumbled. "I liked talking to the operators. They were dependable girls. Some of them were my friends. I hate trusting an automated faceless thing to get the number when I'm in a hurry. But everyone wants to be so 'modern.' I still say, 'If it ain't broke don't fix it.'" She swallowed down the last of her wine as the phone stopped ringing.

I ate until I thought I'd bust. Mercy had made lamb with mint jelly, mashed potatoes, string beans and butternut squash. Then she turned off the lights and left Shirl and me in the dark. A few minutes later, she returned carrying a flaming Baked Alaska. Our exclamations of amazement almost made Mercy burst her buttons. I liked pleasing Mercy, and it was so easy to do.

While we finished the Baked Alaska, the phone rang again, and both Shirl and I stared at it.

"No," Mercy said. "Finish your desert."

We finished our meal with an after-dinner brandy that Shirl and I took into the living room while Mercy did the dishes. Shirl lit a cigar to go with her brandy and sat in her chair. The phone on the table next to her rang, and she reached for it. "Yes, she's here. Are you all right?"

I mouthed, "Juliana?"

Shirl nodded.

"Good?" I whispered.

Shirl shook her head no.

"Damn!"

Shirl held out the phone. She put a big grin on her face and whispered, "Smile."

I mirrored her grin as I took the phone. "How nice to hear from you. Now? I'll take a cab. Not needed. I can pay for myself." I took a deep breath. "It's going to be okay. Yes, I'll be there in no time."

"Not good," I said, to Shirl as I hung up the phone. "I have to get over there right away."

"It could be nothing," Shirl said. "Panic. A loss of faith in her talent."

"Your coat," Mercy said, hurrying into the room. "Give Juliana my love." I slipped my arms into my overcoat. "Button this top button. Don't let anyone see that tie. Shirl takes such chances, and after what happened it gives me the shivers."

"I'll be fine." I kissed her on the cheek and dashed out the door. I was running up Juliana's stairs in less than a half-hour.

* * *

"It's terrible," Juliana squawked at me as soon as I walked through her door. "Awful, horrible." She paced back and forth.

"What's terrible, awful, horrible?"

"The play. Did you read it?"

"Uh … no."

"Then why did you tell me to do it?" she yelled at me.

"I didn't."

"Then who did?"

"Richard. And Ben, your agent."

"What did *you* say?"

"*I* wasn't consulted. Richard's your manager."

"Richard doesn't know anything about theater. Why weren't *you* consulted?" she yelled like it was my fault Richard hadn't contacted me. "*You're* supposed to make sure you're consulted about everything."

"You've got dirt on your forehead."

"It's not dirt. It's ash. From a priest."

"Oh, the mumbo jumbo."

"It's not mumbo jumbo. Ash Wednesday is a holy time. I'm giving up cigarettes for the next forty days."

"Well that's a huge sacrifice, considering you only smoke about one cigarette a year. The play can't be that bad. You're nervous. This is something new. How are things going with your acting coach?"

"All right, I suppose. Maybe you're right. I'm upset for nothing. I read it when Richard first suggested it and liked it."

"See? Nerves."

"Would you read it and tell me what *you* think?"

She had to be wrong; it couldn't be terrible. Shirl wouldn't back a bad play. "I'll take it home tonight and—"

"No. Now."

"Now?"

330

"Sit here and read it." She handed me the script. "Richard'll be home in an hour. You can tell him what you think. Oh, but you can't be dressed like that when he gets here. Give me your tie and jacket. I'll get you a blouse and a skirt to wear." She ran into her bedroom.

"What does your acting coach think of the play?" I tore off my jacket, shirt and tie.

"He won't tell me," Juliana called from the bedroom. "Do you think that's a bad sign?" She came back with a blouse and skirt draped over her arm. "He says a good actress never judges her character. A good actress doesn't think about what is good or bad; she makes whatever it is into something wonderful—even if it's shit. He said 'shit,' not me. Does that sound right to you?"

"I don't know anything about acting or plays."

"Yes, you do. Take your pants off."

"I wish you'd say that when Richard *wasn't* on his way home. It's been months, you know." I uncinched my belt and let my pants fall down around my ankles.

"You studied acting and even had a part on Broadway." She snatched up my pants and threw a skirt at me.

"And now I manage a nightclub and some cabaret performers. Does that tell you anything about my expertise in theater? These don't fit. I'm smaller than you."

"That's right, rub it in. You look fine."

"I look like Little Orphan Annie. I'd kill to have tits like yours."

"You do have tits like mine. Mine."

I rushed to kiss her, but she backed away. "Richard. Soon."

"Oh, him."

"Sit, take the script. I'll put the kettle on and make you a nice glass of hot Turkish tea. You read."

I sat on the couch, balancing the script on my lap.

When it was done, Juliana placed the glass of hot tea on the coffee table. She sat in the overstuffed chair opposite me as I pored over what seemed to be an unwieldy script with too many pages. Unless this kid was Eugene O'Neill, I was worried.

Juliana tried to divert herself by looking through *Vogue*, but her page flipping and sighing made me feel like we were in a soap opera doctor's waiting room about to be told she had an incurable disease. Cue in melodramatic music. "Juliana, please. I can't concentrate."

"Sorry. Do you want more tea?"

"If I say yes, will you spend the next ten minutes in the kitchen?"

"Yes."

"Then I'll take more tea. And, could you whip me up a batch of brownies so I can get this done?"

She gave me a smirk and took my glass into the kitchen.

It was a relief to have her out of the room. I was finishing the first act, and I was not impressed. How could Shirl have wanted to invest in this? The plot was dull, the characters unbelievable. The thing was terrible, like Juliana said. I hoped it'd pick up in the second act.

As I opened to the page that announced Act Two, the phone rang. Juliana tiptoed toward the bedroom. "Sorry. Keep reading. I'll be quiet."

I read, hoping to find something inspiring, uplifting, or simply *interesting*. I looked up to see Juliana standing outside her bedroom, not saying anything.

"Why are you standing there?"

"That was God."

Oh, no. She'd completely gone over the edge this time. "Who?"

"Well, maybe not God, but like him. It was Cardinal Spellman's secretary. The Cardinal wants me to sing *Ave Maria* at St. Patrick's for Easter."

"That's good. Isn't it?"

"No, it's not good." She paced in the center of the room. "Sing for The Blessed Virgin? What if I botch it up?"

"You won't."

She looked dazed and miserable.

"Oh, honey, you won't." I got up and reached out to touch her hand. She shook me off. "Richard will be home any minute. What am I going to do? I can't say no to the Church, but how will I ever get ready in two weeks with play rehearsals going on, too? He saw my act in Chicago and heard I was a good Catholic. I'm not a good Catholic. I'm a sinner. I can't do it."

"You can. *If* you want to. But you don't have to."

"Yes, I do. You don't say no to the Pope."

"He's not the Pope."

"He's close. What am I going to do?" She flopped onto the couch.

"If you feel you have to do it then you can. Are you telling me you don't already know *Ave Maria* right now, this minute?"

"Of course, I know it. But knowing it and *knowing* it are two different things."

Richard came through the door. "Oh, Richard," she said, hurrying toward his outstretched arms. "Cardinal Spellman wants me to sing *Ave Maria* at St. Patrick's for Easter."

"That's wonderful." With his arms around her he walked her to the couch. "Such an honor. That'll show my mother."

They sat down on the couch together. I got up. My arms were filled with the play; his arms were filled with her. "I'm worried I won't be able to do it," she said. "What if I forget the words? It's for the precious Virgin."

I moved to the overstuffed chair across from them, knives shooting through my stomach. She put her head on his shoulder, and he patted it.

"I better go," I said, choking back my rage. "I'll talk to you later, Juliana. You should tell Richard what you think of the play *he* chose for you."

Chapter 62

"EAT YOUR BREAKFAST," Max said as we sat in the breakfast nook. I stared past the living room through the French windows and the patio, watching the clouds in the distance. "Scott spent a lot of time on that breakfast, and you're letting it get cold."

"It's okay," Scott said. "I didn't spend that much time." He whispered to Max, "I think she's feeling blue."

I shoved a forkful of cold scrambled egg into my mouth. "I didn't get much sleep last night."

"Al, you have to face facts," Max said. "Richard is her husband." He took a sip of his coffee. "This coffee is wonderful, hon," he said to Scott.

"I added a little almond flavoring."

"Very nice. Look, Al, I don't mean to defend her. Juliana's lifestyle is indefensible. But what did you expect her to do when Richard hugged her? Push him on the floor?"

"Don't be so hard on Al," Scott said. "She's in love. Let me have your plate, Max. I'll get you more egg."

"No, I'm stuffed," Max said. "I wish you'd find someone else, Al. Shirl must know ..."

"I don't want someone else! Dammit, Max."

"Okay. But don't forget, Richard and Juliana have something in common that you can never share."

"What's that?"

"Their religion."

"Oh, that."

"That's not minor. *You* make fun of her religion."

"Not much." I put a few crumbs of scrambled egg in my mouth, so Scott wouldn't feel bad. "Do you think she sleeps with him?"

"Yes," Max said without hesitation.

"Do you think she likes it?"

Scott jumped up, tightening the tie around his robe.

"Who knows?"

"I better clear the table," Scott said. "Are you finished with this, Al?"

"Yeah, it's very good. I'm not up to it today."

"I understand." He balanced an armload of dishes and hurried to the adjoining kitchen.

"You shouldn't talk like that in front of him," Max whispered. "He's uncomfortable with talk about people's sex lives."

"You two seem to be doing well since he moved in last month."

"I don't think I've ever been this exquisitely happy. He's so much better. I want that for you too, Al, and it won't happen with Juliana."

Scott stood in the doorway. "Al, the phone for you."

"Is it?"

"Uh, huh."

I picked up the phone in the kitchen, only to hear Juliana tell me she was furious with me. "You're furious at *me*? I didn't think you even noticed I left. I didn't want to interrupt your *private* moment. Oh? Do I sound mad? I can't imagine why. Yes, dammit, I know he's your husband. I'm so sick of that sentence. Yes, I can come over today and talk to you and *Richard* about the play. In the afternoon. I have some things to do this morning."

* * *

That afternoon, I dragged myself to Juliana's house. I had barely gotten two hours sleep. I'd tossed and turned thinking about Juliana in Richard's arms doing the things that I ... I didn't want to think about that. I plodded my way up her stairs and wondered what in the world I was going to tell her about that clunker of a play. As I got to the top, Richard burst through the archway, carrying a suitcase. "Al. Sorry I can't stay. Got word my mother's taken ill. Catching a plane to Omaha."

"That's okay," I said. "Go take care of your mother. Take as long as you need."

"You're so kind," he kissed me on the cheek.

Not *that* kind, I thought.

He gave Juliana a quick kiss on the lips and buzzed down the stairs.

"Well, come in," Juliana directed. "You look terrible."

"Gee, thanks."

"I meant you look exhausted. That skirt and blouse combination is pretty. Even in style."

"I'm not sure how to take that, but I can barely see straight, so I'm going to have to let it go. I don't think I'm awake enough to talk sensibly about the play, and since Richard isn't here, maybe there's no reason to talk about it. But I know I'm awake enough for you and me to ..." I moved toward her. Then backed up. "You're wearing trousers."

"Don't they look good?" She twirled around, showing me from all angles. "I put the kettle on. The tea will be ready soon." She headed toward the kitchen.

I followed her. "But you're wearing pants."

"They show off my derrière nicely, don't you think?" She bent over and shook her rear at me.

"Don't do that in public. It'd be bad for your career."

"Al." She straightened up. "We're in my kitchen, not Times Square." She poured the tea into the little Turkish glasses and put them on the silver tray with the sugar bowl and some butter cookies.

"I know, but pants could ruin your career."

She sighed. "Let's go and talk about the play." She carried the tray into the living room.

"Sure, but couldn't you put on a dress first?"

"I'm sorry if these slacks don't do anything for you, but they're comfortable. I don't even have to wear a girdle. What a relief."

"Well, okay," I said, sitting on the couch, "As long as your public doesn't see you."

She sighed.

"It's quite a surprise that Richard had to go off like that," I said. "Leaving us—alone." I put my hand on her knee. "We haven't been alone in months." I inched my hand up her thigh.

"Sweetheart, I can't."

"What?"

"Yesterday I woke up with a yeast infection. I went to the doctor, so I have medicine, but ... right now, I don't want to stir things up down there. You understand."

"Sure." I took my hand back. I don't think I sounded terribly convincing.

"That doesn't mean I can't do something for you."

"No. We'll watch TV." I hopped over to the TV. I had to move away from her. I was past the pants bothering me; her perfume was driving me mad. I grabbed the TV Guide. "What's on tonight?"

"Come drink your tea. We have a play to ..."

I turned the TV on. I couldn't sit next to her without something to distract me. *The Guiding Light*, a fifteen-minute soap opera, came on.

"What happened to Richard's mother?" I asked, walking back to the couch.

"The way I hear it, she had some type of fit."

"Fit?" I sat on the couch as far away from her as I could get.

"She has a nervous condition. She's had it most of Richard's life. But this is the first time they put her in the hospital for it. She's a nervous person, and sometimes she comes close to fainting. Richard's worried about her heart."

"You don't seem to like her very much."

"She's not my favorite person. She thinks her son married a dance hall girl, which to her mind is close to a prostitute."

"That's not good."

"Not very."

"This is nice, isn't it? The two of us sitting here, the TV on, like we're a family. You know, 'So how are the kids, Ma?' 'Fine, Paw.' Have you ever thought of us—I know we can't, but what if *we* were married? Of course, we couldn't ever be, but Shirl and Mercy are married. It's not real, but they had a ceremony and a party afterwards, and they've got rings."

"I know. I was there."

"You went to their wedding? Was it nice?"

"Very moving."

"Have you ever thought that maybe someday you and me …?"

"Even if Richard weren't in the picture, my religion …"

"Yeah." I sighed.

"Are you all right?"

"Frankly, no. I'm acting like I'm calm and lady-like when I'm really going out of my mind with you sitting right next to me and Richard not here, but you can't do anything, so instead, I'm watching this dumb TV show that I'm not *really* watching, imagining the two of us naked, and you touching me in all those places while at the same time I'm so exhausted I could die. I know that's selfish of me because with all the rehearsing and plane hopping you've been doing over the past few years, you've got to be ready to collapse, and now you've got this play and the singing at St. Patrick's, so why am I telling you my problems when all I really want is for us to get into each other's clothes—*and*—I'm sorry I'm so selfish."

"My goodness." She laughed. "Come here. I don't mind. Let me do something for you."

"Nah, I'd feel like I was at the doctor's."

"What kind of doctors do *you* go to?" She laughed. "And how can I get an appointment?"

"You know what I mean." I laughed, although I didn't want to.

She deepened her voice, "Well, Miss Huffman, let Dr. Jule take a good look at you. Let's get those clothes off." She pulled at the zipper on my skirt.

"No, Jule. Really. When we do it again, if we ever do, I want to do it *with* you. I'm tired and cranky."

"Why don't you take a nap on my bed? Richard'll be away for a week or so, and I'll be better in a few days, and then you and I can 'get into each other's' clothes together. When you wake up we'll talk about the play."

"You wouldn't mind?"

"Not at all. I have plenty to do."

"I need an hour and I'll have energy again." I hurried toward her bedroom. "Oh. Can I use your phone?"

"Be my guest."

I dialed the phone in Juliana's bedroom. "Bertha? What are you doing picking up my phone? Hatcheck girls don't pick up telephones. And they don't do filing. Put Bart on. Bart, why are you having Bertha answering phones and working in *my* office? No. You will not hire her as a secretary so you can do less than nothing. If we need a secretary *I'll* hire one. Get Bertha back to hatcheck and far away from *my* office. I am not being a hysterical woman, and I am not jealous of her. She's a goddamn hatcheck girl. I never expected such sentiments from a *queer* duck like yourself. Look, I'm not going to be back for a few hours. Do the set-ups. I'll put an ad in *The Times*, 'Help Wanted—Female,' on Monday."

I placed the phone back in its cradle and returned to the parlor, my mind on Bertha. Something in the back of my head told me I should fire her, but on what grounds? Doing too much work? Helping me too much? I should've fired Bart ages ago, and I didn't do that. I just can't do that to anybody.

"Everything all right?" Juliana asked from the couch.

"Sure." I pushed Bertha out of my head. "I'm going to collapse on your bed for a few minutes." I walked back into the room and flopped onto the bed.

Juliana suddenly stood in the doorway. "Do you want to go to sleep, or do you want me to relax you?"

"*You* relax me?"

Without speaking she walked into the room, smoothing out her slacks as she sat beside me. I watched her unbutton each of one of my blouse buttons.

She spread apart the two sides of my blouse and stared a moment at my blue bra with the lace on top. She slid one of her hands around to my back and unclasped the bra. She bent my arm to remove the blouse; I sat up to help, but she whispered, "Let me do it. Go limp in my arms."

I never would've been able to do it, I would've laughed if it hadn't been for the seriousness in her eyes, and her gentle care as she held me. I let go of myself, and her arm supported me around my back as she removed my blouse. I was fascinated with how intent she was about completing this task. She gently laid me back on the bed and pulled the bra straps down my arms. I felt a shiver of excitement. She held the bra in her hand and looked closely at the heart-shaped locket I'd pinned inside—the gift she'd given me for my birthday—and smiled.

"Sweet," she said looking at my breasts.

"Too small."

"Shh. Don't do that," she whispered; then ever so lightly she brushed her fingertips over one of my nipples.

I gasped. "Uh, Jule, I don't think this is going to relax me."

"Breathe deeply."

I did as she instructed. "That's making it worse." I laughed.

"Breathe deeper," she said, as she ran her fingertips over the nipple of the second breast. "Get past the excited feelings to something else, something deeper inside yourself." She put her hand on my stomach and pressed down lightly. I was aware that three of her fingers rested under the waistband of my skirt. "Breathe right into my hand."

A rising crescendo of excitement.

"Keep breathing," she whispered; I did, and gradually a kind of peace came over me, a safety, like there was a communion between us, unspoken. As my mind faded into a haze of sleep, I thought—to lay open in front of another person, tits bare, while she's fully clothed, and still feel safe. To feel mildly sexual and do nothing about it, but enjoy the pleasant drifting of it down your body. To no longer be ashamed. This must be it. Love.

When my eyes opened again, a warm breeze from the window above the bed drifted over me. I laid there dressed only in my blue underpants and a thin sheet she must've put over me. The door was ajar, and I could hear her playing and singing *Ave Maria*. I had no idea what the words meant, but the love she put into it made me shiver. When she finished the song, everything went silent.

I continued to lay in drowsy comfort, the breeze light against my skin as I drifted off again.

The next time I awoke, the sunlight in the room was duller and the breezes cooler. The smell of spaghetti sauce drifted in through the door. I stretched, feeling deliciously rested. I looked over at the alarm clock perched on the end table next to the bed. "Six o'clock!" I sprang up. I'd slept through the whole afternoon. I bounced off the bed and grabbed the toothbrush I kept stored under the floorboard covered by the rug. I showered before I made my reappearance.

I stood on the threshold of her bedroom in one of her robes. Juliana sat on the couch, studying her script. "Well hello, Sleeping Beauty."

"I'm sorry."

"It's okay. You look rested now."

I came into the room and noticed an open magazine on the coffee table. I picked it up. The title of the article was "Women Who Fall for Lesbians."

One sentence was underlined: "Many young women, however, are not so lucky as to escape the designs of female sex deviates."

"Why's this out?" I asked.

"Did I trap you? Force you into something you didn't want all those many years ago?"

"Of course not. You think you made me into a 'deviate?'"

"You were very young."

"So were you."

I was *born* older than you. I'd been sleeping with girls since I was eleven."

"Eleven?"

"I was precocious. So, did I turn you into a ..."

"Well, you certainly did ruin me for all men."

"I knew it. Why don't you hate me?"

"Juliana, stop. The first time you kissed me—how do I find words to ... a feeling I'd never known before shot through my whole body. I didn't know it was possible for your whole body to feel a kiss. That never happened with Danny. And then the first time you touched me you-know-where, and the first time I saw your breasts—whoa, I have to stop. I'm getting myself worked up. Jule, you're the best thing to ever happen to me. Stop reading this crap. I'm going to throw it in the garbage."

I walked into the kitchen, tore the article out—*why do they have to keep writing this stuff*—ripped it up, and threw the whole mess into the trashcan. I leaned against the doorsill. "Can I come to the Easter service when you sing?"

"Richard'll be coming, but I'm sure he won't mind if you join us. It'll be very Catholic. Latin mumbo jumbo and all."

"I'm sorry I said that. I want to come."

"Then, you'll come. About the play. It's bad, isn't it?"

"Yes."

Chapter 63

April, 1954

"THANKS FOR SEEING me, Miss Huffman." Lucille Wadwacker sat in the chair next to my desk. She was dressed more demurely this time. No big flower across her rear, only a simple gray pencil skirt. Her breasts were still sticking out like two lethal points, but the blouse was plain white with a Peter Pan collar. The rose-colored cardigan over her shoulders was almost demure. Her box-style handbag sat atop a large, brown envelope lying on her lap.

I shouldn't be sitting opposite her after what she and her friend pulled. My heart knocked against my chest, but the way she sounded on the phone—desperate, apologetic, I don't know. Something made me say yes, she could come to my office. Maybe I wanted to prove what she and her friend thought of me wasn't true. I had a business to run; I couldn't have a rumor like that running around town.

"When I saw your ad in the paper," she began. "I knew I had to try. I wanted to impress on you—I didn't know what Ethel had planned till it was over and she told me."

"Ethel. That's the young woman who demonstrated her 'wares' here a few weeks ago, accompanied by your piano."

"Yes, but I had no idea she was going to do *that*. When she asked me to accompany her while she auditioned for you, I couldn't say no. Well, I suppose I could've, but I wanted to audition for you too."

"But you left. Standing guard, she said, to make sure no one entered."

"Isn't that ridiculous? During our rehearsal, she told me I should leave because she wanted to talk to you alone. She didn't tell me she was going to do a striptease. She was so mad you kicked her out. What did you expect you to do? I had no part in this plan."

"Miss Wadwacker—am I pronouncing that correctly?"

"Yes."

"Thank you for coming in. I appreciate your taking the time to apologize." I extended my hand toward her, but she didn't take it.

"Miss Huffman, I've come about the job." She opened her handbag and took out the newspaper clipping.

"Oh. Well, you must know I'd have doubts about hiring you."

"I'm hoping you won't let my misjudgment of Ethel ruin my whole life."

"You're young. There are lots of other jobs." I stood, ready to end the interview.

Not moving, tears rolling down her cheeks, Miss Wadwacker said, "I want to work with you. I know the kind of work you do. I've watched you build your clients' careers. I've read about you in the magazines. Juliana is the most wonderful singer I've ever heard in my life, and Lili Donovan is doing good. Peter McQuill and Patsy LaRue are coming along too. But I do think Patsy would do better if she changed her name. Forgive me, but that name makes her sound like she's a stripper."

I laughed and sat down again. "Maybe *you* can convince her. I haven't succeeded yet."

"I'd love to try. I'm an excellent typist. I take short hand. I graduated from Katherine Gibbs at the top of my class. Here. My references. They're very good."

She handed me the envelope. "My resumé is in there too. I also studied piano privately. Besides the secretarial tasks, I could also play rehearsal piano, and you'll only have to pay one person. Please, Miss Huffman, all I want to do is learn how to be a good talent manager like you."

"We didn't get started on the best foot."

"How can I make it up to you? I'll do anything."

"Young women need to be careful about saying *that* in this business."

"You're right. I wasn't thinking. Couldn't you check my references? If they're not as good as I say, then you needn't see me again. But if they are, my number is at the top of my resumé."

Chapter 64

"OH, THIS IS funny," Max said as we finished our morning coffee in the breakfast nook. "Juliana hot to sing at St. Patricks because Cardinal Spellman, the old queen, asked her?"

"Come on, Max, show a little respect." I said, "The cardinal's not gay." I took a sip of my coffee.

"Sweetheart, he's as queer as the proverbial three-dollar bill."

"Don't use that word. It's the straights' word for us," I said.

"I would never use it—except for someone like him. On Sundays, he prances around in holy robes, spouting pronouncements from the altar damning homosexuals to hell, while on Saturday night, he's bent over and taking it up the ass like a good little Catholic boy."

"Max!" Scott admonished. "Don't talk like that in front of Al. She's a lady."

"Yeah!" I said. "Am I?"

"I'm sorry, Al, but if you don't believe me, ask Tommie when he gets back from L.A. Or better yet, call him."

"Are you certifiable? You know what that would cost?"

"You can afford it now. Remember? The way Tommie tells it—His 'Eminence' used to send around a car to pick him up during the war. Tommie said the cardinal had 'special skills' in the mouth department."

"Max!" Scott admonished again.

"What? I cleaned it up for her."

"Oh, yeah, real clean."

"It's okay, Scott. I can handle it. Juliana would die if she knew this."

"Juliana *does* know it. She just doesn't let herself know it. I wouldn't suggest bringing it up unless you want to be permanently barred from her home. Hey, that's not a bad idea. Go ahead. Tell her all about how the dear cardinal used to get on his knees and suck Tommie off."

"Max!" Scott scowled.

"Juliana'd love that story," Max said. "Tell her."

"Thanks a lot," I said. "Max, have you ever heard of Lucille Wadwacker?"

"My God, what kind of name is that?"

"So, you haven't heard anything about her? I'm thinking about hiring her as my secretary."

"Aren't you getting fancy?"

"I can hardly keep up with the paperwork, and—"

"Hire her if you think she'll do the job."

"She's got great references. Her resumé is stellar."

"So why the hesitation?"

"No reason, I guess."

Chapter 65

RICHARD AND I made our way to the front steps of the Cathedral. We'd dropped Juliana off at the back door. Getting through the hundreds of Easter paraders strolling down Fifth Avenue showing off their expensive new hats wasn't easy.

We had to wait in line to get past the heavy doors. With tourists treating themselves to a church service at St. Patrick's, it was even more crowded than usual. Richard and I filed into the sanctuary with its cavernous dome and ivory statues lining the walls. Stained glass scenes from Jesus's last days blocked out the morning light.

Richard genuflected in the aisle while I stood waiting near a pew. All around me, people genuflected while I stood there feeling awkward. Still, I couldn't follow them, even though I thought it looked rather comforting, like doing that would make you belong to something bigger than your small self. Throughout my childhood, my father had told me Catholics were bad because of the phony-baloney rigmarole in their religion, so ...

Richard guided me into a pew and knelt on the padded kneeler. Again, I sat watching, out of place. I didn't feel an urge to make fun of it, though. Not the way I had back home in Huntington. I remembered Thanksgiving when I'd pretend to be a priest speaking Latin by saying the words, "Hut-Sut Rawlson on the rillerah and a brawla, brawla sooit" from "The Hut-Sut Song." Everyone would laugh. Then Mrs. Wright, my friend Aggie's mother, would hold up the turkey's rear end and say, "Look, the pope's nose." I didn't want to make fun of Juliana's feelings anymore.

Richard rose from his knees and sat down. "You know she's upset about this," he whispered. "She had her vocal coach working with her all week."

"She did?" I hated Richard knowing things about her I didn't.

"She had him come over to the house. I had to listen to that same song over and over, hour after hour." He smiled. "If that's not love, I don't know what is."

I smiled back at his little joke even though I didn't want to.

Surrounded by the sound of chanting and incense, a quietness overtook me. I wanted to kneel with the rest of them. But I couldn't.

Cardinal Spellman, in red robes, prayed and spoke in Latin. Then he sat down on his throne, and Juliana, looking holy in a white choir robe, walked gracefully up the steps to stand on the platform with the choir.

Juliana nodded at the organist, and the introductory notes played as she stepped forward and sang. She sang with all the love she had inside her, all the love she had for "The Holy Mother." Her love lifted and soared over and through us. She was no longer a plain, ordinary human being. She had become someone from another world, holy. When she finished singing, the serenity of the song lingered in the air, caressing us in a wordless love.

Chapter 66

November 1954

"MAX, SHE WON'T even come out of the house. Because of these." I put my hand on top of the pile of reviews from *Summer Dandelions* that lay on my desk. "The damn thing only lasted four lousy days. Doesn't seem like something so short should have this much impact."

"Can't you book her somewhere? One bad play shouldn't sink a whole career. She was going great guns before this."

"It's not the clubs; they're a little hesitant, but I think I can get them past that in a few weeks when these reviews are ancient history. The biggest problem is her. She's convinced no one will show up if I book her. She feels humiliated; she doesn't want to face the public. Some of these critics *were* pretty brutal. There's no excuse for that. Did you read Kerr in *The Herald*?"

"Yes."

"*The Bronx Chronicle* gave the fairest depiction of her performance."

"*The Bronx* what?"

I picked up the phone and pushed down a key switch on the dictograph box, then I pressed the ring switch. "Lucille, could you bring me that copy of the *Bronx Chronicle* I gave you to file this morning."

"You hired her—Wadwhistle."

"Wadwacker. She's doing a terrific job. So efficient. I don't know how I managed—"

Lucille knocked on the door, and I opened it to receive my paper.

"You see, Max?" I said as I closed the door. "She's completely stupendous, magnificent—"

"She brought you a newspaper, not the combination to Ft. Knox. That's what secretaries do."

I thumbed through the pages till I got to the review. "I'll read you my favorite part. 'Miss Juliana showed a real theatrical spark, and as a newcomer to the boards, this is no small thing given the dullards who often grace our stage nowadays. This critic hopes to see more of Miss Juliana, both on Broadway and in the nightclubs where she got her start.'"

"Al …" Max tried to cut in.

I continued to read, "In time she might—"

"Al! Stop reading. It's *The Bronx Something or Other*. Nobody cares what *they* think."

"Don't you see a problem with that? These other papers were prejudiced. Because Juliana is a nightclub singer, they think she can't or *shouldn't* act. It was that damn script."

"I agree. She didn't have enough experience to pull a bad script out of the sewer, but moaning over the unjustness of the New York Theater is not going to get you anywhere. You've got to do whatever it takes to pull Juliana back up."

"At least Shirl loves me. I saved her a bundle. You know, I asked her how she could've wanted to invest in such a bad play, and she said she'd never read the script. Can you imagine that?"

"Yes. I don't have time to read the script of every show I invest in. Often, I don't even have time to go to Philly or Boston to see it before they bring it to Broadway. My decision is based mostly on the summary of the story, and the reputations and track records of the people putting it together."

"That's what Shirl said, too. What do I have to do to save Juliana's career?"

"Send her to Paris."

"Paris?"

"She knows people there, good friends, family; that'll make her comfortable. The French will love knowing she lived there with her mother as a child and is completely fluent in their 'beloved' language. Most of them will be unlikely to know about this four-day fiasco. You can set her up to sing in a few big nightclubs, one in Paris and the others in the provinces. She'll get good reviews from the French critics. Americans love that. Everyone thinks the French know more about art and culture than anyone else, so whatever they say, everyone here will believe. She may have to take a small pay cut when she comes back. Americans also think they're best at everything, especially since the war, but you'll have a fistful of great reviews for building your PR campaign. It won't be long till she's back on top again. That's what Hildegarde did in the thirties when she was a nobody, and look where she is now, the most sought-after supper club singer in the world. While Juliana's away, people will forget that silly play, and she'll come back with confidence."

"This is good. No wonder you're a big success. Paris, wow! I've never been there before."

"And you won't be going any time soon."

"What?"

"I need you here. You can arrange everything from your office. You even have a secretary to help you. The telephone is a marvelous invention. So is the telegram. You can't take off. You have a club to run, clients to manage. Richard is her manager."

"In name only."

"The way *you* wanted it. She's his only client. He'll take care of everything in Paris. You can be in touch with him from here."

"He could screw it up."

"That's a chance you'll have to take, a chance you've been taking all along, but you have work to do here. I have some Paris contacts back in my files at the Mt. Olympus. I'm heading over there now. I'll call you with the info, and you can get started."

He left. I sat back in my chair, seeing Juliana and me in Paris. I thought of the movie *An American in Paris*. I was Gene Kelly, and Juliana was Leslie Caron. We danced together on the dark bridge that covered the Seine. Of course, I wouldn't really be able to dance that well. Their dance had some ballet in it. I would've tripped over our feet and knocked us both into the water, but hey, it was *my* fantasy, so I could do whatever I wanted.

I was graceful as a swan dancing with Juliana, pulling her toward me in grand, sweeping movements until we were chest to chest. I kissed her in the moonlight, and she kissed me back. We kissed in public, like Gene and Leslie, and nobody cared. The music swelled around us. Then I looked. It wasn't *me* who was kissing Juliana; it was Richard. *Dammit, get out of my fantasy!* He danced with her, and *he* kissed her under the bridge, and the music swelled for *them* while Parisian lovers walked by, nodding their approval.

I sat up straight in my chair. It would be the two of them seeing the sights while I stayed home making it possible. Another thought—what sights? They won't have time for sights. I grabbed my memo pad from the desk drawer. I'm going to book her so solid, they'll never have time to see a single thing. They'll never even have time to see each other.

Chapter 67

December 1954

"AL, GET OVER here right away," Max ordered as I sat in my office, holding the phone to my ear.

Marty was opening the midnight show with *Because of You*. After the bad reviews, the only thing I could get him were rare spots opening for our headliners. We had lots of up-and-comers clamoring to be on our stage, and most of them came with their own fans. With business slow, we had to use them on our off nights. Marty didn't have many fans to come see him, so we couldn't pay him much, and we couldn't hire him often. At least it was a little something to keep him going while I talked him up to my own contacts. It was a challenge trying to explain what happened without badmouthing The Dame; that would be career suicide for both of us. I knew tonight he'd be melting a few hearts, so I tried to get Kilgallen to come to the show. As soon as I said the name "Buck Martin," she chuckled. "Oh, dear, you can't be serious. I certainly couldn't subject myself once more to the antics of Buck Martin. I think my review of the play said it all."

"Get over here where?" I said into the phone. "I still have another show to get through and Marty feels better when I'm here. He's been depressed lately."

"Let Bart handle it."

"You certifiable? Bart *causes* depression."

"I need you here. Now. St. Sebastian Emergency Ward. Scott."

"Oh, my God." I jumped out of my seat. "What happened?"

"Get here."

I rushed toward the door, unthinking. Bertha ran after me, my fox stole thrown over one shoulder. "Wait. It's cold out." She put the stole around my shoulders and hooked the fox's tail into its mouth.

I was strangely warmed by her gentle gesture. "Thank you. I'm a little rattled. Scott Elkins has been taken to the Emergency Room."

"Oh, no."

I turned back to Bart's office to tell him to take care of things, but he wasn't there. I went to Lucille's office and found her at her desk feverishly typing. It was long past her hour to go home. "Lucille, have you seen Bart?"

"Not yet. When does he ever come in on time?"

"I hate to ask you this, but I have an emergency to attend to. Could you stay till Bart gets here? Scott's been taken to the emergency room."

"Not Mr. Elkins." she gasped. "Why?"

"I don't know. I have to get to St. Sebastian now."

"Don't worry about a thing." She threaded her arm through mine, leading me toward the exit. "I'll take care of everything until Bart wanders in. Take care of Mr. Elkins, and let me know how he is. And ..." she leaned close to me, whispering. "I'll keep my eye on Bertha. I don't like being suspicious, but she—there's something."

* * *

I flexed my ankle in back of the cab, afraid I'd sprained it. This was not a good night to be called out for an emergency. Saturdays, Max wanted me to dress-up. What he really meant was wear something more feminine than my usual suit jacket, skirt and flats. So on Saturdays, I wore a simple black Balenciaga dress and heels. Nothing as high as Juliana's, but high enough to slow me down in an emergency.

I pulled my stole tighter around my shoulders to keep out the night air. The cab careened down Broadway, swerving around buses, other cabs, and cars. We passed the *New York Times* zipper as it spelled out the last news of the evening—"The New York Times Wishes You Good Night"—and went black.

The cab sped around it, and jerked to a stop; we were stuck in a bottleneck of honking traffic. I sat on the edge of my seat as the hack inched the cab forward. "I'm in a hurry," I told him.

"Ain't everybody dese days?" he said, chewing on the end of his Camel.

"Can't we get out of this? Go a different way?" I pleaded.

"We're jammed in, lady. It's always like dis on a Saturd'y night. You might as well set yourself back, and enjoy da scenery. By da by, watcha doin' out here at dis hour all by your lonesome anyways?"

"I run a club. I have a friend waiting for me." Why am I explaining myself to this man?

"A *boy* friend?" He winked at me through the rearview mirror.

"Uh ... yeah, sure, why not."

"He gotta be a real loser if he ain't pickin' ya up. Ya shouldn't be out here in a cab all by your lonesome. Someone could get da wrong idea."

"Keep trying to get us out of this mess, okay?"

"You the type dat likes doin' in *t'ings* in cabs? Ya know what I mean? I heard 'bout dem types of goils gettin' friendly with cabbies, and—"

"No, and if you say one more word like that, I'm getting out of this cab. Don't talk to me anymore."

"Oh, Miz High and Mighty." That was the last thing he said. I suppose I should've gotten out and stuck him for the fare, but there was no direct subway route to St. Sebastian from Broadway.

As we inched away from the squealing cars and picked up speed, anxiety rippled through me. I pictured Scott's body all mangled from a car accident, but Scott doesn't drive a car. A bus! A bus ran over him, oh God.

I ran down the sidewalk that led into the St. Sebastian ER. The waiting room was packed with people. The smell of stale cigarette smoke and rubbing alcohol floated through the air. One man I passed held a cloth dripping with blood from his arm.

"You finally got here." Max ran up to me, an Old Gold without its holder dangling from his lips, his tie hanging loose. "What took you so long?"

"I got stuck in traffic. What happened?"

"I think you're a little over-dressed for this place."

"This wasn't where I planned on spending the evening. What happened to Scott?"

Max bit on his cigarette. "Come over here." He leaned against the wall. "I got a call tonight at the Mt. Olympus. Some guy. Didn't tell me his name, sounded drunk, but he said I should get over to this sleazy hotel room uptown around West Ninety-Sixth Street, or he might not make it through the night. I knew right away it was about Scott, so I went."

"You went into that dangerous neighborhood by yourself? It could've been a trap. Someone who found out you're ... You could've been hurt or worse."

He waved his cigarette at me. "I thought about that later. In the ambulance."

"You've got to be careful. There are people who hate us so much they want to—"

"You think *I* don't know that? I've been at this a lot longer than you, but nothing happened. Okay? It was Scott. I found him in this rotten hotel room with rats crawling around. The whole room smelled of liquor, and there were empty scotch bottles all over the place. Scott doesn't drink, so it didn't make sense. I looked over at the bed and there was Scott, a sheet covering him, his eyes closed like he was sleeping or ... I was scared. I lifted it off him slow, but all I saw was a couple of small cuts on his chest, nothing deep, no blood. He was only wearing undershorts. I found a broken scotch bottle near the bed. I tried to wake him, but he didn't move." Max paced. "He didn't move, Al. Not at all. I called the hospital immediately, and they sent a doctor over, Dr. Rollins, and he called for the ambulance and ..."

Max was shaking. "Come. Sit down." I took Max's arm, guiding him into a chair, and sat beside him. "Do you think he did something to himself, or do you think that guy did something?" I asked.

"What difference does it make? Any way you look at it, Scott did it to himself." Max ran a hand through his hair. "Even if that guy did it—why was he with a guy like that? Because he hates what he is, and he hates me because I'm that too."

"No, listen. He loves you. It's just, he listens to all that stuff from his religion and thinks he's doing something evil."

"You know, sometimes I think about his grandma who raised him, and I want to go down to West Virginia and kill her. Actually kill her. Can you imagine that? Me wanting to kill some old lady? I've actually made up scenes in my head where I've got my hands around her scrawny neck, and I'm tightening ..." He flexed his two hands. "He's a good man. Funny sometimes, but mostly too serious. That's his problem. But he's a warm kind of guy. You've seen that."

"Yes."

"It's wrong what's she done to him. There's where the evil is. *That's* the sin. We were doing good, him and me. And you too. The three of us were a little family. Why'd he do this now?"

Max and I spent hours pacing the floor, kicking cigarette butts out of our way, hoping Dr. Rollins would appear to tell us Scott was fine. No one at reception seemed to know anything, so we'd sit back down, imagining the worst. I couldn't pray. I stared at Max, slumped over in his chair, and wondered if he could.

"Max, it's three. I'm going to go call Bart. Make sure everything's okay."

"That's a good girl," Max said, sounding numb with exhaustion and fear.

"Well, where is he?" I said into the pay phone. "Oh, Lucille, you must be out of your mind with exhaustion. I wish I could tell you to go home, but there's that special 4 a.m. show and … Will you? You're such a trouper. You'll be well-compensated for this."

"Bart never showed up," I told Max as I sat back down. "He called Lucille two hours ago to say he was on his way, and he's still not there. Of course, we all know, including Lucille, where he is. He makes no secret of it. He's with a *paying* customer."

"Fire him," Max said with a yawn.

"You see, that's the problem. I can't. Would you?"

"Sorry. You're the boss over there."

"But …"

"Mr. Harlington," the doctor said, coming up to us, a folder in his hand.

Max and I jumped up. "Dr. Rollins! How is he?" Max asked.

"Step over here so we can speak privately."

I started to follow them. The doctor stopped. "And you are?"

"Oh." Max looked at me, momentary desperation crossing his eyes. "Scott's wife."

"Really?"

This was where Mrs. Viola Cramden's acting class had to help me out. "Yes. I'm Mrs. Scott Elkins."

Such a strange thing to say, that *I* should be a Mrs. Anyone.

"Very good." The doctor nodded, leading the way to a small alcove off the emergency room, and standing behind a desk.

"How is he?" Max asked.

"Mrs. Elkins." The doctor began directing all his statements to me. "Your husband's wounds are superficial, a few scratches."

"Then what's the matter with him?" Max demanded. "Why didn't he wake up when I shook him?"

"Mrs. Elkins, won't you please sit down." He pulled out a chair for me. "This sort of thing is never easy to tell a wife."

"Is there some sort of problem, Doctor?" I asked.

"Mr. Harlington would you please step outside so I can speak to Mrs. Elkins in private?"

"I will not. Scott Elkins is my friend."

"Whatever you have to say to me you can say in front of Mr. Harlington," I told the doctor.

"Not this. Please, Mr. Harlington."

"Max, maybe you should go, if this is how the doctor wants it."

"But ... all right. I'll be right outside, and I expect a full report." He glared at me and stormed out to the waiting room. Through the milky glass partition, I could see him lighting a cigarette.

"Please, Mrs. Elkins, have a seat." He pulled a package of Parliaments from his inside pocket and hit the bottom so a few cigarettes popped up. He extended the package toward me. "Cigarette?"

"No, thank you."

He pulled a cigarette from the pack for himself and lit it as he sat on the edge of the desk. "Mrs. Elkins, is your husband a drunkard?"

"He doesn't drink at all."

"Well, he drank himself unconscious tonight. I have reason to believe Mr. Elkins ... This is hard to tell you, but I believe from some things the nurse heard your husband mumble that he is—a homosexual."

"Really?" Mrs. Viola Cramden had been right. You had to be prepared to step into any role.

"I see by your lack of shock you've suspected this yourself."

"Somewhat."

"Yes, we find alcoholism is common with homosexuals. Their sickness makes them so miserable they drink to forget. This may have even been a failed suicide attempt, common among homosexuals; it's easy to understand why they would want to die, but there are cures for this malady. I know you'll want to save your marriage, so hopefully our psychiatrist can be of help to you. Mrs. Elkins, have you ever considered that this friend, Mr. Harlington, may be your husband's homosexual lover?"

"Do you think so?"

"I think there is a very good chance, and if you're a wise woman you will forbid Mr. Harlington from coming anywhere near your husband. That's my professional opinion. We'll let Mr. Elkins sleep here tonight, and in the morning, we'll transfer him to the psychiatric ward."

I jumped up. "You can't!"

"Mrs. Elkins, your husband attempted to kill himself. That makes him a danger to himself, and because he is a homosexual he is a possible danger to others. Our psychiatrist will evaluate him and decide if he is well enough to be released."

Chapter 68

"BRING HIM THIS robe," Max said as he yanked it off the hanger in Scott's closet. He caressed the collar. "He looks better in the blue one, but he prefers this one. Gray. It's so dowdy. I can't imagine *why on earth* he likes it, but ..." His fingers gathered more of the robe into his arms, as if he were pulling Scott close. He sat on the bed, holding the robe. "Why would he want to kill himself? Why can't *I* make him better?"

"Ah, Max." I sat beside him and put an arm around him.

"When no one's around, be sure to tell him I love him. No! Don't."

He stood up and folded Scott's robe into the overnight bag he'd laid on the bed. "That might upset him. Bring him these slippers." He put the slippers into the bag. "Let's see. Which pajamas?" He lifted a folded pair of red and white striped pajamas from Scott's chest of drawers. "I don't want them putting him in one of those shortie hospital gowns with the thin ties in the back. They make you feel vulnerable. He doesn't need that. These?" He held up the striped pajamas. "What do you think?"

"Nice."

"What do you know? You have no taste."

"Thanks a lot."

"I didn't mean that as an insult." He folded the striped pajamas and put them back into Scott's drawer. "It's a simple statement of fact. You're good with music and singers. Lousy with clothes and decorating. I'm a genius at all four. But we're both awful at picking mates. Bring him these and ..." He put a pair of blue pajamas in the bag. "Why aren't I enough for him, Al? Why does he need this God too?"

"I don't know."

"Now, you be sure to see his psychiatrist."

"Me?"

"You're his wife."

"No, I'm not."

"They think you are, so they'll talk to you. You've got to find out when they plan to release him."

"Max?"

"I don't know how many pairs of underpants to put in." He leaned over one of the open dresser drawers.

"I think we should call his grandmother," I said.

"I guess three will do for now. They can't keep him longer than—"

"Max, did you hear me?'

"I heard you." He stuck the underpants in Scott's bag. "Let's see, undershirts." He went back to the drawer and gathered up three undershirts. "One short sleeve and two sleeveless. The sleeveless shows off his muscles. I love those muscles in his shoulders and upper arms. Oh, and that chest. Pure art. When I touch him, hold him close, I feel such a ... It's difficult to put into words. It's not only about sex. I mean, it sort of is, but it's also something more, a closeness, a—"

"I know what you mean, Max."

"I suppose you do."

"Max, Scott's in real trouble. He attempted to kill himself."

"Half-heartedly. A couple scrapes. What's that?"

"He drank a fifth of scotch, and he doesn't drink. What if he gets better at it? Tries again? Uses a more lethal method? That's what my mother did. It was like she was practicing."

"That was your mother, not Scott."

"Neither one of us knows a thing about this. He's her grandson. They're family."

"*I'm* Scott's family. I thought you were, too."

"She should know. *She's* the one who should speak to the psychiatrist. What if there are papers to sign?"

"Don't sign anything."

"I don't intend to. I don't look good in stripes."

"Stripes?"

"Prison uniform. But his grandmother may have to sign."

"Scott can call her if he wants."

"He won't. He's ashamed. He's not in his right mind to make that decision. Don't you think, if we love him, we should pick up the slack and make the call for him? She's very important to him. I don't feel right leaving her out of this. What if it gets worse?"

"It won't. He's gonna be okay."

"Max, we don't know that. My mother—"

"Your mother was crazy!" he yelled. "Don't compare Scott to your crazy … I'm sorry. This cologne." He picked up a small crystal bottle. "Caron's Poive. He likes this on me. One night, I took him to Birdland to hear Charlie Parker. He was so impressed I knew Bird. Scott's more cornpone than you were when you first came to the city. He loved listening to jazz even though that religion of his didn't want him to. That night, Gary Cooper stopped by; I got to be a big shot and introduce Scott to *him*. Scott was so excited. Such a wide-eyed kid." Max opened the bag and put in the bottle of cologne. "Be careful with this. It costs \$342[6] a bottle."

"What? What if I drop it?"

"I'll have your head. Maybe … if he wears it he'll remember that night, and …" A tear slid onto his cheek and he quickly wiped it away with the back of his hand. "When will you call her?"

"Now. Can I have the number please?" I held my hand out.

Max opened Scott's top bureau drawer. "He keeps his important numbers in this book." He took the book into his hands and ran his palm over its rough leather cover. "I'm in here, you know."

"Of course you are."

He held out the book for me to take. "It's under Martha Bond. She's his grandmother on his mother's side."

* * *

"Well, she's coming," I told Max, as I placed my handbag on the couch and started pulling on my gloves.

"Don't put your handbag on the sofa." He stood near the piano, looking out at the skyline, a glass of sherry in his hand.

"Oh, for Pete's sake," I said, putting it on top of the mantel. I stood in front of the fireplace and used the mirror above the mantel to adjust my round hat to the center of my head. I hoped it made me seem like somebody's wife. My diploma hung framed under the mirror. "She's getting the first bus out of Lake Ambrosia. Actually, they don't have buses in Lake Ambrosia. She's making arrangements to get to Mount Hyatt. She thinks Mr. Stubbs, the owner of the General Store—that's the guy whose son drove out in his pick-up to get her when I called because she doesn't have a phone in her house—she thinks he'll drive her. Anyway, after she gets to Mount Hyatt I'm not sure what she has to

---

6 1\$342 had the same spending power in the 1950s as \$2,000 does today.

do. It sounded complicated, but she said she'd wire us with her exact time of arrival when she knows it so we can pick her up."

"Pick her up? I have no intention of even looking at that bitch."

"Max! You're speaking about Scott's grandmother. I can't do this alone."

"I told you I've been picturing myself killing her. If I see her, there's no telling what I'll do. It was your idea to call her. You deal with her."

"I will. I'm bringing her here."

"No."

"I pay a third of the rent. A third of this place is mine. We can put her in my part of the apartment."

"She can stay in a damn hotel."

"You can't stick a woman like her—someone who doesn't even have a phone—in a New York hotel by herself. Have a heart."

"Did she have a heart when she did what she did to Scott?"

"I'm leaving now to see him. I don't want to be late for visiting hours. We'll talk about this more when we get the wire."

"There's nothing to talk about."

I stood at the door. The Christmas tree Scott and Max had bought together still lay off to the side of the room, tied up in twine. "Why don't you put up the tree? It might make everyone feel a little lighter. She's going to be in a lot of pain; maybe a little Christmas—"

"Good. I hope she *is* in pain. I'm not putting up our tree for *her*. That's Scott's and my tree. Our very first Christmas living together."

"I know," I said as I walked out the door.

* * *

I stood outside of the reception room, a few steps in front of the locked door that would lead me to Scott. It was almost 2 p.m., the visiting hour. I waited with a few others, wondering if I looked wifely enough in my pastel-blue skirt with the slight flare and the cardigan sweater covering my white blouse. I threw my sensible cloth coat over my arm as I entered the over-heated reception area. My heart beat in my stomach as I waited, facing the locked ward. I didn't like locked doors. Mom had locked me out too many times. Standing in the cold rain, I'd stare at our locked door, hoping she'd …

Then there were the days and months when the doctors locked *her* in. Dad never made me visit her when I was little, but when I got to be thirteen, I had to go. I hated it. Shrill screams behind curtains, the smell of loose bowel movements, excrement thrown against walls. Each time I went—and I went a lot between thirteen and fifteen—I walked close beside my father. One time, they were moving a bunch of patients down the hall past us, Dad and I got separated. I was alone in that place, and everywhere I looked I saw toothless ladies in loose hospital gowns hardly covering them. I ran in no special direction, yelling, "Daddy, Daddy, help!"

My father slapped me hard across the face. He'd never hit me before. "Don't yell in public," he scolded. He dragged me to my mother's bed, where she was tied up in a strait jacket. She looked like a witch, her hair a matted mess, babbling words that made no sense. I prayed to God he'd give me another mother, but I knew I was too old to be praying for things like that.

The woman behind the desk collected Scott's overnight bag. She rummaged through it and removed the bottle of cologne. My heart leapt. "Hey! Be careful." She shook the bottle at me. "He can't have this." I thrust my hands out, ready to catch the most expensive bottle of perfume I'd ever heard of. "After all, Mrs. Elkins, he *did* try to kill himself." Did she have to say it in front of all these people? She handed me the bag. "You can collect the cologne after your visit."

"You *will* treat it gently, won't you?" I said, unable to hide my anxiety.

I joined the throng who followed the muscular young Negro in a green uniform who brandished a large circular set of keys. We waited as he unlocked the door and held it aside to let us pass. "They're in the recreation room, down that hall," the Negro orderly said, pointing. Then he locked us inside. My stomach tightened.

I followed the others down a brightly lit hallway—brighter than the hospital where they'd put my mother. An old man, his pink scalp peeking out of strands of gray hair, walked by. You could see the outline of his bones pressing against his paper-like skin. He held his calloused fingers close to his dry lips as he mumbled something to himself.

The recreation room was crowded with men in pajamas and hospital gowns sitting at tables in twos and fours, some playing board games, others sleeping. Some sat in corners alone with blank faces, drool oozing from their mouths. There was a steady din of voices and pounding on tabletops. I scanned the room, but I didn't see Scott. A Negro orderly with a towel in his hand breezed by me. "Excuse me," I said. "Scott Elkins?"

"Over there, Ma'am."

I followed his pointing finger to a man who had Scott's general features and dark hair. But the man sitting behind the table, his mouth hanging open slack, couldn't be Scott, not the Scott *I* knew.

I ran to him. "Scott? It's me."

He didn't look up. I took his head in my hands and forced him to look at me. "Scott?"

He blinked. "Al?"

"Yeah. What's the matter? You look strange."

"Uh, noth, nothing." There was slight slur to his speech. I sat at the table opposite him.

"How are you?" What a dumb question. Look where he is. "Max sent you some things." I pushed the bag across the table toward him.

A tiny half-smile creased his face. He pulled the bag into his arms like Max had done with the robe. "He didn't want you to look dowdy. You know Max."

Scott laid his head on top of the bag and fell asleep.

"No. Don't sleep, Scott. Where's your Doctor?"

"Doctor?" Scott repeated as if he were trying to figure out what the word meant. "Doctor?"

"You've talked to a doctor, haven't you?"

"No. I—don't think so, but—Al, it's hard to think."

"I'm going to try to find him. I'll be back."

I left Scott to find the doctor, but nobody seemed to know what I was talking about. I ran to a male nurse I found at the end of the hallway leaning against the wall having a smoke. "Excuse me," I looked closely to read his nametag. "Mr. Donahue. I'd like to see Scott Elkin's doctor."

"His what?" He coughed out a cloud of smoke.

"I want to see his psychiatrist."

He laughed, waving his cigarette through the air. "Hey, Murch, get this one," he said in a falsetto voice, "Little Miss Muffet here wants to see the psychiatrist on a Saturd'y. Ain't that a scream?" Murch, behind the desk, got a good laugh at that one too. "Look, sweetie," Mr. Donahue said with a cock of his hip and a few more puffs of smoke. He pulled a piece of tobacco from his tongue and delicately flicked it from his fingers. "*We'd* like to see that man, too, dearie. But it's the weekend. You ain't gonna find that one nowheres near here today, tomorrow or—"

I rummaged in my bag for a paper and pen. "Give me a number where I can call him for an appointment?"

That was a signal for another fit of phlegmy laughing and swishy arm waving. "If you find that phone number, you be sure to let me and Murch know 'cause we got quite a few bones we'd like to pick with that man." He licked his finger and ran it across his eyebrow. "Well, I'll be gosh darned, you must be some sorta magician, honey." He threw the cigarette down on the floor and twisted his foot on it as a man with graying hair and wide shoulders hurried toward the locked door like a bank robber trying to make his getaway.

"That's him?"

He nodded and I tore after him. "Doctor. Doctor."

"Yes?" He stopped his dash for the door and smiled pleasantly.

"I'm, uh, Al—Alice Elkins." I got it out without choking. "I believe my, uh, my husband, is under your care, and I'd like to speak with you."

He glanced at his watch and sighed. "You know, it *is* the weekend? I only came in for a book I forgot." He sighed again. "Certainly, Mrs. Elkins. Come this way." I followed him down a corridor. "My name is Dr. George Shim," he said as we walked, "and I oversee this floor of about five hundred men."

"Five hundred!"

"Less than usual. Makes it hard to get around to everyone." Dr. Shim took out a key and pushed through his office door. He turned on the light and motioned toward the chair across from his desk. "Have a seat, Mrs. Elkins. I'm afraid I'm not familiar with your husband's case. Allow me a few moments." He took a slim folder from a file cabinet and sat behind his wooden desk. "Well, let's see." He thumbed through the few pages in the folder. "Ah, yes. The homosexual. I heard something about him at our meeting. He attempted suicide by drinking himself to death."

"Scott is not a homosexual. He's my husband. And I can assure you everything's just fine in that department."

Dr. Shim chuckled. "I see."

"Why is he so groggy?"

"It's the medicine. A brand-new drug. We've been getting miraculous results. Some seriously mentally ill patients used to spend their whole lives in a hospital before this new medicine, but now we've been sending more of the mentally ill back to their homes to lead productive lives."

"Scott isn't mentally ill."

"Well, he *is* diagnosed with homosexuality, which *is* a mental illness. *But,* I can take him off the medication. I don't think he needs that. Will that make you happy?"

"Very."

"Good," Dr. Shim started to rise.

"Then you'll be sending him home soon? When?"

"I'm afraid, Mrs. Elkins, he won't be going home for quite a while." He sat down again.

"Why?" I thought of Max and his pain if I didn't return with something hopeful. I remembered Moshe being locked up in one of these places for *three* years! "You can't keep him here. I need him home with me *today*. You can't do this."

"Mrs. Elkins, I'm not doing anything to your husband. He committed himself."

"What?"

"I have his signature here on this paper." He pushed the form across the desk toward me. "He admitted to being homosexual and asked us to cure him."

"Then have him fill out the form to un-commit himself so we can leave."

"There is no such form," Dr. Shim said. "In New York State, you can commit yourself, but you cannot *un*-commit yourself. That has to be done by a doctor."

"Then do it."

"I understand your anguish, but your husband wants to be cured."

"He'd been drinking when he signed that. He wasn't in his right mind."

"Exactly. All the more reason he shouldn't be released. Mrs. Elkins, I know this is painful,"—he leaned toward me in a fatherly way— "but your husband is not only dangerous to himself. Suicide sometimes becomes homicide, and homosexuality *does* pose a threat to society. What if your husband were to force himself on a young boy?"

"Scott would never!"

"But we can't take that chance, can we? And obviously, your husband doesn't want to take the chance either. That's why he committed himself."

"I told you, my husband is not a homosexual."

"Your husband seems to disagree with you. Perhaps you should accept the wisdom of his decision. The sexual psychopath law allows us to keep all potentially violent sexual perverts confined to the hospital until we deem them cured."

"Scott's not violent. He's the gentlest, kindest—"

"He was found in a hotel room with a broken ... I believe it was a scotch bottle." He picked up Scott's folder and nodded. "Yes, a scotch bottle. There were broken bottles all around his bed and there were scratches on his body. He tried to drink himself to death. You don't consider these things violent? As soon as your husband is cured we will send him back to your loving arms."

"What cure?" My head felt light and I feared the room would spin.

"A daily regimen of psychoanalysis—except, of course, on weekends. Next week we have a new doctor arriving to share the load. He has a national reputation. New methods, new research—very exciting. I'm sure he'll be of great assistance to your husband."

"How long will it take?"

"It's difficult to say. Much depends on your husband's cooperation. It isn't a speedy procedure, but it is effective. Still, under the best of conditions, it could take a few years."

"Years? No. *Please*, you can't do this." A grasping desperation rose in me. I was fighting for my mother. I was fighting for myself. I had to calm down; I had to … what? Keep up my demure housewife pose. I put on my sweet, ultra-female smile. "There must be some other way, Doctor. Surely a strong, intelligent man of science like yourself knows a quicker way." Mrs. Cramden was right. You never knew what part you'd be called upon to play. Of course, she meant on the stage. "I just don't know how I will *ever* manage without him." I wondered if I should faint?

"Well, there *may* be something else we could try," he said.

"Yes?"

"The latest research studies are showing positive results. In one study, fifty-eight percent of homosexuals were completely cured."

"What is it?" I couldn't keep up my helpless pose. I was too excited.

"We're setting up a new program. The psychoanalyst I told you we're expecting next week, Dr. Krimsky, a bright young buck, is trained in this other approach. Besides doing the usual psychoanalysis, he will be training a few of our residents in this new procedure. But he plans on starting small. With only a very few patients in the beginning. Those who show the most promise."

"How long will it take to get started?"

"It's hard to say." He touched his pencil to his lips. "Perhaps a week, perhaps less."

"And this way would be faster?"

"According to the research. I myself have had no real experience with it. And we don't know if Dr. Krimsky will choose your husband for the first study."

"He must. Tell him he must, Doctor. Scott can't stay here for years."

"I'll do my best, Mrs. Elkins." He stood, extending his hand to me.

I went back into my helpless female pose, holding his hand for support and awkwardly fluttering my eyelashes like a sick pigeon about to burst into flight. "Oh, please, Doctor, I know I will just expire if you don't help me." My insides began to quake for real.

"I promise that I will do my utmost." He smiled one of those smiles a man gets when he knows a woman can't get to the next moment without him. He took my arm to help me from the room. Unfortunately, by then, I really needed it.

* * *

When Archibald, our colored elevator operator, left me off outside my apartment, I didn't want to face Max. I wondered if the wire from Scott's grandma had arrived yet. Had Max left the poor woman standing alone in that cold, dreary Port Authority Bus Station? I didn't want to deal with any of it. I wanted to curl up under my covers and listen to one of Juliana's albums, or better yet, curl up under Juliana.

I pushed open the door, dreading my first sight of Max looking to me for hope and me dashing it into smithereens. I was greeted by a burst of Christmas carols playing on the hi-fi in the living room. Max and an old woman in a striped dress straight out of the thirties were decorating the Christmas tree and laughing. Tinsel rain draped both of their heads.

"Merry Christmas!" Virginia called over *Santa Claus Is Coming to Town*, as she entered from the kitchen carrying a tray. "Eggnog, Al?" She was dressed in green and red and sparkled like she might be all right. I'm sure she must be. After all, it'd been three years since the incident with Moose Mantelli. But I wondered why, if everything was so fine, Virginia and I hardly saw each other anymore.

Virginia put the tray on the table. "Help yourself, everyone, but be careful. I didn't hold back on the rum."

"Al, this is Martha Bond," Max said, coming around the Christmas tree, pulling tinsel rain from his hair. "You know, Scott's grandma."

I stared. "Yeah?"

The woman came toward me with her hand extended. "Call me Mattie. All my friends down home do." Her accent was thicker than Scott's. Instead of shaking hands, she squeezed my left hand in her left hand. "You're the one who called me, ain't ya?"

"Did you know, Al?" Max said, excitedly. "Mattie is the number one bingo champion in her county?"

"Is she? Bingo. How nice."

"My mother was a champion bingo player, too," Max informed me. "In Cincinnati."

"Was she?"

"This is Scott's wife," Max told Mattie.

"Huh? Oh, yeah," I agreed. "That's me. Mrs. Elkins."

"You're Scott's wife?" Mrs. Bond said. Her brow furrowed into a question. "If I rightly recollect, on the phone you said you was his friend." She took a sip of her eggnog. "Virginia, this is good. You did say you was his friend. You didn't say nothin' 'bout being his wife."

"Uh, I guess I forgot."

"You forgot?"

"She sure can be forgetful sometimes, Mattie," Max said. "Why don't we all sit down and enjoy our eggnog."

Virginia looked at me strangely, but knew well enough not to give voice to her question.

Max sat in the overstuffed chair near the couch and Mrs. Bond sat on the couch; Virginia sat beside her, and I sat in the overstuffed chair closest to Virginia.

"Al, tell us about your visit to Scott," Max said.

I raised my eyebrows, trying to signal Max not continue that discussion.

"How is he?" Virginia asked.

"...Fine."

"When are they going to release him?" Max asked.

They faced me with hope in their eyes. "Well, you see—"

"His wife, huh?" Mattie said. "Scottie never wrote me about you."

"It was fast," I offered. "We couldn't wait a minute longer. So in love."

"Was ya? And he *wanted* to marry the likes of *you*. How queer. I never figured my boy'd wanna marry no girl, but if that's what makes him happy ..." She drank from her glass while we all leaned toward her, staring. She finished the drink and put the glass down, noticing us watching, and said, "Yeah?"

"Uh, Mattie," Max began. "You never figured Scott would marry a ... girl?"

"Nah. But I wanna see him happy, and if he is with you, then God bless him. Still, it seems strange for him to suddenly take up with a gal. I always thought he was, uh, well how's the polite way of sayin' it?"

"Gay?" Max offered, nervously.

"Oh, no, Scott ain't gay," she said with a laugh. "He's the least gayest person I ever did knowed. Such a serious child. Thinking, stewing, trying to be too good. It gave me the worries he'd never get one bit of fun outta his life. No, my Scottie ain't someone anybody'd call gay." She chuckled. "Do you have any more of that eggnog, Virginia? I can't say when I tasted better."

"Certainly, Mrs. Bond." Virginia took her glass.

"Please. Call me Mattie. My husband's been dead so long I can't hardly recollect what he looked like."

"Can we go back to how Scottie never seemed interested in girls?" Max asked.

"I always thought he were a homosexual, myself."

"You did?" Max said, breathless. "And that didn't bother you?"

"Heavens, no. Another part of nature. I'm an old farm girl myself, and anybody with eyes to see with and ain't scared of lookin' can see what's plain as the nose on your face. On a farm ya see it everyday. Homosexual sheep, cows. I had a couple of lesbian cats once."

"You did?" I gasped.

"If I didn't know you was his wife, I woulda guessed my boy woulda preferred you, Max."

"Uh, Mattie," Max began. "I hope you're serious because ..." Virginia stared off into space, like she did sometimes. I held my breath. "I *am* the one Scott prefers. Al's not his wife."

Mattie chuckled and slapped her knee. "Do I know my boy or do I know my boy?" She feigned wiping her brow. "Phew, I thought I had really gone and lost my sense of things."

"And you don't mind?" Max continued.

"Why should I? I don't put much store by what other folks say, if that's what ya mean."

"No. It's Scott. He hates himself for this. He says he's a sinner."

"That why Scott tried to do this awful thing to hisself?"

Max nodded and Mattie continued. "My daughter. She got herself 'converted' a long time ago; Scott was a young'un. Her husband run off with another gal, and my Cady-did were searching all over for somethin' to replace that son of a gun. Unfortunately, that religion were what she found.

"Now, don't get me wrong. I'm a church-goin' woman myself. I sing in the choir, and I'm head of the Ladies Auxiliary, but it seems to me ya gotta pick and choose what ya gonna live by. Ya can't go swallowin' up everythin' whole ; otherwise, why'd God put brains in our heads to be thinkin' with ? But my daughter felt so lost after her husband run off, she took to this religion like it were her life preserver in a ragin' stormy sea.

"She raised poor little Scottie on that joyless religion, and there t'weren't nothin' that boy wouldn't do for his Mama. He loved her. Always trying to please her, but I swear my Cady was so filled with the misery she couldn't see it no how. And there t'weren't nothin' he done that make her happy. Then she up and died of the influenza when he was ten. I tried to school him different, to be a little more carefree, but he hung onto Cady's religion like she done. I guess it was a way of hangin' on to her. Now, it seems he were even gonna let it kill him."

"Well, we don't know for sure he tried to, uh, you know, …" I began. "But now the hospital says he can't leave because he's a violent homosexual. They've got some law that says they can keep him till he's cured because—he committed himself."

"He done that?" Mattie said, making a tight fist around the handkerchief. "What can I do 'bout that?" She looked to Max.

"Don't you worry," Max said. "They have lawyers, but so do we. We'll get him out of there. And if he needs some special treatment we'll get him into a private sanitarium. Don't you worry, Mattie." He looked over at me, agony creasing his face and whispered like was too painful to talk any louder, "Committed himself?"

Chapter 69

"SO, LUCILLE, I thought we'd have lunch together today," I said as Lucille and I sat at a table in Child's. The windows were decorated with Christmas wreaths. "I've been at the club so little this week with Scott being sick, and making the arrangements for Juliana to go to Paris, I thought the least I could do was buy you lunch in gratitude. You've been a gem."

"I love doing it," Lucille said, sliding off her gloves. "I've always been very organized. Even as a child, I had my toys ordered on the shelf in alphabetical order."

I smiled. Lucille was often hard to read, so I wasn't certain if she was making a joke or not. The waitress stood at our table. "How about a cocktail to start?" I opened my drink menu.

"I'd love a cocktail, but I don't think I should go back to the club tipsy."

"I doubt one cocktail from Child's will make you tipsy. I'll have a sidecar," I told the waitress.

"The Child's Special sounds yummy. Have you ever had that?"

"I haven't. I've always been a sidecar drinker."

"That's Juliana's drink too, isn't it?"

"Uh …" I hesitated. "Yes, I believe Juliana does drink sidecars." I turned to the waitress. "One sidecar and one Child's Special." I handed her our drink menus. "You've met Juliana?"

"Heaven's no," she squealed. "If only I could. Is she as sophisticated in person as she is on stage?"

"I'd say so."

"I think I was in love with her a few years ago." She giggled and hid her face behind her hands. "It seems childish now, but I had one of those girl crushes on her. My girl friends and I would go to her shows, both sets, whenever she appeared at the Copa. In between shows we'd go ordered a drink, and sit at one of the tables, pretending we were sophisticated ladies. We'd watch Juliana, the way she moved, the way she held her drink, and the way she laughed with the men. We wanted to be just like her. Sometimes, we'd see her with her husband, Mr. Styles, and a couple times, you were drinking with her."

"Was I?"

"We couldn't stop giggling. My boyfriend laughs at me when I tell him how I used to be about her. But I haven't told him this part." She leaned toward me and whispered, "I may be a little the same about her still. I have all her records: *My Romance* is my favorite."

"I like that one too."

"I hate to ask you, but … no, I can't. It would be a bother, and I don't want—"

"Would you like to meet her?"

"Could I? I mean, I wouldn't want to bother her, but if there was any chance …"

"I'll see what I can do. With getting ready for Paris, she's a little distracted right now, but we'll see."

"I wouldn't want to disturb her, but if there was some way I could—maybe help her. Oh! I can feel my heart beating so fast."

"You'd better slow it down. I can't promise."

"I know." She took a deep breath and opened her menu, then closed it again. "I almost forgot. I gave my word." She reached into her handbag, drew out three envelopes, and handed them to me. "Mr. Marty Buchman, or Buck Martin—he likes that better—has been calling all month and leaving messages for you. Sometimes he comes in looking for you." I opened the envelopes and found numerous little paper squares with notes scribbled across them. "He gets so disappointed when you're not there. I kept promising to give you these, but you always needed to talk about other things so … I'm sorry, I should've told you. I told him I was having lunch with you today, and he made me promise to give these to you. They're in the same order he gave them to me—starting with the envelope marked #1. He worries me. He's been very despondent lately."

"Marty's basically a happy guy, but I haven't been attentive to the office recently … Excuse me. I want to skim through …"

"Certainly."

I quickly thumbed through the notes, while Lucille looked over the menu. They all had the same theme, but with each passing date, they grew more desperate. "Call me. No one will hire me after those reviews."—"Help!! Help! Agent useless. Find me a new one."—"Where are you?"—"Can I sing at The Haven or don't you want me there, either?"—"Lots of jobs opening in TV, none for me."—"This FBI guy keeps following me. I can't go anywhere without him. Help!"—"Don't you care anymore?"—"Did those reviews convince you too I'm bad?"—"Where are you dammit!"—"Help, drowning! Starving! Dying."

Then I came upon one at the end of the pile, which was less desperate, more deliberate. "I think I have no choice but to come clean."

Come clean? "I'll call him today." I slipped the envelopes into my purse. "Lucille, there was something I wanted to speak to you about."

She peered over her menu. "Oh, no, did I do something wrong?"

"No. You're doing a terrific job. But you must've noticed Bart hasn't been around this past week. You've had more to do."

"I don't mind. I think at heart I'm a career woman like you, and a woman can't have a career *and* a marriage. You know how men feel about their wives working."

"You're still young. You have time to decide. At some point, you'll want children."

"A little boy and a little girl."

"Well, you can't have them without being married."

"Was deciding not to have children a big sacrifice for you?"

"It wasn't something I ever thought about, so I never really made a decision. But most women want children."

"I might be like you. I really think a career might fulfill me. I know the world thinks women like us are horrible, selfish creatures, but there must be another way to give to the world besides babies."

"What about the boy and girl?"

"I like helping you put out good entertainment for people to enjoy. Maybe it lifts them out of the blues, and gives them hope. Having babies isn't the only way a woman can give to the world. Giving good entertainment is giving too. Don't you think?"

"I've never thought of my job like that, but I like the idea." Maybe this work *is* the absolutely, completely wonderful thing I dreamed of doing when I was eight. "We'd better order. I have to see Scott this afternoon." I signaled for the waitress. "Oh, and I still haven't told you. Bart."

"Is something wrong?"

The waitress walked up to our table.

"What are you going to have?" I asked Lucille.

"I'll take the vegetable plate."

"You don't want some meat or fish? Did you look at the Child's Suggestions section? It's on me. Live a little."

Lucille smiled as she folded her menu. "Dieting. I'm doing the DuBarry Success Course. The works, the diet, the skin care, the make-up."

"I don't see why you need it, but everyone seems to be doing the DuBarry these days. I'll have the deviled crabmeat cakes with Newburg sauce," I told the waitress, handing her our menus.

"It's my rear end," Lucille whispered after the waitress had gone. "The rest of the program is extra. Don't you think my rear end is too big?"

"Uh—well, I never thought about it. So ... Bart. I had to fire him."

"Oh, no. How awful."

"Please don't make me feel worse than I already do."

"I meant how awful for you."

"I've never fired anyone before. It didn't feel good." My mind wanderered back to the day I told Bart. He stood over me and said, "Nobody fires me and gets away with it." He slipped his hand into his pocket and I jumped out of my chair. He grinned an ugly, knowing grin and slid a nail file out. "What on earth were you thinking?" Filing his nails, he sauntered backwards out of my office, all the time grinning at me. He talk-sang, "There'll come a time, now don't forget it; there'll come a time when you'll regret it ..." The sound of him repeating that refrain floated ghost-like into my office as he walked down the hall and out the door past Georgio. It continued to haunt my dreams.

"You really have nothing to feel bad about," Lucille said. "Bart was a nice man, but he was irresponsible. I don't see anything wrong with, well ..." she whispered, "I personally don't care if he's a homosexual. Is that why you fired him?"

"No. I fired him because I couldn't count on him to show up for work."

"Being homosexual doesn't make a person *automatically* irresponsible, but the two might go together."

"Uh, yes. And since Bart is gone, I'd like to offer you his job."

"Oh, Al, I—don't know what to say. This is a dream come true."

"You may not think so once you've started. Lots of work with long hours."

She sat up straight, shoulders back. "I'm ready. And now that I'm your assistant, I can keep an eye on Bertha for you."

"Bertha? Why would you need to 'keep an eye on her?'"

"I don't know; there's just ... something."

Chapter 70

"THIS IT?" MATTIE said as we stood outside the gates of St. Sebastian. "My Scottie's in there?"

We stood before a giant iron fence, which wrapped around the dusty buildings of St. Sebastian Hospital, Psychiatric Division. We could see through the bars into a yard covered with patches of dying grass in front of a gothic building. It looked like the set of a Hollywood haunted house movie. I practically expected to see ghosts floating out of its roof. The words "Abandon all hope ye who enter here" came to mind as the guard opened the gate, and we stepped through.

The stairs going up to Scott's floor were steep, and murals covered the surrounding walls. The guard told us the murals had been painted in the thirties as part of Roosevelt's New Deal. They once were rich in color, but now were dull and faded behind a layer of dust. I was glad to have a companion to climb these steps with me this time, but I worried the stairs might be too much for Mattie's seventy-seven-year-old legs. She was pretty tough, though.

At the top there was an elevator, and we squeezed in with the other visitors. A woman behind us said to another woman, "Did you know the higher the floor the more seriously ill the patients are?"

"Really?" the other woman said.

"The ones on seven are the criminals. I'm sure glad my son's not there." The door opened, and she got off on the fourth floor. A man in a business suit got off on five. The woman getting off on six turned toward Mattie and me briefly with a look of pity or scorn, I wasn't sure which. When the door opened on seven, fear shook my insides more this time than before. The first time, I hadn't noticed the policeman sitting on a high stool near the door. The policeman's hand rested on his gun handle, his billy club hanging from his belt.

"Mattie, why don't you visit with Scott alone for a while. He'd probably like to see you by himself. I'll stay by the door."

Mattie gripped my hand. "Don't leave me alone in here. I'm scared half outta my wits."

We walked toward the visiting area, the smell of ammonia and diarrhea surrounding us. Faint laughter. Men sitting at tables smoking cigarettes, the air surrounding them a thick yellow. A laughing man being wrapped in a strait jacket by two bulky Negro orderlies. A white man jumped up on his chair and recited as if he were a politician running for office. The words he threw at us had the rhythm of language. They seemed like they *should* mean something, but they were strings of made-up words like my mother would recite when she was locked up in a place like this. Mattie wrapped her arm around mine. "Where's Scottie?"

Our eyes scanned the crowded tables. No Scott. "I'll ask someone. You wait here."

"Don't leave me." She choked my arm. I spotted Mr. Donahue, the male nurse from the day before. With her arm still wrapped around mine, I dragged Mattie with me. "Excuse me, Mr. Donahue."

Mr. Donahue turned, coughed, and blew cigarette smoke in my face. "What can I do ya fer, honey?"

"Scott Elkins. Do you know where he is?"

He looked at his watch. "Hey, Murch!" he called across the hall to his friend behind the desk. "You see that cute Elkins boy anywheres?"

"Right there," Murch yelled back, pointing down the hall.

A large Negro orderly had one of Scott's arms around his neck, and a skinny Negro orderly held him on his other side. Scott's feet, covered in thin slippers, scraped along the floor as his head bounced up and down like he was asleep. Mattie and I ran to him. "What'd you done to him?" Mattie cried out. "My boy, my boy."

"We ain't done nothin' to him," the skinny orderly said. "We jes' be bringin' him back."

"It's the medication," I told Mattie. "They said they were going to take him off it, but it looks like they didn't."

"Ma'am," the large Negro man said, "If ya moves aside we can gets him so's ya can talk to him jes' fine. He a little wore out."

We followed behind as the two orderlies dragged Scott past the men sitting at the tables. In the back, there was row after row of metal beds hanging from the walls. The large Negro pulled one down, and the other man hoisted Scott onto the wrinkled sheets.

Scott curled into a ball, wrapping his arms around his middle, moaning.

"Scottie?" Mattie whispered, leaning close to him. She jumped back. "Oh! He smell somethin' awful."

"They does after the treatment," the large Negro said.

"Well, can't you clean him up?"

"No, ma'am, not yet. That be part of the treatment."

Mattie leaned over Scott, "Scottie, honey? Can you sit up?"

Scott moaned more.

Mattie turned to the Negroes. "What's wrong with him?"

"Ain't nothin wrong with him, ma'am," the large Negro said. "It be the treatment. They all gets like that."

"Come on, Abe, we gots to get outta here," the skinny Negro said to the large one.

"Yeah, I's comin."

Abe started to move back toward the tables when Mattie asked, "What treatment?"

"Ya gots to talk to the doctor, ma'am," the Negro called Abrahan said.

"Come on, Abe," The skinny orderly said. "We can't stays back here. You knows what happen last time."

"You be his grandma, ma'am?" Abe asked.

"I surely am. And I'm none too pleased with how my boy's bein' treated here."

"Well, it be a pleasure meetin' ya, ma'am. I's Abraham, and the fella over there are Randall."

"Abe, we gots to go," Randall said, his eyes darting back and forth. "If I lose this job Daisy won't never speak to me no more."

"Go, then. This are the man's grandma." He turned back to Mattie. "I's sorry, I can't explain ... Ya needs to be talkin' to his doctor, ma'am, but ..."

"But?"

"He left a little bit ago. Sorry."

"Abe," Randall called.

"Okay. I's comin. What ya wants with that skinny assed womens anyways?"

The two orderlies walked past the men sitting with their visitors in the recreation area.

"Ya sure 'nough don't get no privacy round here," Mattie said. "Where's the walls?" She grabbed a chair from the recreation area and put it next to Scott's cot; he was starting to stir.

"Grandma?" he said with one eye open. "Is that you?"

"Yeah, it's me, boy. What they done to you?"

"Oh, Grandma." Scott began to cry. "It's awful here."

"We're getting you out." I said. "Max is working on it, but you gotta be strong."

"What are they doin' to you?" Mattie persisted.

"They're giving me the treatment, so I won't be homosexual any more. It's awful, but I gotta take it. Once it's over, I won't be condemned anymore. Oh, no, I'm gonna be sick." Mattie jumped out of the way in time. Throw up landed all over Scott and the bed.

"What kinda treatment is this?" she cried out so loud everyone turned to look.

I ran down the hall and called to Abraham. He came running with a bucket. Mattie and I left the area while Abraham cleaned Scott up.

"What are they doing to him?" Mattie asked. "We gotta make them stop."

"We will," I said.

Dr. Shim was heading toward his office just then. "Dr. Shim! Dr. Shim! Remember me? Mrs. Scott Elkins."

"Yes, Mrs. Elkins. You'll be pleased to know your husband is in the faster treatment program we talked about, and he's making marvelous progress."

"Progress? He's deathly ill," I shouted.

"Oh, that. It's part of the program, but this method *is* faster and very effective."

"What *is* this treatment?"

"You wouldn't want to clutter your pretty little head with theoretical principles and research studies."

"Try me."

"Look, all you need to know is it works. Like I told you when *you* insisted I get your husband into this program, 58 percent of homosexual men are cured this way."

"Get him out of it."

"Do you know how hard it was to get him *into* it? Only a few were chosen. I had to pull strings for you."

"Now, pull strings to get him out."

"I will not. I have a reputation to protect."

Abraham pushed a cart at the other end of the hall. I rummaged through my purse, pulled out a memo pad, and scribbled a note on it. I hurried to catch Abraham before he turned a corner and slipped the note onto his tray.

* * *

I was on my fifth cup of mud, and still no Abraham. "Ya sure ya don't wanna order somethin'?" the waiter asked. "Don't look like your friend's ever gonna show up."

"No, thanks, I'm fine. I'll have something when he arrives."

"Suit yerself, but seems to me, the guy yer waitin' for ain't worth much, leaving a sweet girl like you here by yerself."

Sitting there alone made me stand out, something I hated. It was a neighborhood diner not far from the hospital, but all the women were either seated with a man or a female companion. That was true for both the white and colored women. A couple of men, one white, one colored, sat alone at their own tables, drinking coffee and reading the paper. People look strangely at women who sit at diner tables alone. Abraham had seemed so kind, I thought surely he would meet me here, but I guess ...

I was pulling on my coat, ready to leave, when I saw him standing in the doorway. At first I wasn't even certain it was him. He wore street clothes, dungarees and a lumberjack shirt. He ambled over to me and stood at my table without sitting. "You gots somethin' you wanna say to me?"

"I, uh, hoped we could talk. Won't you sit down?"

"You sure ya wants *me* doin' that?"

"Of course. Why not?"

He pulled out the chair and sat heavily. He lifted a pack of Spuds Mentholated from his shirt pocket and hit the bottom. He sucked out the cigarette with his lips, lit it, and sat back, making a big production of exhaling the smoke. "Now, what?"

"Why don't we order something? Waiter, oh, waiter! Have whatever you want. It's on me. Waiter, please ..."

The waiter stood on the other side of the room. He looked over at me briefly, then left to serve a Negro couple, which had just come in.

"Menus, please," I called to him, but still he didn't come to our table.

"What's happened to him?" I said to Abraham. "A little bit ago he was very attentive." As the waiter left the Negro couple's table, jotting down their order on his pad, I called, "Waiter. Menus, please."

He walked by us and into the kitchen as if we were invisible.

"Has he suddenly gone hard of hearing?"

Abraham laughed. "Forget it, lady. That cracker ain't comin' over here no time soon."

"But we're customers."

"You jes' gets off the pickle boat or somethin'? That guy ain't comin' over here to serve *us* with me sitting here with you. What world you been livin in?" He chuckled to himself and blew smoke over my head.

"I sit with ... well, gentlemen ... like yourself all the time. I manage a night club, and I've had dinner with Charlie Bird, Dizzie Gillepsie—"

"Cel'brities. They ain't no *gentlemens* like me."

"This isn't the south. Look, he's serving those two women over there."

"You mean them *colored* women? Ya can say the word. They's with their own kind. It's the mixin' the cracker don't like. Look, lady, I ain't gots time to be educatin' you. Jes' asks me what you wants so I can gets on home to my fam'ly. Yeah, I gots a fam'ly and I just finished a double."

"This treatment. What is it? What are they doing to Scott?"

"I ain't no doctor."

"But you know. You've seen it."

"Lady, how cans you be with a mens like that? He ain't no mens. He's a twinkle-toed homo. You oughta be glad them doctors trying to turn your mens back into what he were born to be. Unless you're one of them manified girls?"

"Tell me what they're doing to him. I'll pay you." I unsnapped the clasp on my purse.

"I doesn't need your money. I gots my own. And I ain't sittin' here bein' insulted by the likes of you. I gots only one reason for bein' here."

"What's that?"

"His grandma. I feels bad she gotta have a boy like him. Grandmas is important."

"Then for her. Tell me."

He looked away, uncomfortable. "They make him drink beer."

"But Scott doesn't drink."

"First, they give him a shot of some medicine, and it don't mix right with the beer, so he get real sick and throw up all over hisself, and while he be like that they ... Look, I's can't talk about this with no womens."

"Please, Abraham."

He took a couple of deep breaths. "They shows him pitchers of mens with no clothes on and mens doin' sick homo things. Every time they puts a slide on the screen they makes him drink more beer, and he get sicker."

"That's horrible. Why?"

"You aksin' me? I ain't no doctor. It's part of the treatment."

"What do they do next?"

"This next is the hardest, and I doesn't like stayin' for that, but sometimes I has to straps them in the chair."

"Tell me about it."

"Miss, I's tellin you, it ain't right for me to be talkin' this way with no womens, especially no white ones."

"His grandma needs to know."

He squirmed in his chair, obviously uncomfortable. "They puts these … things—wires, on his arms and legs, sometimes on his, uh, privates. Every time they shows him a naked man pitcher they push a button. It shoot 'lectricity into him."

"My God."

"They screams. Then they shows him some pitchers of gals, you knows, in some kinda way that would make a real man get …" He looked away, beads of sweat forming on his forehead."

He pulled a handkerchief from his back pants pocket and wiped away the sweat. "Once he be lookin' at the gals they shuts off the 'lectricity. Sometimes they cleans him up so he be feelin' real fine. After some days he get to hit whichever button he want: the one with 'lectrictrity and pitures of mens or the one with no lectricity and pitures of gals." He stamped his cigarette out in the ashtray. "I gots to go. I ain't gonna do more." He stood up. "You okay?"

"Yes. Thank you, Abraham." He walked out. I couldn't move. It all sounded like something the Nazis would've done, not our own American doctors.

As I pulled on my gloves, I became aware everyone in the diner was staring at me like I'd done something terribly bad. I walked out hiding my face in my coat.

Chapter 71

THERE WASN'T A moment to waste. We had to get Scott out of there. I took Mattie to meet with the lawyers Max got for her. She signed all their papers. Meeting with high-powered New York lawyers couldn't have been easy for her, but she was determined to do whatever she had to do to get her boy out of the "loony bin." I couldn't bring myself to tell her the details of the treatment.

When I could, I broke away from work and took her to the theater or a club. I wished I could've brought her to Juliana's act, but Juliana still wasn't working. I took her to Ruth Wallis's show of sophisticated songs. Mattie enjoyed how the maître'd and waiters tripped over their feet trying to please me. We were shown to a special table and given drinks on the house. Ruth was pretty bawdy that night, and I was afraid Mattie would be put off, but not Mattie. The bawdier the better.

Marty's notes piled up, and I knew I should contact him, but I didn't have anything for him, and it was hard telling him that. I thought maybe I could get him something Off-Broadway, but ... between Juliana and Scott I was rarely in the office.

One morning, I stopped in at The Haven to see if the contracts from Paris had arrived yet. As I was flipping through my mail, Marty burst through my door. "At last! What kind of manager are you? I've practically been on my knees for a month, but you never call me."

"I know, I know. I'm sorry. I've been going back and forth to the hospital and—"

"I have no money left!" He flopped into the chair next to my desk. His clothes looked even more rumpled than usual, and his hair was a knotted mess. "What do you want me to do? Be a store clerk like my father? Is that all I'm good for now?"

"No. But Marty, those reviews do make it harder."

"TV is hiring. Everyone I know is making great careers and me ..."

"What did you mean in your note 'you were going to come clean?' Are you a communist?"

"No. But I figured out what they might mean. In my freshman year, there was this guy. Really handsome. No, gorgeous."

"Stop drooling and tell me the story."

"*He* was interested in communism, so … I went with him to a couple meetings."

"Oh, Marty."

"I didn't know. This guy was hot, but he was more excited about communism than me. For me—the more I learned the less I liked. Then I found out, with all their talk about equality for all people, communists hated homosexuals as much as anyone, and if they found out you were one, they'd kick you out like everybody else. The guy I liked didn't care. He wasn't crazy about being homosexual, anyway. So, I just stopped going. I only went to get him into bed, and since that wasn't going to happen—well, it happened once—there was no reason to go.

"I think they want me to tell them that guy's name. All I have to do is ruin his life, and I get mine back. I think he's teaching in a university down south. You know what they do to teachers for being a communist *or* a homosexual? But I was all set to do it, Al. I made the call. All you have to do is meet with these guys, tell them your story in a private room and say you're sorry. They write it up, and you sign your name. Nothing to it. But—I couldn't. I couldn't do it. I hung up before I said anything. Jesus, he'd get fired. I heard he has a family now, a couple of kids. No one would ever hire him again. Don't you have any damn work for me?"

"You're quite a guy, Buck Martin. I'm glad you're my friend. But Broadway is dead right now. I've been thinking maybe Off-Broadway—"

"Off-Broadway? I really am finished, aren't I?" He jumped out of his seat and ran a hand through his hair.

"Off-Broadway is doing important work."

"Who'll see me there? I'm a song and dance man."

"Lots of people are going there now with Broadway prices becoming outrageous. And *Pennies from Heaven* is a musical. Off-Broadway is experimenting, they're … oh, what's the use?" I was tired of defending the Off-Broadway movement. I didn't have an Off-Broadway part for him anyway. "What about Arthur? Isn't he your agent these days? *He's* the one who's supposed to get you auditions. I'm only advisory."

"He won't talk to me either."

"I'm not not talking to you. I'm over my head."

"You know those reviews weren't my fault. Dame Margaret kept tripping me up, throwing me lines that weren't in the script, playing to the audience. Unprofessional. Then *she* gets the accolades—that damn English accent makes everyone think she's brilliant—while I get pies in the face."

"You slept with her, didn't you?"

"What does that have to do with the price of eggs in China?"

"I knew it. I told you not to, but you did it anyway. Some of this *is* your fault. For not listening to me."

"Terrific. Make me feel worse."

"That's what she does. She tries to get her leading man to sleep with her. She finds desperate gay guys especially enticing."

"I'm not desperate."

"Sleeping with her lets her know she can make you do anything for your career, and she hates you for it. She tells you she wants to guide your career, but then leads you in the wrong direction during rehearsals. Oh, but she is oh-so-forgiving when you trip up. When the director gets furious with you, she comes to your defense. Privately, she tells you how to 'handle' the bullying director. How close am I?"

"Right on the mark." He sighed, stuffing his hands into his pockets.

"She finds little ways to alienate the cast from you, subtle, so you and they never notice *she's* pulling the strings. When the rest of the cast gets quietly sore at you for being her favorite and starts isolating you, like going out for drinks without inviting you, you begin to feel alone with a very big part. She tells you they're jealous of your brilliance. You start to depend on her. Yes?"

He flopped back into the chair. "Oh, man."

"And then when you really trust her, she goes after you. Opening night, you feel like you've walked into a different show. The lines she feeds you have changed, the blocking is different. A preset knife you expect to be there isn't when you go for it."

"It was a gun. And the phone rang when it wasn't supposed to. I didn't know what to do. It kept ringing and I'm standing there like an idiot. Then she says, 'answer the telephone.' So I did, but of course no one was there because it wasn't supposed to ring. I didn't know what to do!"

"Why didn't you say, 'It's for you'? Put it back on her."

"Oh, that's good. I never thought of it."

"Of course you didn't. She had your adrenaline working against you."

"I fell into every one of her traps." He leaned way back in the chair, looking up at the ceiling. "What am I going to do?"

"Why didn't you listen to me?"

"She seemed so nice."

"And you weren't sure I knew what I was talking about. Maybe you'll trust me in the future."

"I trust you, Al. I want this so bad. I love developing a part—really becoming another person. If I can't do it anymore I don't know what—"

"Now you sound like someone who belongs on Off-Broadway, where the real theater is happening. I know you're going through a hard time now, but if you wait it out, Broadway tends to have a short memory. In time, I can—"

"I don't have time! I'm going to be kicked out of my apartment in two weeks. I can't live with my mother. She moved into a one-bedroom last month. What am I going to do?" He jumped up to pace.

"Well ... I do have something. It could help you through this crisis."

"What? Anything. Is it a part? It's not sweeping up the city, is it?"

"No. It's a part. You'd get to meet an important Broadway producer, and it pays well."

"Fantastic! Why didn't you tell me about this before? What's the part?"

I picked up a notepaper lying on my desk and took a deep breath. "It's, uh ... the Easter Bunny."

"The Easter Bunny? Broadway's doing an Easter show during the Christmas season? That's odd."

"Well, ... it's not Broadway. But it's for Harry Brooks, and he's big. You'd be working for him."

"And he's putting up an Easter show now? Jeez, a Jewish Easter Bunny? Where?"

"It could be a real opportunity for you. Harry Brooks is known to be a generous man."

"Where's it being done?"

"In his backyard."

"What?"

"In Long Island. The Hamptons. Lots of money'd people there. He wants someone to play the Easter Bunny for—his kid's party."

"A kid's party? You gotta be kidding."

I couldn't look at him, but I tried to sound hopeful. "His kid's afraid of Santa Claus, but she likes rabbits. It pays really well, and if he likes your, uh, well, performance, you could get other jobs."

"As the Easter Bunny."

"He knows a lot of rich people with kids who'd hire you. And he *is* Harry Brooks, so who knows …?"

"Does this means wearing the outfit?

"Uh, huh."

"The ears?"

"Yeah."

"The—the—tail?"

"I'm sorry. I understand if you don't want—"

He snatched the paper from my hand and ran from the office, letting the door slam behind him.

Chapter 72

AT LAST, IT was done. The lawyers made it happen, and the week after Christmas, Scott was to be released from that piece of hell. I buzzed into the club on my way to the hospital to pick him up. I had to check my mail, mostly for a letter from Pierre Louis Guerin, the director of the Lido in Paris. I threw the garment bag with Scott's clothes over the back of my chair and proceeded to attack my mail. Lucille had it piled so high on my desk, when I reached for it, pieces tumbled to the floor. I worked my letter opener like a knife, slicing through the white and brown envelopes, searching for an onion-skin airmail. Time was ticking, and I pictured poor Mattie pacing in our living room, waiting for me to bring her grandson to her.

As I finished chopping through the first layer of mail, I saw a book lying on my desk. One I had not put there. One I did not own. *Female Homosexuality*. It might as well have been a ticking bomb. I sank down into my chair. I didn't want to touch it. Who could have put that there? Shaking, I stuffed it into my drawer and picked up my phone. I flipped the switch on my dictograph. "Lucille, could you come here, please."

"Lucille," I said, as she came through the door. "Was anyone besides you in my office during the last few days?"

"I don't think so. I'm the only one besides you and Max who has a key. Aren't I? Oh and the cleaners. And Mr. Buck Martin sometimes comes by—I guess you gave him a key—but I haven't seen him in awhile."

"And I never got my key back from Virginia and ... My God, everyone has a key to my office!

"Has something happened?"

"No. Everything's fine. I'm heading to the hospital. Scott's coming home."

"I'm so happy to hear that. Give him my love."

She left and I opened my drawer again. I almost expected it not to be there, but there it was staring up at me. *Female Homosexuality* by Frank S. Caprio, M.D., subtitled, *"A Psychodynamic Study of Lesbianism."*

There was an embroidered bookmark in the book, with the words: "Sugar and spice and everything nice." I took a deep breath and opened the book to the page. One paragraph was underlined in red pencil.

"Crime is … associated with female sexual inversion. Many crimes committed by women … reveal the women were either confirmed lesbians who killed because of jealousy or were latent homosexuals with a strong aggressive masculine drive. Some lesbians manifest pronounced sadistic and psychopathic trends."

Who could've left this in my office? Lucille? But why? To tell me she was like me. But how could she know I'm …? I'm very careful. Bertha? She's always snooping around, cleaning things that don't need cleaning. And Lucille thinks there's something up with her too so… No! Bart! Of course! Could he get into my office? Would Lucille let him… Damn! I jumped out of my seat. I never got my key back from him. In my mind, I saw Bart sauntering from my office, filing his nails, singing, "There'll come a time when you'll regret it." My heart thundered. His revenge.

I heaved the book back into my drawer. I'd throw it out after I got Scott out of the "looney bin." I marched to the door, ready to storm out, but— stopped. I looked back at my desk. No, that book has nothing to teach me, I thought. I opened the door about to … I shut it and ran back to my desk; I lifted the book out of the drawer. *What am I going to do with this thing?* I dropped it on my desk; opened it and began to read: "A lesbian is the victim of a defective emotional development …"

Chapter 73

"I'M SCARED TO see everybody," Scott said on our way up in the elevator. He'd lost a lot of weight and looked haggard with dark circles under his eyes. The blue sports jacket and blue tie Max had me bring him helped some.

"Everybody loves you, Scott."

"I'm so—ashamed," he whispered.

I looked over at Archibald, our elevator operator. He faced the door. He always faced the door. We never exchanged more than the briefest pleasantries. Yet, he was doing work my father might have done. When had I begun to take living like this for granted, forgetting it took people like Archibald to make it possible?

Standing behind him, I could see he wasn't very tall, and his maroon uniform with the gold epaulets was a little big for him. He was balding in the back. I never noticed that before. I wondered if he had a wife, kids. He was one of the very few Negro elevator operators in the city. What was it like for him to be such a credit to his race? Who was he when he wasn't our elevator operator?

"Archibald, how was your Christmas?" I asked.

"Fine, Ma'am," he answered without turning around.

"Good," I said to the back of his head. He only answered me because he had to. It was his job to be polite to me.

We reached our floor, and Archibald pulled the rod to open the elevator door; he stepped aside so we could get out. Scott and I moved past him. I turned back toward him wanting to say … something … He'd already stepped back into the elevator, and the door was closing.

Scott took tiny steps away from the elevator. I put my key in the door. Mattie and Max stood near the Christmas tree waiting for us. Scott stood in the foyer, his hands shoved deep into his pockets. Mattie poked Max. "Well? Get yerself over there."

Max, hands in his pockets too—something he never did—approached Scott. He looked like a schoolboy on his first date. "Hi, Scott."

"Hi, Max. Are you mad at me?"

"Oh, Jesus," Max said, tears sliding down his face. He grabbed the two sides of Scott's head and kissed him on the lips.

They fell into each other arms, crying and holding each other.

"Now, Scott's goin' to play for ya'll," Mattie announced.

"Grandma," Scott whined.

"You get yerself over there, and sit yer rump down and play. It's the only dang thing's gonna keep you outta the looney bin. Play one of them bouncy ones I like."

Scott sat on the piano bench. "I don't feel right doing this, Grandma."

"But killin' yerself do feel right, heh? Play. How you can think God would give ya the gift of music and then expect ya to not use is beyond me. Play."

Scott played a passionate piece by Beethoven.

"He's good, ain't he?" Mattie whispered to me.

"Very good," I said.

"And he can play show tunes and jazz too. Don't ya think ya can use him in that Paris show yer puttin' together?"

Chapter 74

July 1955

"LUCILLE," I SAID into the phone from the rehearsal studio. "You know how you keep telling me almost every day you would *love* to meet Juliana? Yes. Today's the day. Now, calm down. All I want you to do is bring me the sheet music I left on my desk. Then, you have to go. It's a private rehearsal, but I'll try to fit in an introduction if Juliana is up to it. Don't hurt yourself running over here, but get here fast."

I hung up the phone, laughing to myself. I remembered the goofy, wide-eyed kid I used to be. My heart would practically thump out of my chest whenever I saw Juliana. With the right look, or the right touch, Juliana could still get a good thump going in me.

Juliana sat on the edge of the low stage, her white and green kimono thrown over her rehearsal leotards and tights, talking to Billy Preston. The overhead fans whirred through the humidity. Billy was the new director I'd hired for her. He was only twenty-five, but he'd had a few big hits in LA and Chicago, and he was being wined and dined by Broadway producers who wanted young talent to revitalize their shows. I wanted him to pull together a powerful show for Juliana to bring to Paris. Le Lido was to be her first engagement anywhere since the Broadway flop. This show had to be magnificent, but Juliana was tense. She wasn't satisfied with some of the songs Billy had chosen. She wanted most to be in French. Billy wanted most to be in English.

"Juliana. I've sent for three songs we had translated. They'll be here soon," I told her.

"Who's the translator?" She asked, jumping off the stage to pace back and forth. "The translation must be impeccable. You're an American. What do you know about the delicacy of the French language? I will not be made a fool of in my own country."

"I thought the US was your country?" I said, a little insulted.

"Of course, but you know what I mean. The French are much more particular about their language than Americans are about English. It must be precise."

Billy crossed his arms over his chest. "I think you should only sing in English. You're a goddamn American. What are you doing singing in someone else's language?"

"See? See? What does this child know about what those people suffered?" Juliana said to me.

"Suffered? They let Hitler waltz in and take their country. Am I supposed to bow down to these gutless frogs who needed the Yanks to save them?"

"Get him out of here, Al. Or I swear I'll—"

"Billy, I'll talk to you in a few minutes."

"Sure," he said, walking away.

"I can't work with this boy who has no respect for—"

"It's going to be okay, Jule. He's getting a good reputation around Broadway. Working with him will help your career."

"I hope *something* helps it."

"Look, in a few minutes I'm going to introduce you to someone, and I want you to be nice."

"Not today. I can't be nice today. I feel like killing someone. Him."

"Be nice for a few minutes. She's bringing your music, and she's a big admirer of yours. All you have to do is smile and say something nice."

"I can't. I'm too upset. I'm sure I'll say something mean and scar your friend for life, like I did you."

The middle-aged, chubby wardrobe mistress, Madame Herbert, charged into the room. "Madame Juliana," she called, "please to take off zat—zat—how do you call—zat zing? Off, off. Zee coat." She pointed to the dress coat she held in her arms. "I must ..."

Juliana slipped out of her kimono, revealing her leotard. "No, no, zat will not do," Madame Herbert squeeled. "Zee blow, zee blowse. How you call?"

Julliana said something to her in French. I had no idea what it was, but the sound of those words floating from her mouth into my ears made my knees melt.

"No! English alone," Madame Herbert returned. "I have new English boyfriend." She blushed like a teenager.

I brought Juliana the tuxedo shirt and she put it on. Madame Herbert helped her into the dresscoat. She tugged at the sleeves and under the arms, pushing Juliana around like a rag doll. She pulled at the tails, then stepped back to thread a needle. As she was about to push the needle into the coat sleeve, Lucille ran through the door, letting it bang shut. "I got here as fast as I could," she announced, breathless.

Madame Herbert turned toward her, venom in her eyes. "Who iz zis noisy people!" she bellowed.

"Oh. Sorry," Lucille whispered, tiptoeing toward me with the sheet music in her hand. Her eyes were totally focused on Juliana, who could not have looked sexier in her stockings, tuxedo shirt and dress coat.

"Oui," Madame Hubert sighed, turning back to Juliana, "Madame Juliana, you—what is zat American expression? —will knock zee shoes in zee air!" She hummed as she sewed something near the edge of the sleeve. She finished her sewing and stood back from her creation. "Voila! C'est magnifique! Paree will kiss your feet, Madame Juliana. Off. Off. I take. Off." She skipped from the room, jacket in hand.

"Al," Juliana whispered. "Your friend is staring at me. You know I don't like that."

"You didn't mind when I used to do it," I whispered.

"Because I wanted to get you into my bed. I don't want her in my bed."

"I'm glad to hear that."

"Uh, here, Al," Lucille said, extending the sheet music toward me, but still staring at Juliana.

"Thanks." I turned to Juliana. "Juliana, I'd like you to meet my assistant, Lucille Wadwacker."

"Oh, Miss Juliana," Lucille gushed, holding her hand to her chest as if checking to see she were still breathing. "I ... I ... I ..."

Juliana stuck a smile on her face and looked over at me. Her eyes seemed to be asking, 'Do I really have to do this?' I nodded my 'yes' at her.

"It's a pleasure to meet you Miss Wad ...?"

"Wadwacker," I put in.

"Yes. It's a pleasure." I could see in Juliana's face she was struggling to be kind by not making a joke about her last name."

Lucille burst out with, "I can't believe I'm standing this close to you, and you actually had half *my* name in *your* mouth."

Juliana looked at me, and I knew she wanted to say something she shouldn't. I shook 'no' at her. She tossed her hair over her shoulder and kept smiling.

"So—" I said. "Thank you, Lucille, for bringing these. You better get back to the office now."

"Oh. Yes." She was still staring at Juliana. "Uh, if you ever want me to play the piano for your rehearsals, I could. I'd *love* to."

"Thank you," Juliana said.

Lucille backed out of the room, a huge smile on her face. She was happy. Happy just because she'd met Juliana. I had a little something to do with that happiness. My heart swelled with gratitude.

Chapter 75

September 1955

"AL HUFFMAN HERE," I said into the phone. "Yes, Richard, everything's set. You just need to get yourself to the dock on time and everything'll —. Hold on a minute."

I held the phone away from my ear and listened to the sound of Chopin drifting through the door. Scott was playing. He rarely played. It was good to hear him.

"Uh, Richard, I have to see about something. I'll call you back. I promise. When have I ever *not* called you back? Try to relax. Have a cup of tea."

The song changed from Chopin to a piece Johnny had written, one of the songs Juliana had recorded a couple years ago.

I stepped into the main room, empty tables, the chairs all awry. On the stage, in shirtsleeves, Scott sat at the rehearsal piano playing. The sounds he made of Johnny's song were magical. He smiled as I approached. "Did you know Johnny used Chopin as a model for this song?"

"No, I didn't."

"Very skillfully."

"You're much better than Pete."

"Pete's not bad."

"But he's not growing at the same pace as Juliana. He can't keep up with her, and Johnny goes in and out of the drunk tank. We can't send either of them to Paris. I'm really hurting for a pianist."

"I'll work with Pete. Get him ready."

"There's no time. They're leaving next week. *You're* going to Paris."

"I can't." He stopped playing. "I'm the accountant for Max's two clubs. What's he supposed to do if I take off for Paris?"

"He'll find another accountant. They're a lot easier to find than accomplished pianists. While he's looking, Lucille can take care of the books, but *you're* going to Paris."

"I can't play jazz and pop in a nightclub."

"Your grandma asked me to hire you way back in December. To keep you out of the looney bin."

"Grandma doesn't understand."

"You're going to Paris," I told him. "Go home, tell Max, and pack. You don't have much time."

"But Al—"

"Excuse me, Al," Lucille said through her half-open door. "Mr. Styles is on the phone."

"That man will be the death of me. I ran to my office. "Yes, Richard," I said into the phone. "I told you, everything is set. At the dock at three. No, I can't see you off. I wrote the whole itinerary down in the notes I gave you last night, so I don't think there's anything more to talk about. How about I have Lucille meet you down there? Will that make you feel better? Good. Of course, I'll miss you. I'll miss you both. I know she's going to be a hit. Call me when you get to your hotel." I hung up the phone. My heart fell into my stomach. *She'll be gone soon.*

* * *

A ringing cut through my unpeaceful sleep. I groped for the phone. "Richard? What time is it? Five? I went to bed at four. I run a club, remember? What's the matter?

I sat up in bed. "I can't. I have to stay here. Or … well … if it's an emergency. Hang on a minute."

I jumped out of bed and threw on my robe, yelling, "Max! Max!"

I ran down the stairs and into the living room. "Max! Max!"

Max and Scott charged out of their room and met me in the living room. Scott was tying his robe. Max stood there naked, flapping his arms. "What happened? Is there a fire?" Stalks of his hair stood straight up. "Are you hurt?"

"No. Richard's on the phone."

"Jesus, Al, you woke us for *that*?"

"It's important, but you probably should put something on. I can't talk to my boss when he's dressed like that."

"But this is my best outfit." He turned and sprinted into his room. He came back with one of his dull bathrobes on. "Okay, so what's so urgent?"

"Richard can't go to Paris. His mother got admitted to the hospital with a heart attack. He wants me to go. Please, Max!"

"Can't Ben go?"

"Ben's just her agent. With about a thousand clients. He's not going to take off for Paris. I have to look out for her. She needs that. Lucille can handle things here. She'll do a terrific job. And I can give her instructions from Paris."

He crossed his arms over his chest. "Maybe Lucille will do such a 'terrific' job I won't need you when you come back."

"Don't be like that," Scott said. "Let her go. She can look after me, too."

"You want her to go?" Max asked.

"Yes."

"I'm going to lose both of you at the same time?"

"Oh, honey," Scott said, putting his arms around him. "We'll write and call so often you won't have time to get lonely."

"Lonely? Who's talking about lonely? I need someone to work in my clubs." He pointed at me. "You're going to be working extra hard when you come back. And you ..." He put his arms around Scott's neck. "You're going to be working extra hard too." They kissed.

I dashed back to my room. "Richard, yes! I can go," I yelled into the phone, jumping up and down like a kid. "Oh, that's right. You did only book the *one* stateroom on the ship for you and Juliana. And there is only the *one* suite in the Paris Hotel. Oh, well," I sighed. Quite dramatically. "It will be horribly inconvenient and crowded, no privacy, but we must all sacrifice for Juliana's career, mustn't we? Please do give my love to your mother."

End of Book III

Get JULIANA (Book 1: 1941-1944)
and a new story

Building a relationship with my readers is one of the best things about writing. I sometimes send newsletters with details about new releases, special offers and other bits of news relating to the Juliana series and other writing.

Sign up to be a VIP reader and receive your free copy of the new novella at: http://www.vandawriter.com

Juliana (Book 1: 1941 – 1944) is available **free** at:

https://www.instafreebie.com/free/pOK3K

Reviews are Important

They let me know what you're thinking. I want to be in communication with you.

Reviews also help to sell more books, which helps me to write more books and that will mean more books for you to read and I hope to enjoy.

Reviews can be left under the title of the book at:
Amazon.com
www.goodreads.com
Amazon/co.uk
Amazon/co.ca
Amazon/co.au
Amazon/co.de

Thank you!

Behind the Scenes of a Book: The Well-Deserved Thank Yous

I WANT TO thank all of you who read the first novel in the series, *Juliana (Book 1: 1941-1944)*. Coming from a background of playwriting, publishing my first novel has been an exciting adventure, and you have been very encouraging.

Writing a book and creating characters is very much like having a child and preparing that child to meet the world. You want so much for that kid to be accepted and embraced, even when their behavior is sometimes not the best. The comments I received from readers who wrote to me personally and/or those who wrote reviews of the book let me know, that yes, my child was being accepted and sometimes loved. No writer or Mother/Father could wish for more.

Just like with the first book, a great many people were instrumental in helping me turn this second book) in the series, *Olympus Nights on the Square: LGBT Life in the Early Post-War Years* into a reality. Some of these people I even met on the Internet. It's popular today to malign the Internet, and certainly, it has caused a great many problems, but I think it is important to remember that the Internet is a tool. How this tool is used is up to us. For a researcher, the Internet is a blessing. One reason is that it puts me in touch with so many experts I would never meet without it. One of those experts that helped with the current book was *Tom Genova*.

Tom has a website, http://www.tvhistory.tv, which is filled with fascinating facts about the evolution of television, from before 1935 to the present. As helpful as his wonderful website was there are certain questions a novelist can only get answered by interacting with a human being. One such question was, "What was it really like to get your first television set during those early days, and maybe even be the only one on your block to have one?" That type of knowledge is rarely recorded in research texts. Through email, Tom did a marvelous job enlightening me with the kinds of details that spark a writer's imagination. I could not have written my two "TV chapters" without him.

I also met _Arlene (Friedman) Simone_ on the Internet, and she has enriched my life. I introduced Arlene to my readers in the first book under the subheading "The Experience of a 'Normal' Who Lived During That Time Period." For _Olympus Nights on the Square_, she taught me just how difficult it was for women in the fifties. Arlene attended City College of New York at about the same time as my main character, Al. City was considered a progressive school with progressive ideas. They were the first to have an on-campus fraternity that accepted members of any religion or race. Former Secretary of State Colin Powell attended City in the 1950s. City also produced more Nobel Laureates than any other public institution.

However, this progressive institution wasn't progressive enough to know that all women did not want to be schoolteachers. Yet, that was the only major open to them at City in the early fifties. Arlene was drawn to the theatre arts and music. While at City she took mostly theatre courses and performed in most of the school's productions. She played the part of "Miss Turnstiles" in _On the Town_, a demanding singing and dancing role.

Ultimately, she left City without receiving her degree, along with a number of her female classmates. They had no interest in becoming schoolteachers, either. (Arlene later received her bachelor's and master's degrees at another institution.) She pursued her singing career until she married. And wow, can that woman sing! I had the honor of meeting Arlene in person when she came to New York to sing in a cabaret. She's currently working on an album dedicated to her daughter. The working title is: _Together/Wherever_.

I didn't meet _KT Sullivan_ on the Internet. I met her after she'd completed a set of songs celebrating Doric Wilson's (the first produced gay playwright) fiftieth year in theater. KT is a professional singer, often seen around the country in cabarets and theater. She took time out of her busy schedule to talk to me about her life as a cabaret singer. She later invited me to her home for an evening in which her friends gathered to listen to her try out a few new numbers.

KT is a marvelous singer and comedienne. What an honor it was to be part of that. One of her friends who happened to be there that night was Tiger Lily. The honest-to-goodness original Tiger Lily (really Sondra Lee) from the original live TV show of _Peter Pan_ with Mary Martin. I'm sure a lot of you are too young to understand the significance of that, but it was one of my big WOW moments. We even exchanged a few emails. I actually emailed Tiger Lily! Oh, my God

So much can go wrong in the long process of writing a book, and I am grateful to the people who volunteer to keep me on track. One of these people was my Beta Reader: _Arran H. Kendrick_. He read this book while it was still an unedited Word document and let me know about typos, grammatical screw-ups and all my other errors. He also had the job of letting me know if any part of my story wasn't working. He was very thorough, which I am very grateful for.

Then there was my Editor: _Danielle O._ from Write My Wrongs Editing (danielleo@writemywrongsediting.com) I so much appreciate her hawk-eyed vision for checking every detail of my work and her efforts to make it flawless. But most importantly I appreciate her tremendous support. Her cheerleading of _Olympus Nights on the Square_ came at a time when I really needed it. Danielle's support gave me the courage to continue despite adversity.

This year like last, we continued The Juliana Project. Actors performed chapters from the novel at the Duplex Night Club for an invited audience. However, this year we ceased the grueling task of trying to put up the show once a month. This time, we put together one big show that covered (with cuts) most of _Juliana Book I: Before the War_. This performance was entitled: _Juliana: In the Beginning_.

We performed the show before a sold-out audience. The person most responsible for getting this longer, more elaborate show up and running was our director, _Ray Fritz_. There would have been no show without his creativity, persistence and hard work. Thank you, Ray. It was a great show!

We also had a marvelous troupe of dedicated actors involved with the show: Allison Linker (Al), Annie-Sage Whitehurst (Juliana), Ray Allen Fritz (Danny) Ali Ryan (Aggie), Tyler Gardella (Dickie), Matt Biagini (Max), Lucy McMichael (Virginia Sales), Sharlene Hartman (Nan Blakstone), Radio Announcers: Hilary Walker & Jacques Mitchell (Veronica Hudson & Guy Cooper). Kathleen O'Neill was our videographer, Armando Bravi our lighting technician and Thomas Honeck was the ever helpful general manager of the Duplex. A special thank you to Maria Varvaglione at Metropolitan College of New York for arranging space at the school so we could rehearse this monster show.

The actors and I were also graciously invited to other venues around town to read from _Juliana_. The places where we read were: The Kennedy Center (From page to stage). Thank you, Deb Randall, Artistic Director of the Venus Theater, The Bureau of General Services—Queer Division @ The LGBT Community Center. Thank you, Donnie Jochum and Greg Newton; The

Lesbian Herstory Archives. Thank you, Flavia Rando; Hudson Community College. Thank you, Michelle Vitale, Director of Cultural Affairs & Jacques Mitchell; Henrietta Hudson Bar. Thank you, Liz McMullen; Metropolitan College of New York. Thank you, Beth Dunphe and Directors of Metropolitan College Library, Directors: Kate Adler and Emma Moore.

Actors, not mentioned above, who joined us in these venues and added their talent by reading from the book were Molly Collier (Al), Colleen Renee (Aggie), Sarah Sutliff (Aggie), and Lisa Shelle Davis (Mrs. Viola Cramden). Thank you!

As always, I depended on the astute feedback from my writers' group, The Oracles. The Oracles are some of the best writers in the country, so their comments were extremely valuable to me. Thank you: Liz Amberly, Edgar Chisholm, Bill Cosgriff, Stuart D'Vers, Elana Gartner, Nicole Greevy, Marc Goldsmith, Nancy Hamada, Olga Humphrey, Penny Jackson, Robin Rice, Donna Specter, and Mike Vogel. I don't think they're aware of just how much our discussions helped me to make vital changes within the chapters.

I also want to thank <u>Dean Adele Weiner</u> of Metropolitan College of New York who granted me a scholarship leave, which allowed me to complete this novel.

About the Author

I WAS BORN and raised in Huntington Station, New York. This town shouldn't be confused with Al's home town of Huntington. They are two different places, and it's too long a story to explain the significance of that difference. Now, I live in New York City, and I have for quite some time. I've been a professor at Metropolitan College of New York for over fifteen years, but I don't teach writing like many people guess. I teach psychology because my advanced training was in psychology, and I am a licensed psychologist.

I was a writer long before I was a psychologist. I wrote my very first novel in eighth grade, with encouragement from my teacher, Mr. James Evers, who would meet me before school every week to discuss the latest pages I had penned. He wrote in my Junior High Yearbook, "My children will read your words." Unfortunately, others were not quite so encouraging, and I wandered away from my writing.

I spent a lot of years going from job to job because the work-a-day world could not satisfy a restlessness in my soul. Along the way, I found playwriting and was a playwright for about twenty years. I found a place to hang my hat at Metropolitan College of New York where today I am a full professor. The desire to tell the story of LGBT history with fictional characters who live through that history brought me back to my original form, the novel, but I learned a lot about dialogue from playwriting.

I'd love to hear from you. My online home is: http://www.vandawriter.com

You can connect with me on Goodreads at https://www.goodreads.com/drvanda

Or on Facebook at http://www.facebook.com/vandawriter or Twitter at @vandawriter

You can also contact me directly at vanda@vandawriter.com